AROUND ROBIN
THE RETURN

AROUND ROBIN
THE RETURN

John Bolstridge

authorHOUSE®

AuthorHouse™ UK
1663 Liberty Drive
Bloomington, IN 47403 USA
www.authorhouse.co.uk
Phone: 0800.197.4150

Published by AuthorHouse 05/30/2015

ISBN: 978-1-5049-4291-1 (sc)
ISBN: 978-1-5049-4292-8 (e)

Print information available on the last page.

Contents

Chapter One

You are about to read a very erotic Story about the sex antics of a long haul coach driver, who is a relieve driver on a coach tours, that goes to European destinations. Who gets up to all sorts of sex antics, with passengers and guest aboard the coach?

If you read the first book entitled AROUND ROBIN you will already know about Pete West, one of the relieve coach drivers who went on to have many sex encounters, until he went on to find the true love of his live, who is Spanish and her name is Sofia. They finally did marry and live in Tossa-De-Mar Spain.

A little more about Pete West, when he married Sofia, he was a twenty eight year old very well built, and might I say a very handsome Young-man. Who is well endowed with a 10 inch penis? And he thinks he is God's gift to Women. When he lived in the U.K., he worked for a Bulwell bus company called Summer Sunshine Line bus Company. Now with living in Spain he works for a Spanish bus company, and life is rosy with having a cliff top house, which is overlooking the Ocean. Sofia and Pete have been married for just over two years, when Sofia started to have problems with going to the toilet, and this had been ongoing for about 3 months, and she had kept it to herself with being frightened of telling Pete, then one morning she collapsed, and she is rushed to hospital with Pete by her side.

Pete is in the waiting room waiting for the news about his wife, who is undergoing having tests and check-ups, when out comes a house Doctor and asks for Mr West. Pete makes himself known to the Doctor, and the Doctor smiles, and asks Pete to come with him. They go to a room and the Doctor asks Pete to sit down.

"Right let me start Mr West, by telling you that we have conducted the entire tests on your wife Sofia West, and I'm afraid it is not very good news."

"What do you mean Doctor not good news?" Pete looking at the doctor with concern.

"Well the test show that your wife has stomach cancer, and it has spread to other parts of her body becoming secondary, her brain, and lungs, and that is not all." The doctor turning a page on his note pad.

"No-No you must be talking about someone else, this cannot be my Sofia, please tells me this is not true." Pete looking at the Doctor with eyes wide open.

"I'm afraid it is true, and her kidneys are closing down." Pete sits there completely dumfound with all that he had been told, and is head is spinning around with what the Doctor had told him and he asks the Doctor.

"What are we looking at, 2 years, or maybe one year?"

"I'm afraid within the next couple of days." Well now Pete is completely dumfounded, and he is thinking to himself. "My Sofia please God not my Sofia."

The Doctor can tell that Pete was just sitting there looking into fresh air, and he asks him.

"Are you OK Mr West, or would you like to go and see your wife." Pete looks up to the Doctor with a glaze in his eyes, and just came straight out with.

"Please take me to my wife." The Doctor opens the door for Pete and he goes with a look that told you that his whole World had fallen apart. The Doctor takes Pete to where Sofia's room is, and they enter, and Sofia is in a coma and looks peaceful.

The Doctor in a soft voice tells Pete.

"She is in no pain Mr West for we have her heavy sedated, you are welcome to sit with your wife and talk to her." The Doctor puts a reassuring hand on Pete's shoulder and leaves, Pete with his wife. Pete sits down on a chair and holds Sofia's hand, and the first thing he noticed is that her hand is cold, he puts one hand on her forehead and brushes back her long blond hair and even her forehead was cold. Into the room comes a nurse and he points this out to the nurse about the coldness of his wife and she came straight out with.

"We find this with most people who are dying; the blood goes inwards to protect the inner organs. Would you like me to bring her a blanket?" Well Pete could not believe what she had just said and in an abrupt voice tells her.

"This is my Wife you are talking about, please be more respectful." Then Pete burst into tears and just sat there with his hand on his face and one hand holding Sofia's. The nurse leaves the room with knowing that she had said the wrong thing at the wrong time.

Pete sat there all-night and the next morning he awakes with having his head on Sofia's bed and suddenly notices a rather loud rattle from Sofia and this made him come out of his sleep and he starts to shout out.

"Nurse-nurse comes quickly, my wife." A nurse comes into the room and asks.

"What is a matter?" The nurse looking first at Sofia and then Pete.

"It's my wife she is choking."

"No Mr West that is what is known as the death rattle, it is up to you if you stay until the end or leave and let your wife pass away."

"No I will stay, I'm here for her and always will be." Pete holding Sofia's hand and he just could not take is eyes off her. Two hours he sat there and all of a sudden Sofia takes one long intake of breath and falls silent. Pete knew that she had gone he stands holds both sides of her face and gives her a long loving kiss and tells her.

"You will always will be in my heart wherever I go you will come with me, I love you sweetheart so much." He takes one last look at Sofia lying there at peace and goes, without saying anything to anyone on the way out of the hospital. Talk about being alone, but Pete passed everyone with tears flowing down his face at his loss. He takes a taxi home and straight into the fridge and pulls out a can of beer, and goes out into the garden and walks down to the bottom where you just look straight out to sea. He is thinking of the times he and Sofia spent sitting looking out to sea in the summer nights and starry skies. He start to weep even more, takes a sip of beer and looks at the can and he tells himself.

"No way will I get drunk for my Sofia would not want that." He throws the half full can of larger over the cliff top, looks back at the garden and swimming pool and he tells himself.

"After the funeral I`m back off home for I cannot stay here for it will crack me up." Over the next three weeks he had the funeral and sorting out the house that is up for sale, and he soon had a very good offer, all sorted and he was off back home to Bulwell and a life back home in the UK.

The first thing back home is to look for somewhere to live and he soon found a house not far from where he lived before. All moved in and the first thing he did was go upstairs and into his bedroom, he opens the window that over looked his garden and he put out a little tin for the birds, that he filled for them with little treats and he is wondering.

"I wonder if I will be visited by my little friend the Robin Redbreast." The time is approaching 7pm and Pete sitting in his living room just after watching the news tells himself. "from tomorrow I`m going to put all my energy into building up my body even more, so for now why not go for a drink back in my local the Horseshoes." Pete goes and enters the Horseshoes where Terry the Landlord is pulling a pint for a customer. After he asks Pete what he required without even looking at Pete. Pete answered.

"Pint of mix if you would Terry." Terry then looks up to see who had said his name and he sees its Pete an old customer of his.

"Pete my old mate how the devil are you and what brings you back from Spain to this shithole of a country."

"Homesick I suppose." Answers Pete with a smile on his face.

"Well where is that gorgeous blond wife of yours Sofia." Terry looking round to see if she was with Pete.

"She's dead sorry to tell you, she died about 3 months ago of Cancer."

"You are fucking kidding me, Ho my God. Come here." Terry leans over the bar and they both are in a man's hug with Terry telling Pete.

"If there is anything that I can do for you Pete don't hesitate to ask."

"Thanks for that Terry you are a true friend."

"That's what I'm here for." With Terry spending time with Pete there is one or two of the old folk waiting to be served and Pete noticed and he mentions it to Terry. Terry looks to see who is waiting and he turns to Pete and tells him.

"Fuck them they are all piss-heads anyway." Terry turns smiles at them and goes over to serve them. After he had served them Terry comes back to Pete and asks.

"Is that the real reason you are back home Pete with you knowing what happened to your wife."

"You have hit the nail on the head; I did not want to be out there on my own, so that is why I have come home."

"Well if you need anywhere to stop my home is your home Pete."

"Thanks for the offer Terry but I've brought a house just across the Road on Cantrell Road."

"What about work Pete."

"I've got an interview on Monday back at my old job Bulwell Sunshine Line Buses. I will see you soon Terry, just going to sit down and rest awhile." Pete leaves the bar and sits in the window seat and watching a little TV. When into the bar comes this bird and stands at the bar waiting to be served. Pete looks her up and down from the back and he thinks to himself she has a nice arse, I`m sure I've fucked that. She turns around to see who is in and looking towards the bar did not see Pete. Pete straight away tells himself. "Well if it's not Donna one of my regular shagging pieces."

"Donna babe over here." She turns to see who is calling her and her eyes light up when she sees Pete. Straight away she goes over puts her drink on the table and out stretches her arms and Pete stands and they are in one big clinch and one hell of a kiss. Tongues and the lot, after she asks Pete.

"Are you over for a holiday and is Sofia with you."

"No babe she`s passed away."

"What do you mean passed away where?" Pete's thinking thick blond.

"You know died from Cancer three months ago."

"My God you must be heart broken." Donna sitting there stroking Pete's leg.

"I`m over it now but if you carry on stroking my fucking leg like that, I`m going to burst my jeans for I`ve not had my leg over for three months."

"Donna smiles at Pete and looks to see if anyone is looking and straight away puts her hand onto Pete's cock, and she could tell that he was getting a big hard on.

"Well tonight big boy we will have to remedy that, you can come back to my place and I will give you a good seeing too. That should make him happy." Donna stroking his cock that was now starting to go down his jeans inside leg.

"Fine Donna just wait or I`m going to be wet through in a minute if you don`t stop doing that.

"What would you like to drink?" Donna removes her hand smile while taking her hand away for she did not want to go and spoil something that she wanted later.

Chapter Two

They sit drinking and in general chat and Pete was starting to get a little fed up with everyone who knew him approaching and asking either how is Sofia or giving their condolences. In the end at 10.30pm Pete asks Donna if she was ready to go, for he had enough of people coming and talking about his past. They leave the Horseshoes and start to make their way to Donna's home for it was only a 15 minute walk. They reach her front door and enter, on removing their coats Pete turns Donna round and kisses her at the same time picking her up and going up the stairs. At the top he stops looks at Donna and kicks the door on the left and at the same time saying to Donna.

"This is the room if my memory serves me right." Donna just smiles and they enter. Pete walks to the bed and gently puts Donna onto the bed. She lay there as Pete started to undo his shirt and Donna is starting to get excited at what is about to come and she just lay there and is franticly taking her clothes off and throwing them onto the floor. Before Pete had removed his shirt she lay there completely in the nude and Pete carried on stripping and looking at Donna. Pete finally takes off his boxer shorts and stood there with the biggest hard on and Donna looks at his fine frame and comments.

"Fucking hell Pete just looks at you, you are bigger than last time and might I say that thing in-between your legs even looks bigger." Donna licking her lips at seeing Pete's throbbing cock.

"Well starting tomorrow I`m off to the gym and hope to build even more." He starts to walk to the bed and Donna's arms out stretched grabs hold of

Pete's shoulders and helps him onto the bed and she made him lay on his back and she tells him.

"Just lay back and enjoy for you are going to pop your cork like never before." Well Pete just lifts his eyebrows and did what he was told. Donna straight away is down onto Pete's 10 inch cock, pulls back his foreskin and opens her mouth as wide as she could, and her tongue starts to wrap and flick his bell end. Pete is looking at Donna and every now and then he is screwing up his face with the pleasure that she was giving him. Donna by now is really going up and down on Pete's cock and he knew if he did not stop her he would defiantly blow is cork, so he gently puts his arms onto Donna's shoulders and tells her.

"Come on babe my turn now." Well Donna straight away is on her back with legs wider that the channel tunnel, Pete slowly starts by kissing her tits and sucking on her nipples and after a few minutes' starts to kiss her stomach and then the top of her legs and she knew what was coming next. For Pete starts to flick is tongue around her fanny and she gives off one deep breath at the feeling she was receiving, and Pete starts to really flick away at her clitoris and even more groans come from Donna. Her juices by now are really flowing and Pete's tongue goes deep into her cunt and she lifts up with the pleasure that she was receiving and shouting out.

"Fucking hell Pete you are bloody good, for fucks sake get that big fucking dick inside of me, for I want every drop of your fucking spunk" Pete starts to straddle Donna and slowly starts to insert is dick into Donna, and as soon as she feels his prick penetrating her she starts to stiffen up with the feeling that she was getting. She straight away puts her hands onto Pete back and trying to pull him closer and stars to tell him.

"God you are one hell of a pleasure fucking giver, Ho my God you are big." Pete looking at Donna and slowly then fast goes deeper into her cunt. Her legs by now are well into the air and wide as she could get them.

"Just tell me when you would like me to give you the lot." Pete trying to tease Donna by going slowly withdrawing and then giving one hell of a thrust deep into her cunt with every inch of Pete going into her.

"Bloody hell Pete spunk me now, for I cannot take it much longer." Donna starting to look down at Pets cock thrusting her and she is breathing in deep and starting to give off one hell of a moan of pleasure. Pete starts to speed up and suddenly he pops his cork and thrusts deep into Donna leans upwards and just looks at Donna as she lay there with the biggest grin and eyes shut tight and screaming with pleasure and receiving all of Pete's warm spunk.

They both flop back onto the bed and Donna just lay there completely satisfied at what she had just received. Pete lay across her with one hand on her left tit and he was gently rubbing it around.

"Bloody hell Pete don't start again for I don't think I could take it again. Let's just snuggle up and fall asleep." Donna turns and cocks her arse up into Pete's front and she could feel his cock resting on her arse. Pete raps his arm around Donna and he tells her.

"Donna I really love you for that is the first time I've made love since I lost my Sofia, can I just say." Donna turns round and faces Pete and she tells him.

"Don't say it, for what we have just done I will always be here for you for I love you too." Then Donna could feel Pete starting to get another hard on and she tells him.

"Bloody hell do you really want to fuck the arse of me again."

"Well if you would like me to, I think I would be able too." Pete smiling at Donna and kissing her.

"Come on then one more time than defiantly to sleep." Donna turning back onto her back and opening her legs for Pete to enjoy. They do make love again and after just like Donna said they are in the fetal position and both fall fast asleep being shagged out.

The next morning it was up shower and they are both down stairs and Donna had made a full English breakfast and she asks Pete what were his plans for the day. He tells her.

"Well just like I told you last night it's off to the gym and start to build up my body."

"You have got to be kidding you are biggest enough now, I mean just feel." Donna trying to squeeze Pete's biceps.

"No way, I could be a lot stronger with training." Donna just sitting there shaking her head and she tells him.

"Well me it's off to work, will we see each other later for a drink."

"Yes Babe about 7pm in the Horseshoes." Donna stands and tells Pete.

"OK see you tonight at 7pm I'm off to work, don't forget to wash the pots before you let yourself out." Donna making her way to the front door and leaving Pete sitting in the kitchen with the look on his face telling you I don't bloody believe it. He does wash the pots and Pete just like he said is off to the gym for his daily work out.

Pete arrives at the local gym in Bulwell goes in and at the reception desk he tells them that he was once a member of the gym until he went to live abroad, they look up his name on the computer and tell him.

"Welcome back Mr West nice to see you back." The guy on the reception looks Pete up and down and he tells him.

"Looks like you have kept in shape while abroad."

"To true once a body builder, always a body builder." Pete flexing is biceps at the fellow on reception. All signed up and Pete changes into his shorts and goes into the equipment area and starts to put weights on one of the machines. There are two instructors in the gym and they see Pete and his physique and they comment between themselves.

"That guy defiantly works out boy just look at the size of him." Pete on one of the machines and with large weights on, is really pumping Iron. For well over two hours he is on the machines and finally decides to go and cool of in the sauna and cool pool. He dives first in the cool pool and starts to swim up and down and in there is a young woman who herself-pumps Iron see's Pete. She is looking at him at the end of the pool stopping standing then diving forward for another length. She is saying to herself. "My I would not mind a bit of that." She no more than gets out of the pool and when Pete comes swimming to the end where she is, she jumps back in and nearly knocks Pete under water. Pete stops comes up and is saying.

"What the fucks going off." She comes up to Pete and stands in front of Pete and she is telling him.

"I`m totally sorry for I entered the water not seeing you."

"Don`t worry sweetheart no harm done." Pete stands there looking at her firm body and muscles; she had long blond hair and a figure any woman would die for.

"You certainly work out for you have one fine body, Ho I`m sorry my name is Pete West and you are." Pete smiling at her in the look of pure innocence.

"My name is Tracy, and might I say you are one of the fittest men I`ve seen around here." She out stretches her arm to put onto Pete's chest and she asks him.

"You don`t mind if I feel do you."

"Help yourself Tracy, feel what you like." She stands in front of Pete and feels his two firm breast and her long finger nails feel his nipples, Pete tells her.

"Boy if you carry on you will have a different muscle getting bigger." Pete looking down at his shorts under the water. Tracy did no more than put her hands under the water and start to feel his cock and balls.

"My you do work out, it`s a pity we cannot do anything about it." Pete straight away tells Tracy.

"Well we could always go and have a sauna in our own cubicle and lock the door so not to be disturbed." Pete looking to where the sauna cubicles are.

"Lead on big boy." Tracy taking her hands off Pete's cock. They go to the sauna and Pete looks round to make sure no one is looking, and they enter and Pete locks the door and picks up the scoop and puts more water onto the coals, then faces Tracy. They are facing each other and Tracy puts her arms around Pete and they are in one hell of French kissing each other. Pete starts to remove Tracy's bottoms and then her bra by unclipping it and she stands fully in the nude and Pete presses up to her and she could feel his 10 inch prick poking into her. Pete starts to kiss her neck and then down to her breast and he had a mouth full of her tit and sucking profusely on her nipple. Then he starts to kiss her tight belly and then down to her cunt. Tracy is feeling all the pleasure that Pete was giving her, she no more than walks backwards and sits on the edge of the bench with Pete by now on his knees and between her legs starting to kiss around her fanny. Tracy leans backwards and opens her legs wider for Pete to receive more of her cunt. Pete starts to flick away at her clitoris and Tracy starts to give off one hell of a moan of pure pleasure at feeling Pete's tongue working like hell at her, and her juices start to flow. Pete could tell by the taste that she was having on hell of an orgasm. He then stands facing Tracy and she had a full frontal view of Pete's enormous cock and she reaches out and pulls him towards her, and her mouth disappeared onto Pete's cock and he stood there leans back at the feeling Tracy was giving him, as she is sucking away by lifting up and then going deep as she could back onto Pete's cock. After about five minutes Pete puts his hands onto Tracy's face and tells her.

"Come on babe let me feel that lovely fanny of yours." Tracy leans back laying across the wooden bench with legs wide open in the air and looks at Pete and tells him.

"Come on big boy fuck the arse of me please." Pete starts to straddle Tracy and all the time she is looking at Pete's cock as it starts to reach its goal, and when he starts to penetrate her she gives of one hell of a satisfied scream of pure pleasure.

"Fucking hell Pete that's one hell of a prick there, where the hell have you been all my life." As she was saying this Pete gives one hell of a deep thrust and Tracy screams out loud.

"Pete please spunk me, for I want to feel all of you." Another scream of pure pleasure and the dirty talk made Pete really start to speed up and after about ten minutes Tracy is really screaming with pleasure and shouting out.

"For fucks sake now comes please." Then Pete gives one hell of a groan and blows his top and he is ejaculating like no tomorrow inside her, with Tract digging her nails into Pete's back.

"That's beautiful I can feel every drop of your warm spunk, Ho God the feeling." They both flop back and with being in a sauna the sweat starting to discharge off them. Pete tells Tracy.

"Come on babe I think one's pours are wide-open now, let's go outside and jump in the cold tub." They put their bathers back on and Pete unbolts the door and just outside the sauna there is a cold tub that is just round that looks like a well, and Pete just jumps straight in. Comes back to the top and tells Tracy.

"Come on jump in its invigorating."

"Fuck of Pete I'm off for a shower." After they meet up and sit in the cafeteria and sit having a coffee and they decide that they will meet up next week. But Pete tells her that he had an interview for a job and if it comes off might after to phone her to confirm the date. They both exchange phone numbers kiss and they both separate with Tracy looking back at Pete and blowing him a kiss.

"Pete comes out looks up to the sky and he is saying to himself. "Please forgive me Sofia but you are not here for me, I love you."

Chapter Three

Monday morning soon comes round and it is the day for his interview for the job at Bulwell Summer Sunshine Line Bus Company. Pete's interview is at 10.30am and he goes to the depot and knocks on the secretaries door and he is thinking wait till Jane sees me. (Jane is a bird that he was shagging in-between birds, and the secretary of Summer Sunshine line.) Pete opens the door and enters and his eye light up for sitting there in Jane's seat is this absolutely gorgeous blond bird and he is thinking. "Boy I've got to shag this." He smiles at her and asks where Jane is the secretary.

She smiles at Pete at the same time looking him over and answers.

"She left over 3 months ago and you might be."

"Sorry my names Pete West and I have an interview with the manager at 10.30am." She looks in her diary and she tells Pete.

"Ho yes that's right he will be along shortly, with knowing Jane have you worked here before."

"Yes about two and a half years ago, and if I might be bold enough what is your name and why is someone like you working in this place."

"My name is Sandy, and what do you mean working in a place like this."

"Come off it Sandy you are absolutely gorgeous, your boyfriend must keep you on a chain when you are not working."

"Boyfriend you have to be kidding, and thank you for the complement." Pete plonks himself on her desk and he leans forward and tells her.

"Well if I get this job, you beware I will be the first in the line at your door to take you on a date."

"You're on, let's hope you get the job for I will look forward to it." Pete smiles at Sandy just as the door opens and in comes the Manager of the depot looking at his clip board and he said.

"I've one Pete West to interview? Pete West it cannot be." He looks up and see's Pete sitting on Sandy's desk and he looks straight at Pete, and Pete stands and looks at Tom with the biggest smile on his face.

"You have to be kidding me Pete West what the hell is you doing here."

"Me what about yourself I mean Manager you have to be kidding me, bloody come here." Well Sandy did not know what was going on for her Manager just goes up to Pete and they are both in one hell of a man hug and Pete kissing Tom Small. Tom returning the complement and while they were in the hug Pete looks at Sandy and tells her.

"He's really my Dad and goes like this when he sees me." Sandy just sat there smiling at Pete. After the formalities it was back down to earth and the interview. Tom takes Pete into a room and Tom shuts the door and of course the first thing he asks Pete is.

"What the hell is going off why are you back from Spain and where is that lovely wife of yours." Pete explains and Tom gives his deepest condolences at the loss and Pete try's to change the subject by asking Tom.

"That's enough about me Tom, how is that bubbly wife of yours Doris."

Well Tom's face changes and he tells Pete.

"Me too Pete I've lost my Doris and I would rather leave it at that for it still hurts and hard to keep talking about it." Tom sitting there with a different face. Pete stands puts his arms out and they both are comforting each other when the door opens and in walks Sandy to see if they would like a drink. Well when she sees them in another hug she could not believe it. Pete tells her.

"He`s always like this when he sees me." She makes an early exit and Tom breaks away and asks Pete.

"I hope you are not trying to get your leg over Sandy for she is a nice girl."

"No not me Tom. Well would you like me back and working for you?"

"Too bloody true you can start tomorrow, if that`s convenient for you."

"Thanks Tom but before you go one question."

"Yes out with it."

"How the fuck did you become the Manager." Tom smiles at Pete and tells him.

"Believe it or not but you can remember the Depot Manager Rick Blakemore."

"Yes what about him." Pete looking at Tom with the look at what is to come.

"He was no more than moon lighting with the depot buses and doing night jobs on the side, and making a penny or two out of it."

"Well-well Blakemore, who would have believed that," Tom gives his leave and tells Pete that he will see him tomorrow at 7.30am. And leave`s. Pete goes back to where Sandy is and starts to chat her up.

"That went well Sandy my Dad gave me the job and I start tomorrow."

"He cannot be your Dad really, for you are Pete West and his Sir name is Mr Small."

"It`s a long story I will tell you about it tonight over dinner." Pete smiling at Sandy.

"Tonight you mean you would like to go out with me." Sandy leaning back in her chair looking at Pete.

"Bloody well to true, how about 7pm tonight where would you like to meet."

Sandy hesitates with things happening quickly and came straight out with.

"How about you pick me up at my home?" Pete asks Sandy where she lived and he would pick her up in his car." She tells him and he leans forward and gives Sandy a peck on the cheek and tells her.

"Tonight you are going to be Alice in wonderland." He stands and goes to the door and turns back to Sandy smiles and blows her a kiss. Sandy sat there in confusion at such a butch and handsome man asking her out.

Pete leaves the depot with an extra step at getting the job and having a date with Sandy. He is back at home and opens a draw and finds an old diary with all his old numbers and the first thing he said is.

"Well I will be dammed if it`s not my old diary with all my numbers in it, of old girlfriends that I`ve fucked." He sits there looking at them and he thinks for a moment and suddenly said.

"Let`s see if I can beat my Round Robin when I shagged twenty hen party birds in Portugal." He sat there and starts the new chapter with the names of Donna-Tracy and puts Sandy`s name down with a question mark. The day goes quick and at 6pm Pete starts to get ready for his date with Sandy, he showers shaves and dons his pure white clinging T-shirt leather jacket and blue jeans. All aftershave and deodorant up and he stands looking in the bathroom mirror and arms out and saying to himself. Birds just love what they see, and they just die for what`s here. Pete standing looking at the image looking back at him, and he had one hand on his manhood and squeezing it. He leaves jumps into his car and heads for Sandy`s home and outside bleeps his horn to let her know that he add arrived. Sandy comes running down her path and waving at Pete sitting behind the wheel and she opens the door and gets in. well when Pete sees her getting in with the littlest mini skirt and short blouse exposing a lot of tit Pete comments.

"You look absolutely stunning Sandy, and you smell divine what are you wearing."

"Just one of my perfumes and thanks for the comment, and where are you taking me to this evening."

"Well I know this nice quiet country pub that do meals and I thought we would enjoy a meal and a chat and of course an early night, for I start my new job in the morning."

"Sounds lovely Pete, let's go." Sandy leaning towards Pete and kissing him on the cheek. Pete looks at Sandy smiles and they drive off.

Pete takes her to a restaurant on the main road to Mansfield not far from Nottingham called the Hut, he pulls in and Sandy comments.

"God it looks posh, are you sure they will let us in."

"Of course for I've booked a table for two at 8pm." They both step out of the car and Pete goes round to Sandy's side and puts his hand out for Sandy to hold and they go walking towards the restaurant hand in hand. Just before they enter Pete stops puts his hand into Sandy's back with her hand still in his pulls her to him and gives her a full kiss on the lips, and Sandy puts her tongue into Pete's mouth and he responds and they stand in a long lingering French kiss, with Sandy with her other hand feeling Pete's firm breast. They part look at each other in a loving way and Pete tells her.

"Come on babe let's go in and enjoy a meal and a talk." They are escorted to their table and the waiter asks what they would like to drink. Pete looks at Sandy and suggests.

"How about a bottle of wine, for I will not be drinking a lot with driving."

"That's fine by me Pete but could we have white wine." The waiter with hearing what Sandy had said suggests to them.

"How about the house best white wine Madam." Sandy looks at Pete and he tells him.

"That will do fine, one bottle of your finest white wines if you please." They sit there looking around at who were in the restaurant and another waiter arrives to take their order. They both deicide on Rump Steak even yet they have ordered white wine with their meal. The whole meal is one success and after they sit talking and you can imagine Sandy wanting to know all about Pete's past. He tells her the true about being married to Sofia till her death three months ago, and now he is back in the U.K trying to rebuild his life. He reaches out to Sandy's hand holds it and tells her.

"Please forgive me for being formal but the day I walked into the office and you sat there, I felt a feeling and I cannot describe it for I think you are one hell of an attractive girl, and I would like to make ago at a relationship with you." Pete sitting there rubbing the back of Sandy's hand and just looking straight into her eyes. We all known what he really meant and that is. "I'm dying to get into your fucking knickers." Sandy smiles back at Pete and she tells him.

"I the same when you walked into the office and asked where is Jane I to had this feeling of what an handsome man, and might I say wanted to get my hands on you." Pete smiles at Sandy leans forward and kisses her and at the same time touching her face and telling her.

"You are absolutely stunning Sandy, would you like to come and stop at my place tonight and then we both could go to work in the morning together." Sandy looks at Pete and tells him.

"On one condition will you take me home in the morning so I can get my work clothes?" Sandy still holding Pete's hand and smiling at him.

Pete smiles back at her and we all know what he is thinking. "Boy you are going to get the arse fucked off you tonight." Another victim for his sick diary.

Chapter Four

They leave the Hut restaurant at 10pm and start to head for Pete's home and Sandy is leaning on Pete in a romantic mood and every now and again holding his hand that was on his gear stick as he changed gear, Pete looks at Sandy and tells her.

"Wait till we get back you will have something bigger than this to hold." Sandy did know more than put her hand in-between Pete's leg and when she felt Pete's cock starting to rise she comments.

"What is this fucking great thing in here?" Sandy starting to rub a little harder at what she is feeling.

"What you are feeling is one hell of a satisfier, for I have never had any complaints before." Pete turning while driving and looking at Sandy who just screwed up her face and her tongue licking the outside of her mouth.

They pull up outside Pete's house he turns off the engine and turns to Sandy and they are in one hell of a kiss, and Sandy starts to get a little frisky and Pete tells her.

"Come on babe let's get you into bed for you look like you are gagging for it." They walk up the drive and Sandy is all over Pete, he stops at the door and is trying to get the key into the door and Sandy is trying to kiss Pete, and he just manages to turn the key and they enter. Sandy starts to flick her shoes off and Pete just manages to take off is leather jacket, while Sandy is trying to remove her blouse. Pete just takes a deep breath and picks her up and he tells her.

"Now the night for Sandy begins, just calm down babe you will soon be in bed." Sandy sitting there in Pete's arms tells him.

"Take me to bed and be gentile with me." She giggles and then starts to kiss Pete as he gently walks up the stairs and puts Sandy down on the bed. She straight away is franticly removing her clothes, and all the time looking at Pete who was standing and looking back at Sandy and removing his garments in what could be described in a sexy way. Sandy laid there completely in the nude and Pete looks on and fully approved at what he sees, with Sandy laying there and he could not take his eyes of her shaven pussy that looked very inviting. Pete starts to get onto the bed and Sandy leans up and gently pushes Pete down onto his back and she tells him.

"Please let me start first." She straddles Pete and slowly lowers herself and starts to kiss Pete and her tits are gently resting on Pets chest and he could feel her stiff nipples gently rubbing on his. She moves down to Pete's chest and on the way by gives his well firm nipples a flick with her tongue. She is soon down to Pete's firm and standing proud cock. She looks up at Pete and he looks at her as she opens her mouth and starts to flick his bell end and starting to swallow him whole. Pete closes his eyes at the feeling he was receiving from Sandy working on his cock. After five minutes Pete could feel his cock starting to surrender to the pleasure it was getting, and he knew that he had to stop Sandy or she would get a right gob full of spunk and Pete wanted to get into her lovely juice cunt. He holds her shoulders pulls her up gently and at the same time telling her.]

"Come on babe my turn roll onto your back." Sandy turns and lay there and Pete straddles her and he starts by giving her one hell of a deep throat kiss. Sandy starts to really get randy for she could feel her juices flowing with the pleasure she was getting and she breaks away from the kiss and tells Pete.

"Please fuck me now Pete for I'm tingling all-over." Pete starts to work on her tits and her nipples that are standing proud like two chapel hat pegs, he starts to go deep down and he comes to her fanny and Pete straight away starts to flick away at her clitoris with his tongue and then starts to really get down to some serious tonguing of her fanny, and he could taste her warm juices flowing from her. Sandy just lay there tensing back with the feeling and pleasure that she was getting, and keeps looking down and all she could see is Pete's head working overtime. She is now screaming with delight and finally shouts out loud.

"For fucks sake Pete fuck me now please." Pete stops comes up and lay across her and she could feel his manhood starting to press up to her fanny. She opens her legs wide and it works its way into her, and with every gentle thrust that Pete gave she could feel the size and the feeling she was getting made her tense up and start to pant.

"You are big Pete, Fuck me as hard as you can." Sandy whispering into Pete's ear and then a gentle bite of his earlobe. Pete speeds up and they both are in one frenzied of love making and suddenly Sandy starts to scream out loud as she came, and Pete too at the same time blows his top and they both enjoy one hell of an orgasm together. They both flop back onto the bed completely shagged out and Sandy tells Pete.

"I've never felt like that before you are really great at satisfying a woman."

"I the same Sandy you are fantastic and that was for you and no one else for I love you babe." (What he is trying to say is that's another one for the list and roll on the next.")

Sandy goes to clean up herself, comes back out of the bathroom and looks at the clock that showed it was 12.45 am. She starts to get into bed and she tells Pete.

"We had better get some shut eye for just look at the time for we have to be up at 6.30am for work. They snuggle down and soon both are well and truly fast on and it seemed only an hour when the alarm rings out at 6.30am. Pete awakes with a big yarn turns to Sandy and gives her a big kiss on the lips and he tells her.

"Come on babe time to rise and hit the road for work." Sandy murmurs and tells Pete to go and shower first and then she will come in five minutes. Pete goes to the bathroom shaves then jumps into the shower and starts to shower when all of a sudden the door opens and in comes Sandy and asks Pete.

"Hope you don't mind shearing it will be quicker."

"Pete smiles at Sandy and starts to rub soap onto her back and then while she had her back to Pete he puts his hands to the front and starts to soap Sandy's tits. Sand turns to Pete and she tells him.

"No bloody way Pete, don't you start to get randy Pete for we have no time for that for you still have to take me to my home and we have to be at work by 7.30am." Pete still tried and Sandy puts her hand onto Pete's balls and squeezes them a little and tells Pete.

If you cannot stop yourself I could help out with a little squeeze."

"OK you win just a shower." Sandy kisses Pete and they carry on showering and of course rubbing each other down with the soap and sponge. After it was out and Pete dry's Sandy off and they both start to dress and are soon down stairs and a quick cuppa before Pete drives Sandy to her home to pick up her work clothes. They pull into the depot car park and they kiss and go their separate ways with Sandy off to the Office and Pete to the depot canteen.

"The time is approaching 7.30am and in the canteen there are a few drivers waiting for the day's runs and Pete knew one or two of the drivers and the rest he introduced himself to the ones he did not know. Just after 7.30am Tom Small comes into the canteen with his clip board and giving out the drivers their runs for the day, and they start to leave for their coaches. Pete is the last and Tom looks at Pete and tells him.

"I've left you until the last for I would like a big favour of you, if you don't mind."

"Come on Tom you know me I would always be there for you, so out with it what is it you want me to do."

"Well do you fancy two days of short runs then Thursday off, and Friday we have a party going down to Faro in Portugal for one week. I would like you to be one of the relief coach drivers."

"Fine by me Tom who is the other driver."

"His name is Frank Bond and the same age as you, but he does not have the experience like you so you will be the senior coach driver. He's off till

Thursday and I will explain to him about you, and I'm sure you will both get on well together."

"All sorted then Tom, where am I off today then."

"Just a local run for you, can you remember when you went to Matlock with the School From? Kimberly hilltop."

"Ho yes is that where I'm going today Tom."

"Yes 8.30am, so you have half an hour before you go, maybe you would like one of Mabel's special breakfasts".

"No not me Tom watching the figure." Pete standing there and flexing his muscles at Tom.

"Well if you get any bigger you are going to bloody well explode." Tom turning and leaving Pete still posing. Pete relaxes and the alarm bells are ringing and he suddenly remembers, I wonder whether Sandy would be up to it. He is thinking of before he went on a coach trip he used to go into the office and give Jane a good seeing too. Pete is straight into Sandy's office and when she sees him her eyes light up.

"What are you doing in here, has Tom given you you're run for the day."

"Yes sweetheart but I just cannot get over last night and I'm still frisky, would you like to help a poor man out with the problem." Pete looking at the toilet that is in the office. Well Sandy looks at what Pete is looking at and she tells him.

"Well Tom as gone to see one of the drivers that has broken down, it looks like you're looks in." Sandy smiling at Pete and lifting her eyebrows. She stands locks the office door and they both make their way into the toilet and Sandy bolts the door and they are both in one hell of a frantic kiss. Pete is pulling her shirt out and straight away lifting her bra and goes down kissing her nipples and Sandy is franticly pulling down Pete's trousers and within minutes they are making love standing over the sink. Sandy goes down on Pete and sucking away at his erect cock and Pete is trying to pull her up so he could have a taste of her fanny. In the end he lifts her up and turns her over so he is holding her in the air and she is sucking away at

Pete and him with her in the 69 position, he is licking away and flicking her clitoris. They must have been at it for ten minutes and they both are growing and Pete turns her back so she is upright lifts her onto the sink and inserts his cock into her fanny which is flowing with juices.

They are franticly moaning and groaning and Sandy tells Pete.

"For fucks sake spunk me now, please now you bloody big son of a pitch." She is digging her nails into Pete's back with the feeling of pure pleasure and Pete all of a sudden blows his top with Sandy at the same time.

"Ho God Pete you are one hell of a lover, I love you so." Sandy sitting on the sink and holding Pete tight and kissing him.

"Me too babe I love you too." Pete at the same time looks at his watch and shouts out.

"Fucking hell Sandy I'm going to be late for the School trip." He lifts Sandy off the sink pulls up his trousers and opens the door and is flying through the office and telling Sandy.

"See you later babe love you." Sandy stood there looking at Pete hurriedly leaving and said to herself.

"And I love you too Pete." Pete's straight onto the bus starts the engine and is pulling out of the yard and heading towards Kimberly before you knew it.

Pete manages to make it on time and pulls up at Hilltop in Kimberly at 8.40am and pulls up just outside the school gates and he see's someone walking towards the coach and he is thinking I know you.

Onto the coach comes a teacher and she sees Pete and stops dead and said.

"Well I don't believe it, it's Pete if I remember right."

"You are spot on Jenny how the devil are you, and what about your husband Brian is he coming to day."(Pete took the school to Matlock 3 years ago and he tried to make it off with Jenny, but to no avail for she was married to Brian.)

"No we split a year ago, he started to see one of the other teaches here at the school, and they both were transferred, so I'm a free agent now with no commitments." Well Pete grimaces at what jenny told him but under the mask he is thinking. (Another one on the way for the diary and my Round Robin.)

Chapter Five

Pete looks at Jenny and tells her.

"I'm sorry about that sweetheart come here." Jenny comes closer to Pete and he kisses her and tells her.

"Let's get the kids onto the coach and give them a fantastic day. They are going to the same adventure park like they did when they first met and along come three more teachers with the children. All aboard and it was off to Matlock and a fun day for the children, the trip is only about 40 minutes and they pull up and the kids disembark and Jenny is one of the last and she turns to Pete just as she steps off and tells him.

"I will come and have dinner with you back here if you would like me to come."

"To true sweetheart I will looks forward to it." Pete telling himself. (Let's hope you do come.) And we all know what he means by hope you come, translated it means I hope you come when I've my ten inch cock well up you. Pete kips and he is thinking to himself, Jenny is a nice bird and I must impress her when she comes at lunch time. Dead on 12.30pm she arrives and tells Pete.

"I've got an hour's dinner what would you like to do Pete. Pete holds her hand and pulls Jenny to him and she flops into a seat next to Pete and he starts to kiss her, Jenny responds and they are well and truly giving it all. Then Pete feels Jenny slip her hand onto Pete's cock and she starts to pull is zip down and she has her hand on Pete's cock and starts to give Pete a slow wank. Pete tells her.

"Come on babe let's go to the back we will be more comfortable on the long bench seats at the back." They make their way to the back and Pete closes the blinds to make it a little more private. Well Jenny is in one hell of a frenzy and she is straight down onto Pete's cock and sucking away like know tomorrow on it. Pete is surprised that this time he did not have to lead first. He sat there and is really loving the feeling he is getting with Jenny sucking away at his manhood and every now and then flicking her tongue around his bell end. In the end Pete lifts Jenny up and unzips her jeans and pulls them down, then he removes her knickers and she laid down along the seat and this time Pete goes down on her and his eyes light up, when he comes to her fanny for it is clean shaven and he starts to flick her clitoris and his tongue going deep into her fanny, and she gives off a loud intake of breath at the feeling of Pete's tongue working overtime.

"That is lovely Pete God you are one hell of a guy." Another deep intake and she comes while Pete was still at it, and Pete could tell with the different taste of her juices that she was having an orgasm. Jenny by now is well worked up and she tells Pete.

"Please lets fuck now I want to feel that massif cock of yours well inside me." Pete comes up straddles Jenny and her legs are wide open ready to receive Pete's big cock. He inserts it and slowly starts to penetrate Jenny and she is looking down and seeing his cock slowly disappearing into her cunt and the vision makes her give off one hell of a scream of pure pleasure.

"Fucking hell Pete that is bloody lovely faster please." Jenny digging her nails into Pete's back and trying to pull him closer to her, and at the same time she is nibbling on Pete's ear. Pete also was looking at his cock disappear into Jenny and he too is screwing up his face with pure delight and they both are having one hell of a shag. They are well at it and after fifteen minutes Jenny by now her juices are well and truly flowing and she is having orgasm after orgasm and Pete with Jenny moaning and groaning Pete starts to come and Jenny tells him.

"Fucking hell Pete spunk me now I want to feel every drop of your gorgeous spunk." Well Pete with the dirty talk suddenly explodes and they both are having one hell of an orgasm. Jenny shaking at every drop she was receiving and Pete with his cock lifting and jerking giving Jenny all of his spunk is kissing deep into her neck and tells her.

"You are what I call a million dollar girl, for the first time I meet you I knew that there was something there between us, I love you Jenny."

"Ho Pete me too you are one hell of a guy and the truth be known I fancied you the first time we met. And I love you too." They both lay there kissing and stroking each other when Jenny looks at her watch and she tells Pete.

Ho my God look at the time we have been at it for well over an hour and a half, they will be wondering where I have got too."

"Don't worry sweetheart I will come with you now and enjoy the afternoon with the young ones." They both go down into the toilet that is on the coach and clean themselves up and they are soon out of the coach and heading back to where the children are.

Jenny is lucky for now, for no one, mentioned or realised that she was late back, and the whole afternoon is fun for Pete playing with the children and the odd time giving Jenny a kiss. Come three a clock it was time for home for the children to be picked up by their parents. Back at the School the other teachers are escorting the children back to their class and Jenny stops on the coach to say goodbye to Pete.

"Pete you do want to see me again, don't you."

"Bloody well true here sweetheart here is my number, but next week I'm off to Portugal and won't be back for a week, so I will phone you then." Jenny gives Pete her phone number kisses Pete telling him that she loved him, steps off the coach Pete pulls away and they both wave to each other. Pete back home just opens his diary puts Jenny's name next to the other three and tells himself.

"To beat 18 I've only got 15 more to shag for my Round Robin easy." He puts a star next to Jenny's name. Meaning he would shag her again. Pete that night goes into the Horseshoes and who should come walking in but Donna she sees Pete and goes walking over to him and saying.

"Why have you not phoned me Pete, was a nights shagging all that you wanted from me?"

"Fucking hell Donna keep it down babe, no I had an interview with the bus company that I use to work for, and they took me on and would you believe it, I have started already and you will never guess."

"What that they have made you the Company Director."

"No you daft sod, this Friday I'm off to Portugal for a week, so you will have to just use a carrot till I get back."

"Fuck off Pete, I have never seen a carrot that is ten inches long, and congratulations on getting the job." Well with what Donna had said and one or two of the customers looking at them and what Donna had said there is one or two eyebrows being raised?

"I've got to go to work tomorrow, so would you like a quick one round the back."

"Fucking too true come on then let's get too it." Donna grabbing hold of Pete's hands and they start to go up the steps to the outside.

"There is a dark place just under the bridge at the back of the Horseshoes Pete starts to kiss Donna and feeling her tits and Donna with her hand feeling Pete's cock can tell he is starting to rise and she no more than starts to unzip his jeans and exposing his cock. She goes down on Pete and starts to give him one hell of a blow job, and Pete is looking at Donna's head working away at his bell end. He stands there really enjoying the feeling that Donna is giving him and after about ten minutes lifts her head and tells her.

"Come on babe it's time he felt your warm cunt." Donna re-stands and with knickers and her jeans round her ankle Pete lifts her up by her two legs presses her against the bridge wall and his cock goes straight into her fanny, and he starts to really go at her and Donna starts to scream with pleasure and Pete tells her.

"For fucks sake Donna shut the fuck up, or you will have someone coming to see what the hell is going on." Well Donna shuts her mouth and just starts to hum at the pure feeling she was getting and Pete gives one hell of a push and he explodes inside her, and then he is in a loud voice giving it some, so Donna said the same thing to Pete.

"Shut the fuck up Pete." She puts her hand over Pete's mouth and he carried on spunking away while Donna is looking at Pete screwing up his face with pure delight and Donna did the same with the feeling of all that warm fluid going into her. After Pete gives his excuse that he had better go for he is up early in the morning for work. All dressed Donna gives Pete a kiss and tells him she loves him, Pete did the same and tells her he loved her too and he will see her when he gets back from Portugal. Just before Pete leaves Donna tells him just before he goes up the bridge steps.

"You behave yourself in Portugal now Pete, and don't do anything like I would do."

"Fat chance of that when you are a rep, see you sweetheart." Donna looks at Pete going up the steps and turns right and he had gone, Donna return to the bar for her last drink and she was getting one or two looks at her makeup running and hair in a mess. All that Donna did was look at them all and blow them a kiss.

Back home Pete just before he turns in for the night opens his black book and puts Donna's name in it with a little note saying shagged two today, but Donna does not count still four.

The next morning at work on Wednesday Pete in the canteen and sitting with a couple of drivers and in general chat, and about him working there before, when Tom Small comes into the canteen and gives them their runs. He asks Pete if he would take a bus coach trip to the bowl finals in Skegness, with it being you last day with having Thursday off before you go to Faro.

"Fine by me Tom love it, where do I pick them up." Pete under his breath saying to himself. Fuck me a bus full of old folk charming not much chance of fucking today.

"Pick up at 8am at Aspley lane church, bring them back at 5.pm and no later for you should be back for 8.30pm, have a good day Pete and even better one tomorrow on you day off, and I will see you here on Friday just before you go to Portugal. And by the way Sandy would like you to pop in and see her just before you leave to Skegness, but don't be long for you have to be there at 8am for your pick up."

Thanks Tom see you." Tom leaves and Pete makes his way to Sandy's office and he looks at his watch and saying to himself. I wonder if I will have time to giver one in the toilet before I go. Pete enters and Sandy stands and gives Pete a big kiss and Pete try's to take her to the toilet which happens to be in the office for he had already shagged Jane in there when she worked there.

"What are you doing Pete no way for one you have to go and pick up your run and secondly that is why I have called you to see me. Would you like to take me out tonight for I have not to have to be in work tomorrow till 11am for I have time owing? And maybe we could go back to your home." Sandy lifting her eyebrows at Pete and smiling.

"You're on babe meet me here at 8.30pm tonight and we can go straight out, must dash love you see you later." Pete turning and leaving the office Sandy shouts back love you too Pete see you later." Just when old Tom comes walking into the Office with his clip board.

"I heard that Sandy, I hope Pete's not taking advantage of you Sandy for you are a very attractive and sensible looking Lady."

"Why thanks Tom and no he is very charming and handsome young man."

Tom smiles at her and is thinking that's what I'm afraid of for he will soon be in your pants. (Tom is thinking about all the victims he had when they worked together.)

Pete in the coach park looks over his coach and checks everything is Ok and he sets off for Aspley Lane Church and to pick up the old folk for their trip to Skegness.

Chapter Six

Pete pulls up outside the Church and they start to come out of the church and Pete's eyes light up for there is a few old folk but a lot of young men and birds and Pete as they board the coach is thinking to himself. Maybe my luck will be in. He smiles at the old ones and young men but when it came to the birds Pete lifts his eyebrows and tells them welcome aboard sweetheart nice to meet you. Well the girls are well pleased at what they see and smile at Pete and thank him. All boarded and Pete is off out of Nottingham heading for Skegness front and the bowling greens. They start to depart and two of the girls stay behind and get off last and they ask Pete.

"Are you coming to watch us play?"

"I might pop along later when I've secured the coach."

"That will be nice my name by the way is Susan and my friend is Dot she all ways hit's the spot." Pete looks Dot up and down and he tells Susan.

"You are spot on for Dot could really turn me on." Pete sitting laughing at the verse he told Susan."

"You are witty like me and your name is."

"Ho I'm sorry it's Pete and it's nice to meet two gorgeous girls like yourself."

"Maybe we will catch you later Pete." Susan lifting her eyes up to Pete.

"Right on babe me too, I would like the company with it being a lonely job." Pete returning the complement by lifting up his lips at them as they left the coach. Pete watched them walk away and he could see that they were talking as they went across the car park, but unbeknown to Pete they were telling each other.

"He's fucking gorgeous, I would not mind a piece of him." Susan squeezing Dot's arm. Dot tells Susan well if we get knocked out we might have the chance." They both giggle at what Dot had said and head for the entrance into the bowling green.

Pete in the meantime sat on the coach watching the world go by and after an hour said to himself.

"Might as well go and see how the ones I brought are getting on."

He enters the bowling green and on the green believe it or not playing a pair from Skegness are Susan and Dot. Pete sees them and suddenly shouts out.

"Come on Susan and Dot give it to them." Susan see's Pete waves and then turns to Dot and said to her.

"Never mind give it to them, I would love him to give it to me." Susan giggling and Dot tells her.

"Well if we lose this end we might get the chance."

Next up Dot first to bowl and she bowls her first ball down the green and it is just short with the other opponent's bowl just resting off the white jack ball.

Pete sits there not understanding the rules and at the end of the 10 frame Susan and Dot have just lost 10-7 and their opponents go through to the quarter finals. They come off the green and Pete asks them how they got on. Well the girls just drop their faces and tell Pete.

"We lost 10-7 and we are out."

"Never mind girls what would you like to do, I'm all yours." Susan looks at Dot and Dot nods her head and Susan comes straight out with.

"Why not as a consolation prize you take us back to the coach and fuck the arse off us." The two girls stood there smiling at Pete. Well Pete is took back with the request and he tells them.

"Come on then girls let the good times roll." Pete rubbing his hands at the prospects of satisfying two at once. All three of them leave the Bowling Green and head back to the coach and Pete asks them abruptly.

"Hope you don`t mind but what will you wish for when we get back." Susan tells him.

"I want you to fuck me like you have not fucked any other bird before, and you can give me all that you have for I`m on the pill." Well Pete's eyes light up at what Susan said and he turns to Dot and asks.

"What about you sweetheart."

"Well I don't mind a start on my fanny but if you feel like coming put it up my arse." Well Pete cannot believe what they are saying and already he is tingling at the prospect of shagging both of them.

They come to the coach and Pete unlocks the coach door and they enter and Pete locks it behind him and tells the girls to make their way to the back. He pulls down the blinds and Susan and Dot start to remove their green bowling tops and Pete sits there watching and they are soon down to just their panties, and Pete stands up and Susan starts to remove Pete's shirt and when they both see Pete's firm and well-built body they both take a big intake of breath at what stood before them. They are both together removing Pete`s jeans and trunks, and when he stood there fully in the nude and his big Prick standing proud they both turn to each other and both at the same time say,

"Ho my God just look at that big boy." Well Pete stood there and they both put their hands around Pete's 10 inch cock and start to give him a wank, and Pete stood there enjoying their moves and pushing his front further towards them.

Then Susan try's to take as much as she could into her mouth and starts to give Pete a blow job. Then they were taking it in turns to suck on his cock and Pete after a few minutes knew that if he did not stop them there is no way that he would get into their Fannies, so he tells Susan to lie across the back seats of the coach and Dot to stand in front of him. He straddles Susan and starts to insert his cock into her fanny, and Dot stood looking at Pete's cock diapering into her and Pete pulls Dot closer and starts to lick around her cunt and she opens her legs further for Pete to get more. He is bashing away at Susan with her giving of loud sounds of enjoyment and Pete is flicking Dots clitoris and trying to get as much tongue into her. After about ten minutes Susan is screaming with pleasure and he tells her.

"Come on Susan give Dot a feel of my cock." They swop places now it's Dots turn to have a feel of Pete's cock and Susan to have more pleasure with his tongue and before long both are screaming out with pleasure and Pete suddenly could feel that this was it and he tells them both.

"Who would like it quick?" They both sit up and tell Pete.

"Spunk on our faces." Well Pete obliges and standing facing both of them suddenly explodes and they both are having a spunk wash with both of them receiving all of Pete's spunk and sucking every drop out of him. After about five minutes Pete tells them.

"That was fucking fantastic, how was it for you babes." Susan looking up to Pete and still licking her lips.

"All that I can say is I would rather receive that, than play fucking bowls, for we have had the best of both worlds of balls and fucking, I mean bowls and fucking." They both sit there giggling and Pete laughs too. Pete tells them.

"You can go down to the toilet on the bus to clean up and then they will go and see how the contest is getting on."

They all clean up and do return to the bowls just as the winners are announced and it was someone from Skegness that had won.

The rest of the afternoon was Pete walking round the fun fair while the Bowls presentations are made. Pete goes down to the front and sits on one of the benches and looks out to sea. Then all of a sudden with the waves crashing onto the beach it suddenly reminds he of Spain and his Sofia and he suddenly had this cold chill running through him, and he sat there and quivers and he is thinking of Sofia.

"Babe I miss you, please forgive me for doing what I do for I'm lonely sweetheart and miss you like hell." Then Pete gets a tap on the shoulder and it was Susan.

"Pete what are you doing down here all alone, you have not given us your phone number, and I was wondering when we get back would you like to come and stop with me and Dot for the night and carry on where we left off."

"Fucking hell Susan I would love to put it's my mums birthday today and when I get back I've promised to take her for a meal dam it. Look take my number and I will phone you when I'm free for the night, is that a date." Pete writes down his number and Susan does the same and they exchange numbers and Susan tells Pete.

"Shit it will after to be for your Mum defiantly comes first, we love you Pete I will see you back at the coach when we leave." Pete sits there looking at Susan's firm and long legs right up to her bum and he is thinking.

"Fuck it I've promised to see Sandy tonight, and I could have fucked the arse of them to fuckers tonight. Anyway that will be three fucks today by the time I've fucked Sandy tonight. Pete looks back at the sea and said sorry Sofia.

5.30pm Pete back at the coach and they are already for the trip back home and Pete tells them before he pulls away.

"Well I hope you all enjoyed today and I will stop for one drink on the way back and might I say only one drink only, for we have to be back at the depot by 8.30pm. Thank you. Pete pulls away and they have been traveling for about 50 minutes when Pete pulls into a pub where he stops just before you get to Lincoln. Then he suddenly remembers, Ho fuck I wonder if Ruth is still the Landlady, for if she is I might make it four fucks today.

They all disembark and head for the pub and once inside Pete notices that sure enough Ruth was behind the bar, and she spots Pete.

"Well I will be dammed if it's not my handy man Pete." Ruth goes over to where Pete is and arms stretched out approaches Pete with her large tits thrusting into Pete's front and she tells him.

"Well where you have been big boy for the last two years and a bit."

"Along story babe, but I'm back with the same coach firm."

"Well would you like to come and tell me about it up stairs for I'm due for a half hour break." Ruth lifting her eyebrows at Pete and moving her large tits around Pete's front.

"Come on then babe but only 30 minutes for I've got to be back at depot by 8.30pm."

"Long enough I can reassure you, come on tiger follow me." Ruth holding Pete's hand goes to the door that lead to her private quarters, and once up stairs ask Pete.

"Come on get those clouts off and get into my bed, and we can have one of our cuddles and the rest." Well Pete starts to strip and looking at Ruth who is franticly striping at an almighty rate and she is in bed before Pete and she tells him with her legs going up in the air in bed waiting for the hulk that she is hungry for.

"Fucking hell Pete get in this fucking bed for I want that big fucker off yours."

Pete smiles at Ruth and drops his trunks and when she sees his cock standing proud and rather long just licks her lips and she could not take her eyes of it.

Pete slips between the sheets and Ruth straight away had both her hands on Pete's cock.

"Where have you been for the last two years for I've missed this mother fucker. Ruth leaning up and going down on Pete and starts to suck away at his cock. Pete tells her.

"Believe it or not I got married and have lost her to cancer." Ruth stops sucking and tells him.

"You are kidding me, I`m so sorry sweetheart here let my comfort you." Ruth goes back to what she was doing and sucking away. Pete lay there with his arms above his head and looking at the ceiling and enjoying the pleasure that Ruth was giving him he just said to himself.

"Forgive me Sofia." Then he tells Ruth you lay back and let him pleasure her. Well Ruth is straight on her back with legs wider than the English tunnel waiting for the big one to enter. But Pete kisses her neck first then starts on her large Tits and her nipples start to stand proud just like to chapel hat pegs and Pete really is going at them both. Then he is down to her groin and starts to flick her clitoris with his tongue and Ruth starts to open her legs as wide as she could for Pete to really give her fanny a good seeing too. Pete is giving it all and he could tell that Ruth was ready with her juices really flowing and he comes up looks at Ruth starts to kiss her and his cock starts to penetrate Ruth and as soon as she feels it going deeper into her she grips Pete's back and tells him.

"You`ve got the most magnificent cock in the world, fucking hell Pete you are going to blow my mind in minutes." Ruth taking in deep breaths of pure pleasure at the feeling she was getting from Pete and she starts to groan with pleasure at every push Pete was giving her. Pete speeds up for he knew that time was getting on and he really starts to bash away at Ruth and by now she is really flowing with pure pleasure, and Pete could feel her warm juices rapping around is cock and he suddenly explodes and Ruth screams out loud at the feeling of Pete's spunk flowing inside her. She is by now really gripping onto Pete`s back and she tells him.

"I wish I could bottle you for I would be an alcoholic within days at the felling you give, you are fucking magic." she kisses Pete and she was the first to say.

"We had better get back down stairs for you should be back on your way by now."

They both dress and go back down stairs and Pete goes out and the passengers are all waiting to board the coach, Pete apologises telling them that he had to help his friend the Landlady repair her pluming and now it was flowing better, sorry about that please board the coach." Pete unlocking the coach door for them to board. Pete is the last to board and just before he goes into the coach he hears someone shout.

"Love you Pete hurry back please." Pete waves and smiles at Ruth boards the coach and they are on their way back to Nottingham. He drops them of first back at Nottingham and Susan and Dot kiss Pete and Susan tells him.

"Don't forget the phone call." Pete smiles at her and he is off for the depot. He starts to pull into the coach yard and behold Sandy is waiting for Pete.

Chapter Seven

He parks the coach up approaches Sandy and kisses her and looks at his watch and tells her.

"Not too bad only 5 minutes late, have you been waiting long sweetheart."

"No just arrived, I myself how was the day."

"You know old folk going to play bowls bless them." Pete tells Sandy.

"Come on baby let's go for a drink then a meal, where would you like to go."

"You're treat lead on big boy for I'm all yours tonight." Sandy holding Pete's hand and smiling at him with the look that you can have your wicked way with me tonight. Pete opens his car door for Sandy to get in and walking round to his side he is thinking better not take her in the Horseshoes for if Donna's in there, then all hell will take off. He jumps into the driver's side and he tells Sandy.

"I know there is a great pub and restaurant just before you go onto the motorway that serve fantastic steaks, do you fancy that."

"Whatever I'm easy as a cat purring on a rug, and just want to enjoy the night with you." Sandy leaning forward and giving Pete a kiss.

"OK babe let's go." Pete pulling out of the depot and heading for the renamed pub, Miners Retreat. Sandy asks Pete.

"This used to be called the Badger Box."

"That's right babe and before that the Broxtowe Inn." It is only ten minute drive and they pull up and Pete parks and they go in and go to the bar. Pete orders their drinks and turns to Sandy and asks her when she would like to eat, she tells Pete after a couple of drinks then order.

They go and sit in a window seat looking out over the old pit of Cinderhill, and the slag heaps that had been grassed over and now looked a picture to look at with the odd tree starting to grow on the old colliery slag heap. They sit in general talk and after two drinks Pete asks Sandy if she is ready to eat and she tells Pete.

"Fine I would like to go and eat and after we have all night together with us both not working in the morning and a lie in together." They stand and go into the restaurant and are shown to a table and they sit and order their meal with a bottle of wine. And the whole evening is one romantic evening together and the conversation between them was just like any other courting couples. The time is approaching 10.30pm and Pete asks Sandy if she was ready to go and they leave arm in arm and head back to Pete's home. They pull up outside Pete's house and park up and go in and they stand in the hall way, and after they had removed their coats Sandy turns to Pete puts her arms round Pete and they are in a very romantic kiss, and Sandy after thanks Pete for a wonderful meal and night. Pete tells her.

"Thanks babe but the best part is to come." He scoops her up into his arms and starts to carry her up stairs, and Pete his thinking. Boy how many more chicks will be in my arms. As he is thinking this Sandy gives him a kiss while he climbs the stairs. At the top they enter the bedroom and it was in darkness and Pete puts her down, and starts to remover her blouse and then unclips her bra and it falls to the floor. He stands there and kisses Sandy then moves down to her breast and starts to suck on her nipples and at the same time removing her jeans and knickers. Now Sandy is standing completely in the nude and Pete starts to go lower and kissing her belly then the lips of her fanny and Sandy puts her hands onto Pete's shirt and starts to remove it while he still was flicking his tongue around her cunt. Sandy was loving it and she is trying to pull Pete up so she could remove is jeans but Pete carried on and he was unzipping his jeans, and then he pulls Sandy to the bed and she falls back onto it and Pete stood up and removed his jeans and boxers. Sandy lay there legs wide open and Pete starts to get onto the bed, and goes down on Sandy and she pulls him round so he was giving her fanny a good licking and Sandy was sucking away profusely on his dick. Every now and then Sandy stops sucking his cock and gives off on big groan at the feeling Pete was giving her and her juices start to flow for the feeling of his tongue working overtime on her fanny.

Sandy tells Pete.

"Please fuck me now for you are giving me on hell of an orgasm with your tongue, and I want to feel that big fucker of yours inside of me." Pete rises and his mouth his covered with Sandy's juices and he straddles her and slowly starts to put his large prick into her, and every inch that Sandy received she gives off on big groan as it went deeper into her and Pete starts to pick up the rhythm and go faster at her.

"Fucking hell Pete you are going to drown me in pleasure, faster babe please give me it all." Then she tenses up and gives off on loud scream as she starts to have one massive orgasm at what Pete's cock was giving her, and with her warm juices starting to flow Pete also pops his cork and starts to spunk Sandy she was gripping Pete's back and every feel of him ejaculating into her.

"Ho my God you are the bees knees you`re a great big fucker." Sandy trying to push Pete further onto her with the feeling Pete was giving her. After about ten minutes Sandy is back down from the ceiling and they both lay there on their backs and did not say anything for they both had been satisfied out of their minds. Sandy looks at Pete and tells him.

"Where have you been all my life for you are fantastic in bed?" Sandy leaning over and kissing Pete`s nipple. Pete is thinking to himself. (Fucking a lot of other birds me duck.) (Me duck is a Nottingham slang word a man calls a Woman)

"They both drop off and before they know it the daylight awakes Pete and he looks at the alarm and it is 8.30am.

"Bloody hell that went quick." He is lying on his side with Sandy curled up and her arse sticking out so Pete no more than sticks his cock between her legs and starting to push it up towards her Fanny. Sandy awakes and she could feel what Pete was doing and she know more than opens her leg by lifting her right one and Pete slips into her and he slowly starts to speed up and he had one hand holding her hip and trying to push more in. he was enjoying this and he starts to kiss Sandy's back and she quivers and turning slowly onto her belly and Pete followed and she starts to lift her arse of the bed and Pete grabs two of the pillows and puts them under Sandy to be more comfortable, and Pete starts banging away in the doggy position. Pete looking at Sandy's arse made him come more quicker, and they had only had been in the doggy position for ten minutes and Pete blows his top and he just screws up his face while still looking at Sandy's firm and beautiful buttocks, and he is giving Sandy the lot again and she too was having a massive orgasm. After it was up shower and dressed for the day and down in the kitchen Pete starts breakfast and they both sit down at the table and they are enjoying a full English that Pete had made for them. Sandy asks Pete.

"With it your day off what are your plans for the day."

"Pack a few things for tomorrows trip to Faro and then go down the gym, I've just thought, why don't you tag along you would enjoy it."

"No not me I'm not into all that gym stuff and pumping iron."

"Well you could always go for a swim, then after we could go into one of the sauna booths and you never now with it hot in there we might land up in the nude." Pete lifting his eyebrows in a suggestive way."

"Is that all you can think of, haven't you had your fill, then again sauna hot and sticky and owe body's sweating and sticking together." Now Sandy's daydreaming and thinking of the same thing as Pete.

"OK you're on I have nothing to do, and a sauna will open all my pours." Pete tells Sandy he will go and pack and get is trunks and after drop you off for your things." Sandy tells him she will see to the pots while he gets ready and Pete is upstairs in a flash and just before he packs a few things into his bag for tomorrows trip he pulls out the picture of Sofia that he had put away with Sandy coming to stay and he sat on the bed and looks at her smiling back at him.

"Forgive me sweetheart but I could not leave you looking at me while I was shagging Sandy, I still love you sweetheart and always will." He kisses the photo packs and trunks in a towel is soon back down just as Sandy had finished cleaning the kitchen.

"Are you ready sweetheart for a good swim and a relaxing Sauna?" Pete smiling at Sandy.

"The swim yes but we will wait and see if it is relaxing. "Sandy looking at Pete while he still had a smirk on his face. They pull up at Sandy`s home and she is soon back out and they were off to the gym. Once inside they change and meet up in the corridor just before you go into the gym or swimming complex. Well when Pete see`s Sandy his eyes nearly pop out of their sockets for Sandy comes walking towards him in a little skimpiest white bikini and a stunning figure.

"You look stunning sweetheart, you make sure no hulk gets his hands on you or he will feel the raft of me."

"Away will you Pete how long will you be."

"I will have only an hour and if you get tiered of swimming there is a little café that serves coffee and tea."

"OK Pete will see you in an hour."

They go their separate ways Pete into the gym and Sandy into the pool. Pete is pumping iron for an hour and just like he said he goes to meet Sandy and you guessed it she was sitting having a coffee and there were to wolf`s sniffing around her and Pete approaches and asks Sandy.

"Are you Ok sweetheart, or are you`re little friends bothering you are they." Pete standing there and every one of his body muscles is rippling as he glanced at the two fellows. They stood up and give their leave telling Sandy it was nice just talking to you, and they give a little smile at Pete for I think they knew that they were not welcome there.

"Pete they were only chatting to me and I would not do anything, for I`ve got my hunk coming to meet me, and take me to this so called sauna and might I say private." Sandy sitting there with a little teasing smirk on her face.

"Too true sweetheart are you ready to get hot and sweaty."

"Lead on my Prince for your maiden awaits your guidance."

"What the Fuck you on about."

"Come on Pete loosen up, for you are going to take me to this relaxing Sauna aren't you."

"Sorry sweetheart but it was just seeing those too trying to get into your pants."

"Silly man you are the only one and only one who sees my fanny." Sandy standing up and brushing by Pete and having a crafty feel of his dick.

"Come on my Prince lead the way." The go to the Sauna's and Pete finds one that is empty without a window and they enter and Pete locks the door and the first thing he did is throw a scoopful of water onto the coals and the heat suddenly hits them. Sandy tells Pete.

"bloody hell it's hot." She stands there trying to fan herself with her hand. Pete comes up to her and tells her.

"Let me help you feel a little comfortable." He puts his hand on the side of Sandy's bikini bottom and pulls the string on the side and it falls to the floor, and then he puts his hand around Sandy's back and unclips her top. She stood there completely naked and the sweat is starting to pour through her skin. She puts her arms around Pete and they stand there in a loving kiss, and then her hands move down Pete's back and she starts to pull down his trunks and they too drop to the ground and they carry on kissing.

They stand there in a loving clinch and the sweat between them is going all over them and Pete starts to move his hands down to Sandy's buttocks, and he lifts her up and still kissing walks forward and gently puts Sandy down onto the wooden bench where he had put their towels and laid her down. By this time Pete had the biggest hard on for what he is about to receive and Sandy puts her hands onto his manhood and starts to gently give Pete a slow wank why he still stood there in front of Sandy. Well Pete is by now flowing with sweat and Sandy sits up and starts to give Pete a blow job while he still stood there and he looks down and see's Sandy going in and out on his dick. Well he leans backwards with the pleasure Sandy was giving him and after about 5 minutes he tells Sandy.

"Come on babe lay back for it's my turn." Sandy did this and the first thing she did when she laid back on the bench is wipe her brow for the sweat from the heat is getting to her.

"Bloody hell Pete we are going to be ten stone light with this heat."

"Just lay back and enjoy sweetheart." Pete starts to go in-between her legs and his tongue starts to lick around her fanny and flicking her clitoris, well the pleasure Pete was giving her she seemed to forget about the heat and the further Pete pushed his tongue into her she starts to lift her front up towards Pete to get more feeling of his tongue, and she starts to have one hell of an orgasm, and she is starting to moan at the feeling Pete was giving her.

Sandy looks down at Pete and at the same time she is blowing the sweat of her face that is running down to her mouth, and she suddenly tells Pete.

"Come on sweetheart please fuck me know for you are giving me too much pleasure and I want to feel that great fucking chopper inside of me."

Pete rises and goes in-between Sandy's legs and she straight away opens them as wide as she could and legs in the air is telling Pete to straddle her. Pete gives her a kiss just as he was inserting his cock into her, and she suddenly feels the size of it and it takes her breath away, as he pushes further into her and Sandy looking at Pete and screwing her face up with Pleasure and he just looks back at her and it was if he is in another place. For Pete is thinking of Sofia as he starts to go faster at Sandy's cunt. He leans up and looks at the steam in the ceiling and he is saying to himself.

"I LOVE YOU Sofia please forgive me, this is for you." Pete is really going at Sandy and he is brought back down to earth with the noise Sandy was giving why he banged away at her with figure and power.

By now Sandy is having massive orgasms and shouting for Pete to spunk her now Please-please. Well Pete did explode and Sandy's voice is really high pitched and if anyone is in a cubical next to them they would surely be getting an ear bashing from Sandy.

They do finally come back down from their orgasm's and come out of the sweat box to cool down and believe me they looked like two wet kippers that had been slapped around a baking board. Pete takes a cold dip and Sandy a shower and they meet up after and it was if there whole day is going to be one silent time for they seemed to be on another planet. Pete drives Sandy back home and they sit in the car and Sandy tells Pete.

"You have fucked the arse of me well and truly for I think the only thing I'm going to do is go to bed and rest for I'm shagged out."

"Me too baby I will see you at work tomorrow." Sandy stands there and waves at Pete drive off, and Pete looks back into his mirror and see's Sandy waving. Then he breaks down again and all he is asking is for his Sofia.

Back at home he goes up stairs and he picks the photo up of Sofia and laid on the bed clutching it and he drifts off, and starts to dream, and in his dream he is lying in bed still clutching Sofia's photo and he hears a tapping on the window and he looks round and he smiles for there is this little Red Robin redbreast.

He goes to the window and opens it and the Red ROBIN TELLS Pete. "I love you and always will." Then just as Pete is going to say something it flies off just as he comes out of the dream and asking it to come back and shouting Sofia's name. He is sweating profusely comes round and looks at the window and he sees the tray and no birds he tells himself.

"Bloody twat everyone knows you don't get Robins in July." Pete getting off the bed and trying to pull himself together. He puts the photo back down and looks at Sofia smiling back at him and he sits there and tells her.

"When will the pain go away for I truly do miss you sweetheart, and I just cannot stop loving other women but not like I loved you?" He kisses the photo and tells himself, Come on Pete let's look forward to the trip tomorrow.

Chapter Eight

The next morning Pete is up at 6am readying himself for the trip to Faro. Down stairs he checks his bag and the most important thing his passport for he still chuckles at the time he set of with Tom Small and they had to divert to his home to pick up his passport with all the passengers. 7am Pete picks up his bag locks the front door and tells Sofia.

"Well here I go on my first long-haul trip, wish me luck babe." He smiles turns and starts to walk to the depot and to meet up with his co-driver Frank Bond, Pete is thinking. "Most not call him Frank the wank for it rhymes Frank the wank." He tells himself. "For fucks sake pack it in or you will be saying it automatically Frank the Wank." Pete bursts out laughing and he just could not help it and he starts to turn into the depot still laughing when another driver see's Pete laughing and asks him.

"What's so funny mate, you look happy."

"No it's just something I was thinking and he is about to tell him when the driver tells Pete.

"Ho by the way my names Frank and you were saying."

Pete splutters and tells Frank.

"My names Pete West and I'm your next long haul co-driver."

"Please to meet you Pete and you never told me what was so funny." Pete thinks quickly and comes straight out with.

Ho it was the last time I went down to Faro we stopped at one of our regular stops and we see this Drake fucking the arse of a duck, can you just imagine it."

Frank suddenly seeing this Drake fucking a duck in his head starts to burst out laughing and they both go walking into the canteen laughing their socks off.

"Not only that but it was holding the ducks head down on the concrete and the poor thing was being totally dominated and getting the arse fucked of it."

Well by now they are totally in laughter and Frank is buckling over with laughter so much that it bring tears to his eyes.

"Stop it Pete you are killing me." Well they both were brought back down to earth for standing there with his clip board is Tom Small.

"Well it looks like the introductions are out of the question, do you too know each other."

"Sorry Tom it's my fault for I was coming through the gate and had the giggles and the next think Frank joined in."

"Ok settle down now and let's concentrate on the job in hand, for both of you ahead, for you both know that you are taking one coach down to Faro in Portugal for one week and you Pete are the senior coach driver and Frank is the second coach driver, but you both are reps for the passengers on behalf of Summer Sunshine tours. Is there any questions lads."

"No Tom just the one." Pete smiling at Tom.

"Come on then Pete what it is."

"Well are they all assembled and what are the ages of the guest we are taking."

"Might have known your first question is that, yes they are all assembled in the waiting area for boarding and secondly might I have known too that this answer is all you have been waiting for is. Yes there is a number of young ones going." Well Pete nudges Frank and thumbs up telling him.

"You never know Frank we might be in here." Frank smiles at Pete and looks back at the Boss Tom Small.

"OK go and pick the keys up for coach twenty and board your passengers, and I will see you back in the depot in a weeks' time, have a safe journey." Tom leaves the canteen and Pete tells Frank.

"You go and get the keys and I will see to the passengers and welcome them."

Frank goes to the office while Pete goes to the guest lounge to tell them that they are about to depart. Frank goes into the office and he asks Sandy for the keys to coach twenty and she asks Frank.

"Where is Pete I thought he would have come for the keys."

"Ho he is seeing to the passengers, why is there anything you would like me to tell him."

"Please Frank tell him to pop in and see me before he goes."

"Will do Sandy see you in a weeks' time." In the meantime Pete had been introducing himself to the passengers and just like a radar is looking to who is going and especially the young birds. Frank pulls up outside the waiting area and Pete tells then.

"Please follow me and please have you're boarding passes, this way please."

He takes them to the coach and Frank opens the holding lid on the side of the coach for their cases. Pete is helping with the loading and checking their tickets and they start to board. The first dozen or so are middle age passengers and then standing next to Pete as he is throwing a few cases in bending at the time, looks round and all he could see is 8 legs standing in front of him and all in short miniskirts. Well Pete's eyes light up like Blackpool illuminations at seeing all that flesh. He stands and is saying out loud.

"What have we here the spice girls?" They giggle at what Pete had said and they tell him.

"We are from Manchester and decided to instead of flying try a coach and see what it is like."

"Well you won't go wrong with myself and my mate Frank, for we look forward to giving a great service to our beautiful young ones like you're self's."

Pete looking back down at their legs and as they are boarding up the steps one turns round as Pete is looking up to her and might I say showing a little of her panties.

"Let's hope we do get a great servicing from you this week."

"Don't worry about that love you will all be satisfied with what you get." Pete smiling at her and lifting his eyebrows in a suggestive way.

"Will look forward to being introduced to you later," She turns and returns the complement that Pete showed her by lifting her eyebrows at him.

All boarded and it was time for the off and Pete tells Frank.

"Did you see the four in short miniskirts that boarded last."

"Fucking to true what fine legs they have."

"Well I think our week is going to be one hell of shagging the arse's off them four, roll on when we get there Frank, get this show on the road let's go."

Frank with being the first coach driver for their trip down to Dover, starts to pull out of the depot and heading for the M1 South for Dover, while Pete stands and on the bus loud speaker tells them by introducing themselves to the passenger.

"Good morning Ladies and Gentlemen may I welcome you aboard Sumer Sunshine Tours of Bulwell." Well as soon as he said Bulwell the four girls giggle and Pete looks at them with a little screwed up face at why they are giggling. Then he continues.

"We are going to travel down to Dover and the first turn at the wheel is your driver Frank Bond, and I the second driver Pete West, and we do welcome you aboard today. Then a ferry crossing and then we will continue the overnight run down through France then Portugal and hopefully have you in your Hotel by mid-afternoon. Any questions don't hesitate to ask us, Thank you Ladies and Gentlemen, sit back and enjoy your run down to Dover, thank you." Pete puts the microphone back in its holder and he goes to Frank and he tells him.

"I will go and chat the four birds up and see how the land lies with them." Frank puts his thumb up to Pete and he turns and starts to go down the coach and asking the question if everything is alright. He comes to the four birds and Pete kneels down so he is looking at their legs and they notice that Pete's eyes are looking down and then back up at their faces. One of the Girls called Kay opens her legs a little to show a little panty and Pete straight away noticed and he seemed to tense up and Kay asks Pete.

"You are one hell of a fit bloke Pete, you must work out with what I`m looking at."

Too true and your name is."

"Kay and might I say I would like to wonder around at what I'm seeing but tell us one think Pete."

"Out with it what is it." Pete thinking she is going to ask him about his body.

"Are you from this place Bulwell?"

"Yes why Bulwell is a great place to live."

"Well who the hell named it Bulwell, did a bull fall down a well or something." Kay looking at the other three and giggling.

"Hay never mind laughing let me tell you that the word Bulwell, is a great place to live and many moons ago, yes you are right in one way but no the wife's tail did say that a bull being brought to market did fall down a well hence Bulwell market but this is not true. For Bulwell goes back centuries and in the early years in around the ten century they built a bridge across the river lean and it was notorious for highway robbers and then the place was called Buleuuelle. Pete smiling at Kay.

"Fucking hell Pete I wished I never asked, I mean how the hell you pronounce Buleuuelle. Anyway forget all that crap, me and the girls were wondering are you two interested in sharing a little time with us at the hotel for we like what we see." Kay putting her leg into Pete's front as he was bending down and telling them the bull shit about Bulwell.

"Well we will be stopping at the services in what." Pete looks at his wristwatch and tells Kay.

"Then the four of you and Frank and myself in about an hour and a half could have a coffee with you and rally get to know each other before we board the ferry for France." Kay looks at the other girls and all nod their heads and Kay tells Pete.

"You have a date, in an hour and a half we will have a little chit-chat." Kay still rubbing the inside leg of Pete and he is thinking to himself. "Boy you are going to get the arse fucked of you on the ferry tonight."

Pete touches Kay's leg to help himself up and looking at Kay puckers up his lips at her, and then goes to the front were Frank is concentrating on driving. He tells him about when they stop and Frank turns to Pete and tells him.

"Well I will drive till we get there at the services and after you can take over for the last haul to Dover."

Pete resits and every now and again looks back to where Kay is sitting with her mates and she smiles at Pete and gives him a wave. Pete tells.

"Frank how long now Frank for I think they are gagging for it."

"About half an hour for fucks sake don't keep asking or you will have me putting my foot down to the boards and sitting with a hard on."

"That's my boy just keep going for the quicker we get there the better we will know who we are going to shag on the ferry." Pete sitting back on his seat and with the biggest smirk on his face.

They do eventually pull into the services and Frank parks up and Pete stands and tells them that they have an half hour break before they set of again for Dover.

Chapter Nine

They start to disembark and Pete is helping the passengers off, then the girls and they wait till everyone is off and all six of them head for the services.

Once inside Pete sits the four girls down and he asks them what their drinks are, and he and Frank go to the counter to be served. While they are going Kay asks the three other girls.

"Who do you fancy for I tell you now I want that Pete to fuck the arse of me for I tell you girls when he bent down by my seat I brushed up to his cock and might I say it was some fucking tool." Well that brought one or two giggles from them and two of them tell Kay that they fancy Frank. It looks like the boys will not after to work hard on these birds. They start to come back to the table and out of earshot Frank suddenly stops and he tells Pete.

"Ho my God you fucking wanker." Pete stops dead and looks back at Frank and he asks him.

"What's up with you, you isn't got cold feet have you."

"No you are going to fucking kill me, for Sandy asked me to ask you to go and see her before we go, and I totally forgot."

"Never mind I will ring her and tell her what a fucking plonker you are." Pete in a friendly way slapping both sides of his cheeks tells him.

"Come on mate more important things to do than phone some bird up, when we have four chicks here." They come to the table and dish out the drinks and all of them sit there and Pete looks at Kay and he asks her.

"Are you an item or free-lance." Kay looks at Pete and tells him.

"No I'm a free agent and I think I'm looking at my next conquest." Kay feeling Pete's leg under the table. Pete tells her.

"Wait till we board the ferry for the night crossing I know one or two hidden spots were we could get closer together." Pete lifting his eyebrows in a suggestive way.

"Roll on when we are on the ferry." Kay still rubbing Pete's leg.

"Come on then introduce you're three other mates then." Pete looking at Kay and noticed that Frank was getting well into one of the other birds. Kay tells her friends.

"Listen up for you will have to tell Pete and Frank you're names, Carol you start.

"Hi Pete and Frank my names Carol and this is." Carol pointing to her mate sitting next to her who Frank had an interest in.

"My names Rosemarie, and over to you." Rosemarie pointing to her mate. Her mate smiles and in a quiet voice tells them.

"Hi Pete and Frank my names Lorraine, please to meet you." Pete looks at Lorraine and it reminded him a little of Sofia with her long black hair and petite figure. They carried on chatting and Pete and Frank are well into the girls and the ice had truly been Brocken when Pete tells them.

"Come on girls the sooner we are in Dover the sooner we will be on the ferry for the night crossing." They all stand and make their way back to the coach and would you believe it Pete had Kay and Lorraine hanging of his arm, while Frank brought up the rear with Carol and Rosemarie on his arm. They reach the coach and the four girl's board while Pete and Frank stand outside the coach waiting for the stragglers, and Frank tells Pete.

"Fucking hell Pete I think we have scored there." Frank rubbing his hands together.

"Scored I tell you now when we reach Dover and aboard the ferry that Kay is going to get the fucking arse fucked of her, and if I get the time and chance that Lorraine is going to get it too."

"What both of them in one night, no fucking way will you achieve that."

"Come on then but you money where your mouth is, I bet you I fuck the arse of both off them before we get off the ferry."

"You're on a ten pound note say's you will not do it." (Little does Frank know about Pete if he had the time I think he would fuck the arse of all four, plus anyone else who wanted it.)

They set off and Pete is at the wheel for the final run in to Dover and about 9pm they arrive and pull into the dock and they all disembark for Passport control while Pete and Frank take the coach and board the coach onto the ferry and they to go through Passport control and they all meet in the ferry's cafeteria. Pete tells them.

"Come on then girls let's go up top and watch the ferry pull out of port." All six of them go onto the upper deck and look down as they are casting off and Pete tells them.

"Well here we go next stop Calais in France, they are all looking over at the ropes being released and suddenly the ferry's foghorn sounds to tell them that she is pulling out of dock. Well Kay jumps out of her skin as the other's did and she is all over Pete arms wrapped around him and Pete press his front into her so she could feel his cock trying to burst out of his trousers.

"Fucking hell Pete do they have to do that I nearly shit myself, and what is that I can feel, boy you do need me."

"You bet Babe let the rest go back inside and I will take you somewhere where we can sort this bulge that you are feeling out." Kay discreetly feeling Pete's cock and her eyes light up.

"Fucking hell Pete what the hell have you got in there?" Pete presses closer and gives Kay a kiss and she responds and they both are in one hell of a French kiss and they have not noticed that the others have retreated back inside out of the noise of the foghorn bleeping every few minutes. Pete looks and notices and he tells Kay.

"Come on babe this way." He takes her to the spot where the last time he came he shagged another bird and he pulls her into a door way that is set back and he starts to feel her tits. Kay straight away is starting to unzip his zip on his trousers and Pete's trousers fall and she pulls out his rather large cock and with both hands starts to fondle it and she starts to gently wank Pete off.

She looks down and just could see his manhood in the dim light and comments to Pete just before she goes down on him.

"Fucking Jesus Christ what a fucking big fucker you have here, I'm going to struggle to get this fucking monster in my mouth. She is going down to Pete and looks up at his face as she starts to try and swallow Pete's cock and he stood there enjoying the feeling and pleasure that Kay was giving him. Deeper she tries to slowly suck away on his cock going in and out and starting to go faster with every move and after about five minutes Pete tells her.

"Come on Babe my turn." Kay comes up and it's Pete's turn to go down on Kay. She had a small mini skirt on and her knickers were soon down and as Pete puts his head between Kay's legs she opens them wider to receive Pete and she suddenly takes a deep breath as Pete's tongue starts to work away at her clitoris and then her fanny.

"Fucking hell Pete that's wonderful." She starts to pull the back of Pete's head further into her groin and by now her juices are really flowing and Pete could tell with the taste and the groans she is making.

"Please fuck me now Pete, come on babe show me what that big fuck can do." Pete rises and starts to point is cock towards Kay's fanny and she opens her legs and with one hand guides Pete's cock to its goal. Pete starts to penetrate her and his cock starts to go into her an inch at a time, and

Kay takes one hell of a deep breath as every inch went into her, and she had never felt like this before.

"Fucking hell Pete you are a monster that is lovely please fuck me faster for you are going to blow my mind in a moment, God you are fucking good."

Pete puts both his hands under her buttocks and lifts her up so he could really penetrate her, and starts to go faster and Kay is in mid-air with legs wide open and shouting out loud with every thrust that Pete made, and she suddenly explodes with pleasure and Pete could feel her warm juices flowing and he too pops his cork, and he withdraws for he did not know whether to leave it in or not. But Kay shouts out put the fucking thing back in for I want to feel every drop of you spunk. Pete obliges and he ejaculates and Kay is moaning with pleasure at every drop she was getting from Pete.

"Pete you are the greatest fuck ever, boy I`m going to have the time of my life when we get there." She starts to kiss Pete while she is still in the air and Pete`s cock is still moving in and out of her fanny and they both have had one hell of a shag.

After they have come back down to earth Pete suggest that they go back inside and clean up, and then meet the others. They both go and about fifteen minutes later they are back inside and Pete comes to where Lorraine is and she is sitting on her own and he asks her.

"Hi Lorraine where are the rest of the guy`s."

"Hi Pete I don`t really know for I do now that Rosemarie had gone with Frank and I could not tell you where Kay is."

Pete looks round and he suggests to Lorraine.

"Well how about me and you go and take the warm night air around the deck for there is a full moon out there."

"Well it is warm and stuffy in here that would be nice, thank you Pete."

Pete takes Lorraine's hand and leads her to the upper deck and they go onto the decking and go to the rails that look out over the sea. The moonbeams are dancing across the water and Lorraine comments on this to Pete.

"What a romantic place this is just look at the moonbeams and the flickering waves." Lorraine looking straight out to sea and then Pete puts his arm around Lorraine and into her ear whispers.

"Yes and with a beautiful Woman by your side." Kisses the side of her cheek and she turns faces Pete and they end up in a long loving kiss and Lorraine's hands are trying to grip Pete's back. Pete starts to press his front into Lorraine and he breaks of kissing her and he tells her.

"You are gorgeous and the first time I set eyes on you I knew that there was something there, I would love to make love to you in this wonderful setting."

"Ho Pete that will be imposable for we are on a ferry and there is no place to go."

"Ho yes there is come on baby I will show you." Pete grabbing Lorraine's hand and leading to yes you guess the same place where he had just shagged the arse of Kay. He pulls Lorraine into the door way and starts to kiss her and Lorraine responds and they are both in one loving romantic kiss and Pete starts to unzip the back of her skirt and it drops to the ground and he starts to put his fingers into her pants and gently starts to finger her clitoris and then starts to finger her. Lorraine is starting to groan with pleasure and she unzips Pete's flies and she starts to fondle is cock and she suddenly realise how big he was.

"Ho my God Pete you are truly well endowed, for God's sake that will never penetrate me."

"Don't you worry it will and I will be gentile with you being petite babe." Well Lorraine suddenly tells Pete which through him completely Lorraine tells him.

"Fuck me up the arse for you would not find me taking any contraceptives and don't want to become pregnant." This took Pete by surprise and Lorraine no more than turns round bends forward holding onto the door and tells Pete.

"Put it up my arse and be gentle when you penetrate me." Pete did this and guides his cock to its goal and he starts to insert his cock into her arse and

Pete really enjoyed it for the sensation he got when he started to go slowly into her and looking down at his cock disappearing into her arse with the moon shining onto her arse made Pete really tingle and what made it worse was with Lorraine with every thrust Pete made she was really groaning with pleasure. Pete starts to really bash away at her arse and with one hand rubbing her clitoris his thumb and two fingers working away at her fanny and Lorraine with the feeling Pete was giving her suddenly shouts out for Pete to spunk her, and Pete did and he explodes and they both start to groan with pleasure, one with Pete feeling every drop going into her arse, and Lorraine the same with receiving every drop that Pete was giving her. After both stand and are kissing profusely with each other and Lorraine complementing Pete and Pete the same back. In all them both enjoyed the night and the ambiance of the view and moon.

Soon after Pete and Lorraine are back sitting at a table in the cafeteria, where Carol sat and in comes Frank with Rosemarie and they join them and they ask the same question, to Carol where Kay is, well Pete and Lorraine lift their shoulders in a pose saying you tell us.

There is only 20 minutes left on the ferry when into the cafeteria comes Kay looking a little sleepy.

"Where have you been we were starting to get a little worried?" Lorraine asking Kay.

"Would you believe it I went for a drink in the bar and sat down and the gentle sway of the ferry and I bloody fell fast on, you know just like some people do when on a bus or in a car." Lorrain giggles and Pete looks at his watch and tells them.

"Well you four should start to make your way to the gate for disembarking for we will be pulling into Calais France in a few minutes and Frank and I will go to the coach for disembarking and Passport control." The girls start to make their way out and Just as Frank is starting to get up Pete pulls him back down and tells him.

"That's a tenner you owe me for I shagged Kay and that Lorraine you will have to get in there Frank for she takes it up the arse."

"You never did Pete, did you?" Pete with the biggest smug look on his face and he is thinking to himself. That's 8 I've shagged, only 11 more to go to beat my Round-Robin. Frank pulls out a tenner out of his wallet and tells Pete.

"Well worth it for I shagged the arse of that Rosemarie, very nice." Now Frank with the funny looking face thinking back.

"Come on mate let's get to the coach and depart, and roll on when we are there, for I think this is going to be one hell of a shagging trip. YES." Pete putting his arm around Frank and them both go walking off with an extra step and leave the cafeteria smug looking. Down in the lower deck once docked they are allowed back onto the coach when safe to do so and they are guided off down the ramp back onto the dockside, once through Passport control they go to the pickup point where all their passengers are waiting. All boarded and Pete tells them over the microphone the rest of their journey down to Faro. Good evening Ladies and Gentlemen, we are about to start our second half of the journey traveling through the night down to Faro in Portugal and we hope you enjoy the trip and please do try and get a little sleep, for we will not be stopping till 5.50am for breakfast then the final push for the Hotel and hopefully we will have you there and booking in at 10.30am thank you.

Frank is taking the first drive for four hours and the time is approaching 9.30pm and then Pete and so on till they arrive at their destination. Pete tells Frank that he will go and see to the passengers, that they are comfortable and any questions.

"Well don't be too long Pete for you ought to rest before you take over for it will be about 1.30 am."

"Don't worry Frank I will be alright mate."

Chapter Ten

Pete starts to go down the coach seeing to the passenger's needs and any questions they had when he comes to the four girls that are occupying the back seats with three of the seats being obscure to other passengers with having the coffee making bar and the stairwell on the other side for the toilet that is set below. Kay and Loraine are both well out of it with being fast asleep with Lorraine resting her head on Kay's shoulder. Pete looks at them toots and turns to Rosemarie and Carol and tells them.

"Did not take those two too long to nod off, it must be the drone of the engine and gentle sway, bless-um." Rosemarie and Carol giggle and tell Pete.

"Well you are not driving for a while are you?"

"No it's my four hours off and then I take over at 1.30am."

"Well why don't you join us for we could do with the company." Both of them patting the seat between them."

"I don't see why not thanks girls." Pete sits down between them and they cover themselves up with a blanket that is provided for passengers comfort through the night. They are both giggling and Pete seemed to know what was coming for they both put their arms through Pete's arms and snuggle right up to him, and then Rosemarie hand starts to wonder down to Pete's groin and she starts to gently rub Pete's bulge, while Carol puts her hand into Pete's T-shirt and starts to rub his breast and tweeting his nipples.

"Carol comments.

"Fucking hell Pete you are one fit and muscular fellow."

"That's what they like babe and there is plenty more of me to explore."

Rosemarie by now had Pete's cock out and pulling his foreskin back and looking at Carol and telling her and might I say in a darken back seats.

"Never mind what you are feeling you ought to feel this fucker." Carol takes her hand of Pete's chest and goes down to where Rosemarie is working away on Pete's cock. Carol also feels Pete's erect cock and she looks at Rosemarie and asks.

"Fucking hell Rosemarie is this thing real" Rosemarie tells her.

"Well we will soon fucking find out." She know more than lifts the blanket and goes down on Pete who just sat there with a smirk on his face and it was if he was saying.

"Just help yourself girls and enjoy." Rosemarie is giving Pete one hell of a blow job and he turns to Carol and starts to kiss her and with his tongue going deep into her mouth, then he pulls away and tells her.

"If you want some I think you also should get down there and have some." Well she to disappears beneath the blanket and they both land up trying to swallow Pete's cock and they just could not get the whole thing in their mouth but they still enjoyed sucking away on his bell end. Pete just sat there arms above his head and screwing up his face at the pleasure that both of them were giving him, for he is thinking to himself. "Boy this is one hell of an enjoyable blow job." He took it for about ten minutes and he knew that he had better change it or he would not fuck them, so he tells them.

"Come on babes my turn now for I want to fuck the arse of both of you." They both come up and Pete turns Rosemarie onto her front and tells her to sit on his cock while Carol keeps watch.

Rosemarie did this and Pete sat on the seat and Rosemarie straddles Pete and she slowly lowers herself onto his cock. She had one leg on both sides of the seats and starts to slowly lower herself onto Pete's cock.

Every inch that went in she is giving of one hell of a deep breath at what she is receiving and Pete at the same time as she went down his lifting up so she felt more of his cock and it was not long when her juices start to flow and she is starting to ride Pete's cock faster and she starts to moan loud and Pete starts to kiss her to keep her quiet but the more Pete penetrated her the more she wanted to break of kissing and shout out loud. Pete knew that she was having massive orgasms and he tells her.

"Come on babe Carols turn." Rosemarie lifts of Pete and flops back down and she is truly shagged out at what she received and Carol sits in the same position and starts to lower onto Pete's erect cock, and she nudges Rosemarie and telling her.

"Come on your fucking turn to keep watch." Rosemarie in a daze stands up so any passengers wanting to go to the toilet would not see the seats behind the coffee bar. Carol slowly lowers herself down on to Pete's cock and with the noise that Rosemarie had made had turned her on and she was well up for a shag with her juices flowing at what is to come. Pete holds on to her arse cheeks and he is penetrating well into her and Carol is gripping Pete's back at the feeling he was giving her and Pete had only been shagging her for ten minutes and she was about to explode.

"Fucking hell Pete I'm going to explode." Pete tells her.

"Me too if you both want some I suggest you get off and both get down there to receive it." Well Rosemarie is lifting Carol of Pete's cock and he is about to explode, and they both dive under the blanket and Pete with the feeling of them both trying to get a lick of his cock he explodes, and they both get a face full of Pete's spunk and they are licking every drop of his cock, and each other's face. Pete just sat there with a smirk on his face at hearing them both murmuring at what they were getting. They both come back up and land up just kissing Pete and complementing on his performance, all that Pete did is look a cross and see Kay and Lorraine still fast on. The girls go down to the toilet and clean up, and by the time they have come back even Pete with the drone of the engine he too had dropped off. All back and settled down and it was not long when they were all off into the land of nod. 3 hours must have passed and Pete awakes it was if he had an internal alarm clock, for he looks at his watch and it was approaching 1.30am, and it was his turn to drive. He discreetly gets up and leave the four girls asleep goes down to the toilet to freshen up and then down to the front of the coach were Frank was pulling into a layby to be relieved. They swop places and Frank tells Pete.

'"Boy I'm ready for a rest for I'm all in." Pete adjusting his seat tells Frank well if you want a good sleep go to the back were the girls are there is plenty of room and blankets."

"Thanks for that Pete will do." Frank goes walking off up the coach with Pete looking at him go, and he is smiling to himself and saying.

"Yes but first you might get fucking molested and God help you if the other two awake." Pete pulls away from the layby and it was off for another four hours or so until they get to the services for their breakfast break, before the final push to the hotel. Pete driving along the motorway and at a constant 65 miles per-hour, and he his thinking well that is ten only nine more to break my record, then he hears a voice and it is telling him.

"Pete I love you so much, why I had to go."

"Sofia my babe I love you too, and miss you so." Pete is starting to drift and suddenly is brought back down with another voice.

"Please mate where the cups are for the coffee machine maker." Well Pete swerves a little and he tells the person.

"Please do not approach the driver like that you could cause an accident, if you need assistance see the other driver, he should be at the back near the coffee machine. Thank you."

"Sorry mate did not realise, I'm sorry." He walks off with a little bit guilty feeling towards the back and Pete his thinking.

"Thanks mate for if you had not come along I might have drifted off into a world with my Sofia. Bloody hell that was close." Pete sits there driving with a little more concentration and he looks in his rear mirror and sees the man at the back of the coach, and he looked like he was talking to Frank. Pete is thinking I hope they are not up to anything.

The time is approaching 6am and Pete had been driving for well over four and a half hours and he pulls into the services for their hour long breakfast break, and the Sun is just breaking the horizon with it being summer. He is on the microphone and telling the passengers.

"Good morning everyone hopes you all slept well for we have arrived at our stopping of point for you all to have a hearty breakfast before we set off on our final journey in one hour to the hotel. Thank you." Some of the passengers were awake and clapping that seemed to bring those who were still asleep around, and they all start to disembark, with one or two with just awakening stretching and yarning. All off and the last few with being at the rear are the four girls and Frank. Pete and Frank are at the back behind the four birds and Frank tells Pete.

"Fucking hell Pete I don't know how to tell you but when you took over I went to the back and sat with the girls and they started to mess about.

I think at this point with a little smirk on his face Pete knew what was coming.

"The two girls went down on me and were giving me one hell of a blow job when this passenger came up asking for cups for the coffee. Well I just hope he did not see the four legs sticking out under the blanket with the girls going at my cock. But when I told him in the bottom cupboard on the coffee machine, he seemed to bend down and look at the girl's legs and screw his lips up to me and smile." Pete was trying to stop himself from bursting in to laughter and is thinking to himself. He knew all right mate what was going off. Pete tells Frank.

"Don't worry he probably thought they were asleep on the floor." They enter the services and no more is said on the matter and they go and order their breakfast and after sit down with the four birds that they have befriended on the way down.

They have finished their breakfast and Pete tells Frank with the girls listening.

"How about I show you where that fucking drake lived, it's just through an hedge at the bottom of the car park."

"Lead on mate we have half an hour before we set off." Two of the girls Kay and Lorraine ask if they could tag on with them.

"Come on then let's go." They stand and leave Rosemarie and Caron finishing off their breakfast. On the way out Frank sees the punter that caught him on the coach when the two girls were going down on him, and when he sees Frank with another two birds, just puckers up his lips and raises his arm in a suggestive way. Frank whispering into Pete's ear tells him.

"FUCKING HELL Pete that's that block that caught me and did you see what he did."

"Forget it Frank he looks a man of the world and probably wishing it was him and not you that was getting a good seeing too." Frank looking back and feeling a little worried. They all four of them go walking down to the bottom of the car park and the hole in the hedge is still there, the last time Pete came and they go through. And in the morning light they see this duck pond with all the ducks and drakes upon the water and Pete points out to where in the past he had took a photo of the drake shagging the arse off that duck.

Kay and Lorraine are feeling a little frisky and come onto Pete and Frank and Pete straight away tells them.

"Come on babes we have not the time for we are due to get back to the coach in." Pete looking at his watch and telling them.

"In five minutes and I would sooner wait till we are in the hotel and in a comfy bed where I'm sure you won't be disappointed." Pete lifting his eyebrows at both of them. Lorraine tells them.

"That's a date then when we get together and you can have your wicked way with us both." Pete tells them that they are on and all four go walking back through the hedge to the coach where there is one or two waiting to board.

All boarded Pete doing a head count and telling them.

"Well Ladies and Gentlemen I hope you all had an hearty breakfast and ready for the last push to the Hotel, your driver for the last leg will be Frank and I'm sure traffic willing he will have you all booked in and round the pool in what looks like being a gorgeous day." Pete looking out of the window and seeing the sky starting to get lighter with the Sun not long before it will be up. The rest of the trip goes well and like they told the passengers Frank pulls up outside the Hotel, and Pete helping unload their cases is wishing them a good stay and have a fabulous holiday, and he will be there for them along with Frank if they need any help in any event. The girls are the last off and when Pete was bending into the hold for their cases Kay grabs his bum and asks him.

"Are you going to be around the pool when you are sorted?"

"Don't you fret now as soon as the coach is away and locked up and we have booked in we will be right out."

Kay tells them that they will save two Sun loungers for them, and all four go walking off into reception and giggling at something they were talking about. Pete stands looking at them and Frank joins him and Pete tells Frank.

"Looks like we will be fucking the arses of them four all week."

Coach secured and the first thing they do is book in and are told what room they are in and point it out to them. They are on a ground floor complex and with the time just before 10am, Pete and Frank go walking past one of the pool areas with no one out yet.

"Looks like this pool is quiet, let's hope the other two pools are the same."

Chapter Eleven

"Well this pool is nice I mean bar decking you can sit on, and, if the others are like this we will have to put a good report in when we get back." Frank smiling at Pete with approval so far.

"We will see come on let`s get changed and the first thing for me is a dip in that pool to try and waken myself up, come on Frank let`s get changed."

They go to their room and dump their cases and are soon into their trunks and Pete with towel over his shoulder asks Frank.

"Are you ready to hit that pool mate?" Frank comes out of his bedroom and tells Pete.

"Come on, then last one in is a wanker." Well both are dashing out of their room as if it was on fire, and they just throw their towels on to the nearest Sun loungers and dive into the pool. Well by now there were one or too punters settling down and when they see Pete and Frank charging into the pool one of them turns to her husband and tells him.

"Let's hope there are no others like them two for if there is it's going to turn out to be an holiday from hell."

"Don't worry dear I think it's the excitement on arriving here." Well Pete is use to cold water and starts to swim around the pool, but Frank is not and he comes up out of the water and came straight out with.

"Fucking hell Pete my bollocks have gone straight into my belly. It's fucking freezing." Frank is straight out of the pool and picks up his towel, and starts to rub himself down with the old couple looking on. Frank turns and is rubbing his balls and he looks straight at them and tells them.

"You would think that they would heat the pool up." The old man looks at Frank and tells him.

"If you go to the second pool it's heated, that is why we come and sunbathe around this one for it is a little quiet usually." The man giving Frank a little smirk smile. After about fifteen minutes Pete comes out of the water and is rubbing himself down and looking round the pool and it is still quiet, he looks at Frank who by now is lying on his bed and warming up with the sunshine.

"You would think that there would be more punters here by now." Pete tells Frank.

"Maybe they are around the heated pool, that's what that old chap told me" Pete straight away lifts Frank's sun lounger up and he falls onto the concrete.

"Come on then let's find the girls, they said they were going to save us two sun loungers."

"Fucking hell Pete I was just warming up."

"Come on we have more business then lying on our own, when we have our shagging interest sitting alone." They go walking off and the two old couple looking at them and the old Lady tells her husband.

"Well young ones today have no sense of respect, the language was beyond believe."

"Settle back dear they have gone now." Pete and Frank go down to the second pool and sure enough it was swarming with holiday makes and the pool was very fall, with hotel guest and their children splashing about in the heated pool. Pete looking round spots the girls and he tells Frank who was dipping his toe into the pool.

"Come on they are over there." Pete pointing to where he could see them. Frank starts to follow and he is telling Pete.

"That pool is like bath water, so warm."

"Wimp nothing wrong with the first pool good swim and no one to bump into but look at this if you dived in you would probably wipe out half the holiday makers." Pete approaching the girls and Kay straight away asks Pete.

"Where have you two come from, I thought for a moment that you had gone off us."

"No babe we went into the top pool and had a swim and realised that you must be at the heated pool." Pete putting down his towel on his sun lounger between Lorraine and Kay.

"You're kidding us you went into that top pool it was like ice water, that cold it curled you toes up when you put your foot in to the pool."

"It was refreshing and I have swam in colder water than that, very refreshing."

"Bloody hell Pete it makes me shiver just thinking about it."

"They all settle down and it was well over two hours that a word was not spoken for they all were off into the land of nod with the long haul trip over night down there. Pete was the first to come round and the time is approaching 1.30pm he looks at Frank who is snoring his head off for great Britain and Kay opens her eyes and see's Pete sitting up.

"Boy I needed that, what time is it Pete."

"1.30 pm Babe why." Kay looking round and seeing that the rest were fast on, asks Pete.

"Would you like to go and have a beer around the bar, for I'm feeling a little burnt with having a couple of hours in the sun."

"I see why not, come on then Babe let's go." They come to the bar and Pete takes two drinks to a decking table, they sit and are in the shade and watching all the people splashing around in the pool and enjoying themselves. They sat in general chat when Lorraine comes and joins them, sits and with her drink in hand tells them.

"Boy its hot sitting out there for the sun is belting down, and God help anyone who falls asleep sunbathing." Kay looks at Lorraine and whispers something to her while Pete was not looking and they both giggle, and Pete turns round and asks them.

"What's so amusing then girls."

"Nothing Pete just something we were on about coming down on the coach." Well Lorraine smiles at Kay and tells her in a quiet voice.

"Go on then ask him."

"Alright I will." Kay takes another sip of her drink and looks at Pete and asks him.

"Pete while the others are fast on, how about the three of us go back to my room and have ourselves some fun."

"Would love to, but first would you like another drink or." Before Pete finished his sentence Kay had, pulled him up out of his chair and all three of them were off to Kay's room. Once inside Kay locks the door and pulls back the blanket on the bed and as she rises from doing it, Pete puts his arms around her and with one hand unclips her bra and gently pulls down her bikini bottoms and she laid back on the bed. Then he turns to Lorraine and repeated the action and she too gets onto the bed, and they are both looking at Pete removing his trunks and revealing his fine physique and rather large manhood, that was starting to rise at the prospect of shagging the both of them. He starts to come forward to the bed and both the girls had their arms out to receive their prize, and they are starting to get excited at what is about to come.

Pete gets between Kay and Lorraine who are both still on their backs, and their hands are straight onto Pete's dick and he starts to feel their fanny. Pete gently with his thumb is turning it around on their clitoris and he inserts two fingers and he could feel both girls juice's starting to flow. He gently is turning and fingering Lorraine and he looks at her while still kneeing and her face was screwed up and eyes shut with the pleasure Pete was giving her. He leaves his fingers in Lorraine and gently starts to go down on Kay kissing her thighs and slowly making his way to her fanny. Kay opens her legs wider, for she knew what was about to come. Pete starts to kiss around her fanny, and his tongue starts flicking her clitoris. And he starts to really go at her clitoris, and every now and then he puts her clitoris in his mouth. And gently sucking it in and after a gentle blow onto it, Pete really starts to tongue her fanny and Kay by now is lifting her head up at the pleasure Pete was giving her and tells him.

"For fucks sake shag me now for I`m going to explode." Pete starts to rise and he starts to insert his cock into her and Kay is pulling Pete onto her, with feeling his cock going deeper into her. All this time Lorraine is still in heaven with what he was doing to her, and she was oblivious at Kay shouting out with so much pleasure. Pete starts to go deeper into her with his ten inch cock and by now Kay was really pulling Pete and starting to dig her nails into his back.

"Ho my God you are one hell of a fuck, you big fucker." Pete starts to kiss her and his tongue going down her throat, she pulls away from him and she is shouting out.

"Fucking spunk me now, God I`m in heaven."

"Wait a little longer sweetheart for its Lorraine's turn." Pete comes off Kay and straddles Lorraine and he starts to insert his cock, and Lorraine straight away takes one hell of an intake of breath at the feeling of Pete's cock. He starts to go slow and every now and then gives on hell of a push so more went into her and it was not long, before Lorraine was shouting at the top of her voice.

"God I want it all spunk me now." Lorraine turning her face and looking straight at Kay who was screwing her face up with Pete rubbing her clitoris and fingering her. Pete could feel he is about to explode and comes off Lorraine, laid back down on the bed and he tells them.

"He's all yours babes, make me explode all over you." Well they are that worked up with multi orgasms that they have had, and are both in turn sucking Pete's upright cock at a very fast rate. Now it was Pete's turn to start to screw his face up at the feeling Kay and Lorraine were giving him, and he explodes and both girls are sucking away on his cock in turn and murmuring in the taste and pleasure out of it.

All three of them fall back onto the bed and it was silence, it is if all three of them had been well and truly satisfied with the whole event. They are soon fast on and it must have been another two hours when they start to come round, and the first is Kay and she looks at her watch.

"Bloody hell you two wake up, for we have been asleep for well over two hours." Pete in the middle with his arm around Lorraine looks up and in a sleepiest voice.

"What are you on about?"

"We had better get back or the others will be wondering where we are."

"Pete is next sitting up wiping the sleep out of his eyes and then looking at his own watch, fucking hell you are right. Lorraine move that arse of yours it's time to shower and get back round the pool". Pete slapping her arse in a friendly way, she too stirs from her sleep and it was not long and they started to make their way back to the pool.

They are walking passed the decking with the bar on it, when they hear Carol sitting at a table telling them as they walked by not seeing her.

"Where the fuck have you three been, you have been gone ages." Carol asking them with Frank and Rosemarie also looking at them. Lorraine straight away told them.

"We got fed up with sunbathing and went for a walk around the town." Then Frank chirp's in saying.

"Wish you had told me for look." Frank stands and shows them his back, it is completely red raw and it made you squint just looking at it."

"Fucking hell mate you daft sod, you are going to suffer tonight with that, have you got any after sun, for that should cool it down." Frank stood there in a pathetic way looking for divine help, when Kay tells him.

"I will go to the Hotel shop and get him some." Lorraine as Pete are walking to the entrance of the decking to join them tells Pete.

"Looks like they don't suspect anything." Pete smiles at her and goes to the bar to get three beers for them. He comes back to the table and sits and Kay comes back from the shop with the after sun for Frank, Pete lifts his arm and in a gesture with hand out open pretends that he is going to slap Franks back. Well Frank is straight up and pleads with Pete.

"Please don't Pete it's killing me."

"Only kidding mate." Pete smiling at him. Kay tells Frank.

"Get yourself sat down and turn your back to me." She gently puts some cream onto Franks back and it felt really cool, and he takes a deep intake of breath, at the feeling he is getting as his back cools down.

"I will tell you one thing Frank we have had a long trip down here and I bet tonight we will be ready for a good night's kip, and if you are moaning and groaning tonight, you will be straight into the fucking pool."

"Frank giving Pete a gingerly smile at what he said. Rosemarie puts her hand onto Frank's knee and tells him.

"If he kicks you out Frank you could always come round to my bedroom, and we could make mad passionate love, and I could dig my nails into your back."

The girls giggling at what she said.

"Very funny I must admit, but it could have happened to anyone of us."

Rosemarie tells Frank.

"I don't think so mate for we had our towels over us, so we would not get burnt, and what did you have around you, SKIN." Well they are all laughing at Frank's expense and he stands and tells them.

"Well if you don't want me around I know when I'm not welcome." He is about to walk off when they all tell him.

"Come on Frank its only banter, I mean chill out man." Frank sits back down and in away is sulking a little with the girls all rubbing his leg, and even now two of them tell him.

"Well at least you have not burnt your dick, at least there is something to play with." Frank just smiles at them and he tells them.

"Come on then I will get the next round in what will it be." Well they all pass him their glasses and are smiling at the nice offer from Frank. Frank rises and starts to go to the bar, and they suddenly clock on.

"It's all inclusive, what is he on about, I will get them in." Frank turns when he is at the bar and smiles back at them, and he is thinking.

"That's one up for me." We'll all even and they decide to go back to their rooms and have decided what they are going to do that evening, and that is stay around the complex and have an early night.

Chapter Twelve

The time is approaching 6.30pm and Pete and Frank are ready for their evening meal in the Hotel's restaurant, they make their way and Pete in short sleeve T-shirt and jeans and Frank with a silk lose shirt on. ("And we all know why, yes the sunburn.") Pass the lobby and see the evening entertainment and it is a comedian at 10pm, Pete comments to Frank.

"I don't think we will be seeing much of that for I tell you now, even with the rest I had I'm ready for a good night's sleep." Frank thinks for a moment and asks Pete.

"What rest was that then?" Pete suddenly realised what he had said and came out with.

"You know the little sleep round the pool and then we went around the town."

"Ho yes I forgot, anyway let's hope there is something nice to eat tonight."

They go into the restaurant and sit and they make their way to the buffet, and Pete plumps for steak and fries and Frank the same. They have all the trimmings with it mushrooms and grilled tomatoes, with breaded cobs and they really are tucking in. Pete looks up at Frank who is taking a gob full of cob and chips.

"Fucking hell mate this is alright, let's hope it's like this all week, and we won't go wrong." All that Frank did was nod back at Pete in agreement.

They wash it down with a glass of white wine and they had just finished when the four girls come into the restaurant, they see Pete and Frank and go over to them.

"Is it OK then." They are looking at Pete's empty plate along with Franks.

"Fucking lovely girls, the steak was out of this world." Then Kay asks Pete what their plans are after. Pete tells her.

"We will see you at the bottom bar that looks out to sea, and have a relaxing drink in the cool evening air, I think Frank will enjoy that." Then Lorraine asks Frank.

"How is the back Frank."

"Ho it is a lot cooler at the moment, but I'm dreading tonight in bed." Lorraine tells Frank.

"Never mind I will have to find someone else to fuck the arse off me." Well Frank nearly spits his drink over Pete, at what Lorraine had said.

"Take no notice of what she said Frank, she is teasing you. Pete looks up to her and came straight out with.

"Never mind Lorraine when we are at the bottom bar I will take you in the toilets down there, and shag the arse of you twice, once for Frank and once for myself." Pete feeling his manhood and pointing it at Lorraine. Well that seemed to do the trick for Lorraine just smiles back at Pete, in a cheeky way.

Well banter over and Pete and Frank head for the bar at the bottom of the complex and with beer in hand, go and sit at a table overlooking the front and out to sea. They sit chatting and in general taking in the nights cool air, and the slow setting of the sun the time is approaching 7.45pm with about 15 minutes before the sunsets. Frank looks at his watch and he tells Pete.

"The girls add better hurry up or they are going to miss the sunset." Pete looks at the entrance and in come the girls from dinner, Frank looking round at what Pete is looking at and he sees the girls.

"Come on get your drinks in or you are going to miss it."

"They order their drinks and settle down with Pete and Frank, and are looking at the Sun starting to set over the sea. Kay coming a little closer to Pete and putting her arm through his arm and saying. "What a stunning sight, just look at the Sun starting to go closer to the sea."

They are all just looking at the Sun starting to finally end its day, it's if it is starting to say good bye to all that are watching. The sky starting to turn red as it goes further down and Kay moves her hand and holds Pete's. She tells him.

"Its times like this that makes you feel good to be alive, and reflect on lost ones that have passed away, and are not here to see this, Ho Mum I love you.

Pete looks at Kay and in a quiet way asks her.

"What do you mean by that sweetheart, Ho Mum I love you." Pete looking at Kay and he could see that she was crying. Kay squeezes Pete's hand a little more and she tells him.

"I lost my Mum two years ago, and I was only twenty eight year old, and it almost killed me." Pete wipes the tear from her cheek, and gives her a loving kiss in sympathy, at what she had just told him. The others were oblivious at Pete and Kay, in a loving and tender kiss, and are still memorised at the Sun waving good bye, while the darkness starts to creep in.

They sit in silence till the Sun completely had gone, and sit in generally talk and refreshing their glasses, well they were all-inclusive. The time is approaching 9pm and the stars are starting to shine bright, and Kay still with her hand holding Pete's and leaning on him, asks.

"Pete do you think there is anyone out there." Pete looks down to the front and he tells her."

"Yes sweetheart I do, for look there is a man walking his dog along the front."

"No stupid I mean out there, in space."

"Well let's put it into perspective, we live on the Planet Earth going round the Sun at just the right distance for life to evolve. There is bound to be some Planets out there in the millions of stars, with Suns and Planets going round them, just the right distance, and life just like ours might exist, and you never know there might be, six of them all looking up to the stars and saying the very thing you have just asked. And furthermore that is why we have not been contacted for the absolute distance from each other, would take thousands of years to travel here, and even if you bent space and time it would still be the same. For if you did set out to go to another Planet, you would not live long enough to achieve your goal." Kay looks straight at Pete and might I say with a look of amazement at what he has said, and she is sitting straight up and tells him.

"Fucking hell Pete a simple yes or no would have been what I was looking for, not a fucking Steven Hawkins the universe rolled into one answer."

"I thought you would be interested that is all."

"I loved it Pete great answer." Frank clapping Pete. Then Frank asks them.

"Well what if you set off an unmanned spacecraft, and when it finally comes to the end of the universe and into infinity, how long is space, and how long is infinity." All of them were picking up newspapers off the table and throwing them at Frank, all that Frank did was put up his arm, and he is laughing his socks off at their response to his question. The time is approaching 9.30pm and onto the decking comes this old man in a long black robe, Pete standing behind him waiting to be served after the old man. The old man goes walking down the decking, and Pete sees him starting to sit down next to them on the other table. He asks the barman who is serving him.

Who is the old man who you just served?" The waiter looks to where the old man had sat and tells Pete.

"That's old Tom McNeal, he's armless he comes into the complex and buys one beer and entertains the customers with stories and tricks, it is said that the Scotsman is a retired Millionaire living down here." Pete takes the beers back to the table just as the old man starts to tell one of his tails. He is looking at the darkness down on the front and saying out loud so they could hear him.

"Be-warned take heed of the darkness, for it is waiting for its next victim." Rosemarie and Carol who are closes to him, turn and ask.

"Excuse me what did you say." Well that was it he had their attention, and with his finger and leaning forward and with eyes wide open starts to tell them.

"Come closer we hens and be told of the Hotel of darkness and the weird goings on. For it was a howling rainy night, with the tree outside this wee hens room rattling on her window, I tell thee howling, more like the howling of the dark calling for its victims to come, Yes come to me, Come to me." His eyes are wide like to boiled eggs trying to pop out. Rosemarie and Carol sit there and cannot take their eyes of him, as he spoke in this broad Scottish accent, and Carol's hairs on her arm are starting to stand on end, as she grips Rosemarie's arm. By now all six of them are all engrossed in old McNeal's story.

"Come closer just look at the darkness out there, do you see the darkest patch down there, yes look the darkness that you cannot see through, beware keep well away for this is the darkness that the wee hen is seeing, as she gets out of her bed, with the howling wind trying to talk to her, and the tapping on the window from the tree outside. The wee lass is frightened out of her skin, as she opens her bedroom's door to try and find comfort from someone." By now even Frank is holding Lorraine's arm, yes Frank if Pete sees him he would be calling him all the names under the Sun. Kay is as close as she could get to Pete and the old man carried on.

"She stood in her doorway with candle in hand and lifts it a little and she is asking, if anyone is there, please talk to me for I'm frightened. No answer but as she looked down the passageway the darkness seemed to be creeping forward and yes, the darkness that black that even the light from her candle could not penetrate it. Then suddenly from behind her comes this voice, she jumps out of her skin and looks round and it is one of the Hotel staff, and he tells her. "Sorry love about the lights being out it must be the storm, but don't worry there will be an electrician here shortly to fix the fuse box." He smiled at her and carried on down the hall way. Then old Tom stands and tells them.

"Time I was off home goodnight to thee all." He stands goes to the end of the decking, lifts his robe above his head and lowers it and he had disappeared into thin air. Well Lorraine and Rosemarie scream out loud and they are both pointing to where he vanished, and looking round to the others and saying.

"Did you see that, he has gone, puff straight into thin air." Well Pete stands goes to where he had left, and looks down into the sand pit that is for small children below the decking, and he sees Toms imprint were he hit the sand when he left, and foot prints were he scuttled off.

Pete comes back to their table and he sees the look on their faces, and it is if they still believe what had happened.

"Well-well the old faker had you all fooled, or should I call in the old fucker." Kay tells Pete.

"He might be old but he had us all going, I mean look at us he tells a ghost story and we all were taken in by it, I mean darkness. Lorraine the black darkness is behind you." Well Lorraine jumps up screaming and just grabs Frank, and she is trying to pull him towards her.

"Come on now all settle down, just look at the time its 11.pm and I tell you now I'm off to bed, for it is two days since I had a goodnight sleep." They all stand and with Pete with Kay and Lorraine on his arm, and Frank with Rosemarie and Caron they all start to make their way back up to the main complex and every now and then, Frank is still trying to frighten them with saying.

"Just look at the darkness ahead of us." Wrong for them both clobber him over the head and both telling him.

"Bloody well stop it." Back into the Hotel and they all make their way to their bedrooms, and in the corridor with them all being all in are saying their goodnight to each other. And might I say no come on shag the arse off me.

They are soon all striped off and into their beds and soon gone into the world of dreams, let's hope none of them are dreaming about old Tom McNeal and the darkness.

Chapter Thirteen

The next morning the time is approaching 7am, and Pete is starting to come out of his sleep and he sees the time, well might as well get up and go down the gym, for it opens at 7am. Pete showers picks up his kit bag, and going past Frank tells him.

"See you at breakfast then mate, I'm off down the gym." All that Frank did was murmur, and roll over. And tells Pete.

"Give us a kiss babe." Pete looks at him and is thinking, "What the fuck is he dreaming about." Pete leaves and heads for the gym, he enters and there is one Hotel trainer there for the punters, and he gives his good morning to Pete.

"You English then." Pete taking off his top and the trainer looks at Pete's fine physique. Asks him.

"Yes I'm from Liverpool, down here for the season, and might I say it looks like you work out on a regular bases."

"Very true mate it's a bird puller, and might I say I like the looks you get from passer-by's when they see you walk by." The trainer smiles at Pete and asks him.

"Do you need any help on any of the gym equipment with the weights or adjustments?"

"I'll be fine, just one thing, my names Pete and yours is."

"Gary, sorry I should have told you when you first came in." Pete tells Gary that he is going to pump some iron first, and he goes to one of the machines and starts to load heavy weights on to the bar. Gary helps Pete and Pete starts to really go at the lifting, and Gary looks on looking at Pete's muscle in his arms and upper body, really working out. Then onto the bottom half of the body, legs and abdomen. Pete had been at it for well over an hour when two young birds walk by, and they see Pete through the all glass front windows working out, well the wolf whistles and cheering at Pete. One presses up to the window and lifts her front T-shirt and presses her large tits onto the window giving Pete and Gary a really good eyeful.

"Pete stops pumping looks at Gary and he tells him.

"It looks like those two need a good seeing too, I will go and see what the odds are of fucking the arse off them." Well Gary just looks at Pete as he goes walking off to the door where the girls are, and when he open it gets the shock of his life, for they are both talking in cockney slang and Pete could hardly understand what the fuck they were on about.

"Hi Babes you are up early, and might I say you have a lovely pear of tits there, my names Pete." The one who exposed herself to Pete tells him.

"I'm Shelly and this is my skin blister Molly, boy I would not mind a farmers truck, and look at that fife and drum, you could give him a Westminster bank." She is laughing her socks off and tells her sister. Just going for a Patrick McGee. She goes walking off to the toilet that is next to the gym and the other one tells Pete.

"You will have to excuse her she's been on the Paul Weller all night."

"I'm sorry babe I do not understand a word she was on about, it looks like if we cannot communicate in English we might as well call it a day." Pete is about to walk off and the other girl tells Pete.

"We are sorry, you see we are from London and it's a way of life slang, she is a bit under the weather, for we have been out all-night and just on our way back to our Hotel that is next door. You see skin blister is sisters and we are twins, and Paul Weller is Stella beer, and when she told you farmers' truck she meant she would like you to fuck her. And me to give you a Westminster bank wank. And that you have a nice fife and drum bum." Pete tells her.

"Well that was better I understood everything, and when she gets back if you would like me to shower and come with you to tuck you up in bed, I'm all yours and did you say you are twins."

"That's right twins, and OK you're on please don't be to long for I think we are gagging for it." Pete smiles at her and goes to shower, and passing Gary tells him.

"They are twins and I'm off to fuck the arse of both of them." Gary looking at Pete heading for the shower and might I say a very quick one. With Gary under his breath saying to himself. "Jammy bastard, it looks like I'm going to after pump a little iron." Pete comes back out and Molly is still on her own, just as Shelly comes walking back out of the toilet, and she sees Pete with her sister.

"Flowers and frolics you aren't going to sooty and sweep with him are you."

Molly tells her that Pete is coming back with them to their room, but she will have to stop the cockney and talk normal, if you can. Well Molly's face lights up and she goes and holds Pete's arm, and Shelly on the other side. The girl's complex is small outer chalet and they go into their room without causing any trouble. Once inside Molly locks the door and they start to hurriedly start to undress, with Shelly pulling back the sheet on the bed. Pete stands there and he is admiring their large tits and slim figure and he starts to get a hard on just looking at what he is about to receive. The two girls are stripped and in bed as Pete removes his T-shirt and then his boxer shorts and stood there in front of them. Well they both sigh and are telling him that he had a fine body, and what the fuck is he doing with an elephants trunk. Pete smiles at them and asks.

"Well do you approve then." As he approached the bed and without his hands makes his cock point upwards at them.

"Fucking hell Pete get down here and give us both a good seeing too." Pete gets onto the bed between them and kneels looking at them both, well they are straight onto his cock, and Shelly pulling it back and Molly starting to give him a blow job. They take it in turn enjoying Pete's 10 inch upright cock. Pete puts his hands onto both of their tits, and he is having a good rub round and tweaking their nipple and he tells them.

"You both have beautiful tits." Then he starts to go down to their fanny and he starts to work away on both of their Fannies. With his thumb working away on their clitoris, and with two fingers gently going right in and then slowly out. They both stop giving Pete a blow job, and are both flat on their back at the pure pleasure Pete was giving them. They are both telling Pete that it was lovely what he was doing, and Pete just carried on and starts to mount Molly first, her fanny is well lubricated and his cock slides in easily and he starts slowly going further in on every push, Molly is soon moaning with pleasure and Pete could tell that she is having orgasm after orgasm. He comes off Molly and mount Sally and he did the same with her, and she too soon is having orgasm after orgasm and Pete is having his mouth full kissing and flicking Molly's nipples. Then the same with Sally and he could tell that he is about to explode and he tells them.

"I'm going to pop my cork who wants it. Well they both push Pete onto his back and he suddenly explodes with both of them like two mad dogs fighting, who could get the most of his spunk. All that Pete did was shut his eyes and enjoying the feeling they were giving him as he exploded, He had his hand on each of their tit and still rubbing their nipples for they were standing upright like two chapel hat pegs. All three of them flop back onto the bed and Pete tells them.

"That was one hell of a shag you too are magic, we will have to do it again."

"I'm afraid we cannot Pete for we are going home this evening back to London at 9.pm, But if you give us your telephone number we could arrange a date with the hope of more pleasure." They exchange numbers and Pete is about to say something and they are both fast on, snuggled up to each other. Pete gets out of bed and goes and showers, after he comes out of the bathroom dressed and he goes to the front door and picks up his kid bag. Turns and looks at them for the last time, and he could see both their arses and just puckers up his lips and said. "See you girls surf is up," smiles and leaves.

He goes back to his room where he sees Frank had gone to breakfast with the time approaching 9.45am, and Pete changers and he is saying to himself. "Boy I had better make haste for breakfast finishes at 10.am. Pete goes into the dining room and he spots Frank and approaches him. Frank straight away asks Pete.

"Where the fuck have you been, you know that we are on the desk till twelve a clock, doing the rep think."

"I know Frank, I`m sorry I`m late, but you see why I was in the gym I met these London birds and I had to go and fuck the arses off them, and boy they were fantastic, big tits and a figure to die for."

"What you shagged two birds before breakfast, you are not real."

"I know Frank but you must know me by now, a shags a shag." Pete smiling at Frank and going to the help yourself counter to get something to eat." Frank just sits there shaking his head at Pete's comments.

The time is approaching 10.30am and Pete and Frank make their way to the lobby to start their rep duties. Pete asks Frank what's on the agenda for the day. Frank tells him.

"Well we have to try and sell as many tickets for the tour tomorrow around Faro and the visit to a vineyard and wine tasting trip."

"Fucking hell that sounds boring, what about more of a visit to a nudist beach and we strip and stand there, and give the one with the winning raffle ticket, a good seeing too."

"Is that all you fucking think about bloody Sex." Frank had not finished when a Lady standing there coughs and tries to get his attention.

"Sorry madam, how can we be of help to you?"

"Well for one you could put my name down for the nudist beach trip, and I will buy all the tickets now for I fancy that big boy there."

Pete stands and tells her.

"Well hello gorgeous, my names Pete and your name is."

"My names Nicolas Summers, please to meet you."

"Let's hope you are Nicker-less." She smiles at Pete and she tells him.

"Well that is for you to find out, what are you doing afterwards?"

"Afterwards, what about now, I`m due a coffee break." Well Frank just sits there and just looks at Pete and is saying. "WHAT." Well Pete gives him a gentle kick under the table, and smiles at the Lady. Then Pete stands tells Frank he will be back shortly, puts his arm on his hip for Nicolas to put her arm through, and they go walking off through the lobby to the outside. Pete looks back to where Frank is sitting at the table, and just gives Frank a big grin, all that Frank did is put his hands on his head and sat there shaking his head, at what Pete had just done.

Outside Nicolas and Pete go to the decking area and they get two small orange drinks, and sit at a table and Pete asks her.

"If you don't mind me saying Nicolas you are a very attractive Woman, and might I say a very fetching body, you must be married." Nicolas giggles and tells Pete.

"Me married, sorry haven't the time for it, and anyway if I were married I would not be able to sit with such a hulk like yourself. Just look at those large arms, and is the rest of you that big."

"I say it is, and even down there, if you would like why not a closer look at it in private." Pete smiles at Nicolas."

"Would you like to go back to my room, and I could see for myself." This time Nicolas puckering up her lips at Pete.

"Lead on babe I`m all yours." They stand and Nicolas leads the way, with Pete slightly behind her standing up from the table, and he is having a good look at her firm plum shape arse, and he is thinking to himself.

"Fucking hell I can't wait to bash the fucking arse of that." They come to Nicolas`s room, and she turns the key and as they enter she swivels round, and straight onto Pete and they stand in one hell of a kiss, and with Pete with being on the door, goes backwards and it slams shut. She is all over Pete like a mad dog on heat and her hands are all over Pete and she goes straight down to his cock, and she came straight out with.

"What the fuck have you got in there, that cannot be real? "She was very Lady like. Pete tells her.

"Come on babe slow down go and take your clothes off, and we can really start to make love." Well she is straight to the bed and within seconds she stands there completely in the nude looking at Pete. He stands about two feet from her and starts to lift his T-shirt off, and she gets her first look at Pete's fine physique, and Pete looks down at her slim bronze body and shaven fanny, and his cock starts to rise at what it is about to receive. Pete removes his shorts and stands there takes a deep breath and gives her one of his poses, with every muscle in his body rippling and she just gasps at what beholds her.

"You are a true God Pete, I've never seen such a beautiful human being like you before, Please be gentle with me." As she walks towards him and stands in front of Pete, and her hand is straight onto his cock and her other hand feeling his firm breast. She is slowly giving Pete a slow wank and she starts to kiss his firm breast and slowly starts to kiss his abs, and then down to his cock, and Pete stands looking at her slowly trying to swallow is large cock. He can feel her gently sucking on his bell end, then sliding by it and her teeth giving him a very satisfying feeling and he is thinking. "I better not let her carry on for too long, or she will get a face full before we get started." He stands her attention for a few minutes screwing up his face now and then at the wonderful feeling she was giving him, and he suddenly puts his hands inside her armpits and lifts her up and telling her.

"Come on sweetheart my turn to pleasure you, he lifts her up into his arms and takes the few steps to the bed. He is giving her a tender kiss and slowly puts her onto the bed, and starts to straddle her, and going down onto her breast and he sees her all over tan, and starts to kiss and flick her nipples with his tongue. Nicolas starts to lift her tits for Pete to get more and she is already taking deep breaths at the pleasure Pete was giving her. He then starts to move down her belly kissing all the time and with is tongue licking as he goes, she is watching him move down to her groin area, and Pete starts to flicker her clitoris, and this made her tense up and push towards Pete.

By now with what Pete was doing really had her groaning with pure pleasure, and the more she looks and sees Pete working away at her clitoris and Fanny really made her juices flow, and her groans are getting louder and her breathing more heavy, as she starts to have multi orgasms at what Pete is doing, she suddenly shouts out.

"For God's sake Pete, please fuck me now, or you are going to blow my mind." Pete comes up and gently guides his, by now very hard and erect cock to its goal, and Nicolas is watching it come closer to her fanny.

"Ho my God Pete, please get that fucker into me." Pete starts to penetrate her and they both get this warm feeling, as his cock goes further in and he leans forward and starts to kiss Nicolas. She tenses up backwards pushing her groin towards Pete, at the feeling of Pete's massif cock starting to really go at her. By now she is digging her nails well into Pete's back and she is shouting out as Pete goes like a bull at a gate.

"Ho God-God, please come now I want to feel every drop of that warm spunk flowing inside of me, please now Please give it me for God's sake." Nicolas by now her juices really flowing and Pete could feel them, and he too explodes along with Nicolas, and both screaming with pure pleasure. She feeling his warm spunk and Pete feeling her warm juices from her massif orgasm. After they are both just coming back down to earth from the pure pleasure that they had given each other, and Pete looks at his watch. He Jumps up and telling Nicolas.

"Fucking hell Nicolas, we have been at it for well over an hour and a half, Frank will kill me. He goes to the shower and standing there trying to hurry himself up, when into the shower comes Nicolas, and joins him and starts to rub soap onto his chest, and Pete just stood there enjoying the feeling. He looks at Nicolas and he tells her.

"He's not a bad lad, I suppose he will be alright." And before you know it they are at it again having full blow sex standing. After Pete tells Nicolas.

"That's it for now babe for I had better get back, for I am supposed to be working not shagging." They dress and Pete tells Nicolas that he will see her later, and goes hurriedly back to the lobby and to the desk, and Frank had gone. Pete looks at his watch and he realised why, for it was by now 12.05 pm and the desk shuts at 12.00 noon. He goes to the pool area and see's Frank on a sun lounger and might I say with a towel round his shoulders, and we all know why.

"Frank mate, sorry about that, boy she was hot-hot."

"Never mind hot-hot, that was some fucking tea break, you ought to think yourself lucky that it is me, and not some snotty jump up other bus driver with you, for you would have been reported and down the road. And by the way what was she like."

"Fucking Goddess mate, a fucking Goddess."

Chapter Fourteen

Pete with panic over settled down with Frank, enjoying the afternoon Sun.

Frank had not completely forgotten about that morning, and he turns to Pete and puts it to him.

"How many birds have you fucked since you came back to the UK?" Pete thinks for a while and you could see him trying to work it out, and he suddenly tells Frank.

"Nicolas is the thirteenth, why do you ask."

"Why do I ask fucking thirteen, it's a wonder you have not caught fucking knob rot and it had fucking dropped off, I mean thirteen, I've fucked one in how many weeks." Pete smiles at Frank and in a smirked way tells him.

"Less than two weeks, I'll try my hardest for you Frank to make it twenty in two weeks, if that will help you." Frank just laid there laughing his socks off at the answers Pete gave him, and he just tells him.

"Well don't come running to me one morning with your ten inch fucking cock in your hand, and shouting look what's happened Frank." Well now Pete's in utter laughter until he looks round and there is two couples both sides of them and they had heard everything that had been said, sitting up on their Sun loungers. The two Woman were puckering up their lips at Pete, and might I say looking down to Pete's groin area, to see the bulge in his swimming trunks.

Pete standing and just telling them.

"He's only kidding folks, Frank I'm off for a swim." Pete walking by the other couple and the Woman turns to her husband and came straight out with.

"I wish you looked like that, and with the bulge to match." Well her husband tells her.

"Well Mavis I'm what I am." Sticks his chest out, and bends his arm. She looks at him, and just said.

"Pathetic." And laid back down Sunbathing. Pete heard this when he passed and he is telling himself, bloody Frank and his loud voice. Pete dives into the pool and starts to swim up and down the pool. He had been swimming for about ten minutes when he bumps into another swimmer, and unbeknown to Pete it was a young lady, and with Pete doing the crawl, and his arm coming over knocks her top off, and Pete comes up and all that he could see is two very large nipples and Pete is thinking.

"Fucking hell I could dam well give them beautiful tits a suck? For they look like two fried eggs on a baking board." Pete shakes the water of his head and he is looking at this jet black haired bird, that looked a million dollars, and Pete noticed that in his right hand he had her top, and straight away Pete is trying to help her on with her top, and at the same time telling her.

"I'm profusely sorry sweetheart, I did not do it on purpose." She looks at Pete and presses up to him and she is thinking. "What a fucking hulk." She tells him.

"Well normally the boys are trying to get my tits out, not put them back in."

Pete smiles at her, with his arms around her back, and clipping her top back on. And tells her.

"Well with a beautiful girl like yourself, I to would love to take it off and give them a good seeing too, but I bet your boyfriend sees you right in that department." Pete with a bigger smile, and might I say with her standing so close, pushes his groin into her, so she could feel his bulge.

"Well I've no boyfriend, but I'm on the market, and you look like a good investment, that is if you are free, and not committed to anyone." She stands holding Pete's arm muscles and trying to squeeze them, but cannot with Pete being so hard.

"Well what about tonight, we are going to go down to the disco tonight, if you would like to join us."

"Try and stop me, and who is this we."

"That's my mate Frank."

"Great, I will ask my friend if she would like to come and we could make it a foursome."

"We have a date then, 7 30 tonight in the Hotel bar, and please forgive me my names Pete, and you are."

"Bonny Ray, and might I say that what I can feel pressing into me under the water, is you would like to have your wicked way with me." Bonny lifting her eyebrows up to Pete, in a suggestive way.

"You bet Bonny for you are one of the most attractive women, I have ever met, down boy wait till tonight." Pete looking down into the water at his prick. Bonny does know more than, puts her hand on Pete's manhood, and with her hand is feeling his cock and she comments.

"Fucking hell Pete, where the fuck did you get that fucking big thing from, and you promise me, tonight you will be gentle with me, with you being so BIG."

"Don't worry babe you will enjoy, and have one of the best nights you can ever imagine." Pete pulling even closer to her in the water and giving her a loving kiss. They part and Pete tells Bonny that he will see her.

"Till tonight Bonny, will see you in the Hotel bar at about 7.30, and by the way what is your friend's name, for I will tell my mate Frank."

"Sue, a very attractive blond, I'm sure your mate Frank will be pleased, see you later Pete." Bonny goes swimming off with Pete looking at her arse bob up out of the water and he is thinking, roll on tonight for I`m going to fuck the arse off that. Pete smiles and he too goes swimming off. Back round the pool Pete comes up to Frank who is in a sleepy snooze, and Pete sits down on the sun lounger and shakes the cold water onto Franks belly, making him come round and he is saying, what the fuck is that.

"Frank come on lazy bones, let's go and have a quick beer at the pool bar, for I`ve got something to tell you, and you will be blown away by it." Pete getting up and walking off towards the bar, with Frank bringing up the rear and asking.

"What Pete, come on mate tell me, what's going to blow my socks off." They reach the bar and have two small beers and they sit down at a table taking in the last Sunrays, with the time being 5.30pm.

"Bloody come on then out with it, what have you to tell me." Pete tells him about Bonny and knocking her top off, and looking at two lovely tits, and what is going to happen that evening.

"Well Frank we are going to go down to the disco and have ourselves a good night, and after shag the arses of two gorgeous birds, and yours a stunning blond."

"You're kidding me Pete I`ve never shagged two different birds in one week before."

"Well stick with me and you might even try for your own personal Round Robin, and shag lots more." Pete nudging Frank, and all that Frank did was give Pete a funny look at what he had said. Pete tells Frank that tonight.

"Don't bloody well go crazy on the booze, for don't forget that we are both working in the morning at 11am, for the trip to Faro, and the wine tasting trip."

"No chance mate, for if what you say comes about, I will not drink too much if I`m shagging later." Frank standing daydreaming. Pete finishes his small beer and tells Frank.

"Well drink up mate, time we were off and change, then dinner, and then the night's entertainment. They go back to their room shower and shave, and in general spraying themselves up for the birds, Pete stands looking in the mirror and with a short white T-shirt, and blue jeans and leather jacket, looked and smelt like a million dollars that no bird would turn down. Frank comments and asks Pete.

"Do you think this Sue will like what she sees?"

"You will be fine mate, come on let's get something to eat, and then we can meet the birds." The eat and go into the bar with the time approaching 7.30pm and they order a small beer, and dead on time the girls come into the bar and Franks mouth opens wide and drops to the floor, and he is telling Pete.

"Look at those two, they are stunners and fucking hell, look how short their skirts are." For them both are in very short miniskirts low tops that revealed a lot of Cleavage, and they come walking up to the boys and introduce each other. They stand having a small beer before they set of and Pete is giving Sue the eye and she too, is looking a lot at Pete. They set of for the disco and walking in partners, Pete with Bonny and Sue with Frank. The disco goes well, they dance a lot with the girls drinking and the boys taking their time and only having a few half beers. The time is approaching 11pm and they are on the dance floor and dancing to a slow dance and might I say they were dancing very close. When Bonny asks Pete.

"I know it is early but I would like to go back now, and make love to you."

"Well to tell you the truth, Frank and myself are working in the morning, and I too would love to have you in bed, for I cannot wait to feel your body next to mine." Pete squeezing her cheeks and looking her straight in the eye. All four decide to go back to the Hotel and they leave the disco, and just as they turn a corner with a side entrance, two youths come into view and pull two knives and demand they hand over their wallets. The two girls hang onto their escorts and looked shocked. Pete straight away puts himself in front of the youths and in a frightened voice tells them.

"Please don't hurt us, we are on holiday, please here take my wallet." Pete reaching into his pocket, and this seemed to make the youths drop their hands down, with knifes now pointing down towards the ground. And straight away Pete kicks one of the youths straight in his bollocks, and he buckle up with pain, and Pete know more than hits him full in the face, and he goes recalling back into bins, and falls to the ground. The other youth looking at his mate go flying, did not see Pete grab him by the hand with the knife in it, and Pete starts to squeeze it tight. So tight that the youth screams out in pain and drops the knife, Pete kicks it away and carried on squeezing, then you could hear the bones in the youths hand cracking and he screams out even more. He is sobbing profusely and Pete let's go and he goes running off in dire pain. Pete turns to the other three who just did not believe what they just witnessed and he tells them.

"Well I don't think they will mug anyone else, do you." Pete smiling at Frank, Bonny and Sue. Well the three are dumb found and Bonny is all over Pete her hero, and she is telling Pete.

"I just did not believe how a big guy like you could whimper at them, and put them off their guard."

"Let's just get back and settle down, for I just want to make love to you babe." Pete kisses Bonny, and might I say looking at Sue, who in turn is looking at Pete. They arrive at the Hotel and make their way to Bonny's room, and they enter. There is two bedrooms and Pete and Bonny go into one, and Frank and Sue into the other and straight away bonny is all over Pete, so much that Pete slows her down.

"Come on Bonny let's get into bed first." Bonny starts to strip and soon she lay on the bed just in her white thong and white bra, Pete stands looking at Bonny as the moonbeams shinning off her body, made her skin shine in the semi dark of the room. Pete strips and takes off his boxer shorts, and stands in the moon light, and Bonny seeing his massive frame shinning in the moonlight opens her arms for Pete, he goes walking forward and he had the biggest hard on and Bonny licks her lips at seeing such a hulk coming towards her. Pete straddles her as she opened her legs wider and Pete slips off her white thong, and straight away while still kneeling up in-between her legs, starts to flick her clitoris, and rubbing his thumb around it and at the same time pushing two fingers into her vagina, and she takes a deep breath at the wonderful feeling Pete was giving her. Pete had been doing it for about ten minutes and looking at her body tensing up as she arched her back upwards, he then laid back down on top of Bonny and straight away unclips her bra, and he is soon giving her breast a good seeing too, and sucking away on her nipples, and at the same time his cock slips into her fanny, and he starts to push forward and his massif cock starts to penetrate deeper into Bonny's fanny, she is giving off loud moans of pleasure, so much that Sue who was being shagged by Frank could her moans of pleasure, and she is thinking at the same time as digging her nails into Franks back.

"I wish it was me getting my arse fuck off me, instead of Bonny." Pete had been shagging for about 25 minutes and by now Bonny is totally screaming with pleasure and telling Pete to come now and spunk her, Pete goes at her like a bull at a gate and he explodes and he too starts to moan at the same time as Bonny, for they both are having one hell of a climax. It's not long after and they both fall asleep and Pete awakes at about 6.30am and he decides to get up and have a shower, and then go to the gym. He comes out of the bedroom and closes the door, taking his clothes with him, so not to disturb Bonny. He enter the shower and unbeknown to him Sue had heard him go into the bathroom and with Frank fast on, goes to the bathroom and enters quietly with Pete not locking the door, and she can see Pete in the shower rubbing soap onto his back. She opens the cubical and enters and starts to soap Pete's back, Pete just stood there enjoying the feeling, and he turns round and sees Sues long blond hair down her front covering her tits. Pete leans forward and kisses Sue, and after whispers in her ear.

"I'm clad it's you for when you came into the bar last night I fancied you like mad."

"Why do you think I'm here for, please Pete make love to me and make me feel like you made Bonny feel last night." Pete brushes back Sues Blond hair, and exposes her tits, and starts to suck on her nipples with the water running over her tits, and she straight away starts to feel the tingling inside her at what Pete is doing. Next he is kissing her tummy and then down to her fanny and Sue opens her legs wide, and Pete starts to flick her clitoris and pushing his tongue into her vagina, and Sue suddenly starts to feel her juices flowing at the feeling Pete was giving her, and Pete too could tell that she is ready and he slowly comes up and kissing her fully on the lips, pushes back onto the shower wall and he lifts her up by both legs and he is in-between her, and she rises up to his cock and she could feel it on her clitoris, and Pete starts to lift his cock up just with their muscles, and Sue felt every move Pete made. She starts to gasp and she looks Pete straight in the eyes and she tells him.

"Fuck me now Pete, please get that fucking big fuck inside me. Pete starts to slowly penetrate her and moving slowly at first, pushing more and more into her, and she tenses up pushing back on the shower wall, and telling Pete to speed up. Pete starts to go a little faster, and his cock is moving more freely inside Sue with her juices flowing, and she is trying to contain herself from bursting out with the pleasure Pete was giving her, it got so bad that she is biting down on Pete's shoulder. Good half hour Pete was shagging her and by now she could take no more and tells Pete.

"Come now Pete, let me feel your warm spunk swimming inside me, please now. Sue is breathing faster and suddenly Pete explodes and this time Sue does shout out at the feeling, and Pete straight away puts one hand on her mouth to stop her from waking the others up. They both come back down to earth and finish their shower and Pete dresses and leaves, while Sue went back to bed. Pete goes back to his room and change into his gym kit and it was off to the gym.

Chapter Fifteen

Pete's in the gym for well over an hour and a half, and after a shower, and the time being half past nine, he goes to the restaurant for a bite to eat. He walks into the restaurant and sitting there is Frank, eating his breakfast and Pete approaches.

"Hi Frank a good fucking night last night, did you get him away." Pete standing there lifting his arm up in a suggestive way.

"Too true, Sue was a peach, but I could not understand is in the morning, when I woke up, she did not want to do it again, saying she was knackered with all the shagging." Frank looking at Pete puzzled. Pete just shrugs his shoulders, but the truth be-known, it was him that knackered her, with shagging her in the shower.

"All said and done it was well over one good night, are you ready for the trip this morning?

"I suppose so, do you think we will see those two again Pete."

"Well to tell you the truth, I think they were just after what they could get out of us, but if they come sniffing round us again, we might swop and I will shag Sue, and you Bonny, anyway never mind Frank, there might be a couple more on this trip that would like to have their arses shagged off them." Pete lifting his arm in a suggestive way, and lifting up his eyebrows.

The time approaching 10 15 am, Pete tells Frank.

"Come on mate let's go and get the coach ready for the trip." Pete puts his arm around Frank, and they go walking off to the coach park, to check the coach over, and ready it for that day's trip. All done and they pull up at the Hotels entrance, where one or two passengers had already gathered. Frank is going to drive them down to the main shopping area in Faro, while Pete starts to welcome the passengers aboard the coach. There had been about 15 passengers and might I say Pete had already eyed up a couple of birds when the next Passengers comes up to Pete, and straight away puckers up her lips at Frank and said.

"Good morning Pete a lovely day for the trip."

"Good morning Nicolas, nice to see you up early out of bed." Pete looking at her tits while saying this.

"Thanks sweetheart, you have not met my new boyfriend, Graham, he's a sports writer, Graham this is one of the coach drivers that takes you on trips while on holiday, I think his name is Pete."

"Please to meet you Pete, looking forward to the wine tasting later."

"Thanks Graham, hopes you have a great day, they say the fish markets a good place." Pete smiling as he walks off to the back of the coach where Nicolas is just sitting. All aboard and Pete turns to Frank to drive off when Frank asks him.

"That's the bird you fucked the arse off the other lunch, and what's with this the fish market is a good place."

"It's just that bird, you know another bloke, it must smell like a fishmonger's slab, with what's been deposited in it." Pete smiling at Frank. All that Frank did is screw up his face and comment.

"Pete do you have too."

"Just drive off Frank, the sooner we are there the sooner we can get back and do things we love best." Just before Pete could say anymore Frank releases the hand break and they were off to Faro.

They pull up in the main area of Faro for tourist and they start to disembark of the coach, and Pete is helping them off, when he came to the two birds that he had eyed up, and one slips on the steps and Pete is there to catcher.

"Steady sweetheart, we don't want you landing up in bed now do we."

"Why not, am I not to your liking then?" She is looking Pete straight in the eye and giving him the come-on.

"You know what I mean a Hospital bed, but then again with looking at you, I would not mind whatever sort of bed it was, so long as I'm with you." She giggles at what Pete had said, and she asks him.

"Well how about the both of you tagging along with us around Faro, and maybe you could direct us up into the right places." Pete looks at Frank and asks him.

"Are you up for it with these two lovely girls then Frank?" Pete looking at Frank and at the same time lowering the girl back down to the ground, and at the same time pressing you know what into her. She feels her interest and in a soft voice tells Pete.

"Well at least I know one that his." At the same time as rubbing her groin around Pete's cock, and smiling at him.

"Come on then let's go, and by the way my names Pete and you are."

"My names Clare, and my mate her names Samantha, Samantha this is Pete." Samantha smiles at Pete and looks back at Frank and they are chatting each other up, after locking the coach they go off walking hand in hand and in general chit-chat. They walk around a few shops, trying hats on and having a giggle with each other, when they come to a large shop selling suits and things and they enter, and at the back of the shop there were fitting rooms and Pete straight away pick up a pair of trousers and grabs Clare's hand and tells her.

"Come on babe come with me and see if these fit me." They enter a cubical and Pete is surprised at the room you have, he spins Clare round and they are all over each other, kissing and Pete starting to fondle her breasts. He starts to kiss her neck and lifting her short T-shirt and he is soon kissing her nipples and Clare starts to take deep breaths with the feeling. Then he is down to her tummy and he starts while kissing her tummy, while unzipping her jeans and they fall to her ankles, and she is hurriedly taking one leg out. Pete pulls down her thong and he is straight onto her fanny and giving her one hell of a feeling as his tongue is working hard, on her clitoris and fanny and she is pulling Pete's head further to her and giving of big intakes of breath. After she had a good seeing too, Pete starts to come back in reverse kissing her tummy and the kissing her on the lips. Clare like lightning has Pete's jeans down and his massif cock out and she looks down at her prize, then straight back to Pete and in a soft voice tells him.

"Fucking hell Pete have you a licence, for that fucking big thing."

"Too true babe and I can reassure you, that it is one big pleasure giver." Pete walking backwards to the bench where you sit to change, and he sits and Clare straddles Pete, and his cock is standing straight up waiting to be fed. Clare gently sits on Pete's cock and guides it to its goal, and she gently starts to slide down a little further onto his cock then back up, then down a little further then the same back up, she starts to moan at the feeling of Pete's cock going deeper into her. Then she pulls Pete into her breast and she starts to orgasm straight away. Her juices are by now flowing, and she starts to go faster and Pete sits looking at her, and he is looking at her face that is screwing up with so much pleasure, and her eyes were shut tight. Then Pete starts to lift a little and they had been at it for well over fifteen minutes, and Pete could feel that he is going to explode. Clare had multi-orgasm's and Pete tells her that he is coming. She lifts up off Pete, and she is straight down onto his cock, and sucking profusely on his cock, and she is really giving it a good suck trying to get as much of his cock into her mouth. Then all of a sudden Pete explodes and it was his turn to screw up his face with his eyes shut, and it was her turn to look straight at Pete's face with the pleasure she is giving him. After they are telling each other that they had really have had a great screw and in general complementing each other, when all of a sudden there is a knock on the door and someone asking if they were Ok in there. They both were trying not to giggle and Pete shouts out.

"Nearly done just putting my jeans back on, won't be a moment."

They come out with Pete holding the trousers over his arm, and he tells the assistant.

"No to tight and my girlfriend said, it was too long, never mind I might find something more fitting later." Well Clare this time did burst out laughing at what Pete had said and they leave, with the assistant screwing up his face with the whole event. Outside Frank and Samantha are waiting for them and Frank looks at Pete and asks.

"Bloody hell Pete, what did you do try everything on."

"No Frank, just slipped into something nice and warm." Pete smiling at Frank.

They carry on going around the shops, until it is time to return to the coach for the rest of the day's events. Back and they board the coach, with the others coming back, with might I say some large gifts that have to go in the luggage hold underneath, where the suitcases go. Frank this time is seeing the passengers back on, and he did the head count, while it is Pete's turn to take the wheel, to the vineyard for the wine tasting. Frank tells Pete.

"All aboard let's go, for the last leg, then back to the Hotel and catch the last Sunrays of the day." Pete pulls away and they are heading out of Faro for the vineyard, and they are only about twenty minutes away, and they soon pull into the vineyard at 1.45pm. They all disembark, and are unshed to two small coaches that is going to take them to the estate, and grapevines, the attendant is telling them.

"Please to the two coaches for the half hour tour of the estate and wine growing crops. Then back to the large barn for wine tasting. They all board including Frank, but Pete stays behind with doing it a lot of times in the past. The two coaches pull away and Pete is sitting on the coach steps enjoying the afternoon Sun, with a drink of orange. Then from behind the coach comes Samantha, Pete sees her and he asks.

"Samantha you have missed the coach, for the tour of the estate."

"Good for that is not what I need, but it is you. You see Clare told me what you did in the shop, and by the tone of her voice at what you gave her, sounds fantastic, please Pete make love to me like you did with Clare. Pete looks at his watch and he tells her.

"Come on then babe we have only half-an-hour, to the back of the coach." Samantha climbs on board and Pete locks the door and they make their way to the back and Pete tells her.

"Down here babe, we will be more private down there." They go down the steps and into the toilet and again Pete locks the door and they start to kiss with Pete's hand's starting to lift her T-shirt and unclipping her bra and he is straight onto her nipples and flicking away and sucking them. Then he removes her jeans and before long he is down giving her fanny a good seeing too. Samantha leans back on the sink for Pete to get more of his tongue around her clitoris, and she is in heaven, Pete feels her juices flowing and the sweet taste and he comes up with the biggest hard on, and Samantha gets her first look at Pete's cock.

"Fucking hell Pete I see what Clare told me, and you are truly a well big block, please fuck me now. "Pete puts the top down on the toilet, sits down and he tells Samantha to climb on and enjoy. She straddles Pete, and her fanny slides over Pete's big cock with ease, and she sits right down on it, and gives off on hell of a groan at the spine chilling feeling of him fully penetrating her.

"God that's lovely." She is having one hell of an orgasm and Pete as she goes up off Pete's cock them down, Pete pushes up and she shouts out with the pleasure. Pete is thinking to himself. For fucks sake, come Samantha or you are going to bring everyone running, thinking that someone is being murdered. They are both speeding up and Samantha shouts out to Pete.

"Fucking spunk me now, for I'm on the pill, fucking now please." Pete pushes that little bit faster, and one hell of a groan as Pete fills her boots, with both of them having one hell of an orgasm together. They sit there just in one long kiss, with both of them having been satisfied to the hilt, then Pete looks at his watch, and they had been at it for well over forty five minutes, and he tells Samantha.

"Fucking hell sweetheart get dressed, or we are going to get caught with our pants down." They hurriedly get dressed and Pete goes to the front of the coach and unlocks the door, and there is no one there, he takes in a deep breath of air and he is thinking to himself. "Thank fuck for that." When all of a sudden Frank comes round and said.

"You missed a bloody good half hour or so, going round the vineyard, what have you been up-to, while we were away."

"You know me Frank, just up to it, that's all." Then Samantha comes down the steps of the coach, and walks by Frank and just said. "Hi Frank." Well Frank just looks at Pete and he asks him.

"Don't tell me, you have fucked the arse of Samantha, haven't you." All that Pete did is smile back at Frank and tell him.

"You know me by now FRANK, EVERY HOLE IS A GOAL."

"I don't bloody believe you, what would you not shag." Frank with his hands on his head, then turns back to Pete for the answer. Pete just smiles at him and tells him.

"A corpse." Then an even bigger smile from Pete. The passengers are in the barn having the tasting of the wine, while Pete and Frank just stand there talking, waiting for the passengers to finish, and purchase the fine wines on offer. Within half an hour, all are aboard, for the trip back to the hotel, and Frank is at the wheel, pulling out of the vineyard, and Pete is up on the microphone, asking the passengers if they enjoyed the day trip. Then Samantha stand and shouts out.

"Three cheers for the drivers, for they have been up to it all day, hip-hip array, hip-hip array, hip-hip array. All on board are doing it, and Pete stands there with his arms stretched out and thanking them. They are soon back and Pete at the door helping them off, and one or two are leaving a tip in the little weaved box on the front, then off comes the coach Samantha, and she tells Pete in the side of his ear.

"Here is my phone number if you are ever up in Doncaster, you would be given one hell of a night." She kisses Pete, and the next off is Clare and the same, putting her phone number into Pete's hand and telling him.

"You bloody well phone me Pete, and I promise, I will blow your socks off when you come up." She kisses Pete, and might I say with tongues down each other's throat.

"Thanks babe, I`ll always be up for you, you will be straight into my book.
"Pete and Frank do get the last hour around the pool, relaxing and having a little banter with the ones around the pool. They finally start to go back to their room to change, and get ready for their evening meal. On the way back Pete asks Frank what he is going to do that evening, Frank tells Pete.

"Just dinner sit around the bar, maybe a little entertainment that is on in the hotel, what about yourself Pete."

"Well the same as you Dinner few beers in the bar, then a stroll down to the front to take in the evening air."

Chapter Sixteen

That evening showered, dusted down, and they both go for dinner, and after a few beers around the bar, the time is approaching 8-45pm, and Pete tells Frank that he is going to go for a stroll, and he will see him later.

"OK Pete see you later, and if not, try not to make too much noise when you come in mate."

"Will do Frank see you later." Pete stands and goes through the lobby and starts to walk down to the sea front, and to enjoy a quiet drink in one of the sea front bars. On the way down he passes an alley, and suddenly a cat knocks off a dustbins lid that rattles to the ground, which made Pete spin round and he looks down the alley. And what he sees makes the hairs on his arms stand up, and a very cold feeling run through him, the sort of feeling that someone had just walked over you're grave. For he sees his Sofia walk between two buildings dressed in a white long dress and long flowing blonde hair. Pete shouts out her name.

"Sofia-Sofia, he goes running down to where she had passed and stops dead, and looks and to no avail did he see her. Then again the cold feeling and he rubs his arms turns and walks back, and just before he carried on walking looks back and no Sofia.

He finds a quiet bar with tables looking out to sea, buys a beer and goes and sits on his own, deep in thought and just thinking about what he had experienced earlier. When all of a sudden this voice asks him.

"Please could I join you?" Well Pete with being not fully aware turns and jumps out of his skin, and the Girl who asked the question jumps back in fright. For she had only a long white dress and long flowing hair.

"Please-please forgive me, I was miles away." Pete stands, holds her hands, and still asking forgiveness on making her jump.

"Don't worry my fault really I should have caught you eye first, then asked if it is alright for me to join you."

"Please-please, do join me, it would be nice to have someone to talk too, and have a little company, my names Pete, and you are." Pete smiling at her.

"Angie, please to meet you Pete." Angie out stretching her hand to Pete to shake. Introductions over Pete asks her.

"Angie more like an angel, what are you doing out on your own, one would think that you would be out on the town enjoying yourself, with a handsome fellow in tow." Angie smiles at Pete and tells him, not me Pete I have just finished work, and always stop for a drink before I go home, but you are right in one way, I am out with an handsome fellow, that being you."

"Away with you Angie, I'm just an ordinary run of the mill fellow."

"Away with you too, just look at yourself, handsome, good looks, and might I say, a very impressive body to go with it."

"OK please, before my head drops of with the weight of complements, would you like a drink Angie." She asks for a vodka and lime, and they sit chatting and are hitting it off well, Pete telling her about why he jumped when she approached, and what had happened in his life. For well over an hour they are chatting and laughing together, with Angie the odd time touching Pete, and finally she asks Pete.

"Would you like to come back to my home, for I only live a few minutes away, and maybe slip into something more comfortable, and we could carry on with our company together."

"I would love to Angie, drink up and let's go." They both finish their drink and start to leave the bar, Pete puts his hand out and Angie holds his hand. They had been only walking a few minute, and just before they reach Angie's home, Pete stops pulls her closer to him, and they stand in one romantic kiss. After Angie tells Pete.

"We are at my home, over there. They enter and Angie asks Pete.

"I would like to make love to you in my games room, that if you would like to make love to me."

"You are so beautiful, and you're long blond hair, who would not want to make love to you." Angie smiles at Pete, kisses him and tells him.

"Wait here, while I slip into my play suit." She walks off to her bedroom, and Pete is thinking to himself. "Play room, I don't think I've had it over a snooker table, and change, I hope she does not come out in a suit with a snooker cue in her hand." Pete standing there chuckling to himself. When suddenly the door opens and is eyes light up, and are as wide as they could be, with what be fronts him. For Angie had this black leather waist coat, that buttoned up under her breast, that were exposed, then he looked down, and all she had on is a black suspender belt, black stocking, and nothing else, and you could see her shaven fanny, and Pete's eyes got even wider, at what he is looking at. Pete thinks, fucking hell, I'm going to pop my cork, she's fucking gorgeous. Angie approaches Pete and asks if he approved, Pete straight away kisses Angie and his hands start to go for her fanny and she pulls away and tells Pete.

"Not yet sweetheart, first let's go into my play room." She pulls Pete along by his T-shirt and walking backwards, she pushes open the door and they enter. The first thing Pete notices is the very dim lit room, and he could just make out some sort of rack, and everything seemed to be black. He is thinking, fucks sake a kinky woman. Angie lifts Pete's white T-shirt off, and starts to remove his jeans, and then his boxer shorts, and Pete is completely standing in the nude, and Angie could not get over how spectacular Pete looked, standing there in all his glory.

"My you are one hell of a big man, I have never seen one that thick and long." (Well I think we all know, what she is talking about.) Then she drops a bomb shell to Pete telling him.

"You don't mind playing a game, do you Pete, I think it makes the sex we are about to have even better."

"Not me babe, I`m all up for it." Angie straps Pete to the rack, with his arms out stretched and his legs too, on the rack, but might I say not completely tied down, for Pete could release himself anytime he liked, but at the moment, the truth be known I think he is starting to enjoy it. Angie steps back and admirer's Pete standing there all trust up, and under her domination, and she picks up a bottle containing baby lotion, and starts to pour it onto Pete's shoulders, and the lotion starts to run down Pete's breasts. She starts to rub the lotion into Pete's breast, and making sure he is completely covered, while she rubs more into his nipples and kissing them. Then his tummy, and finally down to his groin, and she stops, looks at Pete, then starts to pour more lotion onto her hands, and at the same time looking at his cock, which by now is fully extended and just over 10 inches long. Pete is pulling back his head with the pleasure she is giving him, then looks back to Angie, who smiles while rubbing the lotion in her hands, then starts to apply it to his cock, while looking at him, and leaning forward and giving him a kiss, while her hands are rubbing the lotion into the full length of his cock.

"Fucking hell Angie you are fucking going to make me blow my top babe."

"Not yet sweetheart there is more to come." She just smiles at Pete and goes down, and her mouth starts to swallow Pete's cock, while he is looking at her, and he is thinking at the site of Angie, and her long blond hair covering her face, that she looks just like Sofia. Pete in a quiet voice is saying to himself, "Ho Sofia I love you so." His eyes are closed tight and he is fully engrossed at the feeling of Angie, giving him one hell of a blow job. He could not take any more for he knew, that another minute and he would explode, he does no more than take his hands out of the rack, and pulls Angie up. Then he stands her in the rack, pulls the cord on her hands, then straps her feet that are spread eagled onto the bottom, and tells Angie.

"My turn, to make you're pleasure, a true experience." Pete first did no more than unclip her leather waistcoat, and it drops to the floor, and then he starts to rub baby lotion into his hands, and looking at Angie at the same time moving towards her, so she could feel his massif cock, pressing into her fanny, but not penetrating her. He pours the lotion onto her shoulders and starts to rub it into her breast, and the feeling she is receiving with Pete's hands rubbing the lotion around her breast, make her stretch outwards with the feeling that Pete is giving her.

"You are fucking good Pete, you are making my juices flow, God how much more." Pete by now is starting to rub the lotion around her fanny, and she seemed to be stretching further back with the pleasure, then Pets starts to go down on Angie, and he starts to flick her clitoris with his tongue, which brings a rather large scream of pure pleasure from Angie.

"Fucking Jesus Christ, Ha, God fuck me now Pete please, fuck me now." Pete is really going at her fanny with his tongue, and he could tell that she is ready to be fucked, he comes up and with Angie standing straddled legs does no more, than put his hands on her hips, and kneels a little and thrust upwards and he penetrates Angie straight away, and that was it, the most loud scream of pleasure as she feels, Pete's cock going deep into her, with effortlessness with her being well lubricated. Pete speeds up and they had been at it for well over half an hour when Angie screams out to Pete, and leaning forward and looking at Pete tells him.

"Fucking come now I`m exploding, now, for fucks sake spunk me."

Pete did explode, and they both come together, with Angie looking straight into Pete's eyes and he the same, as they both wallow in the orgasm that they were having. They soon come back down to earth, and still standing in the upright position are complementing each other on their performances and Angie tells Pete.

"Anytime you are back in Faro you must make a bee line to my home for you are the best I have ever had."

"Don`t you worry about that babe, I will come running, lets shower, before I go." All cleaned up, and Pete kisses Angie at the door and he leaves to go back to the hotel. He arrives at about 2.am, and he enters his room and with the light off starts to strip, he is standing there in the nude just before he gets into bed, and he is saying to Frank.

"You are not going to believe me what I have been up to." When all of a sudden the table light comes on, and he hears someone say.

"Wow, what a fantastic man." Pete looks and looking at him standing there in three nude is this bird, who is in bed with Frank. Pete asks.

"Is Frank awake babe."

"Bloody joking aren't you, would you believe me if I told you, he dropped off in to a drunken stupor, as soon as his head hit the pillow."

"Pete smiles at her and getting into bed tells her.

"My names Pete and you are."

"Ellie, and I have not had a shag of him, so I might as well get into bed with you, and hope my lucks in." She know more that gets out of Franks bed, and with her already in the nude, joins Pete, and wraps her legs round Pete, and she feels his cock, and Pete starts to rise at the feeling with her hand on his cock.

"Yes my luck is in, boy you have a large one down there Pete."

"Thanks." Pete starts to fondle her breast, and kissing her nipples and he slowly starts to make is way down to her fanny and starts to finger fuck her. And Ellie starts to stretch upwards with the feeling.

"Fucking hell, this is what I should have been getting last night". Ellie is giving Pete one hell of a wank, and Pete does no more than mount her, for he did not want Ellie to carry on pulling his cock, or she would never get fucked. Pete mounts her, and he slowly starts to insert his cock into Ellie, going in about two inches, pulling out, then back in again. Gradually Pete starts to speed up, and he is well by now nearly fully in, with Ellie wrapping her legs around Pete and lifting up off the bed with every thrust.

"Fucking hell, I'm glad you came along." Then she screams out with the feeling of Pete's cock going to the hilt and Pete stopping and lifting his cock with his muscles, and Ellie could feel it every time he did it, and she is having orgasm after orgasm.

"Ho my God, Pete." She is kissing Pete's neck and breathing heavily, and saying to Pete in his ear,

"Bloody well come now, for fucks sake, you are blowing my fucking brains out with pleasure, Ho God, please." Then the loudest scream of pleasure, and Frank is still snoring away for Great Britain. Then Pete explodes and by now the noise that both of them are making, you would think it would wake up half the hotel. After they lay there just kissing in general, and Pete with his hands tweaking her nipples, Ellie had her hand on Pete's cock, and would you believe it he starts to rise again, and not long they were at it again, but this time Pete laid back and Ellie was the jockey. By the time they had shagged again the time is approaching 4am and they finally do drop off, with being shagged out. The time is just after 8am, and Pete rises with Ellie fast on, and Pete showers and puts on his gym shorts and vest, and is off to the gym. Leaving Ellie and Frank fast on. About 9.30am Frank comes round, and he sits up in bed, and he is moaning like hell with the biggest headache, and he turns round to Pete's bed, and sees Ellie laying there with her tits exposed, with the sheet being low on the bed, he then looks down to her arse that is cocking up, and he is thinking. "Must be Pete's shagging partner, boy surfs up."(Frank talking about the crack of her arse.) He goes to shower, and he had only been in there ten minutes when Ellie comes into the bedroom, and she opens the shower door and looks at Frank. Frank turns and straight away puts his hands on his manhood, and asks Ellie.

"What are you doing, Pete would not like it if he caught the two of us together."

"What the fuck are you talking about, I went to bed with you last night, can't you fucking remember, it should have been you that shagged me, not your mate." Well Frank just stood there in the running water, and he is thinking to himself. "What did I drink last night, I cannot remember a thing." Ellie gets into the shower passes Frank the soap and tells him.

"Here make yourself useful, and soap my back, and if you are a good boy, maybe I will let you rub soap on my front." She holds out the soap and

Frank removes his hands and takes the soap, and just before Ellie turned round she had a look at Franks cock, puts her hand on his manhood, looks Frank straight in the eyes and said.

"Not as big and thick like your mates." Frank straight away with a little wit said.

"Well at least it can fill a pram." He stands smiling at Ellie as she turned round and Frank started to soap her down.

Chapter Seventeen

Pete finishes his workout and goes back to the room to change, ready for breakfast, and the room is empty, Pete thinks well at least he`s up, I will go and see if he is taking breakfast. Pete enters the restaurant and sure enough Frank is sitting with a coffee, and with his hands wrapped around it. Pete approaches and said.

"Here you are Frank had breakfast yet, I`m starving." Frank looks up to Pete and he tells him.

"Not I mate, the coffee will do, and you are not going to believe this, but when I woke this morning, there was a bird in your bed, and would you believe it, when I went for a shower she came in. I`m sorry mate but we made love, but I cannot understand when she said, that I make love not like my mate, for it was like throwing a sausage up an entry, what does she mean by that."

"Bloody hell Frank cannot you remember taking her to bed with you last night."

"No I bloody well cannot, for I do not know what they put in my drink last night, for all that I know, is waking, and seeing this bird in your bed."

"Well she went to bed with you last night, and all that she required was for you to shag the arse of it, but you might not know this, when I came back from a fantastic night of fantasy shagging, I was trying to tell you, and she turned the light on, and might I say she was in your bed, and not mine, with you snoring for Britain, but she just got into bed with me, and the rest is history." Frank just sat there shaking his head, and then looking up to Pete, and asking him.

"What do you mean Fantasy shagging?" Well by the time Pete had told him about the games room, and the rack, Frank's eyes were wide open and he just said to Pete.

"Bloody hell Pete, were you not frightened that you could have become a sex slave to her."

"No way more like she would have become my sex toy, I tell you now if we are back here soon, I will make a bee line there, and maybe you would like to tag on with me." Well Frank just looks at Pete and said nothing. Pete tucks into a full English breakfast, while Frank just sat there screwing up his face, at seeing Pete devouring is breakfast. Pete finishes his breakfast and Frank asks Pete.

"What's on the agenda today then Pete."

"Well it's the last day tomorrow, how about a relaxing day, sunbathing around the pool, a little swimming, and just see what develops." Frank just sat there nodding his head in agreement. They go back to their room change and come into the pool area, and find a place around the pool that had the Sunshine on it all day.

They settle down on their Sun loungers and Pete comments.

"This is the life, sitting here sunbathing, and bloody well getting paid for it, lovely jubbly." Frank laughs and tells Pete.

"You sound like that bloke off the telly, you know that old series, with Del boy, he used to say that, lovely jubbly."

"Just sit back, and make sure you have some sun factor on Frank, I don`t want you dropping to sleep, with already being burnt."

"No worries about that Pete, I've learnt my lesson." They settle down and Pete and Frank must have dropped off for well over an hour and a half, when Pete awakes and sits up, and looks at Frank and just in case puts a towel over Franks chest. Pete is looking around the pool with his radar working overtime, looking for new talent, when his eyes catch site of four young ladies entering the pool area, looking for somewhere to sit. They finally find somewhere, and they start to put their towels down on the Sun loungers, and might I say bending down showing a good view of their arses. Pete's eyes light up and he is thinking, come on my son get in there, for they are truly stunners. He stands and makes his way over to them, and stops and said to them.

"Morning girls, have you just arrived." All four of them look up to Pete and might I say with one of their hands over their eyes, for Pete stood there with the Sun on his back. One of the young ladies tell Pete, and she had long blond hair, and wearing a white bikini.

"Yes we flew in this morning, and just arrived at the hotel."

"Well my names Pete, and I'm one of the reps at the Hotel, and if there is anything you would like to know, or want, please don't hesitate to let me know, for I'm up for it all the time."

Pete turns around and dives straight into the pool and goes swimming off to where he is sitting. The blond girl looks to her mates and comments to them.

"Boy if he is one of the reps, boy we are going to have one hell of a holiday." They all sit there giggling and looking at Pete. Pete comes back to Frank and with him dripping with cold water, flicks some onto Frank's tummy and he jumps up.

"What the fuck."

"Sorry mate but you have missed four gorgeous birds, which have just come." Frank looking around the pool and asking Pete.

"Where are they?" Pete points to where they are lying, and Frank spots them.

"Ho yes, they do look fetching." Pete finishes drying himself off and tells Frank.

"Well I'm off and see if I can get acquainted to one of them, especially the blond in the white bikini. Pete goes walking off and he passes them, and smiles at the one in the white bikini, and she shouts to Pete.

"Pete have you a moment." Pete is straight over and asks.

"What is it sweetheart, what would you like to know."

"Please Pete, where do you go to get refreshments."

"Over in the pool bar, over on the side, on the right, why I`m off for a cool beer myself, if you would like to join me." Well straight away she stands and walks over to Pete and tells him.

"That would be nice, please lead on Pete." They go walking off around the pool, and Pete turns to her and asks.

"You know my name, and I do not know yours."

"She tells Pete, sorry my names Amy, and might I say you are one hell of a fit young man." They go walking off towards the pool bar, and Amy is looking at Pete up and down, and she could not take her eyes of Pete's bulge, within his trunks.

"You look like you work out Pete, how often, do you go to the gym."

"Every morning, here I try and get to the gym by seven in the mornings when it is a little quiet." They come to the bar and Pete asks Amy what she would like to drink, she had the same as Pete and they go and sit at a table in the sun. Amy asks Pete.

"Are you with anyone Pete?" Well at first Pete took it in the wrong meaning and came straight out with.

"Yes my partner over there, his name is Frank." Well Pete see`s Amy`s face drop and then the penny dropped.

"Amy no I don`t mean it like that, Frank and myself are Reps and coach drivers, we have brought a coach load of customers down from Nottingham, you meant girl, didn't you." Amy's face had the biggest smile on her face, and just giggled at the thought of Pete being gay.

"Ho, that's relieve, for a moment I thought what a waste, of a good looking bloke."

"Not me baby, for as soon as I seen you and your friends, I could not take my eyes off you, and might I say I fancied you to bits, and I don't think I would if I was gay." Pete bending down his hand in a gay like fashion. Amy laughs at what Pete had said, and a reaction puts her hand onto Pete's leg. Pete looks down to his leg, looks back up to Amy, leans forward and Amy did the same, and they are sitting there in one long kiss. After they part and Amy tells Pete.

"You are giving me a loving feeling running down my back, you are so handsome Pete." Pete leans forward again and kisses Amy, this time with tongues. After Amy just came straight out with.

"Ho I would love to make love to you right now." Pete stands and tells her.

"Come Amy let's go back to my room, and I will make slow passionate love to you." Amy stands and puts her hand in Pete's and they leave the pool area, just when Frank sits up, and sees them both walking off together, Frank is saying.

"Fucks sake he's at it again, and it must be a world record, for I bet he's going back to our room, to fuck the arse of it." They come to Pete's room and enter and Pete locks the door, and straight away pulls Amy to him, and they stand kissing, and Pete unties her top and it falls to the ground, and then her bikini bottom, and she is completely in the nude. Amy while they are kissing removes Pete's swimming trunks, and they stand in one loving kiss, and Amy feeling Pete's cheeks, suddenly puts her hand onto Pete's Cock, that is pressing into her groin, and when she feels It, breaks away from Pete and looks down at her interest, then back up to Pete.

"Fucking hell Pete, you have one mother fucking cock there." Pete looks at Amy and looking at her body tells her.

"And you have one of the finest, and stunning body's that I have ever seen." Amy bends down and straight away trying to get as much of Pete's cock in her mouth, and flicking her tongue onto Pete's bell end, which makes Pete judder with the pleasure of her tongue giving him one hell of a blow job. When Pete had is fussy out of the blow job, lifts Amy up and carries her to the bed, and slowly puts her down, while they both are kissing each other. Amy is laying on the bed and Pete goes through the motions, by first giving her a good tongue kissing then moving down to her neck, then onto her breasts and giving them a good seeing to, making her nipples stick up like two chapel hat pegs. Then down to her Vagina and his tongue starts to work on her clitoris, and by now Amy is already having her first orgasm, and breathing heavily, and sighing.

"Ho that's lovely Pete, more, more, God you are fucking good." Pete could feel the warm taste of her juices, and he is giving her fanny probably the best tonguing she had ever had. Pete knew that the time is right for him to start to shag her, and he comes up and starts to insert his cock into Amy, and she is watching every inch of Pete's cock disappear into her. And the sigh and scream of pure delight is deafening. Pete is going slow then withdrawing and pushing back in a little faster, then repeating the action. He had been shagging her for well over 30 minutes, and Amy had her fill and screaming with the orgasms that she is experiencing. It got to the point when she screams out to Pete, fucking hell Pete when are you going to come. Pete tells her.

"Anytime now." Well when Pete said this she pushes Pete off, and spins round and cocks her arse into the air, and screaming at Pete to come up her arse. Pete starts to press his cock into Amy's arse, and the tight feeling and the length that went into her made Pete blow his top, and he is giving her all of his spunk, and Amy just screams out with the feeling of his warm spunk, flowing into her arse. They both flop back onto the bed and Pete laying there with his arm around Amy, and might I say holding and foundering one of her breasts asks her.

"Tonight is the last night that Frank and I, can have a drink for Saturday morning we have to drive all day and night, and a little of the next, taking the passengers on the coach back home. And I was wondering if we could make a date for tonight, and all of us go and have a good night down in the centre, and go into night club."

"Leave it to me, they will tag along, in the hotel bar, let's say eight-o-clock." All sorted and, they shower and go back out to the pool.

Chapter Eighteen

Back around the pool, Pete comes back to Frank, and straight away Frank asks Pete.

"You have just fucked the arse of that blond bird, haven't you?"

"Fucking too true Frank, and she took it up the arse, and you would not believe it, with this the last night we can have a drink, for tomorrow night we have to stop sober, for the drive back Saturday, so, tonight we are going to go out with the four of them. You never know you might land up in bed with a couple of them." Pete leaning down and tickling Frank's belly.

"You're not bloody real, but the other three were stunners, and maybe, you never know." Frank sitting there smiling at the thought of taking two of them to bed, in a daydream. Pete tells Frank.

"Well another hour sunbathing, then we will go and start to get ready for tonight." Pete flops down on his sun lounger and he is soon off in a dream, and might I say not the sort you would like. For he sees his Sofia approaching, still in the white long dress with her long blond hair flowing in the breeze down to her bum. Pete by now starts to sweat and all he is saying is Ho Sofia, I love you so. Please come back, and she tells him.

"My darling Pete, I love you, and miss you so, what I would give to feel one more time, your touch, and your warm arms around me, my love, my protector, I love you so." Pete suddenly screams out loud, and wakes up, and he had tears flowing down his face, and Frank looks at him, and sees the state Pete is in.

"Bloody hell mate, what the fuck were you dreaming about."

"You would not believe me if I told you." Pete wiping the tears from his eyes.

"Come on Pete it's me, you're so called mate, you can rest assured it will go no further, what's on your mind."

"Well I have seen my Sofia in her long dress, with her long blond hair, and now she is talking to me, in my dream, bloody hell Frank I'm not cracking up am I."

"No way Pete, you are still missing her, and might I say, what I know about you, she was your soul mate, it's going to take time, for you to come to terms with your loss." Pete out stretches his hand, and Frank grabs his arm and they sit there and doing an arm shake, when Pete leans forward and kisses Frank on the cheek and telling him.

"Thanks Frank I will never forget this, with you being there for me."

"Any time Pete, if you would like to talk about anything, do not hesitate to come and see me." Pete again shakes his hand and tells Frank.

"Come on then, let's go and spruce ourselves up for tonight." They eat first then go into the bar to wait for the girls, and sure enough dead on 8pm the four of them come walking into the bar, and Franks mouth drops at what beholds him, four they all had very short miniskirts on and two had stocking tops showing, with their suspender belt showing. They were stunners, Frank tells Pete as they came walking over.

"Fucking hell Pete, I've got a hard on already, just look at the legs on those two. They approach the boys and order their drinks and Amy kisses Pete and tells the girls.

"This is Pete and his mate Frank, Frank and Pete, this is Linda, Emily, and Joanna. The girls smile at the both of them, and all three give Pete and Frank a kiss, and they stand chatting together, and asking about the club they are going to go to. At about 9pm, Pete asks them if they were ready to go to the club, and they all start to leave the hotel and might I say the night security guards, were having an eye full of them leaving, and it does not take long to know, what they were thinking about at seeing so attractive girls. Pete is in front with Amy on one arm, and Joanna on the other, and Pete is eyeing her large tits up, and thinking to himself. Boy I hope, I`m going to get my head between those two. Pete looking down her cleavage.

They go into the club and the beer is flowing, and Pete when he had the chance is chatting Joanna up, and praising her on her looks and he tells her.

"Don't think I'm being forward Joanna, but I would love to take you and Amy to bed, and make mad passionate love to you both. Joanna comes up close to Pete, and she whispers in his ear.

"Amy told me about the size of your cock, and if she is up for it so am I." Joanna puts her hand onto Pete's cock, and feeling it to make sure Amy is not fantasising over it, she smile and tells Pete.

"Well with what I have just felt, if Amy is not up for it, then you can fuck the arse of me big boy." Pete smiles and he see Amy coming back, and Joanna comes straight out with what Pete had just asked. She looks at Pete and tells him.

"Well if you would like a threesome, so be it." They carry on enjoying the beer and music, with the odd dance. Frank is getting on well with the other two girls and at about 11.30pm, Pete whispers to both Amy and Joanna, if they were ready for some fun back at the hotel, the girls nod their heads in agreement and they sneek out without telling the other three. They go walking back and Pete with his arms around both of them, is kissing each in turn, and already having a feel of Joanna's massif tits. Pete is thinking that as soon as he has them both on the bed, he is going to dive head first into her lovely tits, and work on them. They pass the security guards in reception and when they go by, one of the guards nudges the other and in Portuguese tells the other one.

"Lucky English bastard, he`s going to fuck them both, just look at where his hands are." Pete on purpose is holding both of them by the cheeks. Turns looks at the guards and lifting his eyebrows and smiling at them. They reach the girls room and the first thing Pete asks them.

"What about the other two, what if they come back."

"Don't worry Pete they are together next door." Pete smiles and approaches the both of them, and he starts by lifting Joanna's top off, and then Amy's, Pete starts to kiss Joanna's nipples and Pete is thinking. "Jackpot, what a fucking lovely pair of nipples." While he is pulling down Amy's thong and she then stands behind Pete and starts to put her arms around Pete and starting to play with his cock. Pete feeling the top of Joanna's leg, for she still had her suspender belt on, but no nickers, starts to finger her, and he turns slightly so Amy could give him a blow job, instead of a wank. Joanna's nipples are well and truly standing proud and Pete could feel her juices flowing, and she then goes down, and before long they are both taking it in turns to give Pete one hell of a blow job. Pete stood there looking down at them both, and when he knew when to stop them, he tells them.

"Come on girls let's have you two in bed, for I want to fuck the arses of you." Well like grease lightning they are up and straight onto the bed, and looking back at Pete who approaches, and with his massif build, and might I say that fucking great prick of his pointing the way, the girls start to purr like two Cheshire cats. Pete climbs onto the bed and he starts to give Amy's nipples the works, and he is feeling Joanna's tits and then moving back down to her fanny to keep it nice and moist, till he mounts it. Not long and Amy's tits have had a good session, and he starts to give her a finger job, Joanna is moaning with delight, and Pete while still fingering Amy mounts Joanna, and he slowly starts to penetrate her, first going slowly into her, and then gradually speeding up, and it was not long before Joanna is having multi orgasms, with what Pete was giving her. Pete starts to give Amy a tonguing and flicking her clitoris, and then giving her fanny a good tonguing. Joanna is really shouting, and Pete comes off her and swops over to Amy, and Pete tells Joanna to come up to his face and Pete starts to shag Amy, and now it was Joanna's turn to have her clitoris flicked and a good tonguing. After about ten minutes they both were screaming out with pleasure, and Pete knew that he is going to explode, and he tells them both, and they both turn over and cock their arses up in the air and tell him, to come in both of them. Pete penetrates Joanna's arse first and might I say within a minute Pete explodes, and gives Joanna a little, then mounts Amy and inserts his cock into her arse and gives her the rest. After all three flop back onto the bed and complementing Pete on his performance. And giving him a loving kiss.

At about 1am Pete tells the girls who are starting to drop off, that he will go back to his room for he had to be up at 7am to go to the gym. They murmur and Pete smiles at them both, and he goes and have a quick shower, he dresses, and by now both were fast on, and Pete quietly leaves the room. He closes the door and turns and nearly knocks Emily over.

"Sorry Emily, I thought you were with Frank."

"What you are kidding, we came out of the night club late, and he went to bed with Linda, and it looks like I've lost out." Pete looks at Emily's long slim legs and she was the other girl with the suspenders. Pete presses up to her, puts his arms around her, and he tells her.

"Well if you would like I could see that you are well satisfied." Well Emily feels what is pressing into her, and she smiles at Pete and tells him.

"Well what I can feel, maybe I've won the jackpot." Emily kissing Frank and going to the door and opening it while Pete is still kissing her. Pete is thinking to himself.

"Fuck me three within a couple of hours, I don't think I will be coming with Emily." They enter the room and straight away Emily is stripping like there will be no tomorrow, Pete just stood there in amazement how quick she strips and she stood straight in front of Pete, who just stood there admiring her fantastic body. Pete while Emily is still looking at him, slowly removes his top, revelling his muscular body, then his jeans and boxers, and they both by now are admiring what beholds them, it's like a slow dance, they both go walking towards each other, and stand in one mighty clinch kissing. Tongues and all.

Pete picks Emily up into his arms, and still kissing her, and he walks to the bed and puts her upon it, and Emily straight away laid there and opens her legs spread eagled, waiting for her prize. Pete goes down on Emily, and first kissing her on the lips then neck, and you guessed, giving her tits the works, and then down to her tummy, and by now Emily is contraction up with what is about to come. And Pete starts to slowly flick her clitoris, and going slowly down, and he starts to suck her clitoris into his mouth, and slowly suck in and out, well Emily sure does explode with one mighty orgasm, for she is experiencing some thing, that she had never done with any other fellow.

"Fucking hell Pete, who the fuck showed you to-do that."

"Experience babe, and you have felt nothing yet." Pete looking up to Emily and smiles and then carried on with pleasing her. He then puts both hands onto her bum and lifting her up, and might I say two of his fingers are tickling her arsehole, he goes deep into her fanny with him with his tongue, well that was it, Emily explodes, and she gushes with juices, as she has one of the most fantastic orgasms. Her whole body lifts of the bed, and she is completely wrapped around the feeling that Pete was giving her.

"Fucking Jesus Christ, fuck the rest, you are fucking magic, and I mean fucking magic. Please Pete fuck me like you want to fuck the arse off me. Well Pete did just what she wanted, and comes up straddles her. And she looks down to see what she is about to receive, and when she sees Pete s cock coming towards her, I think her juices exploded again. Pete slips in quite easily, Pete pushing his large cock in, and Emily feeling her fanny expand to receive it, and within minutes she is gushing, and having might orgasms at what Pete is doing. They had only been doing it for about fifteen minutes when they both scream out with one might orgasm each, and Pete's cock going up and down, and Emily feeling like he had come. They both flop back down and are laying there with arms around each other and giving each other a loving kiss. After about half an hour Pete looks at his watch and the time by now is approaching three in the morning and he tells Emily.

"I've got to go babe, don't forget to leave your phone number." Pete dresses and he is thinking, fucking hell I've never had it like that, that was fucking magic, let's go and get my head down." Pete leaves and he is back in his room and it was in complete darkness, he strips down to his birthday suit and is about to get into bed, when the table light comes on, and Pete turns round and it was Linda, that lay there looking at Pete in all is glory.

WELL Pete is thinking of the other night, when another bird turned the light on when Frank was pissed and he landed up shagging her, is thinking.

"For fucks sake no, not four in one night." She looks at Pete, well something on Pete and straight away asks.

"Hi Pete can I come and sleep with you, this boring fart has dropped off, and not even a kiss me good night." Well Pete is saying.

"If you must, but no fucking about, for I`m knackered, and if you want me to make love to you, you will have to wait till the morning." Well she is straight up and into Pete's bed and would you believe it the first thing she does is put her hand onto Pete's cock, and with them facing each other, kisses Pete and tells him.

"Well you promise me, when we awake you will let me feel that big boy inside of me."

"No problem Linda, good night sweetheart." Linda still holding Pete's cock smiles kisses Pete, and they are both soon off into the land of nod.

Pete had been fast on and sure enough he did wake at 7am, and he sees Linda, laying there, and he is thinking, maybe I could get up and go to the gym, but look at her, Pete pulling back the sheet and with Linda laying on her back and her tits looking like two fried eggs on a backing board, and might I say very nice looking nipples to suck, and then Pete looks down to his final goal and his eyes light up, for she only had a shaven fanny, and that is one of Pete's, best views, and he thinks.

"Boy I`ve got to fuck the fanny off that beauty." He leans over Linda and gently gives her a kiss on the lips, and this seemed to bring her out of her sleep, and she straight away puts her arms around Pete, and they are in one French kissing, and it's not long before Linda had her hand on her own interest, yes you guessed Pete's cock. And Pete starts to get aroused and he soon had a full hard on, and he slowly goes down on Linda, and working away on her fanny, but Linda turns Pete over so she could work on his cock, and they both are enjoying oral sex with each other.

Pete comes up and mounts Linda, and they both seemed to look as Pete's cock starts to penetrate Linda's fanny, and the sigh that she gives, as she feels Pete's large cock disappear into her.

"That's lovely and warm Pete, fuck me slowly first, then speed up, fucking hell the feeling." Linda digging her nails into Pete's back, that made him stretch up and go deeper into Linda. They had been at it four well over twenty minutes and by now Pete was really bashing away, like a bull at a barn gate, and Linda had orgasm after orgasm, and she tells Pete.

"Spunk me now, and leave that fucking big fuck in me, now Pete please spunk me now." Well with the dirty talk, Pete does explode, and sure enough he does spunk her, and Linda stretches back with the warm feeling of Pete's warm spunk ejaculating into her. They both flop back and Linda tells Pete.

"That was well worth waiting for, and I bet you did not give the others that." Little did she know that, now he had shagged all four of them in one night?

Pete tells Linda that he is going to get up and go to the gym, she kisses Pete, and she know more gets out of bed, and back in with Frank, who is fast on. Pete just shook his head, and goes to shower, and he is soon out of there, and down to the gym.

Chapter Nineteen

Pete gets a full hour and a half in, pumping iron, and doing what he likes best, and without any more distraction from the females. After the work out Pete is getting dressed after a shower bends down to put his trainers on and he suddenly feels his abs tighten up, and he starts to rub them, and saying. "Looks like with all the shagging and pumping Iron, they are tender." After breakfast it is the last day to catch the rays, and Pete and Frank are around the pool and in general talking about the trip back home tomorrow, Pete asks him.

"I've just remembered the notice for the passengers, I've forgot to put it up this morning."

"All sorted Pete, lay back and relax, I put it up first thing this morning."

"Ho by the way, did you." Frank looks at Pete and asks him.

"What the fuck are you on about, did you."

"What you said, you put it up this morning, and you know with that Linda you were in bed with."

"No, she said I was fucking useless." Pete smiles at Frank and he tells him.

"Probably because I fucked the arse off it."

"WHAT." Well that was it, Pete was up like a flash, and Frank chasing him around the pool, till Pete dived in and swims off. Then turns round and looks at Frank, and Frank stood there shaking his fist at Pete, and laughing at the same time. Pete wipes the water off his face and laughing back at

Frank. They had been around the pool, for about an hour, when one of the girls who Pete had made love to, comes over to him and asked him.

"You are off home tomorrow Pete, I just wanted to make sure you had my number." Pete stands kisses her and takes the number and puts it down the front of his trunks in a suggestive way and tells her.

"This will remind me to definitely phone you when we get back home." Pete kisses her again, and she turns and walks off. Most of the morning they are approaching Pete and handing him phone numbers, and Frank asks the question.

"Pete how many birds have you fucked?"

"Well it depends what you mean by that, since I have been back from Spain, and that is about three weeks. I've been trying to beat my Round-Robin and let me see." Pete with is head up, and you could tell he is counting and suddenly comes straight out with.

"TWENTY THREE, and that is including that Linda you were with this morning. YES, beat it by three, I will have to improve, I must be slowing down." Well Frank just could not believe what Pete had just said, and just sat on his sun lounger shaking his head. Come lunch time they both go up to the decking, where the bar is, and have a light lunch with a couple of shandy's. They are in general talk when this young bird comes over to them and she asks.

"Excuse me, for interrupting you, but I've just arrived here, and back home I've just started training, and I'm wondering if there is a gym here, that I could go to, and with seeing your physique, and might I say a very good one, is wondering if you know one."

"Thanks' for the comments sweetheart and yes, I'm a rep here, and there is a gym, and if you would like I could show you and give you one, that's a training session if you would like to do it." Pete smiling at her and lifting his eyebrows.

"That's most kind of you, are you sure I would not be spoiling anything."

"No problem sweetheart my names Pete, and this is Frank, and you are."

"Emma, from Nottingham."

"So are we Emma, Bulwell, in fact if you are ready we could go now."

"Thanks Pete." Pete with arm stretched out for Emma to walk that way, and Pete walks off behind her, looks at her arse and looks back too Frank and he tells him.

"Make that twenty four to my Round-Robin."

They come to the gym and there is no one in and Pete is thinking, nice one. They go over to the first apparatus and Pete asks her.

"Right Emma how much lifting have you done."

"None, only rowing and sitting on a machine doing leg exercises."

"Well let's show you how to really work out, and do those abs good. Pete looking at Emma's stomach and telling her.

"Your abs look in reasonable shape but could be better. You don't mind do you Emma." Pete starting to move is hand to Emma abs.

"No help yourself Pete." Pete feels her abs, and tells her that they could do with a proper exercise, and tells her to feel his abs. Well Emma really gave Pete's abs a good feel, so much that Pete started to get aroused, so he quickly tells her to stand on the machine, and Pete is behind her, and he puts small weights onto the bar and tells her to pull down then slowly up, and she should feel her abs tighten. Emma starts, and after about ten minutes Pete asks her if she could feel the difference, and at the same time Pete stands that little bit closer to her with his arms around her, and feeling her abs tighten. Pete at the same time is that close that every time Emma releases the weights her bum goes back, and she could feel Pete's penis press into her. She tells Pete.

"Yes I can really feel the difference Pete." She turns and faces Pete and she looks down at his groin and came straight out with.

"With what I can feel pressing into me, I think that if you could hang on till you have shown me the full work out, then maybe you could have a good work out on me." She goes forward and presses her groin into Pete and after, a feel at what Pete is packing. Pete kisses Emma and breaks off and tells her right lets workout on your arms. Pete shows her the exercise for her arms, then legs, and she had a good work out and knew all the exercises, and then Pete tells her.

"That includes the work out." Emma asks Pete.

"Were can we go to conclude the deal." Pete takes her by the hand and tells her.

"Follow me." They go into one of the shower rooms that included a table for working on muscles and injury. Pete pulls Emma to him, and they start to kiss profusely each other, all that Emma had on is a small bikini which is soon off and so his Pete's boxer shorts, and they both are pressed up against the table and Emma could feel Pete's cock searching for the top of her legs, she know more that puts her hand onto Pete's full erect cock, and starts to slowly wank him off and telling Pete.

"You have one of the biggest cocks that I`ve ever felt."

"And you baby are going to have one of the fittest body's, any Woman would love to die for." Pete goes down to her tits and starts to flick his tongue around her nipples, and Emma with the feeling, takes a sharp intake of breath, at what Pete is doing. Then he starts to slowly kiss her abs and finally down to his goal, yes her fanny and clitoris, Pete straight away starts to flick and suck on her clitoris, and this made Emma really intake of breath so much, that she shouts out.

"Ho my God, what the fuck are you doing to me?" Pete looks up and came straight out with.

"You have had nothing yet babe, wait till I get my fucking big tool into you, and then you are really going to scream." Pete going back to work on her clitoris and fanny. With all the dirty talk, and they both seem to be getting into one hell of a sexual frenzy. Pete could feel Emma's juices starting to flow, and he knew that it was time to start to fuck her. He stands up and with Emma on the edge of the table opens her legs wide as he could, and at the same time puts his hand on his fully erect cock, and guides it to its goal, with Emma leaning up and watching it coming towards her, and with the sight that she sees, she is taking in one hell of a breath, for what she is about to receive from Pete.

Pete looks at her straight in the eye, and just when he enters her, they both squint at each other with the feeling, of Pete's warm cock, and Pete feeling the warmth of her fanny, and they both are taking in deep breaths of air at the feeling that they both are getting. Pete plungers deep into her and she gasps and tells Pete.

"Fucking hell, do you have to go home tomorrow, God fucking hell I'm going to explode?"

"Not yet babe, please just feel this." Pete goes to the hilt and then when he is fully in her, slowly lifts his cock inside her and she leans up and looks Pete straight in the eye, and she tells him.

"I can do that, feel." Well Emma squeezes her fanny muscles onto Pete's cock, and it was his turn to tense up at the feeling.

By now they both were taking it in turn, Pete lifting and Emma squeezing, and the feeling the two of them were getting, suddenly they both explode, Emma having one hell of an orgasm, and Pete ejaculating into her, and the warmth of Pete's sperm, made Emma just flop back to enjoy every drop. Pete flops on top of Emma, and they both start to kiss each other, and complement each other on the session, and they both were sweating profusely. Pete tells Emma.

"Well I think we both have had a good work out, and if I could stop I would jump at the opportunity to have more work outs with you, but I've got to drive all the way home tomorrow, but I promise you, give me your phone number, and we could carry on with the gym work when we get back home."

"Fucking too true Pete, for you are bloody out of this world." Pete smacks her arse and tells her.

"Come on babe, let's shower and get back to reality." They both are in the shower, and Emma soaping Pete's massif frame, and Pete gently rubbing soap into Emma, and with them both looking at each other, are soon kissing in one romantic kiss. After they both go back to the decking were Frank is still sitting, and he sees them coming and pulls out the seats for them. Frank asks Emma.

"Hope he gave you a good seeing too." Emma tells Frank.

"Fucking too true Frank, he certainly knows what to give a Woman, and he fucking well made me sweat, with the work out." Emma brushing back her hair with her hand. Frank looks at her and is thinking.

"I bet that dirty fucker pumped the arse off her." Pete comes back with two shandy's and sits, he asks Frank.

"What's the plan for tonight then Frank?"

"Well with leaving early in the morning, shit meal, bit of entertainment in the hotel, and bed early."

"That sound great Pete, do you want me to tag along, with you." Emma lifting her eyebrows up at Pete.

"I don`t think so babe, you just leave you phone number, and I will see you when we get back home." Emma smiles at Pete and tells him.

"Well I had better get back to my mates, or they will think that I`ve come on this holiday on my own, anyway here is my phone number, and you bloody well ring me." Emma stands and kisses Pete, looks at Frank and said goodbye. Pete as she was leaving shouts.

"Don't worry babe you will be the first to call when back home, see you babe." They both watch Emma walkaway and they both were looking at her arse, Frank looks back at Pete and tells him.

"I bet you fucked the arse off that, didn't you." All that Pete did, is look at Frank smile, and then back at Emma`s arse as she walked back to her mates. And he just tells Frank.

"All that I can say is, that`s twenty four towards my Round-Robin."

They go back to the sun loungers and this is the final bit of sunbathing that they will be having this holiday. All afternoon Pete keeps getting girls approach and give him their number and wish him a safe journey home.

By 5pm they decide to go back and freshen up for the evening, and to pack away the clothes they will not need anymore, and by the time they had finished it was time to eat. After around the bar and a little entertainment, the only thing they did not like is everyone who were still on holiday going out for the night, for they knew that they both were driving in the morning, and it is not worth risking, for the strict rules on drink driving, especially public transport drivers. Early night and the next morning up at 6am, check the coach and already and waiting outside the hotel for their guest to arrive, for the journey back to the UK.

Come 9am all loaded, with Frank doing a head count, and Pete decided to take the first four hour stint, back up through Portugal. They travel all day and part of the night, and arrive at Calais in France at 4am in the morning, with it being Sunday they have an hour before the ferry sails back to Dover, at 5am. Frank tells the passengers that the ones that would like a little refreshment could leave the coach and go to the nearby restaurant, and the rest to wait in the departure room, for passport control, while they take the coach to the boarding area for coaches. By 6 am they are back in the UK. Four hour drive back up to Bulwell, and by 11.30am they pull into Bulwell coach park and they all disembark and start to make their way home. Pete tells Frank that he will drop the keys off for the coach in the office, and he will see him later.

Pete goes to the office and to his surprise Sandy is there working and she is straight up and all over Pete.

Chapter Twenty

"I've missed you Pete, and especially him." Sandy feeling Pete's cock and Pete straight away tells her.

"Not now babe, I'm fucking knackered, I have been driving all night and have not been to bed since Friday, and as soon as I'm home I'm going to hit the sack for a few hours."

"Ho lovely I'll come with you." Sandy kissing Pete.

"No babe sleep, why not meet me tonight at the Horseshoe inn, and then after a couple of beers, then I will be ready to ravish you."

"OK Pete you win, 8pm, then tonight."

"We've a date." Pete kisses Sandy and he picks up his bag, and it is off home and into the land of nod. He stirs about 6.30pm from his sleep, and he looks at the alarm clock, and tells himself. "Better get up, shower and go and meet Sandy, for if I stop here any longer, I will not sleep tonight." Come 7.45pm Pete is ready and he starts to head for his date at 8pm with Sandy, at the Horseshoe Inn. He stands at the bar with Terry the Landlord in general conversation, when Sandy comes into the bar, and she looks stunning, wearing a short mini skirt and a low silk top revealing her cleavage, that made one or two of the old men lift their eyebrows, and smile at Sandy.

"Hello babe what would you like to drink." Pete seeing her, and looking at his interest that beholds him. Sandy tells Pete her desired drink and Pete gives his leave to Terry the Landlord, and they go and sit at a table. They had been in the Horseshoe Inn for about half-an-hour when Donna comes in and see's Pete sitting with Sandy. Well Donna with a face like thunder goes over to Pete and came straight out with.

"Looks like I'm not wanted anymore then Pete." Donna looking at Sandy and in not so much a friendly way. Well Pete tells Sandy.

"Please excuse me love." He stands grabs Donna by the arm and tells her.

"Bloody well come with me." He takes her outside and straight away tells Donna.

"What the fuck do you mean by bursting on me like that, she's my fucking boss with Bulwell coach company, and she is telling me about the upcoming jobs, fucking hell Donna, you bloody know that you are top of my list, BABE.

"Sorry Pete forgive me, it's just seeing you with her, I thought, I was your bitch, I love you so much."

"I know you do babe, but I've got to keep in with them with me just starting, look here is twenty quid, go and get yourself a cab, and go into town and I will see you in the week, I will ring you." Donna kisses Pete and apologises and she is straight on her phone for a taxi. Pete waits till she is safely in the taxi and he waves to her when the taxi, pulls away from the Horseshoes Inn. Pete goes back and straight away apologies to Sandy for the commotion, and tells her.

"Sometimes I wish I did not get involved with some of them here, she is a little bit of a nutter, you know you get one in every pub, but I told her that if she just went away, and find another pub, she would be better off. Instead of coming up to people she did not know." Well Sandy changed the subject completely, it was if nothing had happened, and the truth be known, I think Pete just sat there thinking. "Boy I got away with that one." They just stayed in the Horseshoes till about ten thirty, when Pete asks Sandy if she is ready to go, for he still would like an early night, with the long drive back home that he had to-day. They go and Sandy tells Pete.

"It's your day off tomorrow, so don't worry if I've gone in the morning Pete, for I've still have to be at work by 8am."

"No problem babe, I will see how I feel in the morning, with the long haul trip, might just have myself a lie-in, and give the gym a miss." They reach Pete's home and once inside, it was straight up to bed and they both start to undress and into bed, boy you could tell it is not the first time or Pete would have been there up to her putting his touch, and spell onto her. Pete lies on his back and Sandy leans over Pete with her tits resting on his chest, and Sandy rubbing Pete's chest and nipples asks him.

"Pete where do you want our relationship to go, I mean good friends, nights out and of course, the closeness afterward." Sandy putting one of her hands down onto Pete's cock that was responding to Sandy's warm hand, on his manhood. Pete turns his head towards Sandy's and gently kisses her, while she was still foundering his cock, and he tells her.

"What I really would like is to carry on the way we are now, for it is still too close to really start to get into a deep relationship, with not yet over this one, I have just lost, you know what I mean Babe." Sandy looks at Pete gives him a loving and tender kiss, and tells Pete.

"I feel strongly for you Pete in your loss, and will be always there for you, just like this hard fucking thing I'm feeling that is starting to throb for, I know what. Come here babe put him in this warm place." Sandy rolling onto her back and opening her legs wide for her prize that she is guiding towards her fanny. Pete climbs on top and Sandy starts to turn Pete's cock around her clitoris and fanny, at the same time looking Pete straight in the eyes and she is taking in deep breaths at the feeling she is giving herself and asking Pete.

"That's fucking lovely, how is it for you."

"I can feel your juices starting to flow, and Will be better when I feel your warm fanny wrapped around my little todger." Well Sandy burst out laughing loud at what Pete said, and tells him.

"Little todger, more like a coppers truncheon." Sandy letting go of his cock and it enters, and it's both of them that are sighing at the feeling they both are getting.

They are locked together kissing when, Pete starting to speed up and Sandy pushing upwards at the feeling he is giving her, and they are making mad passionate love for well over forty minutes and by now Sandy bringing the house down with the loud groans of pleasure as she is having multi orgasms, and this made Pete shoot his load, and quickly with draws, and Sandy is straight down onto his cock and taking all of what Pete is ejaculating, with it his turn to moan with the pleasure of coming, and feeling Sandy's tongue and mouth wrapped around his cock.

The time is approaching midnight, and they both are just lying there silent with Pete gently stroking Sandy's hair, and Sandy resting back across Pete's chest, and gently rubbing his chest, and before long they both are off into the land of nod. Pete slept well, and at 8.30am wakes turns and Sandy had gone, for like she told him, she had to go and change and be back at work by 8am, she had showered and left quietly, Pete just stroke the sheet were Sandy had been lying and thinking. She is a good girl, but a little too close to home for comfort. Pete is thinking back to last night and the close shave with Donna, and he his thinking, that it is not the first time this had happened. Pete sits on the side of the bed and pulls out his little black book and with all the phone numbers of the birds he had shagged, and enters more of them from the coach trip, and he is thinking. "I wonder if another guy does this, or am I the only sick bastard he smiles and just said, well at least my book is a thick one." He burst out laughing at what he had said, for you could take it in another contexts thick book, or cock.

Over the next few months, Pete is doing school runs, days out, and in general day trips, and the winter months are upon us, and one Monday morning Pete is called into Toms office, and Tom asks Pete to sit down, for he had some bad news to report to him. Before Tom could say another word Pete came straight out with.

"You don't have to tell me Tom, for I know what is coming next. You are going to lay me off, for the work is not coming in with it being winter, and you will let me know straight away when it picks up after winter, and the holiday trips kick back in." Tom just sat there opened mouth, takes the paper he had in his hand and rips it up telling Pete.

"I've been worried sick all-night, dreading to tell you, and you just take it like that." Tom shaking his head and telling Pete.

"I'm truly sorry son, and you will be definitely be back, dam the big wigs for taking these measures."

"Come on Tom it's not your fault, and anyway the rest will do me well, for I've plenty left from the sale of my home in Spain. And just lately, to tell you Tom and you alone, and don't let it go any further, over the last few months, I have been taking it a little bad, over the loss of my beautiful wife Sofia."

Tom shakes Pete's hand and then hugs him and telling him.

"We are both in the same boat, what you with Sofia, and me with my lovely Doris, god bless her. But don't forget Pete, I'm always here and will be, for you are like my son to me, and don't bloody well forget it." Tom hugging Pete again and Pete tells him.

"Thanks Tom, and take care over the winter, and I will try and pop in over the winter and see you." Pete smiles at Tom and leaves, and on the way out he had to go past Sandy, who started to cry when she see Pete. Pete sees her and tells her.

"You know then babe about me, but come on it's not the end of the world, I mean I've a bob or two, and won't go hungry, so cheer up. Well its time I was off to the gym, and do something I like doing, see you later Sandy, and for God's sake smile, your man's well-off, for I've got you to take care of me." Pete kisses Sandy and tells her he will see her later, and goes walking out of the office and off down the gym.

Chapter Twenty One

One Saturday night Pete is in the Horseshoe Inn, and is going to enjoy a boy's night out on the town, and they are all drinking and having a good time in the shoes.

They had gone out early and into the pub, comes old Fred on his chariot of fire, (that being an electric wheel chair, bright red, hence the name), and he always parks it across the entrance. You can see him coming into the pub in the picture.

The lads always have a little banter at old Fred, and Frank who is with Pete shouts out to Fred.

"I bet you have fucking left that fire engine of yours across the entrance, you should be reported to Health and Safety." Well Fred just screws up his face and in a grumpy way just grunts at them, and shouts back at them.

"Give an old solider a little respect." Well the lads nearly spit into their beers while one tells them.

"Old fucking solider, he's been on the dole all his fucking life, till he drew is old age pension." Well a little more banter and they all decide to drink up and head for the City by tram, which is straight outside the Horseshoes, across the way.

They get off the tram in Town, and head for the first bar, and lucky it is not heaving with it being early. They all stand at the bar drinking in general talk, and Pete with his white T-shirt, black leather jacket, and blue jeans, looked a daunting site with his build. You know one of those poses that tell you, you don't mess around with me. Pete is looking around and he notices a man sitting facing them, with note pad and camera, and he seemed to be looking at Pete and taking notes. At first Pete took no notice till he looked again, and this time he is taking pictures of Pete with his camera, and Pete felt uncomfortable with the whole issue. Pete no more than said nothing to the others and goes walking over to where the man is, and straight away starts to tell him.

"What the fuck is your game mate, I do not like what you are doing." Well the man just reached into his pocket with being threatened by Pete, and tells him.

"Please do not take it in the wrong contexts, Please here is my card, and as you will see, I work for one of the top agencies in the UK, I'm a scout looking for perfect men, for our top of the range for celebrities, escort agencies." Pete looks at the card and looks back at the man, and tells him.

"Well come on, what as that got to do with me."

"Well, please my names Ron White and I can tell you now if you are chosen, then you could be earning up to £500 plus a day, looking after top women celebrities needs."

"You are fucking kidding me, bloody £500, what for, shagging the arse off them." Pete looking straight at the man and lifting up his eyebrows.

"Well no not officially, just escorting them for the night to their functions, and if this so called, making love to them, well that is where the bonuses come into play. All that I need is your contact details, and once I report back they will be In Touch for you to attend an interview, down in London." Pete thinks and he straight away tells the guy, all of his details and thinking to himself. "Well with myself being laid off for the winter, you never know I might enjoy this escorting lark. Pete leaves the guy and goes back to the lads, and carried on drinking, on the odd occasion looking to see if the bloke is still there.

Three days later Tuesday, Pete gets a call from the agency down in London, and they ask him.

"Mr West would it be convenient for you, to possibly come on Wednesday to our Office, to discuss contract details for yourself. You will be reimburse expenses for the day, all that is required from yourself, is the time you will arrive on train, and we will make sure there is someone to pick you up." Pete tells them that he will book the tickets and phone them back with the time of arrival on that day. All sorted and Pete is thinking. "Hopes I get a fucking gorgeous singer, I've never shagged a pop star." Pete sitting there daydreaming. That night he is in the Horseshoes and Donna comes in and straight over to Pete, and she stands with him and Pete gets the drinks in for her., Donna asks Pete.

"Are we on for tonight then Pete, I'm gagging for it."

"Fucking hell Donna, I've got to go early tonight, for I'm catching the 5.30am train to London, on a job interview, but if you like, we could go under the bridge outside and have a quick one, before I go."

"I suppose if you have to go, just let me know, when you would like to go outside, and what about this interview then, what it is for." Donna looking at Pete.

"Some sort of giving customers what they want in a hurry, when they cannot get it them self's." Well it's better off telling her that, than he is hoping to shag the arses off them.

"How long will you be gone then Pete."

"Only the day babe, should be back that night all being well." Come 9.30pm Pete tells Donna.

"You ready babe, for I`ve to be off in a while, you know bed early and rise early for the train." Donna downs her drink in one and tells Pete.

"Come on babe, take me and fucking fuck the arse off me, for I`m starting to get wet just thinking of you, up my fanny. They go out the back and it is pitch black, and they go under the stairs that lead up to Highbury vale, and once under the bridge Donna is all over Pete. Pete straight away has Donna's knickers around her ankle, and Pete starts to finger her clitoris and fanny, and Donna straight away starts to moan at the pleasure, of feeling Pete working on her fanny. Pete had a full erection and Donna pulls his cock out, and she takes in a deep breath, at feeling his massif tool in her hand, and she opens her legs wide, and guides it into her, and Pete lifts her up and presses her against the wall, and is cock goes up to the hilt, making Donna give off on big loud groan.

"Fucking hell babe, not so much noise, you will have the pub, out to see where the noise is coming from."

"Fuck them, bloody well shag me like you are going to have your last shag, fucking hell Pete, you are fucking magic, Ho God the feeling, faster, fucking hell I`m going to explode." Well Donna is completely out of it with what Pete is doing, and she does explode and Pete could feel her warm juices flowing, and this made him come too. And he withdraws, and Donna straight away goes down on Pete to take all that she could get of Pete's sperm. They start to come back down to earth after, dress and Pete tells her that he will see her when he gets back from London. Donna watches as Pete goes up the steps onto Highbury Vale and he waves to her, just before he turns and goes walking off. Pete is thinking, there`s one think about Donna, when you need a shag, she will be always there for you, bless her, roll on tomorrow, maybe there might be some other bird to fuck."

Pete brushing back his hair and with the biggest grin on his face. Into bed and at half past four the alarm goes off, for him to rise and get ready for the interview down London. Into the bathroom, shower, shave and splash deodorant on and dress, he decided to go like he would look natural, and that his is favoured black leather jacket, blue jeans, and whit-shirt. He catches the 5.50 train down to London that stops at all the main stations, and 8.30 am pulls up in St. Pancras station.

He stands on the platform where he told them were he would be, and dead on 9am he is approached by a man who asks him.

"Are you one Pete West from Nottingham Bulwell?"

"That be me." Pete out stretching his hand for a hand shake, they do and he tells him.

"Please follow me Pete to my car." They both go and it is only a short drive, when Pete is told where to go, and Pete gets out of the car and his escort drives off. Pete goes up to the reception and he is taken back, with all the photos of famous people around the walls. He goes up to the receptionists and tells her who he is. She tells him to take a seat and someone will be along in a moment to see him. Pete sits there looking round when this woman, and might I say a very attractive woman, with a very short mini skirt, and long legs to match, and very large breast, comes over to Pete, who is just admiring the body that beholds him.

"Might I be addressing one Mr Pete West?" Pete stands up and might I say with chest sticking out, so it showed him in all his glory, and he tells her.

"That's right love, and you might be." Pete making sure she notices him looking her over.

"My names Barbara Yates, head co-owner of Marshalls escort agency, would you follow me please."

"Any time love lead on." Pete out stretching his hand for her to lead the way. They go to her office and once inside she tells Pete to sit down. Pete pulls up a chair and he is facing Barbara, and he could just not take his eyes of her large tits. She takes all Pete's details, and she explains the roll of the job, when she comes to the point, and telling Pete straight-out.

"Some of our client's use the agencies', not only for escort jobs, but jobs of the sexual side, and we don't want to disappoint our client's, and I put it to you, are you well-endowed to cope with this sort of demand." Barbara sitting looking straight at Pete. All that Pete did is stand facing her and not far away unzips his jeans and exposed his cock to her, and Barbara's eyes light up, and she did know more than take her pen and lift Pete's cock up, and this made Pete start to get aroused.

"My God, I don't think I've ever seen one this magnificent before. You would not mind me later having a test of how it preforms would you." Barbara stroking Pete's cock with her pen, and might I say Pete by now is fully erect.

"It would be my pleasure to make love to you Barbara, and I don't think you will be disappointed." Pete without his hands lifts his erect cock at her.

"Please put that fucking pleasure giver away, and I will see you at 5.30 pm, outside this office, and we could go and have a little to eat, then back to my apartment for a little session, and don't worry about an hotel, for you could stop there till tomorrow, before you travel back home."

"Do I have the job then Barbara?"

"Well so far you are 100% there, but let's just wait for the final decision tonight Pete."

Pete leaves the building, and decides to tour a little around London, to kill time till 5.30pm, Pete looks at his watch, and the time is to start to go back to meet Barbara, so he starts to make is way back to the Office to meet Barbara, and dead on time she comes out, and Pete's eyes light up, for I don't think he had ever been out with someone so attractive as Barbara, she comes down the steps from the Office and with her little mini skirt, and those long legs, made Pete's mouth drool, for he knew that later he would be fucking the arse off her. She also had a low cut blouse, and a very short black leather waistcoat style jacket, and Pete puts his bent arm out for Barbara to hold, and he leans forward and gives her a kiss, and he complements her on her fragrant perfume she had on.

"Thank you Pete, let's go and have a drink and a bite to eat, at my club."

"Are we going by taxi, or bus?" Pete looking out for one.

"Silly man, you would not catch me dead, I mean public transport, indeed, no thank you very much." She had only just stop saying this, when this Rolls-Royce pulls up alongside, and a chauffeur steps out and opens the backdoor for Barbara to enter.

"Good evening Charles, hopes you are well, and to my club if you please"

"Very well my Lady, and to your club, so be it." Pete's the last in and Charles closes the door and they drive off, to Barbara's club. On the way Pete asks her.

"This club, will I fit in, with me being a." Pete hesitates then tells her.

"You know Barbara common person" Barbara looks at Pete and she tells him.

"No-one who is with me is a common person, but upstanding, and with a fine looking Young man like yourself, I'm sure you will turn one or two heads, magic." Barbara turning to Pete smiling, and this time giving him a long kiss and with tongues and all.

They soon arrive at the club, and Charles opens the door for Pete then Barbara, Pete helps her out and she turns to Charles and tells him.

"I will call you when I'm ready to leave Charles, that will be all for now thank you."

"Yes my Lady, have a good evening." Charles salutes her gets back into the Rolls and drives off.

Chapter Twenty Two

Barbara and Pete enter the club and go walking through the lobby, and just like Barbara told Pete, there were one or two heads turning, and might I say the Women looking at Pete up and down, and you could almost hear the chatter of the Women.

"Look at the hulk Barbara has on her arm, he must be a film star, and that body, and I wish my man looked like that, the lucky bitch." They are escorted to a table within the club, and the waiter asks for their order, Barbara turns to Pete and she asks him.

"What is your choice of drink Pete?"

"Lager, and a wine glass for I would like to participate, also with a glass of white wine if you please. Well Barbara is well impressed with Pete's answer, and she too orders a house best white wine, and when the waiter goes to fetch their order, Barbara turns to Pete and she tells him.

"You really shocked me there Pete, with your choice of words to the waiter, if you carry on like that, people within the club are going to be well impressed."

"Thanks for that Barbara, and when they ask me, where I come from, I will tell them Fucking Bulwell, in Robin Hood Country, we rob the rich bastards, and give it to the poor." Well Barbara and Pete burst out laughing out loud, and Barbara tells Pete.

"Stop it Pete, or they will think that we are pissed."

Sorry Barbara, but this posh lark is not me, for I`m who I am, a down to earth guy, and just love being with attractive Women like yourself." Pete leaning forward and kissing Barbara fully on the lips, and he puts his hand on her face in a genteel way and telling her.

"All that I want is to be alone with you, and to make passionate love to you." Pete again leaning forward and kissing Barbara again. Barbara just sat there looking Pete straight into the eyes and she tells him, I too would just crave to be alone with you, but please let's just eat and I promise, after our meal we will go back to my home and then you can show me, what others clients are going to have."

"That`s where you are wrong, for we are going to make love together as a loving couple, not an arranged meeting, for I only make love to a woman, not lust on a one off night stand." Again Pete kisses Barbara, and she finally tells him.

"For fucks sake let's eat, and then we can go and ravish each other, for if you carry on talking like you are, well I`m going to be flooding in my knickers, that is if I had any on." Well Pete is straight away trying to look at Barbara's top of her legs, for she had a mini skirt on, and Pete trying to look for a peek view of her fanny. In the end Pete calls time out and just tells Barbara.

"OK, for God's sake let's eat, and then get back."

"What would you like to eat then Pete?"

"Fucking pack of crisps will do, and then I will be ready." Barbara slaps him on the arm and tells him.

"You said time out, so come on, what would you like." Pete looks at the menu and tells Barbara.

"I will have the house steak and french-fries, with side salad, steak medium rear." Finally they do settle down and have their meal, and after with the time now being 9.30pm, Barbara phones Charles to pick them up, for they are ready to go home. 9.45pm they leave the club, and Charles is there to pick them up. Barbara only lives ten minutes away and they arrive, and Pete looks up for it is one of the new high buildings, built only a year ago, and they go into the lobby and Barbara pulls out a key, and they go to the lift and once inside she inserts her key and turns it for the penthouse. They start to go up and Pete asks Barbara.

"This must cost a bob or two, babe."

"Not really I brought it outright, so really it's cheap." Pete is well impressed and they come to the top floor that leads them straight into the penthouse. Barbara tells Pete to make himself comfy while she goes and changes. Well Pete cannot believe where he is, and he is thinking to himself. "Wait till I tell them back in the Horseshoes Inn, they probably will think that I'm romancing them." Pete is trying to look out of the large glass window, when Barbara comes back into the room and Pete turns round and his eyes nearly pop out of his head, for Barbara stood there in this very fine silk nighty, and just nothing on underneath, and Pete could see her large tits and those lovely nipples that were just waiting to be sucked, and then he looks down and he could see her shaven camel toe through her negligée. She approaches Pete and they start to kiss and Pete straight away is trying to get under her nighty to her tits and Barbara stops Pete and tells him.

"Please Pete make mad love to me on my balcony."

"Your joking love, it's winter, and we will have goose pimples the size of eggs out there in the cold."

"That is where you are wrong." Barbara presses a button on a remote control and the patio windows slide open and you could see all over London, but it was warm for in the canopy above a bed there were patio heaters and it really felt like summer.

Barbara stood next to the bed and Pete approached her and stood straight in front of her, and she starts to remove his T-shirt, exposing his muscular chest and top, then she unclips his belt and his jeans fall to the ground, and Pete steps out, then his boxers, and he stood there in all his glory, and Barbara is looking at him up and down and she comments.

"You look truly like a Roman Gladiator, and I'm your prize for winning the days fight in the arena. Take me and do your evil deeds with me." Pete leans forward, puts his arms around her, and pulls her close to him, and starts to kiss her fully on the lips, and his tongue disappears deep into her mouth and Barbara could feel his large cock pressing up against her, and she opens her legs so her clitoris could feel what she wanted to feel. Pete slowly works his way down to her nipples for this is what he is waiting for, and he starts to flick her nipples with his tongue, and sucking them profusely. All this time they are still standing, and Pete then goes down to her tummy and Barbara all the time is looking at Pete, and what he is doing. He comes to her shaven fanny and straight away starts to flick her clitoris with his very large long tongue, and Barbara leans upwards looking to the heavens and she is shouting out.

"Ho my God you are truly fucking magic, Pete puts his hands onto her arse and he moves his hand down to her bum, and from the back starts to insert two fingers into her fanny and his thumb up her arse and she screams out with the tingle and feeling that Pete is giving her, and she could only take about five minutes of this, with Pete still down there working on her clitoris, while his fingers are working on her fanny and arse. She suddenly had one massive orgasm and finally tells Pete.

"Fucking throw me on the bed and fuck the arse of me." Well Pete stood up and did just that and Barbara laid on the bed and looks up at Pete and his massif erect cock, and the truth be known, she nearly fainted on the bed at what she was about to receive, Pete starts to mount her and Barbara had her legs open wider than the M1. Pete puts his hands behind her legs lifts her up and his cock goes straight into her fanny and Pete while pushing down lifts her up so his cock penetrated further, well Barbara gives off on massif scream and Pete is thinking, "Thank fuck we are in the penthouse or she would wake the dead with the noise. Pete starts to go slow then quick, and with what Pete is doing makes Barbara scream even more, well Pete had truly given her a good seeing too, and I don't think she could take any more for she just looks Pete straight in the eyes and tells him.

"Fucking spunk me now, before you fucking kill me with pleasure, now fucking spunk me, Barbara is digging her nails into Pete's back, and with the dirty talk Pete does explode, and they both are having one hell of an orgasms, and Pete popping his cork like no tomorrow. They both flop back down on the bed and just laid there in one might fulfilment on what they both had just given each other, after about ten minutes Pete asks Barbara.

"Well is the job mine then, am I to your approval."

"Please Pete don't take the job, you are truly a great lover, and my clients would pay millions once the word spread around, but I want you for myself babe." Barbara purring like a pussy cat, and turning onto her side and stroking Pete's smooth chest.

"Come on Babe that is not the deal, let me show you what the real me is." Pete turns Barbara onto her belly lifts her up and goes between her legs, and starts to penetrate her doggy fashion, and within minutes she is completely out of it with massif orgasms with Pete's massif cock, giving her a good seeing to again. Her face is pushed well down into the pillows and Pete comes again and she can feel Pete again giving her all his warm spunk and she is in heaven with what Pete had just done and gave her, so much she just tells him.

"The jobs yours and never mind the £500 job, you are our top model and you will get a "£700 starting price, but please Pete promise me you will keep me satisfied, babe please.

"Don't worry about that, anytime you would like me to come running to you, you can rest assured, that you are truly top of my list for you are truly a great lay, and I love being with you babe, come here give me a kiss. They both lay there rapped around each other and kissing each other tenderly, and before long they both are fast on outside in the winter air, and it just shows, when you have the money to burn, you can especially with the heating bill that it must cost to sleep on the outside in winter in Britain. The next morning Barbara takes Pete to the station in the Rolls-Royce on her way to the office, and tells Pete that he starts Monday, and to be there at the office at 10am next Monday. Pete kisses Barbara, and tells her that he loves her, and will see her next Monday. Pete is soon on the train back to Nottingham, and he is sitting at a table seat, and with the rattle of the train wheels, he soon drifts off to sleep, and he starts to dream about Sofia, and he is walking along a sandy shore with Sofia by his side, and a gentle wave crashing down onto the sands, and Pete turns to Sofia and asks her.

"Why did you leave me Sofia, you are my soul mate, and I love you so-so much that it is breaking my heart."

"My darling Pete, I too love you to the bottom of my heart, and you too are my soul mate." Pete holding both Sofia's hands, and she starts to drift away, and Pete is shouting and crying for her to come back, please Sofia, please don't leave me. Pete suddenly comes out of the dream, and he his crying and shouting out for Sofia, and he suddenly opens his eyes and sitting opposite him reading a newspaper is a City gent, who with hearing Pete shout out and crying, lowers his paper looks at Pete and just said to him.

"Looks like you have just had a bad dream, Young-man."

"Sorry, it was about my wife Sofia, who died a few months ago, you see I miss her so."

"My condolence to you, and I'm sorry to hear about you're loss."

"Thank you Sir." Pete opens a paper he had with him and they said know more to each other. The train soon pulls into Nottingham station and Pete gets off and catches a tram, back to Bulwell.

That night he goes into the Horseshoes and there is a slight sleet of snow, into the pub comes Frank and another of Pete's mates and they all stand having a pint, and Frank said sorry about Pete losing his job for the winter, but when Pete tells him about the job he is going to start, at well over £700 a day, and they are dump founded. Frank asks Pete if he would like to tag on with them for they are going on a tram pub crawl." (This is stopping at every stop, at a tram station, and going in the nearest pub. Till they get to the end of the line.)

They drink up and start to go out the back to catch the tram, when Pete suddenly looks up the steps that lead from the back of the shoes to Highbury Vale, and Pete sees a woman in a long white dress and blond long hair walk pass the top on Highbury Vale and Pete shouts out.

"Sofia-Sofia."

These are the steps that Pete shagged Donna, under the steps, that lead up to Highbury Vale, and you can see Saint Marys church on the hill.

Pete like a flash is running up the steps, and looks up and he sees the church, Frank and his mate shout to Pete.

"Pete what the fuck is wrong, where are you going mate, wait we will come with you." Frank thinking something is not right, they too go running up the steps and they see Pete disappearing into the church and they both stand there and Franks mate tells Frank.

"Are we going to wait here, for churches give me the creeps?"

"More like you have been watching to many horror movies."

Chapter Twenty Three

Pete goes into the church and still shouting out Sofia's name, where there is a Vicar putting out prayer books and he sees Pete and asks him.

"What is wrong my son, who are you shouting for."

"Did you see just now, a young lady come into the church, in a long white dress and long blond hair?"

"No my son, no one came in or out, for I would have noticed, anyway who is this young lady." Pete hesitated and just tells him."

"She's my wife, who passed away a few months ago. You see I keep seeing her, it's if she is trying to tell me something." Pete by now is so worked up that he just burst out crying, and the Vicar asks Pete to sit down, and he tells him to wait, for he had something to show him. The vicar goes off and in a few moments comes back and sits next to Pete. He is holding a picture in a frame and he starts to tell Pete.

"What you are experiencing is a very hard case of grieving, for you see your mind can not come to terms with your sudden loss, and maybe playing tricks on you, for take notice of this picture, it might help you in a small way, and if you have a mobile take a photo, and when you are down, take your mobile out and reflect on what you read and see. For the lord is with you, and he will be there for you, in your hour of need" Pete looks at the picture that the Vicar had, and he suddenly looks up to the Vicar, for he is looking at a sea shore with waves washing up on the beach, and foot prints, and it was just like the dream he had on the train, coming back up from London, that very morning. Then the Vicar tells Pete to look at the verse within the picture and it is of, a poem of Footprints in the sand.

Just like a Vicar, he starts to tell him that this is him, at this time in his life, walking along with his whole life flashing by him, and on a beach, and with two sets of prints, and just like yourself at this time in your life you see one pair of prints, and this is when God is carrying you through your trouble times. Pete looks at the poem, and does take a photo of it on his mobile, and he tells the Vicar.

"Thanks for your help, I will look back on this and try and get my life back on track." Pete stands and thanks the Vicar for his help and he tells him that he must be off, for his friends are waiting for him." The Vicar tells Pete.

"Any time you would like to come to mass on Sunday' we are here at 6.30pm, and you are quiet welcome." Pete stands and shakes the Vicars hand, and he leaves. He comes out and the sleet is a little stronger and leaving a dusting of snow on the pathway, at the entrance at the bottom of the hill he can see Frank and his mate waiting for him. Pete approaches them and tells them what the Vicar had said about the footprints in the sand, and for some reason Pete looks back, and he suddenly freaks out. For in the snow there are two sets of prints coming out of the church and going into one.

"Look at the prints in the snow, there is no one in the church, but there are two sets coming out, and going into one." Well Franks mate who's name being Paul tells them.

"I fucking told you, that these fucking churches are fucking haunted, let's get the fuck out of here." Well he did not wait and he is across the road and starting to head back down the steps back to the Horseshoes back yard. Pete turns to Frank and tells him.

"Fucking freak that mate of yours, bloody hell I thought I was freaked out with what had gone on today, but really Frank what do you make of it, I mean dreaming of being on a beach this morning with Sofia, then seeing her go into the church, then having a Vicar show me this Footprints in the sand, and finally those prints coming out of the church."

"Don't ask me Pete, for all that I know, you could fucking write a book on it and make a fucking good fright movie."

"I still cannot get it, for it's starting to make me wonder, if there is a so called God."

"Come on Pete lets catch Paul up the wanker, and have ourselves a few beers to cheer us up." They do catch the tram and go on a station pub crawl and all night Pete could not stop thinking about the events of the day, finally they are back home at the Horseshoes, and Pete gives his byes to Frank and Paul and tells them that he will see them around, and leaves for home.

That night he is tossing and turning in bed, and all that he is thinking is of his Sofia and what had gone on, it got so bad that he sits up bashes the pillows and out loud shouts OUT.

"For fucks sake get to sleep, you are doing my head in." Pete does finally drop off, but in all it is one hell of a restless night, the time is 7am Pete sitting on the side of his bed and thinking.

"Boy I could do with lying in this morning, but the gym comes first." He is about to rise to go to the bathroom, when there is a tap-tap on the window. Pete goes and opens the curtains and it is one of those crispy frosty morning, and Pete looks down to where he keeps a little tin with treat for the birds, and there is his little friend the Robin Redbreast. Pete is thinking the time Sofia stopped at his other house, and one morning opened the window and the Robin steps onto her finger, and she smiled at Robin, looked round and showed Pete. Pete did the same open the window put a few nuts into the tray that he keep by the window, and he did know more that out stretch his finger and the Robin hopped onto Pete's finger, and the difference in Pete he suddenly had this wide broad grin, and a feeling of content running through him, he did know more than lift his finger up to his face.

"Hello my little friend, how are you this morning." Well the Robin leans forward and it is if he kisses Pete on the lip, Pete thanks the Robin and in a jest sort of way tells the Robin.

"I have the same effect on all the girls." and smiles at the Robin. The little Robin flies back onto the windowsill, and starts to peck away at the nuts Pete had put into the little tin tray. Pete closes the window and goes to the bathroom to shave and shower, down stairs a little breakfast on mainly chicken, and a little toast, must keep up the protein intake. Then off down the gym for the day's work out. Sunday night soon comes around and Pete starts to pack for the trip in the morning to start is new role as an escort to the rich and famous. Pete is told to bring with him a dinner suit, for the nights out with the celebrities, Pete is thinking it's a good job I keep the one I brought back from Portugal, when I went with that famous Mafia boss, and may I say unknowing about that side, until I had that visit from the police. What was her name Rosie, Rosanna, Ho yes Madam Rosita, I can still see her now, when I first set eyes upon her, at her home Sunbathing in the nude, what a fucking body she had.

Pete flops onto his bed and still romancing suddenly tells himself, and what about her two maids, Pete thinks for a while, Ho yes Ella and Sarah, fucking great fucks all three of them, especially when I fucked the arse off all three of them in one day. Pete sitting there still dreaming and with the look that said, if he carried on would start to arouse himself, to a point he would have to do something about it. Pete comes back down to earth and carried on packing, making sure the suit is well packed in the lid, Pete is told to bring his passport with him, mainly for proof of his identity, and security reasons with going to be in close proximity to such famous people. All packed and Pete looking at his watch tells himself, well I have a couple of hours to kill before bed and up early, so couple of pints down the pub, and early to bed and early to rise for my train. Pete rubbing his hands together and telling himself.

"Cannot wait to get started, I wonder who will be first." Yes we all know what he means who will be first, which is to be shagged if we are not mistaken.

Pete goes walking into the pub with that extra step, with what is coming up, and he goes to the bar and shouts to Terry.

"Pint of your best mix if you please Landlord." Terry comes walking over to Pete and tells him.

"What's up with you tonight, anyone would think that someone has wiped the cats arse for you to try later."

"No Terry off to London tomorrow, and starting a new job, taking out Stars for the night in London."

"Ho yes, more like taking them out to give them a good seeing too." Terry lifting up his arm while pulling Pete his pint.

"That's the bonus Terry, just the bonus." Pete rubbing his hands again.

"Let us know who you fuck, and the ones that are stuck-up," Pete gets his pint and stands and looks around to see who is in, and the pub is quiet for a Sunday night, and Pete asks Terry.

"What have you done barred everyone, it's a bit quiet."

"You know what it is like, I mean the old fuckers won't come out on cold night like this."

"That reminds me Terry, when I was interviewed down London, the boss took me back to her Penthouse and I fucked the arse off her on her balcony, and in the nude."

"Fuck off Pete, you would freeze the bollocks off you."

"No that is where you are wrong, for this is the point I'm getting at, she had heaters on in the ceiling running all-night, and it was like sleeping outside in Summer, that's what you want outside there, so the smokers could sit in comfort smoking themselves to death, in the warmth."

"Fuck the smokers, I would go bankrupt within the week, if I did that." Then from behind Pete hears someone say.

"If it's not, Pete how you diddling mate." Pete turns round and it is one of his old mates from when he was a kid living down Bailey Street, and played on Whitmore Park with the entrance on Bailey Street.

"Well if it's not my old mate, yes Morris, bloody hell you have a good memory, I probably would have not noticed if you had not said."

"Never forget a face, how are you and are you hooked up yet."

"No not me Morris, been married but I lost her, you no fucking cancer."

"Sorry to hear that Pete, myself shacked up with that bird who lived next door to you, Susan." Pete is thinking, fuck me she was one of the first birds I used to fuck on a regular bases, many a time I had a bloody great blow job on Whitmore Park behind the keeper's tool shed. Then out of the Ladies toilet comes Susan, and Morris shouts her over.

"Susan come and say hello to Pete, you know the one that used to live next door to you." Susan goes up to Pete and kisses him full on the lips and in a quiet voice tells Pete.

"I've missed you Pete." Pete smiles at her and his mobile goes off, Pete answers the call and it is Barbara from down London, Pete tells her to hang on till he is outside and Pete gives his leave to answer the call. Pete goes out the back and talking to Barbara who wanted to know what time he will arrive in the morning, so she personally could pick him up. Pete tells her 9.30am. In the meantime Susan tells Morris that she is going to have a fag. Morris tells her.

"It's about time you gave them up." Under her breath she is telling him, fuck off you big fat twat. She goes out the back and Pete is just hanging up and he turns and there is Susan, who know more grabs Pete's arm, and she takes him under the steps. Pete asks her what she was doing and she tells him.

"I've bloody well missed you Pete, and ended up with that fat bastard, come here give me a kiss." They stand kissing with tongues and all, and Susan pulls Pete's hand under her dress, which might I say with what Pete was feeling she had no knickers on, and she tells Pete.

"Let me feel that fucking big man of yours, for all I have had is that twats little todger, all 4 inches of it." Pete starts to finger her clitoris and giving her fanny a real treat, for she is moaning already at what Pete is doing, she starts to take Pete's cock out and he is fully aroused, and she takes a big sigh, at the feel of his cock, and starts to guide it towards her fanny, and Pete bends a little and pushes up and his whole cock goes into her, with Susan giving off one hell of.

"Ho my fucking God, I've missed this fucker."

"Fucking shut up Susan and enjoy." Pete pushes hard again but this time stops at the hilt and moves his cock inside her and she just goes forward and starts to kiss Pete and Pete could tell, that what he was doing, she wanted to scream out. They had been at it for ten minutes and Susan could not take it anymore and she tells Pete.

"Fucking spunk me now, for God's sake, I'm on the pill so leave him in." Pete does explode and she is trying to grip Pete hard as she could with the feeling of Pete's spunk, and she is kissing him profusely, she comes back down to earth, and it was like nothing had happened, she goes back to the back door and lights up additional cigarette just as Pete comes back and he sits on a bench, just as Morris comes out and he sees Susan and he asks her.

"Fucking hell Susan, how many more cigs are you going to shove down your mouth?"

"Fuck off Morris, I'm talking to Pete, you know long time no see, bloody well go and fetch my drink will you, and bring Pete one. Well Morris goes walking back into the pub and Pete asks Susan.

"It looks like you two get on like a house on fire."

"Well I give him back what he gives me, anyway Pete, now that I know where you live, I will come and see you now and then, here is my number, any time you feel like it, give me a call, and I will come bloody well running." Just as Susan had said it, Morris comes out with her drink and one for Pete.

Pete at about ten gives his leave to Susan and Morris, telling them that he is off down London in the morning, he shakes Morris hand and kisses Susan, and he tells Morris just as he turns to go up the steps that lead to Highbury Vale.

"You've got a good one there Morris, you take good care of her now mate, will see you later bye for now. Pete goes running up the stairs and Susan turns to Morris and tells him.

"Did you see how big and strong Pete looks, and those rippling muscles on him."

"To true, bit like mine really." Morris trying to stick out his chest, but most was sticking out of his gut. Susan just looks at him, and with a big complement tells him.

"You fucking big fat bastard, you can get down that gym, and start to pump Iron like Pete must do, or your little todger, won't be getting any of my pussy, till you look like Pete." Susan with a smile and grabbing hold of what she could of his little cock, and goes walking back into the shoes. All that Morris did was breathe out, and now his whole front is covered by his fat belly.

Chapter Twenty Four

The next morning Pete is up early, and with his bag packed, he shaves showers and is soon off down to the station for the early train to St Pancras station.

Pete on the platform and newspaper in hand is ready for the train that is just pulling into the station, Pete boards and sits at a table seat, and opens his Paper and starts to read, for the two hour journey down to London St Pancras. He is flicking through the pages, when he comes to an article about the Mafia becoming stronger in the British Commonwealth, well Pete straight away thinks of the Woman that he went with in Portugal, for she was a Mafia big boss. He is sitting there with the rattle tat-tat of the bogies on the tracks, and he is thinking of Madam Rosita.

"I wonder how she is getting on, and where she is at this moment in time." Pete looking out of the window, and suddenly he drifts off into a slumber, with hearing the ratter-tat-tat of the bogies, and suddenly he sees Sofia standing there and pleading with him, please do not get involved.

"With what my love, I`m all alone and confused, why do you keep coming to see me, please tell me." Sofia standing there and just shaking her head, and suddenly looks up to Pete, and as she fades away is still saying, "Please Pete don't get involved." Pete again starts to steer from the dream, and this time he suddenly opens his eyes, and he is sweating profusely, but not like the last time, there is no one sitting there with him.

He sits there with his hands on his head and brushing the sweat of his forehead, and he is thinking to himself, What the fucking hell is happening to me, for it is if I'm looking at things that are about to happen, God please

I hope I'm not fucking cracking up, for if I carry on like this, someone is going to feel my raff, and bloody well help them. Pete sitting there and tensing up all of his body muscles, and he looked a daunting sight, one that would make the bravest man walk bye at what he is witnessing. The train pulls into St Pancras, and Pete disembarks and he is walking along the platform, coming to the gates and from the other side he hears Barbara calling out his name.

"Pete over here, yahoo Pete here." Pete sees her smile, comes through the ticket gate and approaches Barbara and kisses her.

"Thanks for being here for me Barbara, where am I stopping at."

"I've put you up in one of the top Hotels in London, come with me and I will show you. Barbara holding Pete's hand and they go off to her car, which is a top model sports car, well when Pete sees what he is going in, turns to Barbara and asks her.

"What about the Rolls then, is it the driver's day off."

"No sweetheart, but I thought this would be more discreet, then having someone there to see what is going off."

"Lead on babe, I'm all yours." Pete smiling at Barbara. They get into the sports car and Barbara goes roaring out of the train station car park, and Pete is well impressed. They drive for about ten minutes and pull up at one of the most expensive Hotels in London, and Pete getting out of the sports car looks at Barbara and asks her.

"You've got to be kidding me, there is no way that I could afford to stop here."

"Ho yes you can, for you are one of our top models, and we always look after our best assets." They go up to the room Pete is stopping in, and they enter, and Pete's eyes light up at the size and room he had, for even the bathroom you have room to put a bed in.

"Surely all this cannot be mine." Pete standing in the bathroom, and he looks in the mirror and from behind him, he could see Barbara starting to strip." He turns and she is down to her knickers and stockings and suspender belt, and Pete just stood there admiring the view that beholds him.

"This is why I've come in the sports car, so I can have you here all by myself for the morning, for this is my job this morning, to make sure you are comfortable, before you start tonight, but first, I'm going to get the first picking, before our client gets her fucking dirty hands on you."

"Well, let's both shower to freshen our self's up, especially me with the trip down by train this morning." Pete stands directly in front of Barbara and starts to remove his T-shirt, then unbuckle his belt and he drops his jeans down to the ground, and just stood there in his trunks, when Barbara approaches Pete still in her stocking and suspender belt, and bra. Pete gently kisses her on the lips and at the same time unclips her bra and it drops to the ground exposing her large tits, then Pete pings one of the clips on her suspender belt, then the other and he goes down and slowly removes her stocking, just leaving her with a short thong on, he gently removes this while still down there, and she stood looking at Pete kneeling in front of her. Pete goes forward and starts to flick her clitoris with his tongue, and Barbara opens her legs further for Pete to get more of his tongue around her clitoris. He puts both his thumbs on either side of her fanny and he starts to insert his large tongue, and Barbara gives off one big sigh, at the feeling. Her head goes straight back and she shouts out.

"Fucking hell Pete, you are going to make me explode, God you're fucking good." Pete gives her a good seeing too, then stands in front of her, then picks her up and carries her to the shower, they enter and Pete turns on the water and starts to rub the soap in a suggestive way, and Barbara looks down and sees Pete's upright cock standing proud. Pete starts to rub the soap into Barbara's tits, and he is tweaking her nipples, Barbara also soaps up her hands and starts to rub soap up and down his cock, she starts to look at Pete and slowly goes down and starts to give Pete a blow job, with the warm water running all over them. Pete tells Barbara.

"Let's dry off and go and get into bed, for I truly do want to fuck you, like you have never been fucked before." Well Barbara is straight out drying herself off, and straight to the bed and telling Pete.

"Come my fucking great beast, come and shag the arse off me, like you have just said." Pete comes out of the bathroom, stands in front of Barbara takes a big deep breath, flexes his muscles, and if you could have seen Barbara at what she is looking at, for Pete stood there with his massif frame, looking like a great worrier figure, and his also massive ten inch cock, waiting for its goal. Well Barbara is wetting herself at seeing such an amazing sight, she did no more than open her legs wide, and with her hand beckoning Pete to come. Pete gets onto the bed and straight away with knowing that she is ready to be fucked, goes between her legs, and Barbara watching his every move, He lifts her up towards him and inserts his cock why still holding her legs, and Barbara at the feeling of Pete's cock penetrating her, gives out a loud scream of.

"Ho my God." She is lifting off the bed and looking at Pete's every move, and she looks Pete straight in the eyes and tells him.

"Don't you dear give your client this feeling?" All that Pete did was look back at her and pushes his cock that little bit further into her, and she straight away falls back onto the bed and tenses up with the feeling, and again screams out with pure pleasure. Pete by now is just telling himself. "You're going to feel something that I've never gave any other."

He suddenly speeds up, that fast that Barbara's tits and her belly are getting shock waves, through the quickness and pressure Pete is applying, and Barbara does explode, and she cries out for Pete to stop.

"Well Pete just explodes and that was it she too, explodes and tenses that much up, and a feeling that made her quiver inside, and she flops back onto the bed and is completely shafted, and exhausted with the whole experience, so much that she could not even speak. Pete rolls of her and lay there just looking up to the ceiling in silence, and Barbara turns and rest her tits on his chest, and her head on his neck, and tells Pete when she had come back down.

"This moment in time, All that I would like to-do is just pack my bags and elope with you Pete, for I've this feeling inside of me, that I want you for myself and none other. What am I going to do, for tonight you will be in someone else's arms and not mine." Barbara lying there and playing with Pete's nipples.

"You can rest assure that no other will get what we have just experienced, that is for you and no one else, rest assured on that babe." Pete stroking her hair and they are both snuggled up, and they must have both drifted off to sleep with them both comforting each other. They both come back into the world at about 11am and Barbara sees the time and jumps out of bed, and telling Pete.

"Come on now Pete, we had better get ourselves showered and dressed, and finalise this evening details." Barbara is first out of the bed and goes and showers while Pete just looks at her arse as she goes into the bathroom and he is thinking.

"That's one hell of a fine arse, and a true good shag, better get up and go and shower." Pete into the bathroom and he steps in with Barbara and he is straight away feeling her arse, Barbara turns round and tells him.

"Please Pete, let's just get showered dressed and talk business, Please."

"Ho babe, you have the cuties arse, I've ever seen."

"Well it won't be the last time you will have it." Barbara pushing Pete's hands off her arse, with Pete trying to reach the goal. They finally get dressed and sit in the lounge and Barbara takes out paper work from her briefcase, while Pete pours two coffees.

"Right finally down to business, tonight Pete you will be picked up in the lobby by one Lorraine White, escort men at 7pm, and taken to her dwelling and then on to the venue, and please no after, if you can help it."

"What is she some famous film star." Pete sitting there rubbing his hands at the prospect.

"No sweetheart, she is a top business Woman, in the U.K, and might I say closely guarded, you know against all the terrorists out there looking for good targets, so keep in mind that you might be searched and treated as a suspect at first."

"Well they had better show me a little respect, or they might find that this Pete West is not you're Joe average, whose going to be pushed around by them." Pete sitting there and tensing up.

"Please Pete be on your best behaviour, for she is one of our top clients, and a large earner for the Company, so please respect."

"Don't you worry, I've a feeling that this is going to be a little boring with nothing out of the ordinary, and not like what we have just had." Pete starting to feel Barbara's leg under the table.

"No sweetie, for I've to be back in the Office for midday, for a meeting with upcoming jobs." Barbara starts to take a sip out of her coffee and looks at Pete, and she asks him.

"You would really have me again, if I was not going to go back to the office, wouldn't you." Pete stands pulls her up, and spins her round and leans her across the table, and he presses his groin into her backside, as she leans over the table, he leans forward and tells her.

"You've one of the fantastic arses I've ever seen, and yes, if you were not going to go back to the office, I would shag the arse off you over this table." Pete pressing that little bit harder and putting his hands on to her tits and having a feel. Barbara sighs and tells him.

"Please Pete, I would love you to have you're wicked way with me, but I've truly have to go, or I would be late and would find it hard to explain." She pushes back on Pete stands and faces him, and they stand in one big kiss and tongues and all. Finally she breaks off turns and walking away from Pete goes to the door and turns round, and just before she leaves she tells Pete.

"Please Pete save your love for me, and not this bitch you are seeing tonight, for I love you so."

"I promise you, what you had is for you and me alone, and I love you too." He blows her a kiss as she closes the door and goes. Pete is thinking to himself.

"Let's hope this Lorraine is a little raver, for she will get a different kind of fuck, but still a good seeing too, roll on tonight." Pete walking off to turn the T.V on and settle down with another cup of coffee.

Chapter Twenty Five

All that Pete did is relax and have a lazy day watching the box, and at 5pm decides to go and start to get ready for the evening entertainment with this so called celebrity. All spruced up, and he stands and looks at himself in the full frontal mirror, Pete standing there in his dinner jacket and he looked just like those film starts you see, you known James Bond. Pete just lifts his hands and tells himself.

"How could she refuse this, I mean come on, I fancy myself," Pete with a big grin on his face, looks at his watch and the time is approaching 6.55pm, Pete starts to make his way down to the lobby, and dead on 7pm, three burly looking guys come into the lobby, and they see Pete in his dinner suit and approach him.

"Are you one Pete West?"

"You are to come with us." Pete goes with them but he feels uncomfortable, and once outside, they approach their car, and suddenly two off them grab Pete by the arm, and the other starts to frisk him. Well Pete straight away starts to boil over, and the one frisking Pete his facing the car, which had the back door open, and Pete did no more than lift his leg up and kick him straight onto the back seat, He tightens his arms up and pulls them together, and the two holding Pete's arms, crash into each other and he pushes them as well into the back of the car, and he slams the door. He opens the passenger door, where there is a driver and Pete tells him.

"You can drive on for I'm clean, and if those in the back would like more, they can wait till we get there." The driver smiles at Pete, and pulls away, he is looking at the three in the back, licking their wounds.

They arrive and Pete is first out and opens the back door for the three guys to get out, and they just look at Pete and turn and ask him to follow them, and might I say not one of them puts as much as a finger on Pete. They tell Pete to wait there in her large entrance hall, with a staircase straight facing Pete and suddenly down the stairs comes the Lady, and Pete had the fright of his life at first, for he thought it was Sofia, for she too had a long white dress and long blond hair, running down the back of her dress. She comes to the bottom when Pete suddenly looks at her and his face lights up, for he recognised her and suddenly shouts out.

"My God if it's not Madam Rosita, Bom-Dia Rosita, how long have you been blond?" Well Rosita is straight up to Pete and she puts her finger on his lips and in a quiet voice tells Pete.

"No Pete my names Lorraine White, and this Portuguese Lady called Rosita, does not exist, for you see Pete, I'm under the radar of Interpol and that is how I would like to stay, so please-please from now on its Lorraine please get used to it. And fucking come here and give me a kiss, for I've missed you so." Well Lorraine and Pete are well and truly at it, and the guards just look at them and did not know what to make of it, for they are looking at two people that have just met, so they thought, and they are all over each other. Little did they know that they go back a long way. Well Lorraine is holding Pete tight as she guides him to her Rolls Royce, they sit in the back and are at it again, Pete brushing back her hair and Pete tells Lorraine.

"Boy you look even more stunning being blond, I cannot wait to see your bronze body, and long flowing hair on the bed, fuck you are giving me a hard on already." Pete looking down to his groin. Lorraine puts her hand on Pete's trousers and she tells him.

"Down boy, you will have to wait till later, and I can feel that I bloody well have missed your cock Pete."

"Whatever happened to the villa you left me in to face the police, when you flew off in your helicopter."

"Ho that, sold it, for 2million Euro's, the cops did not give you too much grief did they Pete, for I told them to let you go, because you knew nothing."

"No I was fine, went to the airport and flew out the same day." Pete thinking to himself, she told the Police to let me go, boy these Mafia people have even the Police on their pay-roll. Then Pete asks her.

"This do we are going to, what is it, and who will be there."

"Ho it's some charity gathering of the rich and famous, you know we have an auction, and the most and highest bidder gets the prize on offer."

"What are the prizes then?" Pete thinking might have a flutter on this. Then he gets a shock for Lorraine tells him.

"Well the auction could be for anything, I mean, if you are picked, it could even be you that is auctioned off to the highest bidder." Well Pete's face changed at what Lorraine had told him.

"You're kidding me, it could not be me, could it." Pee looking at Lorraine for reassurance.

"No sweetheart, for no other in this place tonight, have the wealth like I do, so rest assure Pete, that you will be going home to my bed tonight, and not another bitch in the room." said Lorraine. Pete felt a little more reassured with the answer, just as they pulled up at the evening's venue, Pete opens the door for Lorraine to get out and they go up the steps into the Grand hall, where the venue is to behold that night. They are greeted at the entrance by a man in a uniform more fitting to be at Buckingham Palace, he looked just like one of the beefeaters at the tower.

"Good evening Madam and Sir, who might I redressing." Lorraine tells him her name and her guest Pete. The usher straight away announces them to the others gathered.

"My Lords Ladies and Gentlemen, please be upstanding for, Lady Lorraine White, and her companion, one Mr Pete West." They go walking in with Lorraine holding Pete's arm, and they truly looked a stunning couple.

Lorraine starts to socialise with the other guest while Pete is looking round and the other guest, when he is approached by a maid with a try of red- and white wine.

"Would Sir like a glass of wine?"

"Have you any beer gorgeous."

"Sorry Sir only wine, but I could fix you up with a beer from the waiters drink, back stage."

"You're a star, could you take me to this beer you have, for I'm not like this fucking stuck up lot." The maid steps back at what Pete had said, and she tells him.

"Follow me and I will give you one." Pete looking down at her arse as she walks off in front, and he is thinking, "Give me one, I would love to fuck you're arse sweetheart. The both go back stage and she gives Pete a can of beer, and he tells her.

"Thanks babe, I'm dreading this fucking do tonight, and this so called fucking auction." Pete lifting up his drink and taking a sip.

"You are not from round here, where are you from." The maid asking.

"I'm from a place called Bulwell, in Nottingham, and I would sooner be back there with one of the girls and here in this fucking place. What's you name love"

"Debbie, and you are."

"Pete, and is it me or is it getting hotter in here."

"I know it sometimes make me feel like taking my clothes off."

"Boy I wish we had somewhere to go, I would love to see you without clothes." Pete lifting his eyes up at Debbie, and with what Pete had said, she look back at Pete and his good looks and build, she known more than pull him into a store room and she locks the door.

"Well you are in a room, would you help me to remove my clothes." Well Pete did not answer her question but goes straight up to her and starts to kiss her, and at the same time removing her dress and apron, and then her top, and she is soon standing there, and Pete starts to kiss her neck and working down to her tits and nipples, and Debbie is franticly trying to remove Pete's trousers and within minutes she had Pete's cock out, and starting to give him a wank at the same time as telling him.

"Fucking hell Pete you are truly well endowed."

"Yes babe, and wait till I start to fuck you, that is when your pleasure will truly start. Pete did no more than drop to his knees and he is soon flicking her clitoris, and his tongue working on her fanny. Debbie stood there looking down at Pete working away on her, and she is starting to screw her face up at the feeling Pete was giving her, she is sighing and pleading with Pete to come up and fuck her. Pete stood straight up lifts her up, and it is if he knew where her fanny is, for he just looks at her straight in the face, and starts to go forward while still looking at Debbie and his cock goes straight in, and he just looks straight at Debbie at her face just screwed up at the feeling off Pete's cock penetrating her. Pete could see a chest freezer, and walks forward and puts Debbie onto the lid and starts to really go at her, well she is in heaven and calling for Pete to come, for she is going to explode, but Pete is thinking, a few more minutes, and he speeds up. Well Debbie is biting into Pete's neck and trying to tell him now, and he suddenly explodes and withdraws, and Debbie is straight down onto his cock and enjoying every drop of Pete. They clean up and of course Debbie gives Pete her number, but all it is just another number and conquest to his tally.

Pete finally goes back to the gathering, and goes up to Lorraine and she asks him.

"Where have you been, I wanted to introduce you to some of my friends." Pete tells her.

"I asked one of the waitresses if she had any beer, and we went back stage and she gave me one." Pete lifting up his can of beer, and also lifting up his eyebrows at what he had said. Then the compares stands and tells them.

"Let's get the Auction underway." He had a list of items, and he starts by telling them.

"Right the first one on the list is a full ride, and then a lift home, in Major Tomlinson's Roll Royce. Who will start the bidding?" Well Major Tomlinson standing there tweaking his moustache, and might I say he is not a young one but more like one foot in the grave. Well the bidding goes up and in the end, one Miss Cartwright whole being 68 years old wins the bidding at forty thousand pounds. Pete looks at Lorraine and his face is a picture at such a price, for a ride and lift home.

"You're kidding me, is this real, I mean, I would live like a king for a couple of years on that money, not a ride home."

"Yes sweetie, but you are among the wealthiest people in the UK, and money is no object to them."

"I don't believe it." Pete standing there and suddenly the compare announces.

"And next up is a super prize of one Mr Pete West, a night with a hulk." Well Pete spits his beer out at hearing his name, and he looks straight at Lorraine and he tells her.

"You're fucking kidding me, where did he get my name from." Lorraine just smiling back at Pete and encouraging him to go up. Well Lorraine suggesting with her hands, trying to usher Pete up, and finally he gives up, and goes and stands on stage, and might I say with one or two wolf whistles at seeing Pete standing there and dwarfing the compare. The compare looks at Pete and then back to the guest, and he tells them.

"Right look what we have here, it must be the sale of the century, at seeing what beholds you, who will start the bidding off." A voice shouts out.

"100 HUNDRES THOSAND POUNDS." Pete stood there looks at the compare and tells him.

"One hundred thousand pounds, you've got to be kidding."

"No darling, that is correct, and wait a moment, anymore bids then one hundred thousand." Then Lorraine shouts out.

"Two hundred thousand pounds." Well Pete's mouth is starting to open and drop, at hearing that, and he looks at Lorraine and he is suggesting, don't do it babe.

"Two hundred it is, anymore before the hammer falls." Then the first bidder shouts out.

"Four hundred thousand pounds." Pete looks at who is bidding and he liked what he sees, for she is young, with a nice figure and large tits. Then Lorraine smiles at Pete, and finally tells all gathered.

"Half a million." Well that was it, Pete spins the compare round and he came straight out with.

"For fucks sake stop this charade, for everyone is nuts out there." The compare looks a Pet in a disgusting way at what he had said and tells Pete.

"I don't like your attitude Youngman, for they are all decent people, and the highest bidder of the auction, all proceeds go towards the children's hospital for the terminally sick children." Well Pete apologises to him and tells him.

"Sorry mate, but I did not know, tell them that I will do anything, and I mean anything for the highest bidder." The compare accepts Pete's apology, and he tells the audience what Pete had said. Well that was it, more bidders came into the game and all the bids were coming from the Women in the audience.

Bid after bid is flying in until it reaches 900 thousand pounds, the compare is about to drop his hammer, when Lorraine shouts out.

"ONE MILLION POUNDS." Well there is murmuring among the audience and the compare with hammer raised shouts out.

"For the first time anymore bids, (silence,) second time, (again silence,) sold to Lorraine White for one million pounds, well done Lorraine." They all clap Lorraine for her generosity. Pete comes down from the stage and went back to where Lorraine stood and he straight away tells her.

"Are you real, I mean I'm with you, but you still paid one million for something that you already had."

"All for fun and a good cause, and anyway, now I've got you under a contract at what you said, that you would do anything for the winner, so be it wait till I get you home babe." Lorraine kissing Pete on the lips and lifting her eyes up at Pete.

Chapter Twenty Six

The auction carried on and everyone seemed to donate money, and at 10pm it is announced, that that evening auction had raised over 4 million pounds, for a good course. They all applauded the amount raised, and the party continued with the wine flowing, and people in general chatting and socialising. Come 1am Lorraine tells Pete that she had asked for her car, for it is time they were heading back, for she had to be at working that morning, to sort out one or two important matters. They leave and outside are the three guards that Pete sorted out early, and when they approach the car all three of them smile at Pete as he gets in the back with Lorraine, Pete tells them.

"No hard feeling lads, but if you have, see me one at a time later, not in a group." Pete gets in the car and Lorraine asks

"What's all that about."

"Nothing sweetheart my fault really, they tried to frisk me back at my hotel when we approached their car, but I put them in their place, that being backseat of their car, that's all."

"Please Pete promise me you will behave in front of them, for that is what I pay them for, to protect me."

"Sorry sweetheart it won't happen again I promise you." They arrive at Lorraine's place and when she is out of the car, she calls the three guards over and she tells them, that Pete had apologised over his behaviour earlier, so that is the end on the matter do I make myself clear. All three of them tell her.

"Yes Madam Lorraine quiet clear." Pete going by them said sorry to all three of them, they all tell him accepted, and I think that cleared the air. Lorraine and Pete go up to her bedroom and once inside she asks Pete to give her 5 minutes before he comes into the room, Pete said fine and Lorraine goes into the bedroom and closes the door, Pete is thinking I wonder what she is up to, he looks at his watch and after 5 minutes taps on the door and asks.

"Can I come in now Lorraine?" She shouts back for Pete to come in, and Pete enters and his eyes light up at the sight that beholds him. For Lorraine is on the bed and completely in the nude, and with her long blond hair covering her breast, and the blond locks stopping just after her groin, made Pete think of his Sofia. Her bronze body is just like Pete knew it would be like and he just stood there admiring her stance and tells her.

"You are just like I imagined you would look like, for you are truly a Goddess, and we are not worthy of your presence. Pete starts to remove his top, breaths in and displays his fine figure to Rosita, then removes his trousers followed by is boxers, and he stood there in front of Rosita, and asks her.

"Does my Goddess approve of what she sees?" Rosita tells Pete.

"You are truly fit for a Goddess, approach and show me what pleases you can bequeath onto me." Well this game seems to be going well, and Pete steps towards the bed, and Rosita looking at him approaching with a full erection, can hardly retain herself and tells Pete.

"Come my Prince show me how you will please me." Pete leans onto the bed and straight away opens her legs wide, and he is leaning up at her, looks back down at her, and he sees her shaven fanny and she looked good to eat. Pete takes in a deep breath and tightens all is muscles up and Rosita looks at what beholds her and shouts out.

"HO my God, you be fucking gentle with me, you great fucking big hulk." Pete slowly lowers down and starts to kiss her nipples and he is sucking away till they are standing proud, then down to her bronze tummy, and with his tongue licking all the way down to her fanny, he stars by flicking her clitoris quick, then sucking all of her clitoris into his mouth, and sucking gently. Well this made Rosita scream out with pleasure, and she puts both her hands onto Pete's head and pressing him into her. Pete spends over ten minutes down there and Rosita is having massive orgasms and Pete could taste her juices as he still carried on working on her fanny, it became so bad for Rosita that she just screamed out to Pete.

"For fucks sake Pete fuck the arse off me now, please for I cannot take much more of the pleasure you are giving me." Pete rises and pulls her legs up so Rosita is looking straight at Pete leaning upon the bed, and she with legs wide open looking at Pete's massif frame waiting to bare down onto her. Pete puts one hand onto his massif cock that his full erect, and gentle inserts it into Rosita's fanny and he presses forward, well Rosita could feel every inch entering her, and Pete pressed further down upon her, and he suddenly comes to the hilt, with all of his ten inch cock inside of her.

"My fucking God, you bloody big bastard this is worth every penny of the million I paid for you, God the pleasure, Ho my God." Pete with hearing her scream out with the feeling starts to speed up, and she is truly out of it with the massif orgasms, and Pete suddenly slows down, and then speeds up well that was it Rosita just screamed out at top of her voice.

"Now please come, give it all to me now, please." Pete goes like hell and he did explode, and just looks at her while he ejaculates into her, with Rosita lying there screwing her face up at the feeling of Pete ejaculating into her, and she suddenly had this content look on her face while Pete was looking at her.

She opens her eyes when she had climbed down from her orgasm and looks back at Pete and he looks at her and they draw close and start to kiss in a loving way, but Pete did not look right and Rosita asks Pete.

"Did I please you then my love?"

"You were truly loving and I will remember this day for the rest of my life." But as he said this he hears this voice say to him.

"My love my darling Pete, have you already replaced my love for you, for I love you and always will love you, my darling Pete." With hearing this Pete suddenly said.

"I will also love you my sweetheart." Well Rosita thanks Pete, and Pete looked at her and seemed confused and he suddenly realised that with him answering is Sofia out loud that Rosita had heard him and thanking him. They both flop back down onto the bed and the time is approaching 3.30am and Rosita turns to Pete and tells him.

"Ho my God I had better get to sleep or I will be ratty at the meeting in the morning, please Pete forgive me for I will have to sleep now."

"You drop off now my love, I will just use the bathroom before I drop off." Pete goes into the bathroom and is sitting on the toilet and he suddenly starts to think of his Sofia. Then he hears.

"My darling Pete I love you so, why, Ho why, do you do what you are doing."

"Sofia, what am I supposed to-do, sit back and vegetate, while still on this dam God World without you. I'm a man with needs and will always need these needs, forgive me my love, please don't condemn me." Pete sits there crying and after an hour, goes back to bed and he gets in and snuggles up to Lorraine, for he knows that in the morning he will have to call her this not by her old name Rosita.

9am in the morning Pete awakes and he sees that Rosita had gone, and by his side there is a note for him.

"My darling Pete, you looked a picture of pure love just lying there alone, for I have to go, but my darling please come back this evening, and I promise you, you won't be disappointed, I love you my darling. Love Lorraine." All that Pete did was turnover and back to sleep, for he knew that he had all day to himself.

He finally wakes and at 11am, gets up and showers and shaves, and he goes down to Rosita's kitchen to make himself a little breakfast, He had just sat down when into the kitchen comes one of the guys Pete had a run-in with the other night. I think he had a chip on his shoulder with what Pete had done with him, by manhandling him into the car.

"Well if it's not Madam Lorraine play toy, how the fuck did you become her play toy." He puts his hand into a bowl of popcorn and gulps down a mouth full still looking at Pete. Pete looks at him and just tells him.

"I'm no Woman's play toy, and if you would like to know, we go back a long way, and if you would like to make something of it, I'm willing to kick the living shit out of you. Pete stands pushes his cornflakes over the guy and starts to come round the table to where he is.

"Well the body guard spitting out cornflakes that had gone all over him, and might I say all down his long jacket, tells Pete.

"I'm going to thrash the fucking life out of you."

Pete stands there as the guy approaches and swings a punch at Pete, but Pete ducks and the guy goes sideways with the swing, Pete punches him straight into the kidneys, He goes forward and turning back to Pete, tells him at the same time as drawing his sidearm out of its holster.

"Let's see if you can stop this you fucking bastard." Pete seeing his gun coming out from under his coat, suddenly lunge's forward and one foot forward and one foot back just punches him straight on the nose, and Pete hears this sickening crack as he goes flying backwards straight out of the kitchen door, and landing on a patio outside. Pete goes forward and looks to where he had fallen, straight on his back, and to Pete's horror all the he sees is a sea of blood gushing onto the patio and draining off into the underneath.

"What have I done, God his face I've knocked his nose into his head."

Before Pete knows it he is standing over the guard's body when two other appeared and they see what beholds them. They look at each other and one tells the other.

"The fucking twat, it looks like he had found his match." Pete just stood there and the other guard tells Pete.

"Don't worry mate we will take care of this, it's his own fault, he kept telling us that he was going to sort you out, but it looks like he had come to his own comeuppance." Pete thanks them in a quiet voice and goes back inside and he just could not come to terms with what had happened, and he hurriedly gets dressed and leaves.

All day long he spends back in his Hotel and he keeps wondering what to do, for he is thinking that what if the police should come, well all-day its playing on his mind and at 4.30pm suddenly the phone rings in his hotel room, and this makes Pete jump out of his skin, with what had happened, he gingerly answers the phone and it is Lorraine.

"Pete's hopes you are coming round for I`ve some good news for you, why have you left." Pete thinking tells Lorraine.

"Ho I had to come home to change, you know into some more fitting clothes than a dinner suit, but I must." But before Pete could say anymore, she tells him.

"Well jump in a cab and I will see you in a few minutes, cannot wait to tell you the good news." Pete is thinking what do I do, does she know that I`ve killed one of her guards and she is going to sort me out, fucking hell I might land up in a motorway bridge in concrete. Pete looks down to his hands and they are shaking and he tells himself. "COME ON NOW Pete be a man and face the consequences." He changes and gingerly gets a cab and goes to Lorraine's dwelling and he pays the taxi cab, and goes to the front door and rings the bell. Well straight away one of the guards that was with him this morning answers the door.

"I mate, come in Madam Lorraine is in the lounge, over that way."

"Pete goes in and he sees Lorraine relaxed watching the TV, she turns and sees Pete, and beckons him over.

"Pete my love, have you had a good day."

"Well it started off not well for you see."

"Don`t mention that Burk who confronted you, for it is all dusted and forgot, come sit with me and let's talk about more important issues.

Chapter Twenty Seven

Please sit Pete."

"Rosita, I have to." But before he could get another word in, she turns looks straight into his eyes and tells him.

"No Pete please it's Lorraine, for if you keep calling me by my proper name you are bond to slip it out while we are in company, so no more Rosita, and I can tell by the look on your face, that you are still worried about this morning. Well bloody well forget it ever happened, for he is down a mineshaft, and at rest, so no more on the matter, do I make myself clear."

"Sorry Ros-Lorraine, thanks."

"You silly man come here and give your Lorraine a kiss for I've got good news for you." Pete kisses Lorraine and sits next to her, and she holds Pete's hand while she tells him the news.

"Well tonight we are going to a social gathering for wine and nibbles, for the rich and famous businessmen and Woman in the British economy, should be quite an eye opening for you Pete, to see how the top people of your Country socialise. And furthermore the day after tomorrow, we are going to go down to Portsmouth, board my boat and sail down to Monte Carlo." Lorraine smiling at Pete. Pete tells her.

"Bloody boat more like the Titanic, but there is one problem Lorraine, for you see I'm under contract with the agency and it would be impossible to go, for I would be in breach of contract."

"No Darling that is where you are wrong, for you see I've been in contact with them, and I've hired you for the whole year, so you are all mine, and mine alone." Lorraine with a large grin looking at Pete and puckering up her lips at Pete. Pete sat there gives her a smile back, but is thinking to himself. If she thinks I'm her slave come plaything, she's in for a big shock, Hired for a whole year, that must have been a small fortune. Then Pete asks Lorraine.

"Well who the hell pays me then, if I'm yours."

"No problem, they gave me all your details including your bank details, and you will be paid monthly so don't worry my love." Lorraine tells Pete that she will go and get ready, for the evenings party. Pete sat watching the evening news, waiting for Lorraine, and he suddenly looks at the news with intensity at what the newsreader is telling the viewers.

"This morning at Heathrow airport, a gang of men robbed a consignment being unloaded from a Boeing 747, consisting of over 100 million Dollars of American Gold bullion. Scotland Yard told us in a statement that there is believed to be at least 12 heavily armed men, that where involved with the heist, that occurred in the early hours of this morning at about 5.30am. No one at the Airport were reported injured, and it only took them a matter of ten minutes to load their getaway vehicles, which were later found burnt out about ten miles away from the Airport. Scotland Yard tell us that it is an ongoing investigation, and they will keep us up-to-date if they find any new clues. This is Jeremy Best, for B.B.C from London Heathrow." Just as the news changed to another subject Lorraine comes back into the room and Pete mentions the heist at Heathrow and that they got away with over 100 million Dollars, Lorraine tells Pete.

"No darling it was worth over 500 million Dollars, they do exaggerate on the TV." Well Pete just looks at Lorraine and is thinking, how does she know, then suddenly the penny drops, and he remembers that she is a top Mafia Boss, and I would not put it past her to be involved with the whole issue. They go to the car and are taken to the venue, which is a casual party, and they are greeted by an usher who introduces them to the ones already gathered there.

"My Lords Ladies and Gentlemen, Please welcome Lady Lorraine White and her escort Mr Pete West."

One or two come over to Lorraine and start to chat, and Pete is of course looking at the fish in the sea, by looking at the ones in short low necklines showing a little tit, and the ones in short miniskirts showing nice arses and long legs. Pete drifts away from Lorraine who is truly up to her elements in chat with the others, more like working finding out her next victim to relieve them of their wealth.

Pete notices one girl on her own standing near some French windows and looking out of them, he goes walking by and smiles at her and she smiles back at Pete, well that was the introduction and Pete stops and tells her.

"Not my cup of tea this lot, I mean look at them, lardy tardy, Ho nice to see you, spiffing Ho-Ho." Well she bursts out laughing and tells Pete.

"I can see you aren't of this sort of class of people, and your accent, where are you from. And by the way my names Sandy."

"My names Pete, and I'm from a place that you probably don't even know, called Bulwell of Nottingham, you know love Robin Hood Country."

"Ho yes, I've heard of that football team called Nott's Forest."

"No sweetheart, it's Nottingham Forest not Nott's, come on you reds."

"Well I can see that you're a fan Pete."

"Too true love, anyway that's by the by, were are you from Sandy."

"From here in London, my Fathers a top plastic surgeon of Harley Street. He is always invited to these gatherings, probably changed half the woman faces in here."

"Well with looking at your attractive face and figure, it's obvious he has not had his hands on you."

"Away with you Pete you're flattering me, who would want to go out with me."

"Well for one I would jump at the chance to take you out, for you are truly attractive and an upstanding Girl." Pete coming a little closer to Sandy, and putting his hands onto her hips, and just looking her straight in the eyes. Well that was it, she is dangling on Pete's fishing line, and all that Pete had to do is reel her in. Sandy slowly goes forward and they stand in a full kiss, and after Pete tells Sandy.

"It's a sham we have nowhere quiet to go, for I would love to kiss you more." Sandy grabs Pete's hand and she tells him.

"Come with me." She opens the French doors and drags Pete outside, and Pete looks back and he sees Lorraine laughing and giggling with the guest surrounding her. Once outside Sandy tells Pete.

"Follow me I know a quiet place that I've had a tour round when I came when I was a little smaller. She leads Pete to a very large greenhouse and they enter. She takes Pete down one of the gangways and it opens up in the middle with a large green area, where they cultivate grass for relaying their lawns, she stops on the grass turns to Pete and they are starting to have a loving tender kiss. Pete starts to use his tongue and Sandy straight away starts to get tingles at what Pete is doing. Pete at the same time is pressing his hard on into her groin, and Sandy responds by slightly pushing onto his cock then back and then forward again. Pete starts to kiss her neck and at the same time is hand slips under her blouse, and he starts to fondle her breast, then slips one hand onto her back and unclips her bra, exposing both her breast. Pete starts to suck away on her left tit and nipple, then working on her right one till them both stand out proud. Sandy by now stars to go down onto the grass and Pete follows her. Once down on the grass Pete lifts up her miniskirt and slips her knickers off, and Pete is straight onto her clitoris and takes it all in his mouth, and starts to slowly suck on it, making Sandy groan at the feeling of what Pete is doing, and after a few minutes he lets go of her clitoris and gently blows on it while he inserts one finger and starts to slowly push it to the hilt. Well Sandy by now is completely having an orgasm, and Pete could feel her juices flowing, she tells Pete to get his cock out and fuck her now. Pete drops his trousers and Sandy is straight onto his cock and when she feels the length and thickness tells Pete.

"Fucks sake Pete you be gentle." While Pete is telling Sandy not to worry, she is guiding it to her fanny and Pete gently starts to penetrate her, slowly at first and Pete watching her arch back and her breast rise up, as Pete pushes more into her.

"Fucking Jesus Christ, you are fucking good Pete, I've never felt like this before, Ho my God, a little faster Pete please, fucking God. Well Sandy by now is grabbing hold of the back of Pete's white T-shirt and gripping like mad, it's a good job it is not his bear back or he would be feeling her nails by now at the state she is in, for she is screaming out with pleasure with every push Pete is doing. Finally Pete had fully penetrated her and going like a bull at a gate, and all that Sandy is shouting is for Pete to come now for Fucks sake. Well Pete could feel it coming and he tells Sandy and he withdraws, while he is about to ejaculate, well Sandy is straight up pushes Pete's hands of his cock and she drives her mouth straight down onto his cock and Pete is kneeling and ejaculating and Sandy is sucking every drop and looking at Pete's face screwing up at the feeling he is getting with Sandy sucking and licking her tongue all over Pete's bell end.

Finally they both lay back on the grass and just kissing and cuddling each other, and Sandy tells Pete.

"You're the first guy I've ever responded like that on the first meeting, there is something that I cannot put my finger on, about you Pete.

"It's the same for me Babe, maybe it's probably with us both having the same feeling, it is if I had known you for a while and it was right. But there is only one problem Babe."

"What's that Pete tell me please?"

"Well we meet and I would love to see you tomorrow, but I'm going away for a couple of weeks down to Monte Carlo."

"That's alright, you will have to have my number, and just ring me when you are back, simple."

"I suppose you're right, don't forget to give it to me before I go tonight."

"I will Babe, doesn't you worry." Just has she had said this they hear voices. This made them hurriedly redress and they start to walk down the gangway, when the voice gets louder.

"Just going to water the lawn Bert, get the kettle on will you."

"Right on Fred will do." Sandy and Pete are walking along the gangway when Fred turns onto the gangway, and bumps into them.

"Good evening Miss and Sir, what brings you in here tonight, I thought you would be with the guest back at the house." Sandy tells him.

"Just showing my friend these magnificent plants that you grow in the greenhouses, for you see a few years back you gave me a guided tour round the place."

"That's right Miss I used to, and it was an enjoyable job, anyway can't stop, for I've to see to the lawns, goodnight to you both." Sandy and Pete go walking off trying to contain themselves from bursting out laughing, at the antics that they had been up too. Well when Fred reaches the area that he is going to water, he sees the imprints in the grass that Sandy and Pete had left, for there were two indents were Sandy's arse had been, and two dig marks where Pete had dug is feet into the lawn to get a grip, well Fred scratches his head and comes straight out with.

"That bloody cat must-have brought a mouse into the greenhouse, and had been playing with it, and look at the bloody mess, I will kick the little bogger up the arse if I see it." Poor cat taking the blame for two humans that had made the mess in the first place.

Chapter Twenty Eight

They enter back into the house through the French windows, and straight away Pete looks to where Lorraine is, and he smiles when he sees her still up to her arsehole in chat with the guest. He turns to Sandy and asks her.

"Right babe I had better get back to mingling with the dickheads have you your number." Sandy goes into her handbag pulls out a note pad and puts down her number for Pete, and Pete did the same. After they had put them away, Pete kisses Sandy and tells her.

"I will see you when I get back Babe." Kisses her one more time and goes back over to where Lorraine is standing talking. Lorraine sees Pete turns to him and asks.

"Have you been mingling with them as well sweetheart."

"Not really Love, for they are out of my league, and I am getting a little bored with it."

"Come darling enjoy and unwind, come here, put your arm in mine and join in with the chat." Pete looked out of place and just stood there smiling and looking at them, when one Lady turns to Pete and asks him.

"My you look a fine figure of a man, how do you keep a frame like you have in trim."

"Every day that I can get into the gym, the more I can pump iron and build my body up." Pete with his leather coat by his side and just his white T-shirt on tenses up his arm muscles and tells the Lady.

"Here feel this." Well she know more than put one hand on his arm and trying to squeeze, and puts the other onto his cock and she came straight out with.

"Now I see you are truly a hard fellow, and might I say, one that I would love to workout with you." Well Pete just could not believe what she had just done, for she must have been well into her fifty's, and Pete looks at her and is thinking.

"In your fucking dreams, there is no way that my cock would stand proud for that." Lorraine tells Pete.

"See they are human just like the lower class." Well Pete took exception to the comment and he tells Lorraine.

"Well I can tell you that when I go for a drink, with the so called lower class, I don't get the pensioners touching me in the private parts." Pete looking at the Lady who had touched him. If you could have seen the look on her face, she tells Lorraine.

"Pensioner indeed." Pete just smiles at her, and Lorraine tells Pete.

"Please darling try and relax, we are all friends here."

"Sorry sweetheart, but I would sooner be on my own with you, and not with this lot."

"Soon Babe soon, till then try and have a drink." Before Lorraine could say more her mobile rings and she answers the call, and with Pete standing next to her, could hear what the caller is telling her.

"Madam the eggs, do you need them delivering to the 501."

"Yes, and as soon as you can, use my helicopter if you must, but we leave in the morning." Pete with hearing leave in the morning knew that she is going to have the eggs delivered to her ship, and eggs, would that be golden eggs that the giants hen had laid. The 501 must be code for her ship, boy I would make a great detective. Pete smiling to himself. Pete tell Lorraine that he is going to get a drink and he goes next door and he is taken back, for it was as if he had walked into a bar, for there were two waiters behind a bar, and they had pumps on the bar, well Pete goes up to them and asks.

"Are they fake pumps or do they have beer in them."

"Of course Sir they contain beer, what will be you pleasure."

"Would a pint of lager be out of the question?"

"No problem Sir, one pint of lager coming up." Well Pete takes the beer and takes a large drink and looks at the waiters and just came out with.

"You're a fucking life saver mate cheers." Pete looks at the beer and then taking another swag.

"In the end Lorraine had to come and find Pete who is up to his eyehole in pleasure and Lorraine tells Pete.

"Darling are you ready to go, for we have to be up early in the morning to sail away from the U.K."

"Bloody hell, just starting to enjoy this party." Pete thanking the waiters for their service and they smile back at Pete and tell him.

"It's been a pleasure Sir." Lorraine and Pete leave, and her lift his waiting for them and it is not long and they are both back at her place, Pete suddenly realises.

"Bloody hell Lorraine if we are sailing in the morning, I've not got my things with me."

"No problem babe, my driver will drop you off, and you will have to be back here by 8.30am, for the Helicopter is scheduled to take us at 9am." Lorraine kisses Pete and gets out of the car. Pete smiles at her but he is thinking.

"Ho fuck, I was looking forward to shagging the arse off her, dam women, why can't they be more like men, gagging for it every five minutes." The car pulls up at his Hotel and the driver wished him a goodnight and drives off.

Pete back in his room, starts to gather all is belongings ready for the trip and he just left out is toiletries for the morning, he looks at his watch and the time is approaching 1am.

"Bloody hell I have not got a lot of time in bed, when all of a sudden there is a crash in the bathroom and Pete straight away is saying.

"What the fuck is that." He goes into the bathroom and all of his toiletries are all over the floor, and he is thinking. "How the fuck had this happened." When all of a sudden he hears someone crying.

"Whose there, why are you crying." Pete had this cold feeling start to run through him, and he is thinking of the times in the past, of when he seen the footprints in the snow coming out of the Church in Bulwell, and the sightings of Sofia. Then the shower starts to flow and a voice starts to tell him.

"My darling Pete, please-please be careful, for you are going to come into a lot of problems at what you are doing, I love you so, my darling Pete."

By now the goose pimples are sticking out all over his masculine body, and he draws back the shower blind door, and there is no one there. He just drops to his knees and burst out crying at what had happened, and he starts to pick up all of his things and he is still sobbing. He suddenly stands and tells whoever his haunting him.

"Please-please leave me be, for I cannot bring my darling Sofia back, and I'm here all by myself, please let me rest." Pete comes out of the bathroom and gets into bed and he leaves the light on, for a big man it has certainly got to him. There is no other incident for the rest of the night, and Pete had a full 6 and a half hours sleep, and he pulls back the bedcovers at dead on 7.30am and goes to get ready for the trip on Rosita's boat, Ho sorry Lorraine's boat. He takes a little breakfast and calls the taxi at 8.15am and by 8.40 he is at Lorraine's apartment and he is waiting for her to appear. Deed on 8.55 Loraine comes into the room kisses Pete and tells him.

"Hopes you had a good night Pete, and ready for the trip down to Monti-Carlo."

"Well no not really, babe."

"Why is that my love?"

"Well for a start all that I wanted when we arrived back last night is to make mad passionate love to you, but were did I land up." Pete lifting his arms up in a suggestive way.

"Silly boy wait till what will behold you once we are on my ship, it is going to blow you away."

"Well I hope someone gives me a blow away." Lorraine slaps him on the arm in a friendly way and tells him.

"Come my sweet let's get to the helicopter that awaits us." They come out of Lorraine's room and Pete turns for the lifts to take them to the ground floor, but Lorraine turns for the stairs for the roof. She turns and shouts to Pete.

"This way, the helicopter is not in the street, silly." Pete turns and catches her up and once on the roof they board the helicopter that is going to take them down to Portsmouth where her ship is docked. They arrive and the helicopter lands on the heliport on the ship and they make their way down into the ship, and at the same time Lorraine is telling the Captain who is there to meet them.

"Take us out to sea and set sail."

"Yes Madam, welcome aboard and we will set sail straightaway." They go down a passageway and come to a door and Lorraine stops and turns and asks Pete.

"Well here we are, let's see what you think of my little resting place."

Loraine enters and Pete stops dead in his tracks at what beholds him, for he is looking at a four poster bed sitting in a glass window that must have covered the whole of the front and it just looked straight out over the sea, with no other place on the ship were you could look in. Well Pete with is mouth still open goes and stands in the window and you just look down at the sea below going by. Pete turns to Lorraine and he asks her.

"How does the window cleaner, put his ladders up to clean this big thing."

"Funny it's self-cleaning glass, and once out at sea, you can relax on the bed in the nude, and have no prying eyes." Pete looks at Lorraine and he tells her.

"Let's strip off now and get on the bed."

"Don't be silly we have not cleared the harbour yet, in a few minutes, then we can make up lost time from last night. I will just slip into something more fitting."

"Before you go sweetheart, in Monte-Carlo what is the weather like in December."

"It will be about 14c, pleasant, but don't expect to top your tan at this time of year." Pete thinking this is going to be the first year away from home at Christmas, but again I'm on my own so I cannot see what I'm worried about. Pete standing watching the ship pull away out of the harbour and heading into open water, the sky is grey and it looks cold outside, but aboard the temperature is a nice comfortable feeling. Pete standing in the window had not seen Lorraine come back into the room, and she suddenly asks Pete.

"Well aren't you coming to join me." Pete turns round and there is Lorraine lying on the oversized Queen-sized bed, in a very thin pinkish coloured negligée that left nothing to your imagine nation. For Pete just stood there for a few moments looking at the fetching tigress that beholds him. He could see her golden tanned breast through the negligée, and her shaven fanny that looked very inviting. Pete stood there in the window removed his shirt, then his jeans and boxer shorts, and he too stood there for Lorraine to admire what stood before her.

Lorraine looks at Pete smiles at him, and with her hand taps the bed to beckon Pete to join her.

Chapter Twenty Nine

Pete slowly kneels on the bed and approaches Lorraine, and he starts to lean forward and kiss her lovingly on the lips, then moves down to her neck and at the same time pulling the cord that lay on her breast, and pulls her negligée open exposing her breast, he looks at her golden breasts, looks back at Lorraine, then goes down and starts to flick and suck on her nipples. Lorraine laid back and wallowed in the pleasure and feeling Pete is giving her, he then starts to move down her tummy to her shaven fanny and sucks her clitoris straight into his mouth. He gently sucking and letting go, a little blow on it then sucking it back in, well Loraine is breathing heavily at what Pete is doing and she suddenly explodes with one mighty orgasm, and Pete at hearing her groans moves onto the lips of her fanny, and inserts his large tongue into to her and starts to work on it. He can tell that she had, had an orgasm with the taste of her juices.

After about five minutes Pete rises and laid on top off Lorraine, and they are both looking at each other straight in the eyes, and Pete moves forward and his penis finds its own goal. Well as soon as he starts to penetrate Lorraine they both are still looking at each other, and they both close their eyes at the feeling they were giving each other.

"Ho Pete you certainly know how to please a Woman, for your cock is magnificent, and any Woman would love to have this feeling. I'm glad that I'm the only one who gets this feeling. Pete is thinking to himself. "Yes and not to mention the other 28 or so Women that have felt the same way over the last few months." Pete after they had been in the missionary position turns Lorraine over and he lifts her up and inserts his cock dog style while, holding her hips and lifting her arse up into the air. Well Lorraine feels

199

more of his cock in this position and after about ten minutes, and might I say they had been at it for over an hour tells Pete.

"Please now Pete, please now for fucks sake and leave that big bad boy in and give me all of your love juice." Pete is really hammering away at the talk, and he suddenly does explode and they both are shouting out with groans of pleasure, and Lorraine moving her arse around Pete to get all of his sperm and murmuring at the same time. Finally they both flop back down onto the bed and wrapped around each other are both watching big oil tankers and shipping go by in the English Channel. Pete comments to Lorraine.

"I hopes there has not been a Captain looking through his binoculars, and looking at us through that big fucking window."

"No darling for I forgot to mention it, that it is a one-way mirror were you can look out but not in. Anyway if he did see us, all that he would say is look at that fucking big window over there, and that big fucking cock." Lorraine laughing out loud and at the same time grabbing hold of Pete's cock and gently moving it up and down. Pete looks at Lorraine and kisses her and she is still playing with his cock, and Pete starts to rise again, as Lorraine takes bigger strokes of his cock, she looks Pete straight into the eyes and tells him.

"Looks like he has not finished with me yet Pete, lay flat on your back." Pete did this and Lorraine straddles Pete and gets on top and Pete's cock is standing proud. She slowly goes down onto Pete's cock and before long they are in full sexual contact.

They only manage half an hour this time for Pete is going at Lorraine like a bull at a gate, and before long they both again are having a massif orgasm. Pete suddenly sits bolt up and ejaculates into her and he his kissing Lorraine, who is blowing at the same time as kissing and had to break away for she could not help but scream out with pleasure. They start to come back down to Earth and they both are still in the upright position and Pete still penetrating her. Lorraine kissing and brushing back Pete's locks, and tells him.

"No more sweetheart or I'm going to bust my heart, you are truly a great lover, and friend, I love you Pete."

"And I love you too Babe. What's the plan for the trip then Lorraine.

"Well you know that in two days' time it will be Christmas, well I've invited a few friends down to enjoy Christmas on my ship, and it should be fun and games all the way through the two days festive."

"Great I will look forward to that, and by the way, I hopes they are not all up their own arses like that lot at the party." Lorraine laughing tells Pete.

"No these are more down to earth, and you might know one or two for they are into sport. You know this motor grand prick, and Football." Pete burst out laughing at what Lorraine had said and she asks him.

"What is so funny sweetheart?"

"You said Grand prick, its grand prix."

"Well you've seen one prick, or this so called prix, you've seen them all." Lorraine smiling at Pete who is laughing again.

"Come on Pete get dressed, and lets go and have coffee up in the observation lounge, for it will be a little too cold to go on the outside decking." They both dress and do go and have coffee, and over the next two days the main ongoing thing is readying the ship for the festive party. They finally arrive in Monti Carlo and drop anchor just outside with the ship being too large to dock. Lorraine is approached by two of her guards who whisper to her and she turns to Pete and tells him.

"Pete I have to go ashore on business, will you be alright on your own, while I'm gone."

"No problem babe I will carry on helping to ready the ship for the party tonight." Lorraine leaves and leaves Pete helping out, and he is trying to put up some trimmings and comes to some large reflecting balls and he tells himself, better go and try and find a hammer for this job. Pete leaves the ballroom and heads down a passage looking for maintenance, so he could put up the balls, when he comes to a large door. He thinks, this might be it. He opens the door and his eyes light up for there before him is the 500 million gold bars stacked head high.

"Fucking hell, I was right, she is involved with the heist at Heathrow." Pete quickly closes the door and he is just starting to walk away when from round a corner comes one of Lorraine's guards.

"Hay what are you doing down here."

"Ho we are putting up some trimmings for the party tonight and I require a hammer, you don't happen to know where I could get one do you." The guard tells Pete where to go, and Pete thanks him and he is thinking to himself. "That was fucking close, for if he had caught me, I would probably land up down a pit shaft." Pete returns to the ballroom and he sees this lovely girl trying to reach and pin some trimmings to the ceiling and leaning forward, her skirt is ridding up and Pete is thinking.

"Fucking nice pair of pins there." He goes over to the ladder and supports it and tells the girl.

"Better if I hold this love, we don't want you falling off, do we, and you will have to forgive me love, for the view I've from down here is magnificent." She looks down to her skirt and just tells Pete.

"Well enjoy love, my fat arse, won't put you off your tea I hope."

"No problem and it's a nice arse really love. "Pete gently shakes the ladder and the girl starts to get unsteady, Pete with one hand on the steps and he puts the other onto her thigh from under her skirt to support her, and she just thanked him and carried on what she was doing. Well Pete had the invitation and he is gently stroking her thigh. After she had done she comes down the steps and looks straight at Pete and that was it he had her.

You were really enjoying stroking my thigh up there weren't you."

"Too true love, and my name is Pete, and you are."

"Sally, and my, you are truly a fine looking man, how long have you been on board." Sally looking Pete up and down and likening at what she is looking at.

"Since London, and might I say you too are a very attractive girl, and I would love to have a few moments with you."

"Moments, I hopes you are not that quick Pete, Sally looking down to Pete's groin."

"Well why not find out for I've got this lovely secret place that will truly turn you one." Sally puts her hand onto Pete firm chest, looks at him straight in the eyes and tells him.

"Lead on, show me this so called secret place." Pete takes Sally by the hand and they leave the ballroom and he only goes and takes her to Lorraine's bedroom with the large glass dome window that you could walk on and look straight down at the water below.

Well when Pete opens the door and bacons Sally in her eyes light up.

Surely this is not your room, it's out of this world. Well Sally goes walking by the oversize Queens bed and steps onto the glass and she suddenly jumps back, at thinking that she is about to fall into the sea below, and she is straight into Pete's arms and still trying to stop from looking down.

"You're fine babe trust me." Pete still holding Sally steps onto the glass bottom and pushers her up against the window, and tells her.

"You see love you can look out, but no one can look in." Pete slowly goes forward pressing himself against Sally and starts to kiss her while they both are pressed up against the window, they stand in a kissing embrace and Sally could feel Pete getting aroused. Pete slowly starts to unzip the back of her dress and Sally loving what Pete is doing, starts to unzip his front, and them both are starting to work up to a sexual frenzy. It's not long and Sally is down to her bra and knickers, and Pete soon had her bra off and starts to kiss her nipples while Sally is franticly trying to get Pete's cock out.

They are soon both in the nude and Sally looking straight out of the window and Pete slowly goes down on her and he is up to his old tricks. Yes working away on her fanny till she is shouting out with pure pleasure.

"Ho my God, for fucks sake shag me Pete." Pete comes up and he lifts her legs and starts to penetrate her pressing up against the glass, and they are both enjoying the full pleasure that they were giving each other. It's not long and the glass starts to steam up with the sweat that they both were working up.

Pete suddenly opens his eyes with Sally shouting out.

"For fucks sake now please spunk me." And in the distance he sees the helicopter starting to come into few, and he does explode withdrawing as he is about to shoot his load, and Sally is straight down onto Pete, while he is just looking at the helicopter getting closer.

Pete looks down at Sally who is enjoying her offerings from Pete, and Pete lifts her up kisses her while still looking at by now the helicopter about to land and he tells Sally.

"We had better scarper or we will have the owner coming in on us." Well they are both franticly getting dressed and are soon out of there and back to the ballroom, when Lorraine does finally come in and she sees the results that they had made, and she turns to Pete and tells him.

"You have done well there my love, it looks like you have really had it up and have made a good job of it, well done and keep it up. Well Pete thanks Lorraine on her comments and at the same time looking at Sally and trying not to laugh.

Just before he leaves the ballroom he asks Sally for her contact details and she gives them to Pete and hurriedly goes off to continue her duties.

Chapter Thirty

"Well everything is ready for tonight, are you looking forward to it then Pete."

"You bet sweetheart, I am looking forward to a good drink and a good laugh. What's the entertainment then for tonight?"

"We have a comedy act from England, and after dinner a disco, by Dave Rodgers traveling Disco, he's been recommended, and should be good." Pete thinking, sounds good.

"That evening Pete is ready and goes into the ballroom, where there is a bar and he goes and orders a beer, and standing looking at all the trimmings and he his thinking. "Bloody good job that, and the silver balls look awesome, well I did put them up. Pete smiling, he goes to the window that looks across the bay in Monti Carlo, and he is taken back when he sees a rather large boat go by and on the deck he sees this long haired blond girl, with a white dress and her hair flowing in the wind. He quickly goes out onto the deck and shouts out to Sofia, as soon as he shouts to her she waves at Pete. And Pete had this cold feeling running through him.

"It cannot be her, for she has gone, but why did she wave at me, and I'm convinced it was her. Please God not more nightmares Please." Pete watching the boat disappear into the distance, and he is miles away in thought when Lorraine comes out and asks him.

"What are you looking at Pete?" Well Pete jumps out of his skin and drops his glass of beer over the side.

"God all mighty you frightened me there Lorraine."

"Why so jumpy, Pete it is if you had seen a ghost."

"If I tell you please tell me you won't laugh."

"Try me out with it darling, you can trust me." Well Pete tells her about the sightings and voices, and even the foot prints in the snow at Saint Mary's church. Lorraine looks Pete straight in the eyes, holds his hands and tells him.

"There is only one thing that you have to do and that is stop it, for there is no such thing as ghosts believe me darling. And if you carry on believing what you see, it will certainly crack you up, and send you insane, believe me darling." Pete thanks Loraine and he tells her.

"Come on then let's go back in and start to welcome your guests, for it is Christmas Eve, Ho shit I've just remembered."

"What is it Pete what's wrong."

"I've not been off the ship so I have not had the opportunity to buy you, you're Christmas present."

"No worries Pete, I've been at the meeting and snap me too, we will have to settle for each other for Christmas." Lorraine lifting her eyebrows up in a suggestive way at Pete.

At 7pm her guest start to arrive from shore, and Pete with pint pot in hand stands with Lorraine as they come into the ballroom, Pete is smiling at the ones he fancied, and just like Pete he is thinking every time a cracker comes in, he is saying to himself. "Would you", then smiles at the ones with a yes answer. Just like Lorraine had said at 7.30pm onto the stage comes the first entertainment the comedians and they go down well, cracking adult style jokes, and at 8.30pm they are all addressed by a waiter announcing.

"Dinner is served." They all make their way to the large dining hall and sit ready for their meal, while the food is waiting to come, the waiters are serving them with red, or white wine.

The whole evening is one big success and Pete standing at the bar while the disco is on, is approached by this Lady of about 38 years old and might I say very attractive, she asks Pete.

"Please don't be offended, but I've been told that you do escort evening, taking out Ladies. What would you say by me asking you to taking me out when I come to the UK? And off the record of course."

"I would jump at the chance, here take my mobile number and I live in Nottingham."

"Thanks for that. (She looks at Pete's details and tells him.) I see your name is Pete, might I say you are one hell of a man and you must work out."

"That's right, and you have not told me your name sweetheart."

"Bianca Davenport, from London." Pete looks to see where Lorraine is and she is talking to a few friends' near the dance floor and Pete turns to Bianca and asks her.

"Would you like to take in the evening air, for it is not so cold down here, not like the UK?"

"That would be nice Pete." They slip out of the ballroom and head for the bow of the ship, and Pete finds a secluded spot, and they both stop and Pete turns to Bianca and goes forward, and she goes forward to Pete, and they are fully in a kiss and after Bianca tells Pete.

"If we were back in the UK, I would ask you to make mad passionate love to me."

"There's no time like the present love." Pete knew the ship by now, him no more than goes to the first cabin that was not occupied, and they enter and Pete starts to kiss Bianca and at the same time unzipping her dress from the back, and it falls to the floor. Bianca at the same time is lifting Pete's shirt off and before long they are both in the nude. And Pete picks her up and carries her to the bed. He gently puts her down onto the bed, and Bianca laid there and looked at Pete, and she gasps at the site that beholds her.

"It is true you are truly a gladiator, and your penis, God I've never seen such a wonderful site at what beholds me, come Pete have your wicked way with me and make me scream with pleasure." Pete is wondering how she knew so much about him, and he looks at her and then tells himself.

"It only can be Lorraine, for the other girl that I shagged, would not mingle with this lot." Pete slowly goes down on her and he straight away kisses her on her nipples and she is asking him to work on her fanny. Well Pete did not like her away, and he did know more than still concentrate on her tits, and then slowly working down to her belly. Well this certainly did the trick, for she is by now screaming for Pete to fuck her. But again he takes no notice as he sees her tummy going in and out with the breaths that she is taking. He slowly starts to flick her clitoris and she leans up and sees Pete's head down on her fanny and his large tongue flickering away at her clitoris.

"Fucking God Pete fucking shag me, please-please, I'm going to explode." Pete again took no notice and just told himself. "Well fucking explode, for I'm going to shag you like you have never been shagged before, and probably won't again." He is sucking her clitoris into his mouth and Bianca is exploding with orgasm after orgasm, and Pete is loving the taste of her juices and he suddenly tells himself.

"Now mount her and make her scream like a squealing pig at a slaughterhouse. Pete rises and the moon shining through the porthole lit the room, and Bianca could see this big gladiator about to mount her. Well she had her legs wider than the goal post at Wembley, waiting for her man, and Pete goes down on her and his ten inch Penis finds its goal, and he penetrates her straight to the hilt. Well that was it, if the whole ship did not hear her scream out so much, that she tries to lift up and she know more than puts her arms around Pete's back and trying to push him further onto her.

"You fucking big bastard, your fucking going to make me flood this bed, God please, Pete give me it all please." Pete in a tease mood slows down and takes a long withdraw, then plunges back in and he is doing this for about five minutes and again and she is moaning with pleasure. Pete again starts to bash away at her like a bull at a gate. He continues the sequence for well over twenty minutes and she cannot stand it any longer and she tells Pete to bloody well give it her all, well Pete could feel he is about to explode and just before he does, he whispers in her ear.

"Here I go sweetheart enjoy the feeling I'm about to give you." Pete finally does come and Bianca also comes and Pete starts to ejaculate into her and they both are having a massif orgasm together.

"After they go into the bathroom and clean themselves up and leave, and if you could have seen the state they left the room in, you would think that someone had burgled it. They re-join the party that is now in full swing and the wine is flowing, well it is Christmas Eve.

"The disco is playing some great songs and there is plenty of dancing. Well the party goes on till well past 2am and slowly the guest start to leave, by the time everyone had left Lorraine sat with Pete on their own, and Lorraine is well over the limit and she starts to break her heart to Pete. Well ether it is the beer or does she mean what she is telling Pete, for it truly opens his eyes towards her.

"I truly love you Pete, but this job of mine and you probably have guessed, that I'm a big boss in the Mafia, and I wish I could get out, for I would love to be on my own with you." She had been opening up her heart to Pete for well over an hour and Pete is thinking to himself.

"Let's hope she cannot remember in the morning at all of what she had told me. Lorraine sitting there with glass in hand and starting to drop off, Pete sees this, stands up and tells her.

"Come on Babe, let's get you into bed." Pete picks her up and she falls fast on, on Pete shoulder while he slowly walks towards her birth. Once inside he puts her on the bed and unzips her long dress and slides it off, and she only had her thong and no bra, Pete looks at her, and as he covers her up is thinking.

"So much for my Christmas present. "He strips and gets into bed alongside her and snuggles up, and before long he too be off into the land of nod.

They both start to come out of their sleep, and Pete is the first awake with Lorraine wrapped around Pete, and he starts to kiss her while they face each other and he starts to get aroused the feeling of her warm breast on his chest.

Lorraine with Pete kissing her awakes, and she looks at Pete and she asks him.

"What time is it love, Ho my head, what had I have to drink, last night."

"The bar dry I think, can't you recollect us sitting talking after they had all gone."

"No, and did we make." Then Pete knew what she is about to say and tells her.

"No sweetheart to your question, and you don't feel up to it now do you." Pete pressing his hard on into her front." Lorraine puts her hand onto Pete's cock and starts to wank him off and telling him.

"Not really, I think I would be sick all over you, if you started to bounce on my tummy, this will have to do." She carried on playing and starting to go faster on Pete's cock, and he does come and Lorraine gets an hand full and this sure made her get out of the bed and go to the bathroom. By 10 am they are having breakfast and Pete is tucking into a hearty full English, while Lorraine is trying to force a little toast down her. Pete looks at Lorraine and he tells her.

"Merry Christmas sweetheart, and thank for the present this morning."

"Merry Christmas to you, Pete, What present."

"You know the hand job, one of the best presents for years." Pete sipping a drink out of his coffee."

"Well this evening you will definitely give me my present, I promise you." Lorraine smiling at Pete then tells him.

"Christmas Dinner will be in the ballroom at 3pm, and the Captain and crew members will be there, should be a good afternoon, for the same disc jockey will be playing record.

The rest of the morning it was relaxing and a little watching the satellite programs on the TV.

Chapter Thirty One

The dinner did start at 3pm, and Lorraine had outside catering staff come onto the ship and prepared the Christmas dinner. There were pulling crackers putting on paper hats, and telling the jokes out of the crackers. The whole dinner is a success and like Lorraine said after, the tables were cleared and the disco started up. It was truly in the Christmas mood, and everyone was having a good time.

The time is approaching 5pm, Pete joining in with the festive spirit is dancing with one of the girls and having a good time, when out of the corner of his eye he sees three of Lorraine's Hench men approaches Lorraine, and she did not look right, they had been talking for about ten minutes, when Lorraine suddenly pushed one of her men out of the way and she came hurriedly towards where Pete stood. When Pete sees her, he had this unease feeling. For Lorraine was in tears and tears running down her face were black from her mascara, she comes to Pete grabs his hand and pulls him outside and flings her arms around Pete, and trying to kiss him, but with her crying it did not last long.

"What the hell is wrong sweetheart, why so upset?"

"My darling Pete as soon as I have you back in my arms, why-O-why do things go wrong."

"Like what, why so upset." Pete looking at Lorraine with concern.

"I've just been told that I have to go and will not be coming back, for my cover is blown and they are coming after me. My darling Pete I love you so much, I will have to go my darling, please understand. And don't worry I've organised everything for you." She kisses Pete one more time breaks away still holding his hands, and slips them out and as she is about to turn, she tells Pete.

"I truly love you my sweet Pete." She breaks off and goes hurriedly to where her Hench men are." Pete looks at Lorraine and on the disco the song starts up. The Harry Wilson song. I can't live. (If living is without you.) Pete looks at Lorraine and she looks back, just as the song starts to say, I CAN'T LIVE, IF LIVING IS WITH OUT YOU, and I CAN'T LIVE. Pete looks at Lorraine and she is saying as she left the room, lip reading. I love you my darling Pete. Well Pete just stood there, and he walks to the door and out onto the deck, and he sees the helicopter starting up and he sees several people boarding and it takes off. The song is still playing and Pete just watched as the Helicopter disappeared into the distance. Pete reflects for a moment and just came straight out with.

"Fucking fine Christmas this is turning out to be." He goes back into the ballroom and carried on with the party, Pete is doing is usually thing looking for his next victim to shag, and two hours have gone by when one of Lorraine's guards that were still on the ship approach him.

"Can I have a word with you?" Pete tells him to come onto the deck where it is a little more private. Once outside the guard tells Pete.

"In the morning at 9am it has been arranged for you to be transferred to shore and be put up in an Hotel for the night, and the next morning will be by taxi be taken in the afternoon to the airport Azure International in Nice, which is only 15 miles away. This has all been arranged for you under Madam Lorraine's instructions. Pete is passed paper work confirming the arrangements and the guard leaves. Pete pockets the paper work and goes back to the disco."

Pete that night does not score and he goes back to Lorraine's room alone and he is thinking, I will be bloody glad when I get back to the UK, and proper people. Pete striped and in the large bed soon drifted off to sleep and he had one of the worst nightmares imaginable for he is in the Queen oversized bed when Sofia gets into the bed and snuggles up to Pete and she tells him.

"This is what I miss Pete being alone with you with no one to hurt us. Pete turns round and he starts to kiss Sofia and he is saying to her.

"My darling Sofia, you are truly my only one, and I'm glad we are together. He starts to kiss Sofia passionately and she responds with her arms wrapped around Pete. She tells him.

"Ho how I've missed this holding you tight in my arms my love, you are my world and Destiney together forever, nothing will come between us." Pete starts to come round and he feels for Sofia and suddenly shouts our, for her.

"Sofia where have you gone." He is still in a little stupor from the dream and gets out of the bed and goes to the bathroom and shouting for Sofia, then he comes round and he is back in reality. And he flops onto the toilet and he realises that he had been having a bad dream, and then suddenly he had this very cold feeling that bad that it made him sit there and every hair is standing on end on his arms, and goose pimples sticking proud on his arms. He just sat there and his telling himself.

"For fucks sake they are getting worse, she was definitely with me in bed I could feel her warm body and touch, God help me, what am I supposed to do, if you are real please help me God."

Pete goes back to bed and he still is not convinced that she was not there, and he did eventually drop off back to sleep. The next morning just like he was told there is a boat to take Pete back to the main land back in Monte-Carlo. On the dock there is a taxi to take him to a pre booked Hotel, he steps out of the taxi, and he is about to pay the cabbie when he is told.

"No it is all taken care of," The taxi pulls away quickly and Pete just stood there with his bag and all of a sudden all hell breaks loose, for there is armed men with automatic rifles, and all in black with masks and some with sidearm drawn and pointed at Pete, and in a loud voice is told to drop to his knees. Well Pete drops his bag at seeing these aggressive men, and Pete puts his hands straight out in front of him and just saying.

"Don't shoot English-English, please don't shoot."

"Down on your knees and hands at back of your head now, or we shoot." Well Pete is nearly shitting himself and does as they say and he kneels and hands behind his head. Well he is shaking with fear, and two approach him with guns pointing at his head, and they barge straight into Pete, and knock him straight to the ground head first, and Pete cracks his head on the pavement. Within seconds he is handcuffed and lying flat on his front and his forehead is pouring with blood from the crack onto the pavement. All that Pete is saying.

"What the fuck have I done wrong, please tell me." They say nothing and pull him up and when they see the blood pouring from his wound they again drop him to his knees, and one waves to another officer and he is seen to by a man all in black with a hood, who attends to his wounds.

After they have seen to him he is picked up, and thrown into the back of a van and hurriedly driven off, as if nothing had happened.

Pete is taken to Police headquarters and all the time Pete while being escorted into the station keeps asking.

"What the fuck have I done, please tell me."

He is taken to a room and sat on a chair in front of a table, and they leave him on his own.

"God it's just like what you see in movies, next two guys will come in and start to intricate me." Pete looks to the wall and just like the movies there is a mirror which is one-way and Pete smiles at the mirror. Then the door opens and just like Pete had said, into the room come two guys with paper work and sit down and said nothing, bar just look at their paper work and turning pages. Pete is the first to speak.

"Is someone going to tell me what the hell I have done wrong? One of the men looks at Pete and tells him.

"That's correct the mirror is a one-way mirror, Mr Pete West of Bulwell Nottingham U.K. and you have been working for Barbara Yates Escort Agencies of London, and have been hired by one Lorraine White, nee Madam Rosita. A top boss in the Mafia."

"Bloody hell, you know everything about me, what underwear have I got on."

"Boxer shorts."

"You are good, I must admit."

"Thanks just a guess." Then he puts his head back into his paper work then the other lifts his head and asks Pete.

"What is your roll, working for one Loraine White?"

"Well if you don't really know, I'm hired to shag the fucking arse off her, that's all, bloody tell me what the hell am I doing here and why fucking treat me like this, just look at my face." Pete turning and looking at the mirror and seeing his reflection with two black eyes, and a large bump on his forehead, where he was manhandled to the ground by the special forces that arrested him.

"Please Mr West, act like a proper English man and stop the foul language in front of Police officers. And the answer to your second question is. The Special Forces only deal with men of violence, and cannot take chances for they are family men and do like to go home at night, to their Family, hence the treatment. Sorry for your injury, but just put it down to experience." Well Pete just sat there shaking his head.

"Please tell me that you know that I have not been involved with this so called activities with this so called Mafia boss, for if I knew I would not go near her with a bargepole."

"We know that you are a good by standing citizen, but we must try and stop people like her from making peoples life's miserable."

"Well if I help you, would you let me go, and promise me that what I seen on that ship does not go any further than you two sitting here."

"I promise you, anything you tells us, we will most certainly keep it to this room only, what have you to say.

Well you know that heist at Heathrow, the missing 500 million Gold bullion, I know where it is."

"What you are kidding us, if what you tells us is the truth, you will be on your way home before you know it."

"Well on Christmas Eve we were putting up trimmings, and I had some large silver balls to put up and needed a hammer. So I went off to find one and going down this passage must have come to a hold, for when I opened the door the whole room was full of Gold bars. And I closed the door just as one of her guards came round the corner, and might I say there are still armed guards on the ship."

"You are telling us that the Gold is on her ship."

"Yes out in the sea off Monte-Carlo." They both stand and thank Pete for the information and one is straight on the phone to report what they had found out. Pete is held there for 6 hours and the difference for he is taken for lunch in the police headquarters restaurant, and after a hearty meal, he is summons back into the room where the two same officers are sitting waiting for him.

"Come Mr West sit for a moment, for I would like to bring you up to date with our inquiries. For starters thank you for your information, and we have recovered the Gold from her charted ship the Rose of the Sea, and no one was injured on both sides, and 6 men have been held under the firearms act and helping with our investigation. But the main point I would like to brink to your attention is the reward for information leading to the recovery of the Gold, of one million Dollars."

"Before you go any further, I do not require the reward, please if you would, would you make me anomalous and donate the money to the Special Forces bereavement fund, for they really do a hard task and have to be very brave with their life at risk."

"Well that is very generous of you Mr West, and I will assure you, no one will know who the person who gave us the information. You are free to go and I will make sure you are escorted back to your Hotel."

Chapter Thirty Two

Pete is escorted back to his Hotel and he books in, and the man on the desk hands Pete an envelope and he opens it and inside, are Airline tickets for the afternoon flight back to the U.K. and 500 Euros for the taxi. Pete reads the note that came with the tickets, and is told of the changes, with certain things happening that it would be safer. Pete is thinking well they do not expect me for if they did, boy I would land up down one of their mineshaft.

Pete the next day sitting in the departure lounge at Azure International Airport, near Nice is sitting and he still can feel the bump on his head, and the two black eyes, and in away his ego is at a low point with not looking his best.

Pete sits looking at magazine and a young English girl comes and asks Pete.

"Excuses me are these seat taken."

"No help yourself, Pete gingerly takes a look at who was addressing him and is bruised eyes light up, for as she sat down he could see her lovely legs in the short miniskirt that she was wearing. She looks at Pete and with his build asks him.

"I hope you don't mind, but are you a boxer, with your masculine build you look like one." Pete looks at her and his eyes are even bigger for she had this gorgeous pear of tits and he tells her.

"No sweetheart, believe me or not, but this was done by the Police when I was arrested, and roughed up. But please, it was a case of miss

217

understanding, you have noticed that I'm a fine fit looking man, well used to be until they did this, but I will survive and get better." Bloody Pete is at it again his fishing lines tangling in the water for his next victim.

"My names Caroline, I'm on my way back to London on this flight and you are."

"Sorry my names Pete, please to meet you." Pete taking her hand and kissing the back of it, and just like Pete when he had just finished kissing her hand goes.

"HULCH, sorry just caught my eye on your hand."

Ho Pete let me have a look." Caroline comes closer to Pete and she is looking straight into his eyes and she tells him.

"You are a very attractive Young man, and those blue eyes of yours, are so appealing."

"Thank you Caroline, and you too are very attractive too. Please forgive me." While Caroline is close to him he goes forward and kisses Caroline fully on the lips and Caroline did not object, for she too starts to open her mouth and enjoying a France kiss. They breakoff and Caroline just looks at Pete and gently caressing his face. They sit talking and the odd kiss and Caroline tells Pete.

"I would not believe it if someone told me that you will meet a man, and within an hour will be kissing him like you have known him for most of your life. I would say they were crazy, but it has happened, I feel so at ease with you Pete, what about yourself."

"I the same Caroline, I would have probably told them the same." Pete leaning forward and they are at it again." They are fully locked in a loving kiss when there flight is announced for boarding, and they are told to go to gate 6.

They make their way and with is being the Christmas holidays the flight is only a third full, and they sit at the back with no one around them. The flight taxis to the runway and takes off for the hour and twenty minutes flight back to Heathrow International Airport. Pete puts a blanket over them and they both settle back and are soon at it again kissing, but this time Pete takes it a little further by putting his hands onto Caroline's breast and foundling them, and Caroline responds by, with her hands under the blanket his rubbing Pete's bulge, and she starts to unzip is flies, and slips her hand into his jeans and pulls out is by now erect penis.

Pete after he had his fill of her tits, moved slowly down and lifts her skirt and pulls back her thong, and he is starting to gently rub her clitoris and insert a finger into her fanny and with his thumb still stimulating her clitoris, well it is not long and she is growing with the pleasure and she tells Pete.

"I'm stopping in London before I catch my train back home, let's stop in a Hotel for the night and finish this off, for I truly want to make love to you Pete." Just as she had said this, a stewardess is coming up the aisle with the drinks tray and they break apart, and readdress themselves.

She approaches smiles at them both and asks if they would like a drink, they have a coffee each and sit looking at each other and Pete tells her.

"The Hotel is going to be my treat Caroline and dinner too." Pete pulls out a piece of paper and writes down his details and contact number and passes it to Caroline.

"Here sweetheart, I would like you to have this just in case I get that involved with you that I forget when we are parting, and I would die if I did not have your details before we part." Caroline did the same and she tells Pete.

"No more for let's have a good time together, and maybe tomorrow will never come." She leans forward again and kisses Pete. They sit talking and kissing, then over the speaker comes the announcement that they are approaching London Heathrow and control tower is bringing them in, so please put all your seat in the upright position and window blinds up for landing, thank you Ladies and Gentlemen we will soon have you back down, and a cool 6 degrees, hope you have a safe journey if you are getting connecting flights.

The plane safely lands and they come out of Heathrow, and they get a Taxi to the main part of London, and they do manage to book into a Hotel and the time by the time they had arrived is approaching 7pm. They are shown to their room. Caroline tells Pete that she is going to have a shower and change for dinner, Pete tells her that he too will have a shower and shave and change.

Pete is in the bathroom just in his boxer shorts and having a shave, when Caroline enters and she slips off her robe, and enters the shower, well when Pete sees her in all her glory, his eyes light up at what beholds him, for she had a truly stunning figure and large breast. She smiles at Pete and enters the shower. Pete hurriedly finishes shaving and he is thinking. Can't wait for tonight, and he slips off his boxers and him already had a full erection? Enters the shower. Caroline turns and faces Pete who just stood there admiring Caroline and he start so tell her.

"You are truly attractive." Before he could say anymore she approaches Pete and presses straight up to him, and she starts to rub a little soap into his back and kissing him at the same time. Pete after they had kissed starts to kiss her neck and he finally lands up, and yes he is working away on her clitoris and fanny, well Caroline after about five minutes is trying to pull Pete's large frame up, for she is truly gagging for Pete to penetrate her. Pete finally rises and she looks Pete up and down and tells him.

"What a fine figure of a man you are, or should I say gladiator, for the size of you, and this bad boy, please Pete make mad passionate love to me now, please. Pete smiles at Caroline and he starts to lift her up a little, and Caroline had her hands on Pete's massif cock and she guides it to its goal and Pete presses her up against the shower wall, and he penetrates her slowly and every inch that she takes she is giving off one big sigh, at every inch she received from Pete. They are truly making the most fantastic love a couple could make, and they must have been at it for well over half an hour, when Caroline does finally explode with one massif orgasm, that makes her quiver all over, and Pete does the same but he withdraws and stood there as Caroline goes straight down onto Pete's cock, and starts to take all of him love sperm. Pete stood there screwing his face up with the pleasure. With the water running all down him and onto Caroline, who just looks up at Pete enjoying what she was doing. Finally after they had showered it was dry off and back into the bedroom, and they are just going to start to change when Pete turns Caroline around and kisses her, well they both flop onto the bed and they are wrapped up like sardines in a tin, kissing and foundling each other, when Caroline looks at the alarm clock and tells Pete.

"Come on darling look at the time it's 9.20, if we carry on we will have no dinner, but let's get dressed and go and have a drink before dinner, they decide to dress and do finally make it to the bar, and Pete gets the drinks while Caroline goes to the restaurants entrance and orders a table for two, and they sit at a table and Caroline tells Pete, that she had ordered a table for 10.15pm. They are sitting having a couple of beer when a waiter approaches them and tells them that their table is ready and he escorts then into the restaurant and to their table. They decide on rump steak and the trimmings and the meal goes down well with a bottle of white wine, and after they go back into the bar and sit chatting till 12.30am. They decide to turn in for Pete's train is at 10am, but Caroline's at 9.30am, they go back to the room strip off and are soon tucked up in bed wrapped around each other. But not like early it was just cuddling and chatting for Caroline had asked Pete if it was alright if they make love in the morning and he agreed. Pete asks Caroline.

"Where do you live Caroline?"

"I never wrote my address just my phone contact, I'm from York and you are from."

"Nottingham, a place called Bulwell." Caroline starts to shed a tear and Pete asked her what is wrong.

"Nothing it's just that I don't want tonight to end, I mean it's only been a few hours with you and look at us in bed and it's if you are my soul mate and I've known you for years."

"What's the difference, when I'm not working I could come up to York and you then can come down to Bulwell, it's not like I'm in America or half way around the World. Anyway tonight is not over yet, come here babe." Pete wrapping his arms around Caroline, and holding her tight and kissing her.

"I love you Pete, I really do, promise me you feel the same way."

"Of course I do Babe, or I would not be here doing what I'm doing now." Another squeeze from Pete and a loving kiss. The time must have been approaching 2am and they finally do drop-off still wrapped around each other.

The next morning they awake and the time is 7.30 am and just like Caroline had said, they do make love to each other, but this time it is slow and ease and very emotional, with Pete on the bed and Caroline being the jockey and taking ease plunges down onto Pete and most of all kissing each other most of the time, it was like they will never do it again, and they both do it with a lot of feeling and they finally both orgasm together, and after start to get ready for their journey home.

Finally at the station they are standing on the platform, where the York train is due in, Caroline standing holding Pete's hand and looking at him all the time and Pete turning and kissing her and then looking back down the track to see if the train is coming. Then from around the bend the train is spotted and it comes rolling into the station and Holts. Caroline kisses Pete one more time and enters and just before she goes to sit down turns and tells Pete.

"I love you my darling Pete."

"And I the same sweetheart I love you too." She sits at a window seat and the train starts to pull away and they both are waving franticly at each other until they see each other no more. Pete turns and all the time the Station master sees Pete and Caroline and he tells Pete.

"It's hard when you have to leave the one you love." The station master smiling at Pete. All that Pete said is.

"That's where you are wrong mate, just some bird I picked up yesterday, shagged the arse off her, now she's gone home." Well the Station master is gobbled smacked at Pete's answer.

Chapter Thirty Three

Pete's train pulls in dead on time and Pete boards and sits at a table seat, pulls out a paper and settled back for the journey back home to Nottingham.

Pete is soon pulling into Nottingham Station then it is off home, He unpacks his bag and takes out is little black book and starts to write down the list of names, of birds he had shagged, and he suddenly tells himself. From now on it" not my little black book, but My Round Robin book, I wonder who will be next. Pete sitting on the bed smiling at all of his achievements over the last few months. That evening he walks down to the Horseshoes and on the way his mobile rings and he looks who is calling and he is surprised to see the name Sandy, he answers and she tells Pete, if they could meet for a drink, for she had some news on vacancies that will be coming up shortly. Pete tells Sandy that he is still full of work down London, how about next week. She agrees and tells Pete.

"That she will ring him later, I love you Pete."

"And I love you too Babe." Pete is thinking, don't want to get too involved there, for she looks the type who would jump at the chance of tying you down. "Not a fucking cat in hells chance."

Pete walks into the Horseshoes and Terry sees Pete and shouts the usual Pete.

"Thanks Terry a pint of mix." Terry brings Pete is drink and looks at Pete's face and asks him.

"What the fuck have you been playing at, kicking fuck out of the other birds fellow."

"I's a long story Pete."

"Well it's not too busy in here yet, it's too early, I'm all ears." Terry leaning on the bar for Pete to start.

"Well it starts by, you know that mafia boss that I went with."

"Ho yes the one you fucked the arse off, and her maids then had guns in your face when she scarpered."

"The same, well that Escort Agency I worked for in London, she know more than hired me, believe it or not, and I landed up in Monte-Carlo on her ship." Terry is clued to Pete's story, Pete tells him about the heist at Heathrow and the 500 Gold Bullion and it being on the ship, and then being arrested.

"Yes but who kicked fuck out of you."

"That was when I was arrested, by French special forces, all in black and looking very menacing, and they made me knee, put my hands on the back of my neck, and then the Bastards knocked me to the ground and that was when I fucked my face up on the pavement."

"Bloody hell Pete you are worse than that James Bond bloke, when the book comes out put my name down for one will you."

"Funny Terry, it was not funny at the time, but there is one good thing about it."

"What's that Pete?"

"Well for the next year I'm on her books, so her contract says that she will send me £3.500 pounds every month, for the next year."

"Well I would wait and see if a cheque drops through your letter box in the New Year, and by the way, what are you doing for New Year Pete."

"Well a few of the lads are going to meet in here at 8pm and all have to be in fancy dress, and we are going to go on a pub crawl around Bulwell pubs, and raise money for Children in need."

"Put my name down Terry I'm up for that mate."

"What you going as then Pete."

"That's a secret, but I've a good idea that might come off." Pete deep in thought about the fancy dress on New Year's Eve.

Couple of days go by and Sandy rings and they decide to meet in a pub on Nuthall Road called the Newcastle Arms.

Pete is thinking, nice drink in the Newcastle and the guys are very friendly

The Newcastle Arms Nuthall Road Nottingham

Pete goes into the Newcastle dead on 8pm and orders his drink and within minutes, Sandy comes in and sees Pete, and her face lights up for she had not seen Pete for a while. She is straight over to him and the first thing she did was give him a long lingering kiss.

"Ho Pete I've missed you so, how have you been and your face what has happened. Sandy's face drops when she realised that he had injuries, for the bruising around his eyes have started to fade but not quite gone.

"Come on Babe let's sit down and have a chat, and what is this news you are going to tell me." They find a table and sit holding hands and Sandy tells Pete.

"Please don't let this go any further, but the other day I accidentally over looked some paper work on Tom's desk, and it was a schedule for upcoming trips abroad and on top of the list was your name, to start on the first day of February. What do you think of that Pete, you are coming back?" Sandy looked more excited than Pete and she asks him.

"Well aren't you pleased at the news then Pete?"

"Yes and no sweetheart, for you see that job I had in London was for an Escort Agency and I'm under contract for one year, and I will not know if I'm under the contract still, until January, for if my wages does not go into my bank then the contract will be non-avoid, and then I could find more work, but till then I do not know."

"Bloody escort Agency, what the fuck have you been up to, fucking the arse off wealthy People then."

"No sweetheart I was only getting £3.500 a month, that's all."

"Fuck off Pete, you must have thought I dropped off a fucking Christmas tree, no one pays that amount for you to make tea for them, more like make tea in the fucking nude, you dirty bastard." Well everyone in the Newcastle are looking at Sandy rant at Pete she just stands up and tells him.

"From this time now, if you get your job back at the coach company, bloody keep away from me, you fucking cheating dirty bastard." She stands and storms off, with one or two of the lads saying to her as she barged by.

"Happy New Year love." And burst out laughing and look back at Pete and he just lifts his shoulders and tells them.

"Some you win, some you lose." Pete stands with some of the lads in the Newcastle and had another pint before he rings for a taxi. He is thinking she is the first to be scrubbed out of my Round Robin book. Pete does eventually land back up at the Horseshoes, and Terry tells him.

"Donna is in the bar if you are interested Pete."

"Thanks for that Terry I will go and say happy Christmas and New Year to her." Pete walking into the bar and looking back at Terry and lifting up his arm in a suggestive way. Pete goes into the bar where everyone is singing to the music and Donna sees Pete and comes over to him and wishes him a belated Christmas and a Happy New Year.

Well Donna is all over Pete and she asks him.

"What are you doing after the pub babe?"

"Nothing, but I would like to give you your Christmas present, that I have forgotten to get."

"Wow I can imagine what that will be, and if I'm not wrong it will be at least ten inches long." Donna looking at Pete and with her tongue out and flicking it up and down, and her eyes going up and down. Pete laughs and tells her.

"Spot on Babe you got it, or will do later." Pete returning the tongue bit. They are in the pub till well over 12.30am and Donna asks Pete.

"Do you want to come to my place for the night or yours?"

"Let's go to yours Babe and have how self's a good time." Donna kisses Pete and tells him.

"Come on then Babe let's go home and you can fuck the arse off me before I fall fast asleep." I'm up for that if you know what I mean."

Donna laughs and puts her hand on Pete's cock and she tells him.

"You will have to hold me Babe for the rooms going round and round for some reason." Pete holds her and pulls out his mobile and phones for a taxi, for he knew that if he walked home with Donna the fresh air would knock her out and that would be good bye leg over. They reach Donna's home and Pete pays for the taxi, and they enter her home. Pete straight away picks her up and carries her up stairs and puts her on the bed, and he starts to strip her off, and Donna is enjoying the whole experience. She is completely in the nude and Pete standing starts to strip while Donna looked on.

"Fucking bloody body you have on you Pete, I bloody hope no other sees what I'm looking at, you are fucking the man, the real man, come my Prince take your Princess and shag the fucking arse off me." Pete gets onto the bed and he goes through his routine by kissing her, then her neck and working down to her tits and giving them a good seeing to till they stood out like two chapel hat pegs, that's her nipples. After he is going down to her fanny and then working away on that. Donna feeling Pete's tongue flicking her clitoris then his tongue working on her fanny is already having an orgasms and she tells Pete.

"Please Pete now before it is too late, for you are making me feel so relaxed that I might drop off while you are fucking me, please now Babe give it all to me." Pete comes up and he starts to penetrate her, and Donna is well lubricated that is why his penis slips straight in and goes to the hilt, with Donna reeling back and sticking her front up at the feeling Pete is doing. Donna is kissing Pete's neck with her leaning up and she starts to bite with the pleasure she is getting, so much that Pete tells her.

"Don't bite sweetheart, you will give me a blood blister here feel this. Pete withdraws then plunges straight back down and that was it Donna screams out with the feeling she was getting from Pete.

"Ho my GOD what are you doing, I'm going to explode."

"Not yet here another." Pete repeats the action but this time speeding up and that was it for Donna by now, is wetting herself with multi orgasms and she screams out to Pete?

"Fucking spunk me now, you fucking bad boy, bloody hell now please." Pete does explode himself and they both are screaming out with the feeling, Pete with feeling Donna's warm juices, and Donna feeling every drop of Pete's warm spunk flowing inside her.

They both flop back and breathing heavily with the whole experience and Donna with arm across Pete's chest tells him.

"Let's hope next Year is going to be as good as this one. I love you Pete, and always will."

"And I will be the same way towards you next year sweetheart for I love you too, for you are always there for me."

"Thank you Babe." Well that was it they both fall fast asleep and are well out of it.

Chapter Thirty Four

It's New Year's Eve, and Pete had been down Town, to collect his costume for the night's event going around Bulwell for charity in fancy costume. Pete puts his costume down on his bed, and showers, after he shaves and the time is approaching 7.30pm, and he starts to dress in his costume. Just before he puts it one, he rubs oil onto his body that he used when showing off his physique.

He has swimming trunks on and then the Roman skirt with the leather straps, and when Pete walks it did not leave much to the imagination, for you could see his bulge through the swaying leather straps. On his chest he had crossed bands of leather and a Golden breast plate, and on his lower arms golden arm bands. He had the roman dagger and small round Gold shield. Pete puts the metal helmet on that is very authentic, even down to the feather plumage on the top of the helmet, and the nose shield. Pete looks in the long mirror and just stood there admiring the image coming back to him, he is saying to-himself.

"Eat your heart out, Russell Crowe, and Arnold Schwarzenegger." When Pete walks along he makes a clanging noise and you could tell he is coming. He sets off for the Horseshoes, and as soon as he leaves the front door he comments to himself, how cold it was, well it is New Year's Eve, and deep into winter. He arrives at the Horseshoes and enters, well everyone stopped drinking and just looked at Pete and admired what they are looking at, and the whole of the shoes went silent. For a laugh Pete draws his dagger holds up his shield and shouts out to all present.

"My Emperor degrees that you all get pissed, so stop looking at one of his centurion and get back fucking drinking, that is an order."

"Too true Pete, you are making their gobs open wide and no beer going down it, come on you heard what the Centurion said, get fucking pissed." Terry the Landlord shouting out, and putting his thumb up to Pete.

"Pint of your best mix Landlord if you please, bring it to your champion."

"Straight away my Lord, this one is on the house, for making the peasants drink more in my tavern." One or two of the lads start to gather in the Shoes, and they are all having a laugh as they come in, for they are in all sorts of daft costumes, some dressed as Women in miniskirts, and stockings and suspenders, and the usual. Some of the lads grabbing there nuts, to see if they had a fanny down there. It was all in good fun, then into the bar comes. The mad hatter, well they all stop and look for he had the full costume rabbit head and the waist coat with all the watches on and running around. Pete looks and puts his dagger to the rabbit's throat and orders him to stop in the Emperors name. The rabbit tells Pete.

"Fuck off Pete." Pete asks.

"Who the fuck are you when you are at home." The rabbit takes the head off and it is Frank from the bus company.

"Hello Frank, my you look fine in that costume."

"Hi Pete, yes but it's fucking warm in it, I hope I don't sweat to death."

"Well let's hope by the morning they don't find one sweated to death, and one with frozen bollocks." Frank laughs and orders his drink and he asks Pete.

"What's it with Sandy, I asked her if she was coming and she asked if you would be there, and when I told her yes, she just said. NO thank you very much, and stormed off." Pete tells him about telling her he worked for an escort agency and that a Woman had hired him for the whole year and she just went fucking loopy and stormed off out, saying that I`m a Bastard for shagging the arse off her."

"We'll have you." Frank asking Pete.

"Frank it's a professional Agency and that sort of think does not go off, it's mainly for what the job entails, being on their arms for functions, with being seen with a beautiful man, so they are the envy of her friends."

"Did you tells her this Pete?"

"She was out of the door before I put my drink down, and there one thing I do not do, and that is run after Women when I've done nothing wrong, it's her loss not mine. Anyway forget it and let's have a great time tonight. By 8.15 all with tins and they set off for the pub crawl for charity. They go in all the pubs in Bulwell and every pub they go in they get a great reception and one or two of the girls are swooning over the size of Pete, who shined in the lights of the pubs lights. Terry the Landlord had hired a coach for them, so they could get more pubs in on the way to Town, and they hit town at 10.0-clock and they enter The Bell, and it is one of the oldest pubs in Nottingham and they have to watch their heads with some of the bars having low beams. They enter one bar in the pub and there is four birds standing drinking on a girls New Year's Eve pub crawl. And one sees Pete and she just turns to her other mates and tells them.

"Fucking hell looks at that gorgeous heap of a guy, fucking hell my knickers are flooding just looking at him, and look at that fucking bulge down there. I'm going to get a piece of that action tonight, just you see." She had very short cropped hair, large tits a miniskirt on and long fine legs right up to her arse, she approaches Pete and she asks him.

"Hi my Gladiator, my names Diana, what are you collecting for."

"Well Hello you gorgeous thing, my names Pete, and we are collecting for a Children in need charity, we are from Bulwell, how have I missed someone like you."

"You haven't, told me Pete have you put something down there to make it bulge like that."

"No bloody not, have a feel if you don't believe me." Pete moving closer to Diana, so not to look to suspicious. Well she is very bold and does have a feel and her eyes light up at what she is feeling and tells Pete.

"Fucking hell Pete, I'm going to see the New Year in with a bang, and not that sort of bang from fireworks, but a bang from this hulk of a gladiator that I behold."

"Well if I were you I would take your hand of my cock, before it burst through my skirt and heads straight for your fanny, that I would like to truly give a good seeing to later, just tag along with us and you could spend the night at my place, and have a good time."

"I will just go and tell my mates that I've scored and are going back with you, fucking hell Pete my knickers are flooding." She walks to her mates and Pete is eyeing up her arse and long legs and he is thinking. "Can't wait to have those gorgeous legs wrapped around my back, and I up to her hilt in her fanny, for fucks sake think of something different or my trunks are going to be filled."

They leave the bell and Diana is clinging onto her investment and Pete giving her the odd kiss, and they do finally decide at 11.o-clock to head back to the Horseshoes to see the New Year in. Pete and Dianna sit on the coach and they are all over each other Pete feeling his interest by giving her tits a good squeeze and rubbing her legs and Diana the same, her hand down Pete's trunks and feeling his cock. They arrive back and Terry takes the tins and goes to count the takings, and at 11.30pm he comes down stairs and onto the microphone, and he asks for silence, the pub responds and Terry addresses them.

"Good evening folks, right I would like to thank the boys who have made the effort to go out and raise money for Children in need, and I have great news to tell you that. The Total for the night's event comes to a grand total of £1,300.00. And 34 pence. What tight bastard put the 34 pence in? But fun and laughter you all have had, and I would like you all to put your hands together and give them a Horseshoes well done." Well they raise the ceiling and all the lads that were in fancy costume are bowing bar one and that is Pete, he just pulls out is dagger and stands chest out and raising it into the air. He looked truly the part, and he receives a bigger cheer from those gathered there.

The time coming up to12.-o-clock and they all stand and they have the T.V. on and at dead on 12-o-clock the sound of Big Ben strikes, and they are all cheering and wishing everybody a Happy New Year. Then it is the Auld Lang Syne, and everyone interlinks their arms and all going up and down singing the song, all in all a good night. Diana asks Pete if they could go, for she wanted to be alone with him. They slip out of the back and up the steps and head for Pete's house, Pete still in his Gladiator costume is clanging as he walks and Diana looks at Pete while she is cuddling up to him to keep warm and tells him.

"I wonder what it must have been like back in the days when Romans were here, I wonder if they ever seen New Year in, in taverns."

"Well if they did, they would have certainly had a sheepskin around them, not walking along just in swimming trunks."

"I know for the cold, if we don't get you in doors soon, it won't be that big boy in-between your legs, but the little shivered up little thing." Diana trying to warm is front up by putting her hand down Pete's front.

"Don't you worry babe you are going to start this year with a bang."

"How much further, Pete it's freezing."

"We are here." Pete putting the key in and opening the door and the first think they notice is the warmth for Pete had the central heating on full.

"Ho that's lovely and warm Pete."

"Yes, we don't want to start off on the wrong foot." Pete helping Diana off with her coat from behind her, he slips it on to the coat rack and starts to kiss the back of her neck, and this gives her a shiver down her spine.

"Ho that is nice Pete." She turns and Pete still with the helmet on, and she removes it, and she could see all of Pete's face and his deep blue eyes.

"You are truly a handsome man Pete, please take me to bed." Pete picks her up and she feels like a Princess, with her man in shining armour in his arms, and he starts to go up the stairs carrying her, and giving her a kiss fully on the lips. Into the bedroom they go and Pete gently puts her down and stands directly in front of her and he starts to pull her blouse above her head, and all the time Diana is mesmerised at the sight of Pete, for they are in the dark but the light shining from the landing is just giving of enough light to see what you are doing in his bedroom.

"Ho Pete you are so gorgeous, please take me." Pete removes her bra and then her skirt, he puts his hand onto her thong and pulls it down and at the same time going down with it, and Diana is looking at Pete's back with the leather straps crossing his back. Pete goes forward and he is straight onto her clitoris and Diana opens her legs wider for her gladiator, and she starts to sigh at the feeling already what Pete is doing to her. She had her hands on the back of Pete's head as he worked on her fanny, he starts to insert one of his fingers while still flickering away with his tongue on her clitoris, and she starts to pull his head further onto her, and by now she is groaning with pleasure.

"Ho my God you are fantastic, the feeling, God Pete." She is trying to open her legs even further and suddenly she has her first orgasm, and Pete could feel the difference in taste as her juices start to flow, and her groans of pure pleasure get louder. She cannot stand it any longer and pleads with Pete to put her on the bed. Pete stands and in front of her and she removes his Roman leather skirt then his trunks and Pete slips off the breast plate and he stood there just in his leather cross bands across his chest, and his arm bands. Diana looks at Pete standing there and she sees his full erection and she comment.

"Leave your arm bands and straps on, you are one mighty looking warrior, now it's my turn.

She goes down onto Pete erect penis, and starts to give him a bloody good blow job, Pete stood there looking at Diana going in and out on his cock and she looked a wonderful sight with her very short blond hair, and those lips wrapped around his cock made him feel like a king, in full command of his Woman. When he had is fill he lifts her up and puts his hands onto her tits and they both just stood there admiring each other's body till Diana tells Pete.

"Please put me on the bed and Fuck the arse off me Pete."

He picks her up, puts her down onto the bed and without a word spoken goes in-between her legs while Diana opens them wide and he penetrates her while still looking at her face.

And he sees her screw it up, with the feeling she is receiving with Pete's ten inch cock, going to the hilt and within minutes she is groaning with pure pleasure. Pete is totally giving Diana a good seeing too, and he puts both his hands on the side of her head, and starts to hold her very short blond Hair and starts to kiss her very passionately. Unbeknown to Diana but Pete is thinking of his Sofia, and he is calling her this why still shagging Diana, it's a good job it's in his mind and not shouting it out. Finally they both come together and are both having one massif orgasm. When Pete suddenly opens his eyes and out of the corner, sees Sofia walk past the bedroom and he hears the spare bedroom door slam. Well he jumps straight out of bed and goes hurriedly to see what it was. Poor old Diana is lying there and her heart is going ten to the dozen, well with shagging, and of course thinking that someone had broken in with Pete moving so fast.

Pete opens the door, and it is absolutely freezing in the room, for there is no heating on in that room, and he enters and all of the hairs on his arms stand out, and Pete had this cold feeling going through him.

"Sofia is that you, please babe talk to me, you are frightening me to death, and what is it that you want." Pete looking around and it is deathly quiet, then he hears a sigh, and all of a sudden the room heats up and the cold feeling stops inside of him. Pete comes out sharpest and closes the door behind him, and he just could not work it out what the hell is going on. He comes back into the bedroom and Diana lying there with the sheet up to her chin asks Pete.

"What was it Pete, what's wrong."

"Everything is alright now, it was the sudden slam of the door, and I thought we had an intruder, but it must have been a draft with the spare window being open." Pete gets back into bed and they both wrap their legs around each other and just lay there kissing and foundling each other till they must have dropped off, still wrapped up together.

Chapter Thirty Five

The next morning they both awake and it is 10am and Pete tells Diana that he is going to shower, well Diana tells Pete.

"Let's shower together and save water. They both go into the bathroom and Pete turns the shower on and they both enter. The first thing is get under the shower and they both start to kiss and then Pete is straight down on her fanny and she is loving it, after when Pete comes up Diana tells Pete.

"Fuck me doggy style Babe." Diana leans onto the hedge of the end of the shower and cocks her arse up into the air. Pete approaches and just like any bloke would do, is looking at her gorgeous arse. He points his cock to her fanny and penetrates her, and he had both his hands on her hips and he is pushing her onto his cock, then pushing her away and back again. After about ten minutes Diana is screaming out with pleasure at the feeling of all of Pete's large cock working away on her, so much that she screams out for Pete to come. Pete does and he stood there and gave Diana every drop of his spunk, and Diana is moaning with the feeling of Pete's sperm warming the insides of her. After she stand and faces Pete and they stand under the warm water and Diana tells Pete.

"Last night and this morning have been fantastic, I just hope you would love to see me again."

"What you are joking aren't you." Well Diana stands back and just said.

! WHAT IS THAT?" Pete pulls her back to him kisses her and tells her.

"Let me finish what I was saying. What you are joking aren't you, for you are truly a great lover and I would be out of my head not to see you again, for I have had the most wonderful sex any Woman could give her man."

"Ho Pete I`m sorry Babe, here let me soap my little friend, or should I say my big buddy down there." She rubs some soap together and starts to soap Pete's cock and at the same time seeing if there is any reaction to what she is doing. Pete returns the complement and starts to soaps up her large tits, and yes you guessed it they are at it again, just like rabbits, anyone would think that they had got to get it all in, for the World is coming to an end. They do manage to do go down and have a little breakfast, and with it being New Year's day the first thing they tell each other when they are finally awake in the kitchen is wish themselves a Happy New Year. Pete takes Diana's details and when she leaves, Pete goes back upstairs and adds her details into his Round Robin book.

Most of the day Pete tidies his pad, up and the rest of the day is sitting watching catch up on the T.V. There is one thing Pete did and the most important thing, is go and fill up the tray on his windowsill, for the Robin that comes to his window. He sits there just looking out at the frost still on the roof tops, and he puts his hands onto his head and just sat there steering outside, and he is wondering.

"Where is my life going? Bloody got involved with my Mafia bird, beat up by Police special squad, bloody Sandy walking out on me, and most of all, seeing my Sofia. Maybe I should just sit back and bloody well shoot myself. And last night, I hope my Sofia as not left me, for I would surely die." Pete is going down on a downer, and he puts his hands well into his head, and just sat there with head forward and just pondering to himself. Then all of a sudden there is this tap-tap on the windowsill, and Pete looks up and it is his little friend the Robin Red Breast. Pete straight away opens the window and the difference, Pete lights up with seeing it, but the most important think is when again it hops onto the windowsill and then onto his finger.

"Well-well, you certainly do know when to come and cheer me up, what do you want little fellow, aren't there enough nuts out there for you or what."

Pete smiles at the bright breasted Robin hopping up and down on his finger and this truly brought Pete back to himself, for he is laughing at the Robins antics. And he is saying to himself.

"Can you imagine me going into the Horseshoes and telling them about my little friend, they would definably have me certified?"

Pete by now is completely back to himself and the Robin finally flies off and Pete stands, takes a deep breath and tells himself.

"With the gym shut, I will do my work out here."

The next month Pete is just spending his time in the gym and unbeknown to him, Frank who works for the coach Company had told Tom about Sandy and Pete, and what had happened in the Newcastle Arms when Sandy walked out on Pete. Then Tom seeing Sandy looking down confronts her.

"Sandy you are well down in the dumps, please you can tell me, for I think you are just like a Daughter I would have loved to have had." Well Sandy breaks into tears and she spills her heart out to him all about what had happened that night in the Newcastle." Well with Tom knowing the whole story tells her.

"You silly Girl, did you see what Pete's face looked like when he was arrested down in Monte-Carlo, for being involved with this so called Mafia Boss. Well I can tell you girl that Frank had been told, by Pete that the job he had with the Escort Agency was professional, and it was is first time with him escorting her to the party, so she looked a million dollars with an handsome man on her arm, that is why he gets paid so much, there was none of this hanky panky, don't you think that Pete would have confided in Frank with them both being men. And one other reason, I have worked with that lad, and I can tell you that, yes he is a Ladies man, but when he met his wife he never did go out with anyone else, and he is the sort of guy who if he met someone new that he felt comfortable with, then he would be truthfully to them and not break their hearts. As he ever broken your heart." Well Sandy sat there with tears streaming down her face, and Tom puts his arms around her and tells her.

"Come on now Babe wipe away those tears and get on the phone and ask him to meet you and sort this out, for it hurts me seeing you like this." Tom kissing her on the forehead. Sandy just kisses Tom straight on the lips and tells him.

"Thank you, that is just like my own Farther would have said to me." Well old Tom just blushed and tells her.

"Go on sweetheart phone him." Well Sandy stands picks her mobile up and leaves the Office. Well even old Tom had a tear in his eye, and just looks at her leaving the office and said

"Bloody kids, who would have um" Sandy does phone Pete and she asks him to meet her in the Nags Head at lunch time at 1pm, at Bobbers Mill on Nuthall Road.

THE NAGS HEAD BOBBERSMILL NUTHALL ROAD NOTTINGHAM

Pete agrees and he is wondering what this is all about, he gets to the Nags Head and goes in and it is one of those pubs with just a long bar, and he

see's Sandy and goes walking over to where she is sitting, and the first thing he askd her is.

"Can I refresh your drink Sandy." She asks him to get her another shandy for she had to get back to work. Pete comes back and passes her drink and asks.

"What is this all about then."

"Pete I would like to humberly appologise at my outrage the other night in the Newcatle, for I was completely out of order with coming straight out with what I said to you."

"What that I'm a Bastard, I forgive you, it ain't the first time, for I know that I've been rotten in the past."

"What brought the change of heart then Babe." Pete streching out and holding Sandy's hands.

"Tom had a Fartherly talk and he told me that you confided in Frank, he told Tom and that was it. But at the time with you just coming out with this £3.500 pounds a week, well you know what us girls are like I just put money and love together and got sex."

"Silly girl, that would have made me a male prostetute, I don't thing so, me a prostetute, on your bike. Anyway lets put it behind us and start a fresh, for I have strong feeling for you Sandy." Pete still holding her hands and leaning forward and planting a kiss on her. Sandy pulls her hands of Pete and puts them onto his face and pulls him further closer, and starts to kiss Pete with her tounge. After the kiss she starts to cry, and she tells Pete.

"Don't worry sweetheart, it's because I have missed you so."

"Well we are back now, so lets make a fresh start." Pete is thinking, I had beter put her phone number back in my Round Robin book. Then Sandy tells Pete.

"Ho yes one more thing, Tom asked me to tell you if you could pop in, if possible tomorrow morning, if that is convenient for you."

"Yes no problem, tell him I will be there at 10.am, after my gym work out."

They sit talking for another half hour and Sandy tells Pete that she had better go, for she had tobe back at work, they kiss one more time and Sandy tells Pete that she will see him in the morning. Pete watches Sandy pull away and he waves to her, and she speeds off down Nuthall Road heading for Bulwell.

Pete goes back into the Nags and finishes off his beer, and is thinking to himself. I owe Frank one for that, but lets hope Sandy does not go all clingy, or we might land up having a few words, for I don't want her clamping my style.

Pete goes into Town and does a little shopping and he pops into the bank and sure enough, there had been a deposit of over "£14.000 Pounds for one months saloury. Pete just stood there and did not realise that he is standing right next to the queue and he sees the amount that had been deposited and just came straight out with.

"Fucking hell, I'm fucking rich." He turns see's everyone looking at him and just tells them.

"Sorry folk's, just the shock at seeing so much money." They just smile and when Pete left the bank, one Woman turns to the one next to her and said. These young ones, and their language, he must have just won the lottery with saying he's rich."

Pete goes on a spending spree, buying the latest fashion deals, trainers and more T-shirts. Coming back from Town Pete had arms full of bags, and gets home and drops the lot onto the floor, and he must have spent over an hour trying this on then that.

That night it was off down the Shoes for a few jars with the lads, and Pete goes into the bar and he see's Frank and goes over to him.

"Come on mate drink up I will get that in." Frank downs the bit he had left and asks Pete.

"Why so cheerfull, have you won the Lottery then.

"No mate me and Sandy are back on talking terms thanks to you and Tom."

"I'm glad about that it might be a lot better now in the mornings seeing her smile and not walking around with a cloud over her head and it pissing down."

"That's not all Frank, tomorrow I've got to go and see Tom, and I have a feeling what about."

"Bloody great, I think I know why too, for it's up on the notice board for drivers who would like to go on long haul trips, to put their names down."

"Hope so Frank it would be nice to get behind a wheel and have all the catle behind you, looking forward to their holidays." Well they all stood laughing and having a good drink and might I say night, and all that Pete could think of is the meeting tomorrow.

Chapter Thirty Six

The next morning Pete is up early and away down the gym, he is there before 7am and one of the first in, he starts the day by pumping iron, and on the machine and doing press ups lying down on the machine and with the bar lifting weights, every now and again he would get up and add more waights to the bar, before lying back down and pumping more.

He had an hour then goes to the pool and starts to excercice by swimming the whole lengh of the pool, and he is swimming for well over half an hour, comes out and goes to the café and had a coffee. He looks at his watch and the time is approching 9.40 and he tells himself, better make tracks for the bus company, don't want tobe late.

Dead on 10am Pete arrives and goes to the office and he see's Sandy sitting and typing, he goes over to her and kisses her, just as Tom comes out of the Office and he see's Pete kissing Sandy well Old Toms got the biggest grin on his face at seeing them back together again. He coughs and said.

"Morning love birds, nice morning for it." Pet sees Tom puts Sandy back down and comes over and shakes his hand, and off course one big hug, well they do go back away. Tom tells Pete to follow him, and they go into the office and Tom tells Pete to sit down. First off he asks Pete if he would like a coffee, and Pete tells Tom.

"If you have one then I will have one." Tom asks Sandy to bring them two coffees. And Tom starts.

"Why I have asked you to come in is to ask you." Then Pete interups Tom and tells him.

"YES you bet I would." Well Tom tells him.

"I have not told you yet, we would like you to start back and take the holiday long haul trips again, and we will pay you £14 pound a week." Tom smiling at Pete.

"WHAT £14 Pounds a week, you 've got to be kidding me."

"Well you did say YES Pete, before I finished, a contracts a contract."

"Come off it Tom, you know what I men't the job, not the wages."

"I know Pete, just having a little fun." Tom sitting there and smiling to himself.

"Pete out streches his hand for Tom to shake and they are shaking hands when Sandy comes into the office and sees them.

"You've got the job then Pete."

"Yes Babe I start on." Pete looking at Tom. Tom looks at his paper wotk and tells them.

"This Thursday, a trip down to Tossa-de-Mar, Stopping at the Golden Palace, just off the front, and only 100 yards from the beach." Then Pete asks Tom.

"Who is the relief coach driver on this trip."

"Well it's Framk, you have been with him before, and with you already have been down to Tossa-de-Mar, I thought it will help Frank with another destination for him to pick up more, imfomation on trips abroad.

"I'm glad it's Frank for he truly puts his heart into the job, with driving and helping out with the guest, when we are at the resort."

"Well Pete lets get you signed up, and you can be on your way home, and I will see you Thursday at 7am, and don't let me down."

"Away with you Tom, I've been waiting for your call, for this is the one and only one job, that I like the best." Pete signs on the dotted line, and he now is a fully signed up coach driver for Summer Sunshine Tours Bus Company.

Pete leaves Toms Office and goes back to where Sandy is and she asks him.

"Pete with it being Tuesday and you go on Thursday, please could we have a date for tonight, for it will be well over a week before that I will see you again."

"OK Babe what about 7pm tonight."

"You're on, and I will drive, where are you thinking of going."

"Well the weathers starting to change for the better, how about we take a drive out to Gunthorpe Bridge, a walk along the side of the trent, and a meal in one of the restaurants there and then, well that is up to you. Sandy smiles at Pete and tells him.

"I will come and pick you up at your house tonight, I will peep you twice on my horn, to let you know that I have arrived."

"OK sweetheart till tonight, love you Babe." Pete leaning over Sandy's desk and kissing her. Just as Tom comes out of his Office and he tells Pete.

"Come on lad play the game, let the Lass get back to work, for there is a lot of time tables to type out before she goes home."

"OK Tom I'm off, don't let the old grumpy fart work you to hard sweetheart, love you." Well Sandy giggles at what Pete had said, all that Tom said.

"That's gratitude for you, just given him a job, and he calls me a old fart. Bless him, and just like you Sandy, I love him too." Well Sandy and Tom giggle and look at each other and Tom tells her.

"Ho well lets get back to running a coach Company."

That evening Pete is readying himself for the night out with Sandy, and he dones his new trainers, and blue geans, and white T-shirt, and puts on a new leather jacket that he brought with the money that had gone into his bank account. He stands combing his hair and looking into his mirror and telling himself.

"Come on now, what bird could refuse this, I bet they would be wetting there thongs, and knickers, just looking at what beholds them, YES ME?" Well talk about vain, he is top of the list of self confidence men. And I bet one or two of you reading this novel are putting your fingers down your throats, at his self believes. He most have stood there for well over ten minutes when he hears beep-beep from outside, and he goes down and opens the door and waves at Sandy telling her that he is coming. He comes out lifts his coller and gets into her car, and Sandy tells him.

"Boy Pete you look absolutely gorgeous tonight, were did you get that out fit from."

"Just went down Town the otherday and picked a few things up, so it's to your opproval then."

"Certainly is, boy I wish I could go down Town and do a shop, just like that."

"Maybe when I come back from Tossa, I will take you down Town and the treat will be on me."

"You're on Mate I will keep you to that." Sandy starting to drive off and heading for Gunthorpe Bridge, and there evening together. I's only twenty minutes drive and they pull up and Sandy parks facing the trent, withone or two boats going by, with people enjoying a night on the river. They do go walking along the toepath that leads to Trent lock, and boats have to pull in and go through a lock, so they can bypass the fast flowing Trent Weir, and might I say there as been one or two accident in the past.

"They sit looking at the water cascading over the weir, and Pete starts to go into a little daydream, with being memorised by the water, he suddenly said to Sandy.

"It reminds you a little of life, I mean looking at the water rushing over the wier, and never going back. Just like us humans, rushing along day by day, and never going back." Sandy giggles at what Pete had said and tells him.

"Well if you did go back, you would be the first and only one to have invented the time machine."

"You know what I mean, life is to short to stop and reflect on life, for if you did, time would still be going over the weir, if you get my drift."

"Point taken, come on morbid lets go and have something to eat." They both stand and walk off hand in hand back to the first restaurant. They enter and are shown to a table, where Pete orders two glasses of white wine, for Sandy could only have the one with driving them back later.

They both have rump steak with all the trimmings, and the whole evening is a sucsess, after the meal Sandy asks Pete what he is doing after. Pete tells her.

"Well you could come and stop with me for the night, or we could have a little nooky in your car after." Pete touching her leg under the table.

"In my car indeed, no thank you very much, you won't catch me hanging my legs out of the window and being cramped up, no thank you, when I make love I would sooner be in comfort. But why not come back to my home, for Mum and Dad are away down at the caravan, opening it up after the winter, and readying it for the new season."

"Ok Babe your place will do, are you ready to go now, then we could have a drink back at your home." They start to go and Pete paid the bill and they start to head for Sandy's home.

Sandy parks up and they go in and Sandy goes to the fridge and pulls two beers out of the fridge and pours them into glasses and takes them into the lounge where Pete had turned the box on and had football on.

"I hopes we are not going to watch twenty two men run around a pitch, kicking a bag of wind about, are we." Sandy giving Pete a gleare.

"I surpose not, it is only Manchester United verses Chelsea." Pete puts a movie on and they snuggle up watching. They have a coulpe of beers and start to kiss lying on the long settee, and before long Petes hands start to undo her zip on the back of her dress and Sandy undoing Petes geans and then unzipping his flies, before long they were down to their underwear, and kissing profusly each other. Pete slips her knickers off, then her bra, and starts to fondle her breasts, and going down and kissing her nipples. Sandy removes Petes boxer shorts, and she gets down onto a white sheepskin rug, that was in front of the fire.

Pete follows her down and she had the gas fire on just to take the spring coldness out of the air, and Pete starts to kiss her tummy and sliding his tongue down to her fanny and Sandys legs open wide as Petes head approched. Pete is soon flicking away at her clitoris and he starts to incert his fingers into her fanny, so she could feel the pleasure of his tongue and his fingers, working away and it did not take long for Sandy to have her first orgasm, and she is breathing heaverly and sighing with every move Pete made.

"Pete suddenly rises and goes in between her legs and he had a masif hard on and Sandy with both her hands on Petes cock guides it to her fanny and Pete press's forward and he starts to penetrate Sandy, well that was it, she is shouting out for Pete to speed up. Pete is thinking fuck me she is completely having massif orgasms, it must be with being back together. He does start to speed up and Sandy is already praying to her God, for every thrust Pete makes she is shouting out.

"Ho my God Pete."

By now Pete could feel is cock starting to tingle and he knew that he is about to come, so he really starts to bash away and they both finnaly do explode, Sandy well and trully shouting and Pete blowing his top into her, and Sandy with every drop of his warm sperm is moaning with the warm feeling that Pete is giving her.

They both laid there wrapped around each other, and the warm glow of the fire on their body made it feel really relaxing. They are kissing each other and complementing how good it was.

Chapter Thirty Seven

They must have laid there for well over an hour, and Pete did do it again, and after Pete picks Sandy up and he carries her to her bedroom, and laid her down on the bed and Pete gets in beside her, and they snuggle up for the night, and before long they are both fast asleep. Sandy is the first up at 7am and then Pete, for she had to be at work and Pete as normal is going down the gym for he had only one more day left before he goes to Tossa in Spain.

Pete goes to the gym and on the entrance he is met by a rep, who as soon as he see's Pete asked him.

"Excuse me Sir, could I ask you for your opinion for a moment."

"Well that depends on what you require, mate."

"It won't take long, but I could not notice that you are well into your body building, and I was wondering have you ever thought about taking out life insurance, for any unexpected thing that might happen to you." Pete stood there looking at him straight in the eye's, and the rep, he stood there quivering at the look Pete is showing him, and he tells him. And might I say sticking out his chest.

"The last thing on my mind at this moment in time is, how much waights can I do today, not must fucking make sure I'm covered for DEATH."

"Ho thank you for your opinion Sir, thank you." Pete still glaring at him as he walked away, and Pete saying to himself. "Fucking phoney phone calls from home, now bloody dickheads asking the same thing, while you are doing your normal routine things." Pete goes into the gym and sets up the wights on the bar, while the bar is on the rack. He lays down on the apparatus and puts his arms up onto the bar and takes the weight, and lifts it up and he is into his routine, pumping iron.

Pete is really starting to sweat and the training instructor who is walking around the gym, keeping an eye on the members using the gym are OK, He approches Pete and asks him.

"Please do not over do it mate, you are working up a sweat there, watch you're heart rate, we don't want you collapsing on the equipment now do we."

"That will be the day, just another 15 minutes and I will be done." Pete blowing as he answered his question. Pete compleats the time and comes of the equipment, stands tightens his chest and tells himself.

"Well that was a good work out now for a swim."   Pete walking out of the gym, and going by the trainer who spoke to him and he tells him.

"Thanks for being concerned, now off for a swim."

"You're welcome Sir, all part of the service, enjoy your swim, and catch you later." Pete goes to the pool and does his routine in the pool and after, while getting changed he suddenly thinks, I have not seen my Sofia since the day at Christmas when she walked across my landing and went into the spare bedroom, and it went warm. God I hope she as not left me. He sat there with the towel in his head and he heares someone say.

"You alright Mate, you look like you are not feeling well." Pete looks up and he could nor beleave what he see's for he must have been the most skinniest man walking the planet. Pete stands up and right in front of him, and might I say bloody well towering over him, tells him.

"Yes I'm just sitting trying to come back down to earth with one hell of a work out."

"You are not kidding me, mind the language but you are one fucking giant of a man, boy I wish I could look like that one day." The guy flexing his upper arm and this tiny little lump appeared on his arm. Well Pete could hardly contain himself from bursting out laughing and tells him.

"Well go down to the gym and see the training instructor down there, and maybe in a year or two you too could look like this." Pete bending his arm and the most biggest bulge on his uper arm where is muscele stick well out, and the little guy is just flabbergast at the size of it.

"Thanks mate, I`m off down there now." The little guy walks off and with his little chest sticking out trying to look like Pete made Pete just burst out laughing.

"Bless him, that's what I like to see determination in a guy."

Pete spends most of the day readying his bag for the trip on Thursday, and at the night time, he goes into the Horseshoes, for only a couple of pints, for he had to be up early in the morning to go to Tossa-De-Mar in Spain for the week. Into the bar comes Frank and Pete see's him.

"over here Frank" Pete putting up his arm to catch Franks eye. Frank see's Pete and comes over.

"Hi Pete looking forward to the trip tomorrow, have you been down there before." Frank asking Pete.

"Ho yes Tossa brings back one or two memories, the first time I went down to Tossa was with old Tom."

"What the Manager." Frank not believing what Pete had said.

"It's true, we were in the canteen when into the canteen came the manager and told Old Tom that he is taking me down to Tossa, and old Tom came straight out with. "Sounds about right, TOSSA." Well Frank burst out laughing and said, I cannot see him as a bus driver at all.

"That's because it's before your time Frank, come on lets sit and have a talk at that table over there." They sit and Pete takes out a coin and tells Frank head's or tails. Frank calls heads and he wins, and Pete tells him.

"You win, so you are driving from Bulwell to the services, then I will take second stint driving down to Dover."

"it's one more pint for me, then home and an early night, I cannot wait to get back behind the wheel, and on our wat to Tossa, Pete telling Frank.

"Let's hope that there is one or two dolly birds going, on the trip." Frank rubbing his hands together.

"That's my boy Frank now you are learning, come on lets have one more then home, and roll on tomorrow." Pete standing and going to the bar.

Then into the bar comes Donna, she goes over to Pete and tickles him in his side and Pete turns and see's her.

"Hello Babe, what's your pleasure. Just half I have been summonesed round to Mums so only can have the one then off, but I'm glad I've caught you, for I was wondering if we could make a date for tomorrow night, I'm gagging for it.

"HO Donna, I'm bloody off to Tossa tomorrow Babe for a week, you will have to keep it in the fridge for a week to keep it cool for me." Pete putting his hand onto Donna's arse.

"Shit just my luck, will you miss me Pete." Donna starting to rub Pete's chest.

"I've one think to say to you sweetheart and that is, roll on when we are back, and I will defenatly." Then Pete wispers in her ear, so no one else could hear. "I will fuck the living daylights out of you and make you sqeel like a pig with mad passion."

"Stop it Pete or you will make me say fuck Mum, and take me and ravish me, like you have never had it for months." They both laugh out loud and Donna drinks her half and tells Pete.

"Must dash, for Mum will be wondering where I'm at, see you in a week Pete, and you bloody well behave yourself, watch him for me Frank, loves you both." Donna kisses Pete then Frank and goes. Frank looks at Pete and tells him.

"You two aren't seeing each other are you, for you have Sandy who is your girlfriend."

"Frank remember one thing, I have only one Woman in my life and she has gone, God bless her and she will be the only one, and for the rest. Well just look at what you see, which other Woman could resist this." Pete takes a deep breath and shows off his, physique to Frank, and with one or two of the customers looking at him. Frank looks at Pete and he is thinking, "He's still missing his wife Sofia, but the fool does not realise, that one day he is going to get his comeuppance if he is ever caught out, with messing about with other Women." Frank just shaking his head at Pete who is still turning and showing off his physique, to those who were still looking.

They both finish their beer and say their good night and will see each other at 7am in the morning. Pete heads up the steps that lead to Highbury Vale, and he stops at the entrance to St. Marys church and the time is only 9pm, he just looks upto the door and he just could not stop himself from going up to the door entrance, and stopping, and he stands there and starts to talk to his Sofia.

"My darling Sofia, Ho how I miss you my love, the pain sometimes is overwhelming. Pete leans up against the entrance and starts to sob, when all of a sudden, someone touches his shoulder and asks if he is OK. Pete just jumps out of his skin and came straight out with.

"Fucking hell, what away to get someones attention, my heart." Pete holding his chest and feeling the bump-bump of his heart beat.

"Sorry my son, I did not mean to startle you, you see I 'am about to lock up for the night. If I'm not wrong you are the same Lad that came the other day into my church." Pete realising that he is the Vicar apologizes profusely over his bad language.

"What is wrong now my Son, why the crying and the visit again." The Vicar putting a reassuring hand onto Pete's shoulder. Pete sat down on a very old stone bench that is in the doorway and he tells him about seeing Sofia and now it had stopped. And that he had come over with guilt that he as driven her away, and he now is on his own, with out her. Then Pete asks the Vicar.

"Why a'm I up one minute without a care in the World, and the next down on my knees like at this moment, for you see Tonight I was on a high for I`am going to go back to a job I love in the morning, and that is driving a coach, down to Spain.

"Well my Son your first question is no you have not lost your Sofia, for she is at rest now, and if I am not mistaken she is your soulmate, so take heed that you will one day be together, for it is Gods will. Then we come to your mood swings, this will keep happening until, one day you let her rest and sleep, but till then, maybe she will return for if you are not happy, then it will be the same for your Sofia." Pete just sat there still with hands on his head and leaning forward. Then the Vicar puts his hand in his pocket and holds something in his hand and he asks Pete to look at him. In the dim lit doorway Pete looks at the Vicar and the Vicar tells him.

"If I'm not mistaken your Sofia would have been Catholic, so here my Son take this and when you feel you are going to go on a downer, pull this out and look at it and talk to your Sofia through this and Jesus Christ." He gives Pete a gold crucifix, with Jesus Christ on a cross.

"Vicar you cannot give me this, it belongs to you Sir."

"No my Son, it belongs to the one who seeks help from our Lord, take it with my blessing and the blessing of our Lord." The Vicar with both his hands on Petes and he is saying a little prayer to our Lord to take care of his Son Pete.

Then the Vicar tells Pete that he had to go for he had to lock the church gates. Pete thanks the Vicar for his valuble time and leaves back down the pathway and he felt a lot better.

Chapter Thirty Eight

The next morning Pete is up and the time is 6am and he wakes with the cross that the Vicar gave him and he goes to a draw and pulls out one of Sofias gold chains and puts the crucifix around his neck and tells himself, now like the Vicar told me, if I go on a downer, I will always have it with me.

Pete dresses and dones his blue shirt and company trousers, after he had showered and shaved, down stairs for a little something to eat, and then with bag in hand, and off to the depot for the start of the holiday down to Spain.

Pete arrives at 7.30am and goes into the canteen, and who should come in is Sandy and the first thing she does is kiss Pete, and tells him that she will miss him while he is away.

"Don't worry sweetheart, one week and then back and we will go out on the Monday I get back, and go and have a meal in the Hut were we had our last meal."

"That will be loverly Pete, and don't say anything but Tom's got a surprise for you and Frank when he comes."

"Whats that then Babe."

"You will have to wait and see."

"Well thanks for putting us on our horse then knocking us off again." Sandy walking off and smiling at Pete. Then into the canteen comes Frank and drops his bag near Pete and the first thing he asks Pete is have you the key to the coach, so we can put our bags in."

"Not yet mate and Tom's got a surprise for us both."

"Whats that Pete." Franks eyes lighting up.

"Don't ask me when Sandy told me I had the same answer.

Dead on 8am Tom comes into the canteen and said Good morning to the boys.

"Right Let me see yes, Pete and Frank you two are going to go down to Tossa-De-Mar in Spain, and you are in for a surprise lads, for look what I have." Tom holding up some keys, and Pete shouts out.

"The keys to the vault at the bank of England, then."

"No you daft sod, the keys to the latest coach that had just been brought out."

"Whats so special about that then Tom." Pete looking at Tom for a answer.

"Well you know with it being 2032 and that Europe have been installing the latest technology onto their Motorways, well you are going to drive a coach down to Spain that needs no driver, yes the latest coach on the market. Boy wait till you see it." Tom getting a little excited at showing them the new coach. He tells them that everyone that is going are assembled at the departure point, and tells Pete and Frank to follow him to the new coach in the coach park.

Pete and Frank pick up their bag and follow Tom, into the coach park and they stand next to this brand new double decker coach, and both Pete and Franks eyes are well and truly wide open at seeing such a magnificent Coach.

"Come on lads let me show you before you pick up the passengers."

Tom opening the door to the coach, and all three of them enter and Tom sits down at the wheel, and starts to explain to the boys.

"Right here you see the normal starting procedure for starting the coach, but look at this device here. When you enter the Motorway and go into the coach lane, this light here will turn red and it will take over your controls, and all that you have to do is sit back take your hands of the wheel and the coach will take you to the end of the Motorway. Is that good or what." Tom sitting there with the biggest smile on his face. Then Pete asks Tom.

"Well when we see the red light come on, can we leave the coach on its own and go and make mad passionate love to the passengers then."

"NO you bloody well cannot, for if it's your turn at the wheel, then you have to stop with it just in case of any emergencies."

Pete goes walking back to the back of the coach and he is well impressed with the drinks area, and the extra toilet room that you have, all that Pete is thinking is. "I wonder when I will get the chance to christen this." Pete standing there with the biggest grin on his face. Then Frank comes up and tells Pete.

"Boy we will have to make sure we don't fuck this baby up or we will be for the high jump." Pete tells Frank.

"Come on then lets go and see who the pundits are, I bloody hope we have some young ones going, or it's going to be a boaring run down there."

Pete going back to where Tom is and they tell him.

"This has to be the best coach in the fleet Tom." Pete telling Tom.

"Yes and for Gods sake Pete look after her like you would a new young Babe." Pete takes his cross out of his top kisses it and tells Tom.

"Don't you worry Tom we will bring her back just as we started, believe me." All three of them come of the coach and Pete turns round to Frank and tells him.

"You are first mate back on the coach and bring her round to the departure leaving point, and I will go and pick up the guest list and the paper work."

Tom leaves them and just before he goes just tells Pete.

"Do your best for me Pete, for I will be nerve-wracking till you get back my Son."

"Don't you worry Dad, she's in my hands and you know what I'm like with Women."

"Yes they are normaly naked at the end, when they have been with you. Don't forget that the coach is a different body" Well Pete burst out laughing at what Tom had said and he just blows a kiss at Tom and shouts to him.

"See you in a weeks time Dad, and just sit back and relax."

Pete picks up the passenger list and the job list for when they get there, with trips that have been prearranged for the passengers, and Pete goes to the front of the coach where the passengers are waiting to board.

Frank sitting at the wheel and Pete outside at the entrance and the first passengers start to board and Pete puts their case into the hold, he had boarded about twenty and they were mostly old passenger when Pete is thinking, "Fuck me it's the Derby and Jones fucking trip." When all of a sudden as he is bending just putting the last coulpes cases in gets a squese on his bum looks up and all thet he could see is four birds standing ther in short miniskirts and showing a lot of leg, and Petes eyes suddenly stand out at seeing such loverly legs.

"WHO JUST FELT MY ARSE THEN, Pete standing and showing of his fine body to them.

"It was me gorgeous, I hope you did not mind for I just could not resist touching a hulk like yourself." Pete stands close to her and tells her.

"I don't mind in one bit, so long as we can follow it up later, and I could do the same to your arse, but in a more passionet way, if you get my drift." Pete puckering up his lips and lifting his eyebrows at her.

"We have a date, my names Rita, and your's is."

"Pete, and if one of your mates fancy Frank who is driving first let me know, sweetheart." Rita joins her friends and she tells them what she had just done.

"That fucking big hulk at the front, is going to shag the arse off me when we get there, and he has a mate who is driving first, so if anyone of you would like to make up a foursome let me know." Rita telling them all about the pinching of his arse. All boarded and Pete goes to Frank and tells him that we are fully loaded and ready to rock and roll. Frank still getting used to the new controls tells Pete.

"Have you seen this Pete, look it has the latest selfdrive mode, for when we get on the french and Spanish motorways, that is in force since 2031." Pete looking and he tells Frank.

"We will have to try that out, for it does not start in the UK till next year. You drive off Frank and I will welcome them all abouard the coach." Pete stands at the front while Frank pulls away and it is a double decker, so Pete is on the large screen up stairs for the passengers up there, who could no see their host while he talked.

"Good morning Ladies and Gentlemen, and welcome on board this brand New Coach obtained by Summer Sunshine Lines Coach Company of Bulwell. For your Holiday down to Tossa Spain, I am Pete your co-driver and rep, and driving the first leg is Frank your second rep. If there is anything that you require during your Holiday, then come to myself or Frank and we are up for it at anytime that you require us." Well I don't think Pete worded that right, for all the young ones on the coach, are wolf whistling and cheering Pete and Frank.

"Please-please, you know what I mean." Then one of the four girls shout out.

"Yes we come up to you, you drop a pound on the floor, and when we bend down sticking our arses up in the air, it's bingo time for yourself." Well half the coach are laughing at what she said and Pete tells them.

"Alright that's enough of the banter, please lets get back to the trip. First we are going to go down the M1 heading for Dover, and we will stop just after London for refreshments at one of the services, then head down to Dover for the ferry crossing to Calais in France, then a overnight coach drive down to Spain. We should have you into the Hotel for tea time, for you to catch the last sunrays of the day. So sit back and enjoy the view, you will find that the drinking area for tea and coffee is a lot larger, and also the toilet at the back of the coach on the ground floor. Thank you." Pete goes up to Frank and tells him.

"God these are going to be an hand full, and I just hope that they settle down and sleep tonight, we don't want the young ones spoiling the Darby and Jones lot. What's the coach like to drive then Frank."

"Once you are use to the controls, boy I would be well pissed off if we have to drive one of the old ones again, this seat is so well sprong, you don't feel like you are on a coach."

"I will look forward for my turn then." Pete going and siting down in the well at the front with the driver, next to him. They are travling for just over two hours and they finnaly pull into the services for a short break, just before they leave the coach, Pete tells them that they will only be stopping for fourty five minutes, then back to the coach for the rest of the journey down to Dover. Pete helping them off and the four girls wait till everyone had gone and they come down the steps, Rita is the last off and she stands talking to Pete as Frank and the other three go walking off towards the services. Rita asks Pete.

"I'm not really interested in a drink, how about you showing me the new coach then." Rita putting her leg onto the coach step and her miniskirt riding up reveling a lot more leg. Pete having a ganda tells her.

"Come on then love let me show you the back and all the room you have now in the toilet." Rita smiling at Pete and telling him to lead the way.

Chapter Thirty Nine

They go walking up the coach with Pete behind Rita, and Pete is looking at her long legs and I think he his starting to get an hard on just looking at what he is about to receive. They come to the back and Pete opens the door and tells Rita.

"After you sweetheart." They enter and Rita turns round and straight away gives Pete a kiss fully on the lips, and it is tongues and they are down each others throat. Rita breaks away and tells Pete.

"Ever since I clapped eyes on you I knew that I wanted to shag you, your bloody marvellous, come here." Rita starting to unbutton his shirt and pulls it down his back and exposing his massive chest. Well straight away Rita is rubbing Petes chest and his nipples.

"MY God you are one hell of a guy." She is breathing heavenly and starting to undo his trousers and she soon had them off, and pulls down his boxer shorts and when she see's Pete's erect cock just shouts out.

"My fucking God you are not only well built, but where the fuck did this big fucker come from." She is straight down onto Pete's cock and giving him one hell of a blow job, and Pete just stood there enjoying every mouthful that she was giving him. Pete while she is sucking him off, opens her bra and starts to foundle her tits and playing with her nipples, till they stood out like two chapel hat pegs, and he pulls her up, off his cock, for he wanted it to last a little longer. Pete puts his hand under her miniskirt and to his surprise she had no knickers on, and Pete was straight onto her fanny and clitoris, and he starts to return the complement that she had just given him. Pete's tongue is going ten to the dozen flickering her clitoris and going deep into her fanny, till he could tell that she had come, not only the taste of her juices but also the noise she was giving. He rises and with his hand guides his cock into her fanny, and at the same time lifting her up onto the baby changing board and starts to really bash away at her. They had been at it for well over twenty minutes, and Rita by now was screaming at Pete to come, for she is having one hell of an orgasm, and Pete does start to come and witdraws, and Rita jumps off the baby changing board and goes straight down onto Pete's cock, and he starts to ejaculate and Rita is swallowing every drop of his love juices. After she comes up and they are just standing in one long kiss and after Pete tells her.

"Come on Babe we had better get out and go and get a quick cupper before anyone comes back." Rita cleans herself up and leaves, Pete just stood there and he looks into the mirror and he see's his crucifix around his neck, and he holds it and looking into the mirror, and he could feel himself starting to go down on a downer.

"Please not now, for I could not cope with it, Sofia please forgive me Babe, He kisses the crucifix. He stands there and he could feel himself starting to swell up in the eyes, and he just slams his clench fists down on the board and tells himself. "NO WAY." Turns and goes out of the toilet to the front of the coach, just when the first passengers were coming back from their break.

"Welcome back, I hopes you enjoyed your break and we will soon be on our way to Dover." It is not long and they are all back and Frank does the head count with it being Petes turn to drive. He approches Pete and asks him.

"Did not see you in the services Pete, what did you do."

"Just stayed around the coach, well it's my turn to drive and did not want to knock back tea with driving, or I would be running for a pee every ten minutes."

"OK Pete all accounted for, lets hit the road and don't forget that the controls are different." Frank standing looking at Pete pull away out of the Motorway services.

"You are right Frank she does drive different, and boy this seat is sure comfortable, might just sit here and drive all the way to Spain." Pete turning and smiling at Frank.

"You're on there Pete I will just sit here and put my feet up until we get there."

"In your dreams Frank, just a figure of speech."

They both smile and it was back concentrating on the driving, and in away took Petes mind off his Sofia, and the hard time he seems to be going through, with coping with his lose. They arive at Dover just after 1.30pm and are booked in for the 2.30pm sailing, and Pete pulls up at the bus loading bay, and everyone disembark's to go to customes, while Pete and Frank stop with the coach until it is on the ferry. They all make it through customes and meet up on board with some off the passengers who ask questions about the trip, and with Pete and Frank being their reps answer their questions. They finnaly meet up with the four girls and they sit down. Well Rita had only eyes for Pete, for I think with being with Pete, she had not told her friends, for she wanted him for herself, and of course not a word about Pete fucking the arse off her, so if she did they would be all after him. One of the girls tells Rita.

"Come on Rita introduce us to Pete, and Frank, tell them our names." Rita looks at her mates and starts to tell Pete and Frank.

"Pete Frank, the girl there." Rita pointing.

"That is Sam, the one next to her is laze Jane, for she likes lying in, in the morning.

"That's OK so long as she has her fellow with her." Pete giving her the eye, and she tells him.

"If it was you Pete, we would be in bed until dinner, and maybe a litle longer." Jane returning the complement by lifting her eyes at Pete and puckering up her lips at him.

"Alright lets get back to the names only please, next you have Pearl shes the gem of the party, gem get it." Rita waiting for the bum-bum, but they just sat there looking at her.

"Alright then, girls this is Pete and Frank." Well the boys shake hands and might I say a kiss, and I don't think Rita liked that bit, for they were trespassing onto her territory. Then Jane shuffles up to Pete and leans forward and starts to talk, and by the way her tits were laying across Petes forarm, and I think Pete is liking this for he keeps lifting up his arm a little to feel more. Rita see's this and just came straight out with.

"Get your tits of his fucking arm, any closer and they would be in his face." Rita telling Jane in abrupt voice.

"Ha Rita it's OK she's got a loverly pair of tits, and they are fine laying there, you don't mind Jane do you." Well Jane tells Rita.

"If Pete does not mind then I don't and to your question if Pete would like them in his face well sobe it. She know more stands puts her hands on the back of Petes neck and rubs his face into her tits. Well Rita stands and storms off and the other two girls follow her with Frank in hot pursuit to try and calm them down. This leaving Jane and Pete alone. Pete tells her.

"Your tits are loverly Babe I would not mind a suck on those babys."

"Well maybe when we get there we can make a date for you to feast on them Pete."

"I will keep you to that Jane but keep it to yourself, Rita looked a little jealous at seeing you do that."

"Don't worry about her, she does have mood swings like that, she will soon be alright, you know she's like one of these that likes to keep all her toys to herself, I will go and see if shes calmed down."

It's only an hours crossing and the ferry is soon pulling into Calais France, for then to continue their journey down to Spain. Frank takes the coach down to the customes cleared area to pick up the passenger, and all aboard, and might I say Rita appologiseing to Pete for her out burts, Pete tells her not to worry and he is thinking that Jane is right she soon calmed down.

Frank drives off and he soon hits there Motorway, and he goes into the coach lane that is separate from the other uses and as soon as he starts to go down the coach lane, there is a flashing and sound on his dashboard, and Pete looks confused, then a voice tells Frank who is driving.

"This is One-Start Automatic control, taking over control of the Coach." Frank sitting there and wondering what is going off, when all of a sudden he shouts out.

"Whoa look," Frank feeling his foot being released off the pedal, and the steering wheel doing it's own think, and Frank turns to Pete and tells him.

"Boy this is a queer feeling not being in control." Just as he had said this a voice asks for their destination, and to speek now." Well with Pete standing there tells the voice that they are going down to Tossa-De-Mar Spain.

"CALCULATING ONE MOMENT." Pete looking at Frank and telling him.

"What next androids inviting you on board, and that will be our jobs gone."

"Route inputted, and clearance into Spain, no need to stop at check point, we have clearance to continue, when we reach the Spanish boarder." Frank sitting there like a lame duck looks at Pete and asks.

"Well can I get up and go for a wee then."

"Good point, I bet alarmbells will go off, stand up and see Frank. Yes as soon as Frank stood up off the seat an alarm bell sounds on the dashboard, and when he resat it stops.

"What the fuck is the use then, if we have to sit here, doing fuck all." Frank looking at Pete.

"It's just for safty reasons, you know like the driver of an express train just sits there, but he is there just encase of an emergency. Anyway if you did need the bathroom, it would let you swop drivers, so in one way it saves pulling up and swapping drivers." Well Frank sat back and tells Pete.

"OK you relax and I will give you a shout in four hours." Pete starts to go down the coach seeing to the needs of the passengers and he goes by the girls who ask Pete.

"Will we be stopping in the morning for breakfast then, it will be along journey if we are not going to stop."

"Don't you worry love, we will be stopping off for dinner before we carry on driving through the night, and yes, there also will be a stop in the morning for breakfast, so sit back and watch the film that will be starting in ten minutes, or the scenery of France."

"Sam looks at Pete then back out of the widow, then back at Pete and tells him.

"Fucking scenery of France, we are on a fucking Motorway and wow look another fucking bridge." Well all the girls are laughing and Pete too, and also one or two of the passengers.

"Sorry about that love, but we want to get you there as soon as possible, not taking days going through the back streets of France babe."

"Only kidding Pete, look a nother fucking bridge, I wonder how many more we will see." Pete walking off smiling at her, He goes upon to the upper deck and walks along asking them if they are alright, and after goes back down and to the back and makes himself a coffee. While he making it, Pearl comes up to him and asks if he could make her one, Pete abliges and they sit at a table in the drinks area and Pearl asks Pete.

"don't think of me as forward, but since we got on the coach, I've had the hots for you, and I was wondering if you would like a date when we get there." Pete looks at Pearl draws closer to her and kisses her fully on the lips and at the same time running his hand up her leg onto her knickers and having a feel, and not a movment out of Pearl, but just opening her legs a little wider for Pete to get more of a feel. They break and Pearl tell Pete who by now is fingering her, tells him.

"Fucking hell Pete I Want you to fuck me now."

"Go into the toilet and I will follow in a moment." Pearl is up like a flash and into the toilet and Pete stands looks to make sure no one is looking and enters and bolts the door and Pearl had already removed her knickers and she goes straight for Petes zip, and he to stood there and Pearl looks at Petes erect cock and coments.

"Fucking hell Pete, you bloody well be careful with that fucking big bad boy.

Don't worry babe, you will enjoy believe me. They start to kiss and Pearl playing with Petes cock, and she puts it onto her fanny and starts to rub is bell end around her clitoris, and she starts to groan with the pleasure of feeling Petes massive tool on her clitoris. Pete lets her have her fuzzy out of his cock, and then lifts her up onto the baby changing board, and just like he did with Rita incerts his cock slowly into her, and pulling her forward onto his cock with his hands on her arse. Pete goes slow at first and gradually speeds up as he penetrates her more, and before long Pearl is trying to stop herself shouting out to the world, she is bitting onto Petes neck and she suddenly tells Pete to fucking well come or she is going to scream out, well Pete goes that little bit faster and he does explode at the same time as Pearl who by now is digging her fingers into Petes back with the pleasure of feeling Petes warm spunk inside her. They both had a great orgasm, and they slowly come back down to earth and start to clean themselves up, dress and Pearl leaves first, and Pete stands there with a cloth washing the sink when a passenger enters, and Pete looks at then and tells them.

"Just finnished wipping the sink and everything is fresh again, Pete going by the passenger and leaves. Pete is thinking that was close.

Chapter Fourty

The four hours soon pass and Frank taking back control of the coach and pulling into the sevices, so the passengers could have dinner before setting off for the overnight drive through the last leg of France and down into Spain, then on to Tossa-De-Mar. They all leave and go into the restaurant and Pete had told them that it is an hour stop over, so don't rush their meal. Frank and Pete sit with the girls that they had been introduced to, and they order their meal and sit chatting. Sam asks Pete.

"This Tossa," Pete straight away asks her.

"I beg your parden, I'm no Tossa."

"No not you Pete I ment the place Tossa."

"I know babe just getting my own back, for all the fucking bridges."

"Thanks Pete, right where was I, Ho yes this place Tossa, what's the night life like, I mean is it any good."

"You know what Spain is like, no matter where you go, you will always get a good night life, and Tossa is no difrent from the rest of Spain, so don't worry, I will make sure you get a good time."

"I will keep you to that Pete." Sam sitting next to Pete and rubbing the inside of his leg and might I say going a little to far and having a crafty feel. Pete sat there smiling and he is thinking.

"Shagged two, going to shag Jane when we get there, now Sam looks like she want's it, I think all four of them are going to go into my Round Robin black book." Their meal comes and they sit and all goes quiat as they took into the meal, by the time they had finished the meal, the time for going back to the coach they had 15 minutes left, Pete tells Frank that he is going to go for a walk to take in the early evening air before he takes over driving. Pete starts to go outside while the others go around the forecourt shops. Unbeknown to Pete but Sam had followed him out discreetly so the others did not see her go. Pete is walking along the hedge of the coach park when Sam approaches him. She calls out his name and Pete turns round.

"Sam what are you doing out here."

"I just had to see you Pete, for you see I fancy you, and what I felt under the table boy, I would like a little of that."

"I think you are going to get a shock."

"What do you mean Pete shock."

"Well you said a little of that, well wait and you will see, that I'm not little."

Sam comes upto Pete and kisses him, and at the same time unzipping his flies and when she pulls Petes cock out, in the dim light just had to have a look.

"Fucking hell Pete I see what you mean." She know more than goes down and starts to give Pete one hell of a blow job, and Pete just leaned back onto one of the coaches and looked down at Sam ejoying his cock. It did not take long for Pete to come and Sam comes back up licking her lips and Pete tells her.

"Thanks babe, but we have to get back to the coach, but I promise you when we get there it will be my turn to dam well give you a good seeing to that you will probably have the best shag of your life."

"I will look forward to that Pete, God you are one trully hansom guy."

Pete smiles at her and they start to head back to the coach, when between two coaches he see's the girl in the long white dress with long blond hair go between the coaches, Pete goes running off and shouting out for his Sofia. He gets to where he had seen her and nobody is there. Pete is thinking.

"Shes come back again, ho my Sofia I love you so much. Pete standing smiling and holding his crucifix. They finally arrive back and they are the first and before long they all start to drift back to the coach, Pete sitting at the wheel and Frank doing the head count. Just after the hour, all are present and Frank tells Pete to start to pull away. Well it's Franks turn on the Microphone telling the passengers about the rest of the journy down to Tossa.

"Good evening Ladies and Gentlemen, welcome back on board. Now for the boaring bit, we are now setting off for the overnight drive, and I do hope you will get a little sleep on the new reclining seats that will make it feel more like being in bed. And for those who can not sleep, we have headphones so you can still carry on waching the TV that will be showing shows throughout the night. We will be stopping at 7am for breakfast in Spain, and after a shorter drive into Tossa and with this new road system, we should have you there by 2.30pm, thankyou and have a good night. Frank sits back down with Pete who gets the same feeling as Frank when he hits the motorway again and the one-start takes over the coach.

"Bloody hell Frank I see what you mean, well can you go and fill my flask up with coffee and I will sit back and look at the road ahead and hope that nothing gets in the way."

Pete drives for four hours and then Frankt akes over and they did not stop, just one driver out and another back down and Pete looks up the coach and the time is approching 11.30pm and all seemed quiat, with quiat a few fast on, while the insomniacs just sat there looking at the TV. Pete goes walking back down the coach and he passes the four girls and they are fast on, and Pete just smiled at them and is thinking to himself. "They look so inocent bless them, sleeping like butter would not melt in their hands, until they get their dirty hands onto my manhood." Pete chuckling to himself as he goes walking past and the ones watching the TV, he just smiles at them.

The night goes quick with both Pete and Frank taking cat naps when they are not driving, and the time soon goes and by 7am with Pete at the wheel starts to pull into the Services for breakfast. Pete parks the coach up gives off one big yarn stands in the morning fresh air and tells Frank.

"Go on then, I will let you wake the grumpy old lot up, they can throw their sweaty socks at you."

"Thanks mate, Frank goes back on board and does tell them that they have arrived for breakfast and the ones that were asleep start to come round, and it was off to the toilets in the services to freshen up, then a harty breakfast, English of course.

Frank sitting with Pete and they are tucking into a English breakfast and suddenly Frank asks Pete.

"Pete what do you think of the four girls we are taking down to Tossa."

"What you on about Frank what do I think."

"You know mate, would you ask them out for a date."

"Date I've shagged two of them, and had a blow job of the third, and the fourth as asked me to shag the arse off her when we get there." Well Frank spits the mouth full of beans that were in his mouth onto his plate and said.

"What, the fuck do you mean, how and when." Well by the time Pete had told him he just sat there not believing what he had been told.

Then the four girls come up and start to sit down with them, and Rita asks Frank.

"I hope you are going to join in with the fun when we get to Tossa Frank, for you're quite an attractive man."

"There you go Frank, I think you are on a promise there mate. And might I say roll on when we do get there and get you round the pool, so we can see you in all your glory."

"Yes and we can see those big muscels of yours Pete, have you a body like that then Frank." Frank just looks back at the girls and gingerly shakes his head. Well this brought a little titter from the girls and Jane tells him.

"You look fine sweetheart, you are too an attractive guy, never mind what the rest think."

"Thanks Jane, make sure I buy you a drink when we get there."

"Ho yes Frank that would be nice, and I'm sure her knickers will be off, with you buying her a drink in an all inclusive Holiday." Pearl telling Frank and this brought more laughter. Frank looks at Pete and asks him.

"Come on mate help me out here, they are all ganging up on me."

"Don't worry Frank, I'm sure one of the girls will take you to bed and show you how to make love to them." Well by now they are all in tears and the only one not laughing, yes you guessed that was Frank.

"Come on now lets all kiss and make up and head back to the coach, well Pete standing and he kissses the four of them, and Frank just sitting there looking miserable, and Pete tells the girls, Ho yes don't forget Frank." Frank looks up and before he knows it they are all over him, and might I say one or two were giving him a kiss with tongues and all. And by the time they had finished with him, as they walked off, Frank just sat there in amaze at what had just happened.

They all do eventually get back to the coach and Frank too, and he flops down into the drivers seat, looks at Pete and said.

"They kissed me with tongues and all, I think we are in there."

"Yes Pete head count done, you can drive off now." Pete thinking, what a plonker, we are in there now, I've just told him that I have shagged two and a blow job, and a promise when I get ther, how far does he want me to be in there, plonker." They drive for the rest of the morning and just like they told them by 2.30pm they arrive at the Hotel the Golden Palece, and Pete and Frank off the coach and opening the hold for they could get the cases out, one by one they start to go into the Hotel to book in, Then it's the girls and they are all getting excited and they ask Pete and Frank if they are going to come a round the pool as soon as they have parked up and booked in.

"We will be there sweetheart, so come on here is your case, go and book in and we will see you in half an hour." All fout go walking off and with miniskirts on Frank stands there looking and then turns to Pete and asks him.

"Do you think I''ve a chance of getting my leg over there Pete.

"Well I'm going to shag all four of them, why not you too. Come on Frank lets park the coach up in the coach park, book in and get round that pool with our shagging parners." Pete slapping Frank on the back. The time approching 3pm and Frank and Pete have booked in and in their room, and Pete straight away pulls out his trunks and his oil to rub on him and he tells Frank.

"Come on Frank change and lets get out there." Frank changed and just before they go Pete asks Frank just to put some oil on his back, Frank abliges and Pete looks in the mirror and said.

"What fucking bird could refuse this." Frank comes up to Pete and said.

"What fucking cats in hell chance do I stand with this fucking pathetic looking body." Pete looking at the reflection of Franks white torso looking back at him.

"Come on you will be fine, don't forget that birds don't just look at one's body, but what shines out of it with your personality from within."

They throw their towels over their shoulders and leave the room, Pete looks at Frank and is thinking." For fucks sake, I should have my sun classes on to stop the white reflection from Franks body." Pete telling himself under his breath to stop it.

They go walking round the pool trying to look for the girls when all of a sudden they here wolf wistles and shouting out. "Over here." Pete sees them standing and waving at them, and Petes eyes light up, for they all had very short bikini's on that did not leave much to the imagination, and they looked stunning.

Well when Pete approched them, droped his towel onto a sun lounger and stood there and took a deep breath and gave one of his poses, well with the sun beating down and with him having oils on, he looked a daunting sight with his muscels sticking out. Rita said.

"My God you look like a true hansom man, bloody hell girls I'm wetting myself just admiring what beholds me." Then Jane who is on a promise from Pete is thinking.

"If you are wetting yourself, I'm fucking flooding, just thinking that he is going to give me a good seeing to, fucking hell roll on." Pete said Hi to them and they did not answer for they are still memorised just looking at him. Frank sits down and he might have well been on another Planet, for I don't think they even noticed him sitting with them. All four of them were looking at the bulge on Petes trunks, and Pete stands and tells them, while their eyes are glued to his bulge.

"Come on then girls, lets test the pool out. Pete goes running to the pool and just dives srtaight in and starts to swim up and down the pool. Frank stands and tells them, come on the last one in is a chicken, Frank goes running to the pool and jumps in comes up and just shouts out.

"It fucking freezing."

Chapter Fourty One

Pete comes up to Frank and tells him.

"Come on Frank swim, you will soon warm up."

"Warm up more like freeze my bollocks off, more like." Pete laughs at him and goes swimming off.

Back with the girls Jane asks if they are coming, and with seeing Frank they say no thank you. Well Jane see's her opportunity and tells them that she is going to join the boys in the pool. Jane goes running up to the pool and dives straight in and goes swimming to where Pete is, and as soon as she reaches him, puts her arms around Pete and presses right up to him, and tells him.

"Frank is right, it is bloody cold. Pete you said we could get together when we arrived and I was wondering, how about now, while they are all around the pool." Jane slipping one of her hands under the water and having a feel of Petes cock.

"Well lets go now, we could go to my room 134, I will go and open and leave the door on the latch so you could get in, if that's OK with you."

"Get gone and lets snuggle up together, and get bloody warm." Pete goes swimming to the edge gets straight out and Frank is standing there drying himslf off, and Pete tells him.

"Just going to reception and organise the arrangements for our table, when we do our rep thing."

"OK Pete I'm going to lay down and get warmmed up by the Sun." Pete goes and he only had been back about 1 minute in his room, when Jane comes in and throws her arms around Pete, and she is kissing him profusely, and pulling down his wet trunks. Pete unclips her bra and her cold tits drop out, and her nipples are already standing out like two chapel hat pegs. He then pulls down her soggy bikini bottoms and he press's his now warm body onto Janes and she tells him.

"Ho thats loverly and warm." Pete starts to rise to the ocation and Jane could feel his erect cock pressing inbtween her legs, and trying to get in between her legs.

"Fucking hel Pete that big bogger, is egger." Jane opening her legs a little and she could feel it rubbing her clitoris.

"Oh, that's loverly Pete don't stop." Jane moving back and forth so his cock is rubbing a little faster. Pete tells her.

"Come on babe onto the bed, let me really show you how to give your fanny and clitoris a good seeing too." Jane laid down and Pete straddles her, and her legs are wide open, and Pete looks down and see's that gorgeous shaven fanny, and it looked very tasty. He starts his routine by first kissing her belly and sliding his tongue down to her fanny, and he starts to flick his tongue all around her clitoris and she starts to sigh, with the feeling Pete is doing, next he sucks her clitoris into his mouth and starts to suck in and out, well this is even better, then to top it he gentaly blows on it and that was it, for Jane had her first orgasm at what Pete is doing. He then starts to put his large tongue into her fanny and he could tell that she is utterly enjoying the whole experience. She trys to pull Pete up and saying at the same time.

"Please Pete fuck me now, please." Pete comes up kissing her nipples on the way up and Jane guids his large cock to its goal, and Pete slowly at first starts to penetrate her, the more of his cock that goes in the faster he goes and after about ten minutes they are well and trully at it with jane's legs wrapped around Petes back, and he is really bashing away, and Jane could not help but just shout out with the pleasure, so much that she starts to have another orgasm and Pete could feel her gushing with juices, and she shouts out to Pete.

"Fucking fuck me hard Pete, and blow your cork for fucks sake." Well a little dirty talk and Jane digging her fingers well into Petes back and it did make him blow his cork, and Jane could feel every drop and in-between the groans tells Pete.

"Your a God Pete, where the fuck did you learn to do that to a Woman, God that's warm." Jane twisting a little on Petes cock to get everything he is giving her, and Pete lifting his cock inside her just by his muscel in his groin.

"Ho that's nice Pete, it's just like you are coming, then Jane tightens her fanny muscels and they squeeze Petes cock, and he repeated it again, now they are playing squeeze the cock and fanny, I don't think it will get into the olympics. They get up clean themselves down, and Jane slips her wet costume on and goes to change, and Pete puts on a clean pair of shorts and a T-shirt. Pete goes back and just before he sits back down Frank looks up and asks Pete.

"Fucking hell Pete receptions good you went in bathers, and come back with shorts and a T-shirt, not bad."

"Twat, I went back to our room and changed out of my bathers." The time is approaching 5pm, and Pete tells Frank.

"I'm going back to our room to have a couple of hours kip for we have been driving overnight, and if we are going to go for a drink tonight, we will be fucking nacked, and be the boaring farts of the party." Pete standing and just before he left Rita asks Pete.

"What are you doing tonight then Pete."

"Well I'm going for a coulpe of hours kip, then a little to eat, and will meet you in the bar at 8.30pm."

"OK Pete see you in awile, but don't forget to set your alarm, or you will probably sleep through it."

"Don't fear Babe I will be there." Pete walking off and waving to the rest, Frank stands and tells them that he too is going to have a kip and see you later. Back in their room Pete draws the cutains to keep out the daylight and to darken the room and sets is watch for 7pm, and gets into bed and both Pete and Frank were soon off into the land of nod. With being tiered and the long haul trip Pete starts to dream and he see's is beloved Sofia walking towards him in the long white dress and her blond hair flowing down her back too her bottom, she approches Pete stops and stands in front of him and tells him.

"My beloved Pete, I'm so sorry that I cannot be with you, but my darling why do you so miss behave with others. And not wait for me." Pete drops to his knees in the dream and tells her.

"Sofia, my darling wife, why did you leave me, what am I supposed to do, you are gone and I'm left down here on my own, I need love, but my love is for you and you only." Pete laid in his bed and crying, when all of a sudden he gets a violent shake that brngs him round.

"Pete-Pete come on mate we have overlaid, it's 7.45pm, we had better get ready and have something quick to eat. For we have to meet the girls at 8.30pm." Well they are both up and rushing for the shower and they decide that Frank goes into the shower first, while Pete shaved and then swop round. They do make it for 8pm, and they go to the restaurant and Pete had chicken breast and might I say a few, with mash potatoes and Frank a light salered. They sit back after the meal and the time by now is coming upto 8.30pm, and Frank tells Pete.

"Come on then Pete lets go into the bar and meet the girls."

"Settle down and relax, for they will wait for two hulks like me and you, and further more, look they are over there having something to eat, so they would be keeping us waiting, but now, we can get up and go when they do. Would you like me to get you a beer Frank." Pete standing and beaming at Frank.

"OK bring me a beer." Frank turning and seeing where they were sitting. Pete brings two beers, and Frank asks Pete.

"What and where are we going tonight." Pete leans onto the table and tells Frank,

"Well don't forget that I lived down here and know all the joints, and I will tell you one thing Frank, give me an hour when we get back, for I'm going to shag the arse of that Sam tonight."

"What how the bloody well do you know that she will be up for it."

"Well she gave me a blow job on the way down here, and I told her that I would return the complement as soon as we arrived, so tonights the night."

Frank spitting into his beer, at the first part Pete had told him.

"What you will be telling me that you have shagged one of them already."

"No Frank 3 of them, and Sam will make the fourth." Well Frank nearly chocked on his beer this time, looks at Pete shakes his head and tells him.

"Well I now know that you are fucking mad, come off it Pete four in a day and a bit, what next, all fucking four of them together."

"I must be slowing down, a day and a bit, and yes mate all four of them, lovely Jubbly, lovely Jubbly." Pete standing and ruffling up Franks hair and telling him.

"Come on Frank they are leaving for the bar, lets go and meet them." Pete stands and goes walking out of the restaurant, with Frank walking behind him just shaking his head, at what Pete had told him. The girls are at the bar and Pete approches and Kisses them all, and tells them, come on girls it's you turn to get the beers in."

"Funny Pete it's all inclusive, whats on the agenda tonight then."

"Well Babes, with me living down here for over two years, I know all the good joints where we can have a good time, so if you are up to it leave it to your rep to give you a good time."

"Right on Pete, you're the man." Rita giving him a kiss. I think Frank felt out of it for they are all around Pete, and it is if he did not exist and he goes and sits down, on his own. It's not long and Pete noticed him sitting there looking a little misserable, and Pete wispers in Rita and Janes ear to go and bring him back into the fold. Well they go up to Frank and straight away they both put one leg each upon to Franks seat, and with having miniskirts on Frank is getting an eye full of their knickers, and they tell him.

"If you sit like that and don't join in then this is all that you are going to get and nothing up there at what you are looking at." Well Frank puts his hand on both of their legs, and runs both his hands up to the top and tells them.

"If you like what you are feeling just let me know, for my cock can still fill a pram too." Frank being bold and rubbing both their fannys. Rita and Jane tell him.

"We both will keep you to that, so get your fucking arse back up there and maybe, we might return the compliment by having a feel of our interest, that you have." Well the difrence Frank is straight up and Rita and Jane do have a feel of what Frank had down below and they both tell him.

"Maybe you would like to make us scream then Frank."

"Just name the time and Place and I'm all yours." Frank sticking his chest out that little bit more.

Chapter Fourty Two

"They leave the Hotel and start to head to the front, and Pete walking along with Sam and Jane Rita and Pearl are walking along with Frank and teasing him a little, the odd kiss and a quick feel, more like they are still trying to cheer him up. Pete turns to Sam gives her a quick kiss and tells her.

"Tonight Sam, after we come out of the disco, would you like to come back to my room and we could have that date you wanted."

"Fucking too true Pete, all that I want is to have you by myself and get that fucking big boy of yours well and trully into me, and I don't think you will be disappointed." Sam kissing Pete again and having a crafty feel at the same time. They come to the front and Rita shouts out to Pete.

"Come on then where first Babe."

"Up there we will go in Linekers bar first." They go in and the disco music is blearing out, and Pete at the bar getting the drinks in, while Frank was showing them all his moves at dancing, and all around the bar you had photos of the famous footballer Gary Lineker on the walls. They all stand listning to the music and Rita tells them all.

"It's sure is lively in here tonight, I hope you have a good night club we are going to go to Pete." Jane asking Pete

"Don't you worry Babe, the one we are going to go too, only the rich and well off go there." Pete leaning forward and raising his voice a little over the loud music, and swaying to the beat. They have a couple in Linekers, and they move on to the next Pub, by 10pm they decide to go to the club, that Pete is going to take them too. They arrive and a little tippsy, and Pete tells them just before they reach the entrance that had bouncers at the door.

"Come on now look respectable or you wont get in, for they are very strict here." They walk up to the entance and they are stopped, and Pete straight away in Spanish tells them.

"Evening my distingtive guests from the UK, are the best entertainers that are in Spain at this very moment, and one or two of you highly expensive customers would like to meet them." Well the girls were well impressed at Pete speacking Spanish to them, and the bouncers look at the girls who might I say with having the miniskirts on, their eyes light up, but to top it. Rita did no more than bend down to adjust her shoe and the bouncers could not take there eyes of her long legs, leading up to her arse where she was showing just her thong. The bouncers just waved them in and the girls go by them blowing kisses. Going down the entrance into the club Rita asked Pete.

"Your Spanish is good, what the fuck did you tell them that just made them wave us in."

"Just told them in Spanish that you were UK hookers, and that the rich bastards in the club, want to fuck the arses off them."

"Pete you didn't did you." Pete just smiling at Rita, who looks back and see's the bouncers smiling at her. All that she did was give them the Victory sign.

Once inside it was party time and they are dancing to the disco and the beer is flowing, and everyone is having a great time, and at 12-o-clock Sam comes up to Pete and asks hiim.

"Pete, take me onto the dance floor and dance with me." Just as they go a slow dance comes on, and they start to dance close together, and Sam wispers in his ear.

"Pete I'm getting tired with the travling and the long two days, please take me back and make love to me before we drop off to sleep."

"OK Babe we will discreetly leave and go back to my room, and hope that they just think that we are somwhere in the club." They do manage to sneek out with out them noticing them and head back to the Hotel.

They go through the reception where the night security guard is, and sitting listening to his radio, and they give their goodnight to him. Once in the room Pete starts to kiss Sam who at the same time is slipping her miniskirt off and then her top, and she tells Pete.

"Come on Babe get undressed and into bed, the truth beknown, I think she is going to fall a sleep if not careful. They get into Pete's bed and they start to kiss and all of a sudden Pete could see that she is not responding and he turns the table light on and she had dropped off to sleep.

"I don't fucking believe it, she's fucking gone." Pete quietly calling her name, but no response, well Pete just laid back down and turned over and he too had soon gone. The time must have been about 2.30am and into the room comes Frank and Rita, well talk about giggling, they are falling over things in the room and Frank putting his finger to his lips and saying.

"SHUSH, you will wake Pete. Then a giggle, well talk about clowning around, you have Frank trying to unclip her bra and in the end slipping it down to the ground and Rita stepping out and evensurly they do make it, and with no fourplay Frank is inbetween her legs and starting to fuck her like no tomorrow and it must have only lasted about 4 minutes and Frank had come and with drew, and Rita tellling him.

"What the fuck was that, you were like a mad fucking bull at a gate, what about me, no fucking orgasm, thanks a bunch. Well Rita turns and cocks her arse at Pete and she to fell fast asleep. Pete wakes just after 7am and he is facing Sam, and he starts to slowly to fondle her breasts and gently kissing her on the neck, and this was to slowly bring her out of her sleep. Well it certanly did this for she turns over and starts to kiss Pete, and he wispers into her ear.

"Come on Babe lets go into the bathroom and shower and make love, so we won't have Frank waking and looking at us." They both quietly get out of bed, and Pete nearly stops dead in his tracks when he see's Frank and Rita fast on. He points this out to Sam who nearly burst out giggling at seeing

Rita with her mouth wide open and snoring her head off. Sam and Pete go into the bathroom and Pete locks the door and Sam who had brought her clothes with her drops them on the floor and she goes up to Pete who is turning the shower on and puts her arms around Pete and starts to kiss his back. Pete stood there and comented to Sam.

"That's nice Babe, you are sending thrills right down my back." She moves her hand down to Petes cock that is starting to rise at the feeling Sam is doing, and with her playing with his cock soon had the biggest hard on. Pete turns and pulls Sam into the shower while kissing her, then slipping his hand onto her breasts and tweeting her nipples until they stood proud, and he goes down and starts to suck on them, while Sam just streched back and let the water flow all down her. Pete lands up in his favoured position and that is flicking her clitoris and giving her fanny a good seeing too, after he had is fussy and he knew Sam is ready comes back up and starts to kiss Sam, and at the same time lifting her legs, and his cock finds it's own way to it's goal, and before long they were fully at it and Pete penetrating her to the hilt. Sam was bloody well up to her elements in orgasms and totally gone with pleasure. They must have been at it for well over half-an-hour and they both climax at the same time, with Sam streching back at the feeling of Petes warm sperm, and Pete doing the same with the feeling he is getting with ejaculating into her. They shower and Sam dress's and tells Pete that she is going to sneak out, before Rita awakes. She goes and Pete is coming out of the shower just after Sam had closed the door, and with him now standing next to his bed and facing Franks bed, Rita must have overheard the door go, that woke her, and her eyes light up at seeing such a welcoming sight as Pete standing there completely in the nude facing her. She know more gets out of Franks bed, and stands and starts to kiss Pete. Pete asks what she is doing and she tells him.

"Come on Babe make love to me now, for that useless piece of a so called bloke is fucking useless in bed, please Pete I want satisfying and you are the one that can do that. They get into Petes bed and Pete pulls the sheet over them just incase Frank awakes, who at this moment in time is snoring for Gr-Britain.

Pete slowly starts to work on Rita's tits and then her fany and before long she is having her first orgasm and she tells Pete who is just about to straddle her.

"You're fucking magic Pete, I'm flooding already, and you are only just starting, fuck me hard Pete." Pete starts slowly at first, giving her a few inches on every push and working up to the hilt and speeding up. After ten minutes Pete is really bashing away at Rita who by now is screaming out with pleasure, but Frank just snored on. Rita had her legs spread eagled with her legs high and wide and on Petes back and with every push that Pete gives she streches back with the feeling and she starts to have one hell of a massive orgasm, and totally gone and screaming with pleasure, Pete ejaculates at the same time and she is enjoying every second.

"Ho God let this feeling last forever, MMm, KISS ME Pete." They lay there kissing and coming back down and Pete finnaly showers again, and tells Rita that he is going to go down to the gym in the Hotel complex and pump iron for an hour, if sleeping beauty wakes, tell him where I've gone Rita, see you later sweetheart.

Pete leaves and heads for the gym to do his daily routine in the gym. He spends the hour in the gym and with the time now going on for 9am goes to change for after breakfast he and Frank are on the desk in reception to attend to their Rep work till mid-day. Pete and Frank at breakfast and sitting eating, Frank tells Pete.

"Boy was it a good night or what last night, we certainly pulled did'ent we Pete, what you with Sam, and you will never guess who I pulled and shagged the arse of her."

"Rita, if I'm not mistaken." Pete is thinking, shagged the arse off her, I don't think so mate, that was me." Pete smiling at Frank.

"How did you know."

"Well when I got up this morning to go to the gym, you and her were snoring your heads off."

"Ho I see, she had gone when I woke."

"Probably went back to change Frank. Anyway come on lets get set up for the mornings work doing our rep think." They both go to reception, and set up their table and paper work for the mornigs rep work, Frank asks Pete.

"Whats on the agenda, Pete."

"Well to try and fill the places for the trip to Barcelona tomorrow, but the main one is the trip on Thursday, and of all thinks the long trip to Montserrat Monastery, high up in mountain range of Spain." They both sit down and what a sorryful sight, seeing to lads who would be sooner beter off round the pool with the girls, but tough titties, they are working.

They sit there watching the world go by looking at the commings and goings of people booking in and leaving, when they did not see two young girls come up to the table and one coughs to grab their attenstion. Pete is the first to look and what a diference two birds make.

"High their we are the reps for Bulwell Summer Sunshine tours, how could I help you swetheart. My names Pete."

Chapter Fourty Three

Hi Pete my names Emma May and this is Sandy, we are on our Holidays with us both being 25 years old, and this week believe it or not we share the same birthday, and are looking at any good trips to go on.

"Well Emma May, you have come to the right person for we are taking bookings for a trip tomorrow morning, for a tour of Barcelona and shopping, and back home for 4pm in the afternoon, and then you might be interested in a tour deep into the heart of Spain, to the Monastery of Montserrat, if that interests you."

"Mmm, will you be going, on this trip."

"Only if you go because I'm your guide and will do all of my best to make sure you are well and truly satisfied with the whole day's events." Pete smiling at her and lifting his eyebrow in a surgestive way.

"Well then Pete book us both for both trips, first what time tomorrow would you like us, and second what time on Thursday."

"BOY with the look of you Babe, twenty four seven, and Ho yes tomorrow 9am outside the Hotel, and Thursdy the same time, if you are awake from your beauty sleep."

"Well I will be up for it, so long as you are." Emma May retuning the complement by lifting her eyebrow and brushing back her long black hair. They book the trip and Pete watches them walk away and he nudges Frank and tells him.

"Did you see those two beauty's we are in there mate."

"What are you on about."

"What a'm I on about those two there, look standing at reception talking to the day porter." Frank looks and turns to Pete and tells him.

"I was trying to untangle my headphones and did not notice, what those two, why have they booked.

"Only for tomorrow and again on Thursdy for Montserrat, we are fucking in there mate I can tell you." Pete still looking at them and rubbing his hands.

Frank just carried on untangling his headphones." 12 noon soon comes and they had a full booking for Barcelona with only a few tickets left for Thursday, and they leave the rest at Reception, just in case any late booking. Pete tells Frank.

"Come on mate lets get our trunks on and go and cut a few rays, around the pool." It's not long and they are walking around the pool for a good spot, or where the talent is, and they see the girls all sunbathing. They approch and Pete asks them.

"Have you room for one great guy and one whimp." Rita looks up and see's them and tells Pete.

"Get your arse's down here and no hanky panky, for we are catching up on sleep and rays." Pete sits down but he could not resist on giving Rita a loving slap on the arse, and might I say leaving his hand there and having a quick feel of her camals toe.

"Bloody leave it Pete you can have a bit later." Pete turns to Frank and Frank could not beleave what Pete did. In a quiat voice Frank tells Pete.

"That's my bird, you have just felt."

"Don't be a twat Frank, I've already shagged it and might I say, made her scream out with pleasure." Well Frank sitting down on his sun lounger could not believe what he had just said. Frank taps Pete on the shoulder and Pete turns while laying down on his sun lounger and looks at Frank and asks.

"What."

"Is it true that you have shagged all four of them."

"Yes and if they want more, I'm their man." Well Frank is starting to lay down and he is thinking that Pete had shagged Rita and also he had, well talk about wimp he did no more than put his hand onto his cock, and trying to wipe it with his shorts at the thought that he had been there as well as Pete in Rita. WHAT A PLONKER.

They had been sunning for about an hour and a half when Pete asks Rita.

"Rita Babe, did not see you at reception this morning, arn't you and the girls interested in going to Barcelona and the trip on Thursday." Rita puts her hand up to her head to shade the sun off her eyes, looks at Pete and tells him.

"Are you real, I mean we come from Nottingham down here, travelling for two days, by bus and we are only here for a week. And you want us to sit on another fucking bus for two days, well no bloody well thank you, we are quite happy doing this, getting a loverly tan. Isn't that right girls." Well all of them at the same time saying to Pete.

"Right on no-way OH-say." Then they all giggle, and get back to cutting some rays. Just before the boys go, Rita asks what they were doing that evening and Pete tells her.

"Well dinner, and just the show that's on here tonight, for you see Rita, we are technically are working this week, and tomorrow with driving the public, we can not be late or drink to much, for they are very strict down here just like back home on drinking and driving."

"Never mind, your lose, we are going to hit the clubs again, we will see you in the bar later just before we go out Pete."

"OK girls catch you later." Pete is the first to leave to shower and Frank tells him he will be there shortly, he will give him time to shower before he comes.

Later they both are changed and ready for the night around the bar and Hotel, after they had eaten they go into the bar and Pete asks for two beer shandy's, well Pete asked the barmaid in Spanish and tells her what a shandy consists of, that is beer and lemonade." Frank is well impressed with the way Pete spoke to her and he tells Pete.

"I Wish I could speke Spanish fluently like you Pete, for you are truly into it."

"Like I told you Frank with living down here for two years, you soon pick the lingo up and befor you know it, you are just speking it naturally, I will have to start to teach you the lingo."

"Thanks mate, I'll keep you to that." About 8pm the four girls come into the bar and of course dressed to kill, and Frank just looks at Rita and whispers to Pete.

"Look at her, just think I had my wicked way with her, boy I bet she will never forget." Well the look Pete gives Frank and Pete is thinking. "More like she will try not too, for she does not won't to vomit."

"Hi, babes ready for another exciting night out then." Well if you could have seen all four of them, they are all over Pete and hands going into places that you would not expect a fine young Ladie to go, then again Fine young Ladies, more like four hot hookers. Pete reponding and pressing up to Sam and she in turn feeling his cock, and she tells him.

"I wish you were coming Pete, for I would love to give him a good seeing too, and maybe you would return the complement."

"I'm sorry babe but work comes first, but don't let me spoil the night." Pete kissing her again, well by the time Pete had spoke to them all, and all of them giving Pete a crafty feel, they drink up and head off for the clubs, all singing on the way out. Pete tells Frank.

"Fucking best birds we have had on the trip for a long time, Bulwell certainly knows our to breed good looking birds." Pete and Frank sit talking and Pete telling Frank one or two words in Spanish, and into the bar comes the two girls who have booked for Barcelona in the morning. Pete see's them and goes over.

"Helo Babes where are you off to tonight then."

"Ho Hi, Pete, no where in particular just a few drinks and then into bed early and looking forward to the trip tomorrow."

"We are the same, only a few shandy's then the same early night then up for the trip." Pete turns to Frank and tells him.

Frank this is Emma May and her friend Sandy." Well Frank could not take is eyes of Sandy and he came straight out with.

"Hi, my names Frank and you are absolutely gorgeous, if you will forgive me for saying that."

"Well thank you Frank and no, it was a very good complement." Sandy takes Franks hand and starts to shake it and at the same time leans forward and gives Frank a kiss. Well Pete stands in astonishment at seeing Frank so forward, and not wanting to be out done, does no more than look at Emma May and did the same but with tongues and all, when kissing Emma, who after went all weak at the knees.

Formalities over and they sit chatting about themselfs and where they come from, and in general getting on well. Frank asks Sandy if she would like to go, and have a go in the amusement arcade that are in reception area, and she agrees, Leaving Pete and Emma May alone in the bar.

Pete asks Emma May if she would like a walk through the Hotels gardens that they have in the Hotel compound area just behind the pool, she tells Pete that would be nice in the warm evening air, and they stand and leave, heading for the gardens, as soon as they are outside Pete holds Emmas hand and they go walking off chatting and in general enjoying each others company. They come to a surclueded spot and Pete stops pulls Emma May to him, and they stand in one loving kiss and Emma slips her hand under Petes Shirt, and starts to fondle is large musculour chest and gentally rubbing his nipples. Pete did the same and he too is under her blouse and lifts her bra up and the same fondleing her breast and tweeking her nipples, that start to exstend and Pete goes down and starts to suck on them with Emma holding his head and every now and then pushing his head further onto her breasts, Pete comes up and Emma asks Pete.

"Ho Pete I would love to make love to you, but not here, would you like to come back to my room, where we would be more comfy and will not be disturbed by anyone passing." On the way back Emma phones Sandy, to tell her their intention on going back to her room, Sandy tells Emma that would be OK for she is going to go back with Frank, to his room, and she will see her later. Emma puts her mobile away and tells Pete about the arrangement of Sandy, and they will now not be disturbed by anyone, Emma planting another kiss on Pete as they make their way back up to the Hotel.

Chapter Fourty Four

They arrive back and Emma opens the door and they enter, She locks the door behind her just encase and approches Pete, who had already removed his top and stood there with all is bulging muscels on display, and Emma approches him and with both hands starts to fondle is breast and commenting on his fine body.

"That's one thing that I like doing Emma and that is keeping in shape" She starts to unbuckle is belt and he steps out of his trousers, and then she bends down and at the same time removing his boxer shorts, and now for the first time Pete is the center of attraction, and not himself in control, for he just stood there memorised with the whole think that she is doing. For he looks down and Emma who is working away sucking him off, and Pete instead of the Woman screwing her face up it is himself. When Pete could take nomore he lifts her up and starts to strip Emma who her self stood there in the nude and Pete presses close up to her and starts to kiss her and they must have stood there for awhile and with Pete fondulling her breasts kissing her neck and Emma rubbing Petes chest, he finnaly picks her up and slowly puts her down onto the bed, and goes down on her to return the complements of the blow job that she gave him.

Emma is soon lifting and arching her back at the pleaure of Pete flicking and sucking her clitoris and his tongue working away on her fanny. She orgasms for the first time and tells Pete.

"Come on Pete fuck me now for I`m gagging for the feeling of your cock inside of me." Pete comes up straddles her, lifts her legs up into the air and he pushes down onto her and is cock finds it's own way in, and that was it she is soon screaming with the feeling and Pleasure of the feeling of Petes cock slowly at first going in deeper with every plung onto her. Fast then slow then fast again. Emma starts to talk dirty into Petes ear and telling him that he is a Roman gladiator, and she is the bitch of the prize for the champion.

"fuck me hard now Pete, fuck me like you are going to fuck me to

Death." She no more than tells Pete to stop amoment and Pete withdraws and she turns over and cocks her arse up into the air and then tells Pete.

"Now fuck mw hard." Well Pete seeing that loverly arse just waiting for his cock just looks down, and his cock is lifting up and then going down and lifting up again, it's if it s like a lion roaring and wanting to get into its goal and he inserts his cock and it slides in more easerly with Emmas juicers flowing and he did what she asked, and starts to fuck her like there is no tomorrow and it's not long and she is screaming at the top of her voice at Pete, and might I say a few F-words and God's a few times.

"Now Babe now, let me fucking feel that warm spunk of yours, for fucks sake now, HA NOW. Emma having one hell of an Orgasm, and Pete does explode and he looks down at her arse and feeling himself ejaculating, gives of one loud sigh and at the same time Emma too is giving of a loud scream at the feeling and the orgasm that she is feeling. After they both flop back down onto the bed and just laid there wallowing in the pleasure that they had just given each other, it must have been ten minutes before they both turn and face each other and laid there kissing and cuddling each other. They finnaly drop of curled up and before they know it Petes wrist watch alarm is going off and he awakes looks at his watch and tells himself, better get back and changed. He gets up and Emma too and they both shower and might I say with not having the time no hanky panky in the bathroom, Pete tells her.

"Your friend Sandy must have stopped with Frank for the night, I will discreetly knock on the door, for I would not burst in on them."

"OK Pete I will see you at breakfast or the coach after breakfast."

Pete gets back to his room and does knock and Sandy opens the door said hello to Pete and leave, Pete goes in and looks at Frank and asks him.

"Come on then Frank tell me, have you hit it off with Sandy then."

"Pete we are in love, please-please don't hit on her." Frank looking worried at Pete, who tells him.

"Like I told you mate, if you feel that way fair enough, but you are supposed to shagum and leave um, not fall head over heels." Pete standing looking at Frank and shaking his head at Frank, who stood there with qupids arrow sticking out of his chest, and looking out of this world.

"Ho Frank come on mate we have to drive to Barcelona with the coach, you don't want the passengers seeing you look like that, go and dip you head under the cold tap to bring you back down mate."

"Funny Pete I'm OK, come on lets get breakfast before we get the coach." Both dressed and in their working shirt and trousers go to the restaurant and have breakfast, then the coach check it over, and just before 9am pull up outside the Hotel to pick up those who are going to Barcelona. Frank is driving there and Pete on the way back. Frank sitting in the driving seat and Pete at the door welcoming those who are going aboard, it comes to Emma and Sandy and Emma gives Pete a kiss when getting onto the coach and Sandy kisses Pete too, well if you could have seen Franks face at seeing this, and all that Pete did was lift his arms up to Frank and enough to say. "It was not me mate." Sandy leans over Frank sitting at the wheel and gives him a long loving kiss, and she tells him just before she sits down.

"I love you Frank, drive safely." Well all boarded and Pete tells Frank that they are all aboard and ready to go. He starts to pull away from the Hotel and Pete is up and onto the microphone to inform them on the days events.

"Good morning Ladies and Gentlemen, welcome onto the coach this morning for your excursion to Barcelona and the tour and shopping experience. We do hope you have a wonderful time today. First off we will be stopping at the wonderful Cathedral of Barcelona of the holly cross and Saint Eulalia (Catalan Catedral De-La-Santa Creu-i- Sanint Eulialia, which building work started on the 19 March 1882, and is still on going building the Cathedral, so please take time to tour the Cathedral, and to get involved with the guide, then after an hour shopping. So in all please be back at the coach in two hours time, for the continuation of the tour of Barcelona. Where after the shopping and Cathedral tour we will be going on to the Barcelona olympic stadium of the 1992 spring olympics, then after one for the boys and you Ladies too, the FC Barcelona football club ground, the Camp Nou, for a tour of the grounds." Well all the guys are cherring at the tour of Camp Nou, and they odd boo, from the ladies. Then Pete tells them.

"So settle back and we will soon have you there to start your wonderful day in Barcelona thank you." Pete puts the microphone down and tells Frank.

"Well I think that went down well." Just over an hour and the coach pulls into the coach park close to the Cathedral and they start to disembark and some head for the Cathedral and some to the shops. Emma goes with the people that are going to the Cathedral and Frank and Sandy go of walking hand in hand to the shops. Pete stands looking at him and Sandy and he is thinking.

"Truthfuly Frank I wish you luck, for you look like my Sofia and myself walking along hand in hand." Petes head goes down and he just goes back onto the coach sits down and he starts to go on a downer. He sits there and all that he can see is his Sofia in her long white dress and those long flowing locks and her hair going all the way down her back to her bum.

"Ho my sweetheart why you, please God look after her for I love her so." Pete just looking at the Cathrdral just stands up leaves the coach, lock's the coach and goes walking to the Cathedral and enters and sits at the back and it is a daunting sight inside.

He sits there and talking to God and holding the cross that the Vicar of Staint Marys in Bulwell gave him, and he burst out crying, there is nothing anyone can do for him, but himself, for it is himself that will have to come to terms with the lose of his Sofia and no one else.

The two hours soon pass and Pete is counting the heads back onto the coach for the continuation of the tour of Barcelona. All abourd and it was off heading for the Olympis stadium and they stop for ten minutes for the passengers to take photo's and then head off for the main event as far as the boys are concerned, and that is the tour of Camp Nou FC Barcelona football cround.

They arrive and all disembarg and this time Frank is with Sandy and Pete holding Emma's hand go on the guided tour of the ground. They come to the part where they go down the tunnel that leads to the pitch. On the way down on the right hand side they come to a chapel, that the players use just before they start a game, well Pete just pulls Emma into the chapel shuts the door and he is leaning on the door so no one could enter, and he starts to kiss Emma and they are in a very romanic hold, when he for some unbeknown reason he looks at the altar at the front, and above it there is a crucifix of Jessus on the cross, while kissing Emma just opens his eyes and looks straight into the eyes of Jessus, then he gets the shock of his life for the head of Jessus on the cross is looking down, but with Pete looking at him, it just lifts his head and the exprssion on Jessus face changes to a sad one. Well Pete just freaks out, pulls away from Emma and shouts out.

"Fucking hell he is alive on the cross, LOOK." Turns and goes running out of the chapel and down the tunnel onto the pitch, and drops to his knees on the pitch and starts to cry again and praying for forgiveness." Well when the guide see Pete on the pich just bellows out.

"OFF the pitch now, do you hear me now." He goes walking upto Pete and in Spanish repeats what he had just said, well Pete looks at him and in Spanish tells him what had just happened, and the guide did no more than do the sign of the cruifix and chanting verse in Spanish. Well Pete comes round and he stands and goes walking back to the rest and Emma approches Pete and asks him.

"What the hell, happened in there you scared the living daylights out of me."

"When we were kissing for some reason I opened my eyes and the cross at the front with Jessus on, elevated his head and looked sad back at me and it freaked me out." Well Emma tells Pete.

"Pete you are kidding me you are sending cold shivers down me." The giude tells them all to follow him, for the next part is to go to the trophy room, where they will see all the trophy's FC Barcelona have won, including the European Cup. Please follow me. They all go following the guide and going by the chapel, for curiosity Emma opens the door without entering and looks at the cross and Jesus head is bowed down on the cross. She tells Pete who is at the door.

"Look Pete it is not looking up, it must have been a trick of the light or something like that, that made it look like it looked up." Pete never mind how big he is still looked nerves at the cross, and I don't think he is convinced.

They finally go to the trophy room and all the trophy's and football boots of famous players who have played for FC Barcelona, plus their shirts what they played in, and many other things in all a very good tour, they finnaly land up in the clubs shop where you could buy shirts kits and many other trinkets connected with FC Barcelona. After the tour it is time for the drive back, and this time it is Petes turn to drive, in away it might help him forget the whole experience that he went through during the tour.

Chapter Fourty Five

5.PM they arrive back at the Hotel and everyone thanks Pete and Frank on a wonderful day out, and they all disembark, Pete and Frank look at each other and tell themselves, that was a long day mate and we have to go through it again tomorrow with the trip to Montserrat Monastery.

"Come on mate lets park the coach up and have a beer around the pool, before we go and shower and change for dinner." Pete putting his arm around Frank. They land up sitting in the sunshine and having the well deserved drink and Frank asks Pete.

"Pete on the way back Emma told me about what happened when you came running out of the tunnel and onto the pitch of FC Barcelona, I thought at the time that something was not right now I know, you have to do something about it mate, or you are going to crack up under the preasure and even you could have a nerves breakdown."

"It was nothing Frank don't worries about it, I'm alright mate, thanks for asking. Pete trying to change the subject. Frank puts one hand onto Petes lower arm and tells him.

"It's me you are talking too, you know the one who was with you when you seen your Sofia in Bulwell going into the church, and the foot prints when you were coming out, there is something wrong Pete and don't try to shove it under the carpet, when we get back home promise me you will see someone about the whole thing before in gets out of hand." Pete thanks Frank for his comferdence in him, and Pete tells Frank.

"OK you win buddy, I promise I will see someone on the return, thanks for being there for me Frank, much appreciate your concern."

"Come on then Pete drink up and lets have one more beer before we go." Frank going to the poolside bar to refresh their glasses. Pete looking at him go and Pete is thinking. "He's a bloody well good mate, and in one way I appreciate is concern for me, bless him." Frank at the bar and who should come round the bar but Rita and comes up to Pete bends down and kises Pete and tells him.

"Missed you babe and our little get together, What you doing tonight then, are you free now that you have done the trip, I was thinking that you might like a litle more of this." Rita pushing her front into Petes face. Pete puts his hands on top off her legs and is thumbs were pressing into her fanny area and he is moving his thumbs around so she could feel them on her camel toe.

"THAT'S NICE Pete, well are you going out then."

"Sorry babe but, we are working again in the morning, but if you are gagging for it, then there is no time like the present." Rita thinks for amoment, and tells Pete.

"Well the girls have gone to Town to buy their Mums a gift, so we could go back if you would like too." Pete stands and tells her.

"Come on then Babe lets go and have a little fun, it's been a long day and I think I will beable to make you squeal." Pete feeling her arse and they go walking off just as Framk leaves the poolbar turns and se's Pete going with Rita.

"He will never learn, I bet he's going to screw the arse off her." Back in Rita's room Pete waists no time and strips and Rita did the same and they both stand there in the nude and Rita looks at Pete who stood there and his frame and him standing out proud. Rita tells him.

"What bird could resist you, you are one big fucking handsome guy, who should be put in a glass cage and only let out when your goddest needs you."

"Well I'm out of the glass cage, let me make love to my Goddest, come here Babe." Rita walks to Pete and they stand in one big kiss and Pete after they had kissed picks her up kisses her again and goes walking to the bed. Pete asking her.

"How do you require your God to shag you." Pete kissing her again and stopping at the bed.

"Put me down onto the bed and fuck me as hard as you can, and do make me squeal for more, fucking hell lets stop it for I'm wetting myself already."

Pete gently puts Rita onto the bed and this time no foreplay for she opens her legs wide and she is looking down at Pete's massive hard on, and she sighs at the thought of that big fucker going towards her fanny, and Pete turning his cock around her fanny and clitoris teasing it a little and her juicers are really flowing, and she is sighing and the feeling is really getting to her, she suddenly tells Pete.

"Get that big bad boy inside of me now Pete, fucking hell please." Rita trying to push her hips forward to start to get his cock inside her. Pete suddenly does plung forward and she takes one big intake of breath and the feeling of his cock penetrating her deep, and the first HO GOD from Rita as Pete starts to really go at her, lifting her legs up into the air, and Rita wrapping them around Pete who by now is going at her flat out and boy the noise she is giving and it starts to get to much and she starts to bite onto Petes shoulder, and screaming into Petes ear everytime he plunges.

It's a good half hour and that was it she is totally screaming for Pete to spunk her, and to do it now. Pete gives it one last plunge and he screams out as he starts to ejaculate at the same time that rita is having a massif orgasm.

After they both go and shower and soaping each other down, and still getting a lot of pleasure, and finaly dressed and Pete tells Rita he will see her and the girls around the bar later. Pete goes back and Frank had already showered and shaved and just laying on his bed watching the news on the TV, Pete showers again and shaves and by 7pm they both go for dinner and then into the bar.

They get their drink and sitdown and Pete asks Frank what he is doing that evening."

"Well at 8.30pm Sandy is coming and we are going to go for a walk down to the front, and have a stroll along the front for an hour."

"Nice, but don't you forget that we are off early in the morning, I don't want you wondering back into the room in the early hours Frank."

"Don't be silly Pete, I wolud not dream of it."

"Well you have a good time Frank you deserve it mate, don't worry about me I will be alright sitting on my own and looking at the wall paper." Well Frank felt guilty and he is about to ask Pete to come with them, when Pete could see this and just tells him.

"Only fucking kidding Frank, you bloody well go and in joy your evening with Sandy. And I will see you later." Just as Pete had said this Sandy comes into the bar Kisses Frank then Pete and she tells Frank to fetch her a drink. Frank stands and goes to the bar and this leaves Pete with Sandy and Pete asks her.

"How are you and Frank getting on then Sandy."

"I think he is the one for me, when I first met him, I thought he was a little bid of a blonker, but deep down he is a very loving man and he is going to be the one that I would like to spend the rest of my life with." Well Pete is touched with what Sandy had said, he did know more that hold her hands and tells her.

"To me he is a very close friend, and I would hate him to be let down, please never hurt him, for he would be heart broken, and it would break my heart too." Sandy leans forward and kisses Pete straight on the lips, and Frank is coming back with the drinks and see's this and just before he reaches the table Sandy tells Pete.

"Thank you Pete, for he is totally in good hands with a friend like you, and I would never-never hurt him for I love him so." Well Frank sits back down and you could see that he is uncomfortable with the whole thing that he had seen, and after they had finnished their drinks Sandy and Frank leave, and on the way out he confronts Sandy on what he had seen. Well by the time Sandy had told him the whole story Frank comes rushing back to Pete, and with a tear in his eyes, puts his arms around Pete and gives him one of the biggest hugs and a kiss on his cheek.

"Fucking hell Frank, they will think we are a coulpe of pufffters. Whats brough this on"

"Sandy told me what you said, and I the same would be heart broken if anythink happened to you too."

"Away with you man, look Sandy awaits go and enjoy your stroll but don't be late."

"Yes Dad, I won't be late, SEE YOU LATER DAD." Pete standing and shaking his head, and one or two customers in the bar were looking on. Pete sits back down and just sitting watching the world go by, starts to reflect on the whole events that had happened, and he just cannot get out of his head the times he as seen is Sofia, when all of a sudden he gets a sharp pain in the chest and it seemed to tighten.

"What the fuck is this, bloody hell I must have eaten my chicken to fast, wow a nother tight feeling." He sits looking round and all of a sudden they go and he relaxes again, and sits back and went back to enjoying the tranquility of being on his own.

10.30PM and Pete retiers for the night and he goes back to his room, and in away he is saying tohimself. "Bloody job, on Holiday and you cannot enjoy yourself for you are working, never mind get tomorrow over with and we will have the night time on Thursday to have a good dam drink before we have too again on the Friday stop drinking for the long haul back to the UK." Pete in bed and the time is midnight when Frank comes in and in the dark starts to hiss-hiss at Pete and saying.

"Pete are you awake mate, I've some good news for you, Pete are you awake mate."

"I fucking well am now, what the fuck is going off, get into bed you daft sod."

"I've got to tell you before I get into bed Pete."

"Well bloody well tell me and then we all can get some fucking sleep."

"I proposed to Sandy this evening and she said yes, do you know what that means." Frank sitting in the dark with the biggest grin and waiting for Petes answer.

"Yes we fucking all can now get back to fucking sleep. Ho by the way congratulations mate, bloody well goodnight."

All tucked up and it was all off into the land of nod, the alarm goes off at 7am and Pete is up and down to the gym todo is daily routine on the waights, by 8am it's breakfast and then readying themselves for the trip to Montserrat Monastery, Pete goes and gets the coach and pulls up outside the Hotel were he is met by Frank who comes on board and asks Pete.

"Are you driving first Pete."

"Yes I will drive first, you can board the guests and announce the days events."

All boarded the ones that are going at Frank comes onto the microphone and tells them all.

"Good morning Ladies and Gentlemen welcome aboard the coach this morning for your trip to see the Monastery Montserrat, built into the mountain side, and I can reasure you that you will be amazed at what you see when you get there, and with it set in the mountain range of Spain the views from the Monastery are out of this World. So sit back enjoy the views on the way there, and we will update you just before we arrive, thank you." Frank resits and they start off on their way.

They arrive and pull up into the coach park and just like Frank had said approching the Monastery the views are indeed spectaculour, and the cameras are clicking away at the view. They enter the Monastery and you are taken back by the size and the vastness of it and as you looks up there semed tobe walkways above and Pete is walking through, when he hears someone call out his wifes Name.

"Sofia-Sofia please over here." Well Petes eyes are all over and looking to see if he could spot where he heard the voice coming from and he is looking up and suddenly his heart stops a beat for there walking along the balcony is his Sofia and he calls out to her.

"Sofia it's me Pete, down here, please Sofia down here." Pete goes rushing off looking to get upto the next leaveal and Frank had seen him, and within minutes Pete is running along the balcony where he had seen his Sofia, and again disapointment for he did not catch eyes on her, and he comes back down, and Frank approches him.

"Come on Pete mate, it's not her."

"She was up there I saw her with my own eyes, you must have heard the voice calling for her to stop, please tell me you did." Pete trying to get some reasurence from Frank who just tells him.

"I'm sorry Pete no I did not, and anyway it could have been another Sofia, it's a Spanish name and there must be a lot of Sofia's in Spain."

Chapter Fourty Six

They spend over two hours touring the Monastery and they tell the passengers all to reassemble back at the coach, for it was onto the vineyards and dinner and wine tasting. They pull into the vineyard and the first thing on the agenda is lunch then the tour, and after wine tasting and buying products from their shop on site. They are back at 4pm in the afteroon, and Coach parked up, and Pete and Frank can now let their hair down, for they are free till tomorrow Friday. For they know that Friday had to be a dry day, off the beer for the early start Saturday and the long haul trip back to the UK. Pete and Frank change into their swimming gear and head for the pool and on the way grab a coulpe of beers and join the girls who are there Sunbathing. Rita asks Pete what is day was like. Pete tells her.

"Bloody boaring, we had a coach load of pensioners, and members of the Dearby and Jone club." Well all four of the girls burst out laughing and Sam tells them.

"Never mind boys we will make your night go well." Frank wispers to Pete.

"Not me Pete, I`ve a date with Sandy, we are going to the front and have a romantic meal."

"Never mind Frank more for me, I think I could manage three of them, in one go."

"I thought you would say that." Pete stands and tells Frank.

"Come on Frank lets have you in the pool, it will do you good."

"No thank you Pete I would sooner be warm laying here in the Sun."

"Chicken-chicken, Pete running to the pool flapping his arms at Frank mocking a chicken, he dives straight in and starts to do the length of the pool going up and down, and he is enduring to swim up and down for well over twenty minutes when he suddenly stops, and stands there buckled over, and Frank see's him stugling in the water and goes to the edge of the pool and asks Pete.

"Pete mate are you OK buddie."

"Yes OK Frank just a little cramp in the chest, must have pulled something." Pete coming to the edge of the pool.

"Come on Pete lets go and have a beer, it might help, and you can sit in the Sun and warm yourself up."

"OK Frank go and get them in while I just dry off." Pete drys off and goes to Frank and they sit down and Frank looks at Pete and he asked him again.

"You sure you are fine Pete, it's not chest pains you are getting."

"NO Frank just a little pull, I think it's with the water so cold, you are at your most vulnerable to get pulls when its cold, a good work out in the morning will soon put things right."

"Well make sure you don't over do things Pete, for we have a long trip Saturday, and I don't want you laid up, while I do the driving, for we would be breaking the law with just one driver."

"Bloody don't worries man I will be fine."

They have a couple of beers and Pete tells the girls he will see them later.

In their room Pete and Frank are changing and Pete sits down on his bed and for some unbeknown reason, he just bursts out into tear's, sitting with his head in his hands leaning forward. Frank see's the state Pete is in and he his worried sick, for this is not the first time. Frank goes over to Petes side and puts his hand onto Petes shoulder and gently rubbing it.

"Blody hell mate look at you, you are truly in a mess, you are definitely are going to sort this out when we get back, for I will bloody well make the appointment for you myself, so help me God. What's brought this on Pete."

"I'm so-so sorry Frank, I cannot explain, for one moment I'm up and the next down on my knees, Please Promise me you will do what you said, for you know me Frank, if I'm up it will be hell with you mate, I'm alright Jack."

"Mark my word Pete, that will be the first thing I do when I get back. Come on now lets get you into the shower, it might freshen you up, and bring you back to yourself." Pete stands and goes and showers, and Frank this time, he sits down on the bed, and you could tell that he is totaly worried about his mate.

The time approching 7pm and Pete and Frank are ready to hit the reastaurunt and they go, Frank in the reastarunt asks Pete what he would like to drink and Pete asks him to pour him a glass of white wine for their meal. They have there fill and Pete in is ussal gear white T-shirt blue jeann, and leather jacket sit enjoying their glass of white wine. Pete asks Frank.

"What time are you meeting Sandy Frank." Frank looks at is watch and tells Pete.

"In ten minutes and then off, I don't want to be around here if the girls come in and spoil anything, if you know what I mean."

"To true mate, you go and enjoy your evening, and Frank there's onething."

"What's that mate." Frank lifting his glass and finnishing off his wine.

"Please what you witnessed this afternoon, that's personal and only for you and me to know, if you know what I mean." Frank standing to go and meet Sandy tells Pete.

"Look Pete what I said this afternoon stays there, and I will dam well look after you, for I think more of you just like I would a brother." Well Pete stands puts both his arms around Frank and gives him a man hug and might I say a kiss, and Frank pulls away and tells Pete just before he leaves.

"Careful mate, if anyone see's that, I think you're reputation would be well on a downner, see you later mate." Frank leaves to go and meet Sandy and Pete sits there and he is deep into thought on the whole experience that he had gone through, and he thinks right back to when he first had the visit from his friend the Robin Red Breast, that came and sat on his windowsill, back home. He sits there smiling at his thoughs when into the restaurant comes Rita and Sam, they approch Pete who is still in deep thought and smiling and Rita asks.

"What's so funny Pete, what have you seen." Pete comes out of his thoughts looks at them both and asks.

"Nothing Babe just deep in thought, where are the other two girls, Jane and Pearl."

"Don't ask, they pick up two twats, and what do you know, they have booked another date with them."

"Just our three then, never mind, later we could always go back and have a little fun just the three of us." Pete puckering up his lips and lifting his eyebrows at them. Well Rita looks at Sam and before you know it they tell Pete.

"You're on Pete, later we will come back and go to our room and have this so called fun just the three of us." Pete stand and with Sam one onside and Rita on the other puts his hands on their arses and tells them, while rubbing their arse's.

"You two are in for the shag of your life, beleive me." They go walking out of the restaurant and into the bar, and have a drink before they head off down to the front and a club.

Chapter Fourty Seven

Time to head for the front and the clubs, Pete Rita Sam go walking out of the Hotel and Pete had his arms around both of then and his hand keeps having a crafty feel of their tits, and he looks just like one of those pimps with his Woman, walking down to the front. They have a few in the bars on the front then it was off to the club, for the last night that Pete could enjoy before the long haul back home. It was dancing with the girls, and both get a slow dance and quit intimate, with Pete hands on Sams arse and Rita's and he tells both of them while dancing and having a good feel of their arses, and his finger trying to find the hole, that they are going to realy squeal with pure pleasure tonight.

They both finaly tell Pete at 11.30pm that they would like to go back for his dirty talk has made them feel like gagging for it, for they both have had a taste of Petes cock already. They arrive back and going throuh reception they see the night security guard who knew Pete from when he lived down there, and he tells him in Spanish.

"Looks like Senor has his hands full, does you need help with them."

"No way ombray, I will shag the arse off both of them, buenas-notches." Rita asks Pete what he had told him.

"I told him that you were my niece's and I just are going to see you safely into your room, after a night in town in the night club."

"That was sweet of you Pete, your Spanish is good." They come to Rita's room and they go in and she locks the door, for she did not want the other two girls coming in while they are at it. Pete just stood there looked at them both and told them to both strip, and they did in front of Pete who just stood there sticking out his chest and waching the two girls, thay are both in the nude and Pete what beholds him, just out streched his arms and tells them both.

"Now take of your Gods clothes, and feast on what beholds you." Pete standing in one of his poses, they both are franticly stripping Pete and he finnaly stands there in all is gloury and the girls tell him.

"You are one hell of a fucking well built guy, just look at that fucker down there." Pete standing there and with arms out streched lifting his cock up and down, he tells them.

"Feast and enjoy." They both go down on Pete and take it in turn to give him a blody good blow job, and he is loving the fantasy roll play, after about ten minutes the girls having their fill with fondling his cock and balls tell him to take them and satisfy them. Pete point to the bed and they both get down, Pete gets in between them and starts to kiss and suck on Ritas tits, while he starts to finger Sam, flicking her clitoris and at the same time going down Rita's front and while fingering Sam he is sucking and tongueing her fanny, then he switches round and they both are in heaven with the pleasure. He finally lands up shagging Rita first and when she had a massive orgasm, switches round and the same giving Sam a good seeing too, finally it is Petes turn to have an orgasm and he pulls out and they both are straight down onto Petes cock while he is kneeling on the bed, and the girls having their fill as Pete ejaculates, finally they all three lay back down and Pete with arms round both of them, and his hand gently rubbing ther nipples, looks back on the whole event and tells them.

"That was fucking magic, I've never come like that before, was it the same for you two." Rita tells him.

"You are truly a God, I have never orgasmed like that before with anyone but you." And Sam the same answer that she too had never been fulfilled so much by any other guy, but you Pete. All three of them drop to sleep and it must have been about 3am when Pete awakes and he can here giggling and the other two girls had come in and with Pete on top of the sheets with it being warm, had this massive hard on for the two that had come in, Jane and Pearl were tossing Pete off, he looks at both of them, and tells them.

"What the fuck are you doing, do you want some, I am up for it as you can see, if you want shagging. Well Jane first is on to her own bed and tells Pete.

"Come on then shag me first." Pete quiatly gets our of bed with our disturbing Rita and Sam who are fast on, and gets onto Janes bed and straddles her and his cock slips straight into her, and he starts to slowly at first and building upto fast and it is not long and she is squeezing Petes back and having an orgasm, and all the time Pearl is laying there playing with her clitoris and fingering her self, she tells Pete come on Pete my turn. Pete gets onto her bed and he gives her a good seeing to until she is screaming out with having a massif orgasm. After Pete tells them that he is going to go back to his room and get some rest. He dresses and goes to the door and wispers to Jane and Pearl good night. Well all of a sudden all four of them say.

"Goodnight sleep tight." And they all giggle as Pete left the room and he had the biggest grin on his face at knowing that he had given them all a good seeing too.

Saturday morning soon comes round, and it was time to start to get ready for the long haul back home. Pete showered and shaved sits on his bed just putting on his shoes when Frank comes out of the bathroom to start to dress and he asks Pete.

"How you feeling today then Pete, no more mood swings I hope."

"Fine Frank, cannot wait to get back and see our old mates and of course a good pint of beer in the Horseshoes Inn."

"And the visit to see about your situation, and I don't have to tell you what." Frank showing concern about Pete.

"I know Frank, I don't stand a dogs chance with you onto my case." Pete smiling at Frank. Both dressed and in their working shirt that comes with the job, and it was bags to the coach then back for a little breakfast. The time is approching 8.30 am and Frank is sitting at the wheel for the first stint of driving while Pete is showing the guest back onto the coach, and one or two sad faces at knowing that their holiday is over. Pete trying to cheer them up as he loads their cases into the coach hold. All aboard Pete does the head count and all are acounted for and he tells Frank to hit the road for home. Pete gets up and with the microphone in his hand starts the day off introducing the trip details.

"GOOD MORNING Ladies and Gentlemen, bloody hell it looks like you all have caught the Sun, hopes you all have had a wonderful holiday, have you." They all cherr and shout out yes.

"That's more like it, right today we are going to start our way back through Spain and wonce again onto the Motorway and onto the automatic coach lane, if anyone who is interested to see the coach driving it's self, you are welcome to see me, and come up front and have a look, but I must stress only in the day time, for we have to keep our eyes on the road all the time at night, for safty reasons. We will stop at about 12.30pm for you to take a break, then again 4.30pm, then finnaly at 8.30pm for dinner, then the long haul throught the night, so we reach Calais in France early Sunday morning, and the final briefing will be in Dover back in the UK. So sit and try and have a good trip and if we pass any interesting spots Frank and myself will point them out to you, and one more thing if you requier any sort of film put on, please don't't essetate to come upfront and let us know, so we can pu it on for you. Have a good day thank you.

It's not long and they enter the Motorway system and onto the coach lane and again the voice comes on and actvates automatic and takes over and tells the driver to sit back and enjoy. Frank sitting at the wheel and doing nothing but watch the wheel turning slightly, looks at Pete who is sitting opposite him and he notices Pete with lots of pieces of Paper.

"What you got there then mate." Frank looking at Pete.

"Just names and telephone numbers, for my book when I get home."

"Who's names." Frank looking and not getting his answer.

"You know Frank all the birds that I shagged this week." Pete spaning them out like a pack of cards, Pete had not noticed a Lady standing there with a young lad, as he told Frank about shagging the birds. She coughs, and Pete looks round and he felt a little embarrassed.

"Sorry Madam just a little bannter with my mate, how can I help you."

"My Son would like to see this so called automatic driver."

"Please bring him to Frank." The little lad goes across to Frank who is upto his eyeholes in showing the youngster all that he had to do was sit there, when the Woman turns to Pete and she had writen down her mobile number and tells Pete.

"Maybe you would like to add this number." She stands there looking at the bulge in Petes trousers and then his tight muscular chest, Pete looks at the papper and see's her name.

"Thank's Janet, I will keep you to that."

They come to the end of the first stint and it was pull into Motorway Services for their first break. Pete is helping them off and it comes to the four girls that he brought down and shagged all four of them and they kiss Pete as they leave the coach, and one by one hand him their contact details, they ask him if he is coming for a drink and Pete tells them to save a table and they will be along in a moment, all off and Pete tells Frank that he is going to have a drink with the girls, he ask him if he is tagging on. Frank tells Pete that he is going to phone Sandy and he will see him inside the café shortly. Inside Pete finds the girls and with his drink sits with them and Pete asks Rita.

"Is it back to work for you then next week Rita."

"Yes me and Sam are back on the beat first shift Monday mornig." Pete thinking beat, what are they carpit cleaners, he asks Rita.

"What do you mean Beat."

"Were coppers, we work for Chesterfield Constabulary." Well Pete does spit his drink out and starts to chock for some went down the wrong hole, Rita pats him on the pack and Pete tells them in a squeeky voice.

"Next you will be telling me that Jane and Pearl are Coppers."

"How did you know, Detective Constable Jane, and Detective Sergent Pearl." Well Pete came straight out with.

"Now I know you are pulling my pisser." Rita did know more than put her hand under the table and grab Petes cock and gives it a gentle squeeze and tells him.

"No Pete this is you're pisser, and a large one at that, and secondly why should we lie, here see for yourself." She pulls out her Police Warrant card and so do the other three girls, and Pete just sat there opened mouth and not believing his own eyes.

Chapter Fourty Eight

They all go back to the coach, and standing at the coach door is Frank and Pete tells him.

"You are not going to believe this Frank, you missed a fucking good tail mate I will tell you."

"What you on abour Pete, I could not get to have a drink, for Sandy keep me talking."

"Well you know those four birds that I shagged, and you shagged one of them."

"Yes what about it."

"Well they are only fucking coppers mate, they shown me their warrant cards."

"Fuck off Pete they are never." Just as he had said this, the four girls come back and with Pete and Frank standing on the ground at the coach entrance, they start to go on board, and Pete to rub it in does, curtsey and said to them all.

"Evening all." Salute's and they all slap Pete getting back onto the coach. This time it's Petes turn to drive and they set off again. By 5am Sunday morning they land back up at Calais, for their early morning crossing to the UK and Dover.

Everyone had to leave the coach and go through customs while Pete and Frank take the coach onto the ferry check in and meet the passengers on board the ferry. One hour sailing and they are back in the UK, and this time Frank takes the coach on the first leg back to Bulwell Nottingham.

They finnaly arrive back at the depot in Bulwell at 2pm, and everyone picks up their things and say there fairwell to Pete and Frank and don't forget the girls for they tell Pete that they will be in touch and him to phone them.

Pete finally arrives back home and upstairs drops his bag onto his bed, and sits down, onto his bed. The first think he did was pull out his black Round Robin book and enter all the girls names that he had had, looks at it and closes it and throws it onto the side draws were it lands hanging on to the edge.

He flops back onto his bed and he had soon gone, into the land of nod with the long haul driving back from Spain. In his dream he is with his Sofia and she seemed to be asking Pete, why he does what he does, and Pete is trying to tell her that it is because he has not got her love here. He must have been asleep for well over three hours and suddenly awakes and he is completely sobbing, and he sits on the side of the bed and in a sleepish mood, tells himself.

"Come on now Pete don't slide back into depression, my Sofia is dead and gone, God what am I going to do."

The time is 7pm by the time he had showered and shaved and he gets ready and goes down to the Horseshoes Inn, and into the bar and Terry see's Pete and shouting asking Pete.

"Nice to see you back Pete, pint of mix is it."

"Right on Terry, and the sooner the beter."

"I because all that lager shit you have been drinking down there."

"Got it in one mate, what a fucking week, I can tell you something that will blow you away."

"What's that then Pete, you fount the Titanic and shagged everyone that was on it."

"Who told you then, No mate on our coach there were four birds, and yes you fucking know, I shagged all four of them and that is not all, you see they were fucking coppers all four of them."

"Fucking hell Pete I hopes you gave them one from me, you fucking jammy bastard." They both stand laughing at what they had said. Then into the bar comes Donna and straight away she throws her self at Pete and gives him one long loving kiss.

"WOW you are back, I tell you now Pete my pussy is gagging for you, God I'm wetting myself already."

"Well babe you will be wetting a litle longer, for I've been driving for two days and the only thing I'm going to do tonight is, snore my fucking head off in the land of nod."

"Well promise me Pete you will give me a good seeing too, tomorrow night then." Donna rubbing Petes chest and purring. Pete with his hands on her front lifts her up a little with his hands under her breast and tells her.

"You've a date, and you are going to see stars and fireworks and all tomorrow." Well Donna smiles at Pete and she tells him.

"I love you Pete, fucking roll on tomorrow."

Pete had only three pints and he tells them that he is very tired and he is going to go and get to bed. They all say there goodnights to Pete, as he leaves and he starts to leave by going up the steps and walking towards Saint Marys church. Going by he looks up the hill to the entrance were he had seen his Sofia, takes out his crucifix from under his T-shirt kisses it and said.

"I love you Sofia, goodnight and God bless."

Back home he strips and he is just going to get into bed when he gets this shooting pain in his chest.

"What the fuck is this, How you Bastard, that fucking herts." Pete takes a deep breath tence's up and it seemed to ease, boy that was some pain. He gets into bed and he was soon gone. The next mornig he awakes and the time is 7.30am and he goes and showers coming back out of the bathroom wiping himself off he hears a tap-tap, looks at the window and behold it's his little friend the Robin Redbreast, he opens the window and puts his hand out and it hops onto his open hand and flops down laying there looking sad.

"What are you doing round here my friend, what have you been up to fighting with the sparrows." Pete kisses the Robin and he suddenly notices that it had gone.

"Ho my God not you too my friend, no this cannot be happening." Pete looks again and yes the little Robin Redbreast had died in his arms. Pete sat there and the tears start to roll down his cheek and he is telling himself.

"No one will arm you my friend." He gentaly pulls out a tim out of one of his draws, and puts the little Robin into it and then tapes it up, so nothing could get in. He goes into his garden digs a hole and places the tin into the hole. He stands when he had covered it up and he said a few words.

"Look after my friend Sofia take him into your arms and show him the love you showed me." Pete goes back into his house picks up his gym bag and heads for the gym to work out. He slams the front door and upstairs, the Round Robin book that he throw onto the draws falls to the floor.

Then it lands and opens on the middle pages, where there is only one thing across the hole twenty two lines of the pages, and that is what Pete had wrote.

"There is only one love in my life and that is my SOFIA."

Inside the gym Pete changed goes into the gym equipment room, passes the two instructors and tells them that he is going to pump some iron today, they smile at Pete and he starts to put a few weights onto the bar, stands and lifts the bar of the rack and starts to work his upper arms by lifting them up and down.

The two instructors are watching Pete work out and then he starts to lay down and the same adds more weights to the bars, and he is pumping away and the two instructors are amazed at the weighst he is putting on. Pete must have been at it for well over 40 minutes and adding more weights all of the time untl the bar is bending with the total weights he had on them. One of the instructors turns to the other and said to him.

"How the hell his he doing that, just look at the bar it's bending right over."

Pete is puffing in and out and sweating profusely, but still continued until he suddenly gets this very violent pain shooting and tightening across his chest, and his strenght suddenly goes and he drops the bar with the weights on, straight across his chest and gives off one big sigh.

Pete opens his eyes wide looks forward and coming towards him is his Sofia, with her long white dress, and long blond hair down her back and the little Robin Redbreast sitting on her shoulder, and she with her arm streched out with her hand open, Pete see's her smiles and he puts his arm up and still looking at her, his eyes are gleaming and the smile on his face said it all. The two instructors see Pete with the bar across his chest and his arm out streched, and they go running over to Pete.

They stand both sides of Pete and one tells the other to lift the bar, well it took all their might to lift the bar, and they just manage to put it back onto its rack, and they look back down to Pete's face and the smile he had on it was not real, they both look to where Pete is looking and they see nothing, then back down to Pete, and his eyes wide open and his arm out streched with his hand open.

They go round shouting to the ones that were in the gym to leave immediately, they clear the gym and lock the door. and call the emergency services, Police and ambulance.

THE END

What had really happened in the gym, had his Sofia finally come for him, and now they are finaly forever together.

Or did he have a massive heart attack. Or again had he died of a broken heart, with truly missing his Sofia.

John Bolstridge

Come on now it's your turn to help me finish the story of Pete West, you are now the author, to join me to put an end to the story or beginning of another

Round Robin. Right I will start.

The ambulance and Police comes and they enter the gym, and to their astonishment.????.

Printed in the United States
By Bookmasters